Sacred

For my Nana,

WHO TELLS THE BEST STORIES

Can you understand? Someone, somewhere, can you understand me a little, love me a little? For all my despair, for all my ideals, for all that—I love life. But it is hard, and I have so much—so very much to learn.

—Sylvia Plath

I am supposed to be having the time of my life.

—Sylvia Plath, *The Bell Jar*

ONE

The End

All around me, the island prepared to die. August was ending, so summer had come, bloomed, and waned. The tall, dry grass on the trail through the hills cracked under my mare's hooves as we wound our way up toward the island's heart.

Summer sun had bleached the grass the same blond as my hair, which was pulled into a rough ponytail at the nape of my neck. The straw cowboy hat I always wore when I rode was worn out too, beginning to split and fray along the seams.

The economy had done its part over the past few years to choke the life out of the small island I called home—Catalina, a little over twenty miles off the coast of Los Angeles. This summer, the island had felt remarkably more comfortable, as the mainland's tourists had largely stayed away. But even though it was nice to have some breathing room for a change, it came at a price. Our main town, Avalon, had seen the closure of two restaurants and a hotel, and my parents' bed-and-breakfast had gone whole weeks without any guests.

It was selfish that I enjoyed the solitude. Selfish and wrong, but undeniably true—solitude was a luxury, a rare commodity on a twenty-two-mile-long island that I shared with three-thousand-plus people, all of whom seemed to look at me differently lately, now that my brother was dead.

Yes, death was all around. The dry, hot air of August pressed down on me, my brother would not be coming home, and Avalon seemed to be folding in on itself under the weight of the recession, like a butterfly that's dried up, its papery wings faded.

As if she could sense my mood, my mare, Delilah, tossed her pretty head and pulled at her bit, yearning to run. Delilah was also a luxury, one my parents had been in the habit of reminding me we really couldn't afford—until Ronny died. Then, suddenly, they didn't say much to me at all.

I get it, your kids are supposed to outlive you, it's the natural order of things, but since Ronny had died, it was like I was dead too.

That was how I measured time now. There were the things that happened Before Ronny Died, and then there was Since Ronny Died. It was as sure a division of Before and After to our family as the birth of Jesus is to Christians.

Before Ronny Died, Mom smiled. Before Ronny Died, Daddy made plans for expanding our family B&B. Before

Ronny Died, I was popular . . . as popular as you can be in a class of sixty-four students.

That was all different now. Since Ronny Died, my mother didn't seem to notice that a film of dust coated all the knick-knacks in the front room. My dad didn't weed the flower beds. More than a tanking economy was sinking our family business. We were bringing it down just as surely, our gloomy faces unable to animate into real smiles. We probably scared off the guests.

Ronny died last May in the middle of a soccer game. Cause of death: grade 6 cerebral aneurysm. He was just finishing up his freshman year at UCLA. We weren't with him. The distance between Catalina Island and the mainland seems a lot farther than twenty miles when your brother's body is waiting for you on the other side.

I blinked hard to clear these thoughts. They would stay with me anyway, I knew, but I let Delilah have her head, knowing from experience that while we were galloping, at least, my mind would feel empty.

My mare didn't let me down. Twitching her tail with excitement, Delilah broke into a gallop, her short Arabian's stride lengthening as she gathered speed, her head pushed out as if to smell the wind, her wide nostrils flaring. Her coat gleamed red in the afternoon sun.

Ronny used to joke that *Delilah* should have been named Scarlett, not me. Ronny was a literal kind of guy. And he liked to say that *I* should be called Delilah, because of my long hair. That was stupid, of course; in the Bible, Delilah wasn't the one with the long hair. It was her lover, Samson, whom she betrayed by chopping off his hair—the source of his strength—while he slept, damning him to death at the hands of the Philistines.

Ronny just shrugged when I explained all this to him. Sometimes he could be awfully dumb, for such a smart guy.

I wanted to cut off my hair after Ronny died. I stood in the kitchen the afternoon of the funeral, dressed in one of my mother's suits left over from her days as a lawyer, back before she and Daddy decided to move to the island to open a B&B. In my hands, I held a long serrated knife. There was a perfectly good reason for this: I couldn't find the scissors.

But when my mother came into the kitchen, fresh from burying her only son, and saw me standing in the kitchen with a knife in my hand, she freaked out. She started screaming, loud, piercing screams, as if I were an intruder, as if I planned to use that knife against her. Or maybe she thought I was planning to use it against myself, pressing the blade into flesh instead of hair. Then Daddy ran in and saw me there, and his eyes filled with tears, something I'd seen more times that week than I'd seen in the sixteen years of my life up till that point. He took the knife gently from my hand before leading my mother to bed.

Afterward, I couldn't seem to gather the strength to cut my hair. I had wanted to cut it because Ronny had loved it, though he'd never have admitted as much. He used to braid it while we watched TV. I wanted to cut it off and then burn it.

But my mother's expression had taken all the momentum out of my plans. So as I rode Delilah through the open meadow at the heart of the island, I felt the heavy slap of my ponytail against my back, hanging like a body from a noose in the elastic band that ensnared it.

Delilah tossed her mane and slowed to a trot, heading for a clump of grass at the base of a large tree. I thumped her neck with my palm.

"Good girl," I murmured as her trot became a slow, stretchy walk. I slid down her side and pulled the reins from her neck. She made a contented sound as she began pulling up bites of grass. I flopped down next to her in the tree's shade, her reins looped loosely over my wrist, and allowed my body to relax.

School would be starting soon. Junior year. This was supposed to be the best year of high school, even if the academic load would be tough: too soon to worry about college applications, and since I was no longer an underclassman, all the required PE classes were behind me. Still, I was dreading it. Just a few more days, and then I'd be yoked to school as surely as Delilah was yoked to me.

I tried to remind myself of the good things that went along with school in a halfhearted effort to cheer myself up. Lily would be back; that would be good.

My best friend, Lily Adams, was a member of the small wealthy class on Catalina Island. Her parents could have lived anywhere they chose. Independently wealthy as a result of some smart real-estate purchases in the early 1990s, they had come to Catalina because they thought it would be a safe place to raise their kids: Lily and her younger twin brothers, Jasper and Henry.

Catalina was safe, except for the occasional boating accident. The visitors bureau boasted that "violent crimes are virtually nonexistent on this island paradise." Well, the paradise part was dubious, but as far as I knew, it was true about the lack of crime here.

Because of their money, though, and because their livelihood wasn't dependent on the high season for tourism like almost everyone else's on the island, Lily's family got to travel during the summers. This year they were touring Italy. Her family had offered to bring me along; Jasper and Henry had a built-in friend (or enemy) by virtue of being twins, but Lily's parents thought it would be nice if I could come to keep Lily company.

That had been the plan, Before Ronny Died. Then, suddenly, my parents couldn't stomach the thought of my being so far away from them . . . though they hadn't seemed to notice me much this summer, and the three of us existed pretty much like strangers living under one roof all season long.

It made me angry that I had missed out on the trip. But I felt rotten that I could be mad at my parents for anything right now . . . and that I could be mad at Ronny, who was dead, for screwing up my summer plans. Lately I just wasn't a very good person.

Lily didn't seem to agree. She'd kept up a stream of communication all summer, through email, Facebook, and text messages, even though I rarely wrote back. She understood;

she didn't hold my silence against me. I hoped things were going to get better now that she was coming home.

Friday afternoon. She would be in the air, on her way to Los Angeles from Rome. Then she and her family would come to Catalina by helicopter. They were the only people I knew who could afford to travel this way. Most everyone else took the ferry, and a few of the wealthier families kept their own boats for transportation to the mainland, but Lily's family coptered. Not bad.

I couldn't wait to see Lily again. The last time had been at our island's airport in early June, just a few weeks after Ronny's funeral. Her parents had embraced me effusively, Lily had been in tears at the thought of leaving me, and even the twins had given me shy, apologetic hugs.

"Two whole months!" Lily wailed. "How will I survive?"

I smiled grimly. "Fabulous food, handsome Italians, all the wine you can drink . . . I think you'll manage."

"But without you!" Lily moaned, shaking her short, dark curls. Lily had always been dramatic.

"You'll pull through," I promised. "And I'll be here waiting for you come September."

The helicopter had risen into the sky, Lily and her family growing smaller and smaller as they flew away, waving furiously until they were out of sight.

So, Lily's return. That was one good thing about school starting back up. And there was Andy, of course.

Before May, Andy had been my boyfriend. After May, it seemed silly and self-indulgent to have a boyfriend.

With Ronny's death, it was like I had stepped over some invisible line into a world miles apart from the one I'd inhabited before the piercing phone call from UCLA Medical Center.

I didn't have much to say anymore. It had all been said. Lily understood and was waiting for me to reconcile my brother's death with the rest of life. Andy, on the other hand, wasn't quite as patient.

Andy was lots of things. He was handsome, for one. At just under six feet tall, with the well-muscled body of an athlete—which he was, the star of our school's baseball team, scouted even during his sophomore year by colleges—Andy was taller than most of the boys in our class. His cap of shining light hair looked nice in school dance pictures next to my long straw-colored ponytail. We were blond together.

He was whip-smart, too, taking all the advanced classes our little school offered and doing online classes with Long Beach State College. I had a theory that the teachers didn't even bother grading his papers anymore. I didn't know if Andy Turlington had ever gotten lower than an A in his life.

So we were well suited that way too, since grades were important to me. I was competitive, maybe because I'd grown up in Ronny's impressive shadow, maybe just because that's the way I was made. Andy and I enjoyed our unspoken competition, and though I couldn't keep up with him on the occasional runs we took together, I certainly held my own when it came to things academic.

All of this seemed dreadfully sophomoric after Ronny's death. Suddenly, I could barely force myself to breathe, let alone worry about setting the curve on the latest math test.

I don't know how much my parents noticed my disinterest in school, if they noticed anything at all. Mostly they were drowning in their own oceans of grief, and my teachers basically let me slide, passing me along with gift grades of As and A-minuses.

So there we were, my parents and I, three tiny islands on the greater island of Catalina, and it felt like the weight of the entire Pacific Ocean was pressing on my chest. Sometimes, when I noticed my mother clutching her hand to her heart, I knew she felt the same way.

There was no room on my private island for Andy, which he seemed to figure out soon after school closed for the summer. I failed to return his calls, failed to meet him and the other kids at the beach, failed to thrive.

Delilah was all the company I wanted. Andy had come to the stable just once, at the end of June, determined, I guess, to get some response from me in person. He walked up to me while I stood at the wash racks, spraying the sweat from Delilah after a long run. When I saw him, it didn't register at first who he was. I remember wondering what this tourist was doing out here at the stable, and I called to him, "We don't rent horses to the public."

"Scarlett," he answered. "It's me—Andy. What the hell? Are you all right?"

Suddenly, the ever-present weight on my chest grew just a fraction heavier and I sank to my knees, the hose next to me spraying uselessly into the dry earth.

Andy rushed over, uncertain what to do with this much

grief—with my tears, my wailing, my hands pulling my hair out of its braid. His hand hovered above my head for a while before he kneeled next to me, before he untangled my fingers from my hair and folded them in my lap.

"It's all right," he murmured, a terrible lie, but it was the best he could offer, and so I turned to him awash in grief, wiped my tears on the front of his blue-and-white Dodgers tee, and sobbed in his arms as he stroked my hair.

After a time, Andy kissed my forehead, then my cheeks, and then his lips found mine. I pressed my breasts into his chest, winding my arms around his neck, my teeth pushing hard into his lips as I took what comfort I could from his embrace.

He seemed surprised by my response, and I could feel him vacillating between pulling me closer and pushing me away. The part of him that was a sixteen-year-old boy won out, and he clutched me to him, his hands wandering up and down my back as he kissed me more deeply, his tongue exploring my mouth.

But it was as if his desire had flipped some switch inside me, and I was suddenly achingly cold. Andy realized that I was no longer returning his kiss, that I was sitting in his arms like a rag doll, and with some measure of self-control, he pulled away from me.

His arms were rigid, and his eyes, usually a bright blue, looked cloudy with a mixture of emotions I couldn't read. He stumbled to his feet, off balance, unusual for him, and cleared his throat.

"I don't know, Scarlett," he said. "Maybe you need some time."

Then he'd walked away, though over his shoulder he threw "Call me whenever" before climbing into his pickup and driving off.

Next to me, Delilah pawed the earth, her breath warm and moist in my hair. Sitting with Delilah under the tree, for the first time all summer I had the beginning of a desire to do just that—call him. It was like some part of me yearned to pick up my life where I'd left it. *Could I do that?* I wondered. Could I go back to being Scarlett Wenderoth, ace student, girlfriend, BFF? Or was that part of my life as dead as Ronny?

I sighed and stood, stretching my arms over my head. "All right, girl," I said, patting Delilah's neck. "Let's go home."

I chose a different route back to the stable. I was in no hurry to return to the B&B for dinner with my parents, so I opted to take the circuitous route through the valley toward the barn.

Delilah's barn was my second home—El Rancho Escondido, "the hidden ranch," a breeding facility begun by the Wrigley family way back in the 1930s. It was a private establishment, nestled in a valley twelve miles outside of Avalon. The only reason I could keep my mare there was that my mom was best friends with the manager of the ranch. I got my love of riding from my mom, Olivia, though she'd stopped riding when she got pregnant with Ronny. Her good friend Alice ran the ranch now, greeting the busloads of tourists that came by to see the horses and explaining the ranch's history.

My job was to stay out of the way when I was at the ranch, and not to brag too much around the island about my special privileges. It didn't hurt that my Delilah had been bred and born right here on Catalina, just like me. She and I were two of a kind—trapped on this island, at least for now.

Delilah didn't seem to notice this truth, much less mind it. For a fairly young mare—just five years old—she was remarkably calm. Before she had even been born, she'd been earmarked for me. My parents didn't have a lot of money, but they'd always been dedicated to giving their kids what they needed.

Ronny had needed lots of interaction with the outside world, so our parents had sent him away for part of each summer to stay with friends on the mainland. I needed a horse.

I didn't *want* a horse the way some girls ask for a pony; I *needed* a horse. All my drawings, all the little stories that I'd written as a kid, all my Christmas lists had been about one thing—horses.

And it had never been enough just to be around the Arabians at the stable. I'd felt a pressing need to have a horse of my own.

Delilah was a beautiful foal. I was there to see her birth. She was sired by a tall chestnut Arab named Nomad, and she was out of an unusually large mare named Rainbow. I watched as she emerged from her mother, slick and wet and beautiful, and I watched as she stood on shaky legs and searched under her mother for her first sip of milk.

I'd trained her. She had known me as long as she'd been alive, and she trusted me completely. So today, when I turned her off the main path and toward a rocky decline, her steps didn't falter.

I live in a beautiful place, I thought grudgingly. A fire had ravaged the island's interior just a few years ago, but the blackened landscape was recovering. Some species of plants were actually doing better now than before the fire; there had been too much growth, choking out light, and the plants had had to compete for ground and access to the sun. After the fire, with almost everything dead, there was room. Seeds still dormant under the soil might emerge this year, with the rain. But even dry and somewhat barren, Catalina was beautiful. Native sage and chaparral danced as the late-afternoon breeze picked up, and I took in a deep breath of the clean, salty ocean air. Delilah seemed invigorated by the breeze too, and she broke into an energetic trot even as we started downhill.

I leaned back in my saddle and pulled gently on the reins. "Easy, girl," I murmured, but Delilah tossed her head, eager to move forward.

I laughed, happy she was so spirited. After all this time, I barely noticed how strange the sound of my laughter seemed. "All right, then, if you insist," I said. "Giddyap."

I loosened the reins and dug my heels into Delilah's sides. With the grace that only a purebred Arabian can manage, Delilah loped down the hill, her neck long and loose, her haunches tucked tightly beneath her. As soon as she reached a flatter space on the trail she really let go. The pounding of her hooves on the hard soil became all I was aware of, da-da-*dum*, da-da-*dum*, and I leaned forward with the joy of the ride, my cowboy hat blown away and forgotten behind us, my heels pressed down in the stirrups, the waistband of my jeans pushing into my hips as I moved with the rhythm of her gallop. I felt my mouth pulled wide in a smile, and I felt *alive* and *free*, my heart full of something other than pain.

Then we rounded a corner defined by a wide oak tree, and my life irrevocably shifted.

TWO

Alice Butts In

*H*is face was white with fear as Delilah came at him at a full-out gallop, but he stayed stock-still and as solidly rooted to the ground as the oak tree that had hidden him from my view.

His nostrils flared, not unlike Delilah's, and even as my mare and I barreled toward him, his gaze did not waver. At his sides were his hands, clenched into fists.

His eyes were green. Not some version of hazel that people call green, but actually green—flashing green, beautiful, like the color of fresh grass in the spring.

Unflinchingly, he stared at me and held up one of his hands.

"Stop."

It was just one word, and though his voice was not raised, it resonated somehow, and without consciously deciding to, I obeyed. I leaned back in my saddle and pulled firmly on the reins. "Whoa!" I told Delilah. She tossed her head, unwilling, but I increased the pressure on the reins.

In front of me, the boy didn't move. Good thing Delilah stopped, or we would have collided.

Tall and slender, but not filled out with the muscles that would probably bulk up his frame in the coming years, he looked strong. The tendons of his arms and neck were strained with tension as he stood in the middle of the trail. He wore khaki hiking pants and boots, and under his arms his gray T-shirt was stained with circles of sweat, as if he'd been hiking hard before he'd found me on the trail.

I couldn't quite decide why it seemed that way, as if he'd *found* me, but I was certain, somehow, that he had been searching for me. As I stared more deeply into his eyes, I saw mirrored there both fear and pain, though he was no longer in any danger of being run down by Delilah. Then he raised his hand to his forehead and closed his eyes.

"Are you all right?" I asked. I was still annoyed by his interference; Delilah snorted as if she heard my thoughts and echoed them. But I was concerned, too. The way he was acting was definitely not normal, and I found myself wondering if there was something seriously wrong with him. Maybe he was about to have a stroke or something. An image of Ronny, eyes closed, hands folded across the chest of his best suit, flashed in my mind, and I felt the beginnings of one of my panic attacks coming on.

I forced myself to breathe regularly, pushing Ronny's face out of my mind.

"What the hell are you doing out here in the middle of the trail?" I snapped, throwing my right leg across the saddle and sliding to the ground. "You could have gotten both of us hurt."

He didn't answer at first, but his hand dropped from his forehead and his eyes slowly opened. He had eyelashes that any teen girl would murder for. And up close, his eyes were an even more brilliant green than they had seemed to be when I had sat astride Delilah.

He searched my face as if looking for the answer to some riddle, and I felt my anger seep out of me, leaving in its place a warm, soft feeling that I didn't have a name for.

"I'm sorry," he murmured at last. "I didn't mean to cause you trouble. That is the last thing I want to do."

He fixed his eyes on me. "I'm Will," he said, offering his hand. "Will Cohen."

Will tilted his head slightly to one side, waiting with his hand extended while I tried to diagnose his motives before I finally gave up and thrust my hand toward his.

"Scarlett Wenderoth," I murmured in the second before our hands connected. Then our fingers touched, and for a long moment I don't think I could have told anyone my name at all.

His grip was warm and firm, and he held my hand rather than shook it, as if sealing a promise. His other hand came up to grasp mine too.

Then Delilah nudged me with her muzzle, her warm breath sending shivers down my body, and I felt a colder breeze than I'd felt all summer. Fall was coming. I smelled it all around me. I pulled my hand free.

"I'm really sorry," Will said, his eyes pleading. "But I thought . . . I thought you were in some kind of trouble."

I snorted. "Trouble? I don't think so. I've been riding these trails all my life. I know this island better than my bedroom."

Somehow, saying "bedroom" to this boy sent a blush across my cheeks, though he didn't seem to notice.

"Yeah," he said softly, as if contemplating something very important. "You did seem in complete control . . . and I don't see anyone else nearby." His eyes scanned the terrain as if searching for predators.

"What's the matter with you?"

Will shook his head. "I don't know. Something . . ."

He stopped abruptly and walked away, stumbling as if drunk, his head bowed in what looked like pain, his hand once again massaging his temple.

I watched him as he wandered back along the trail and rounded the corner of the large oak tree. Then he disappeared from view.

I wanted to call out to him—what for, I didn't know—but I bit my lip instead, hard, until I tasted my blood, a bad habit I'd developed in the months since Ronny's death. The pain and the metallic taste of my blood did what I knew it would—it cleared my head.

I took a deep breath and turned to Delilah. She stamped her hoof, probably eager now for her oats. It was nearing dinnertime.

"All right, girl," I said, rubbing her wide, red forehead with the hand that Will Cohen had held. "Let's go home."

Effortlessly, with the ease of years of practice, I swung myself back into the saddle. I made a clicking sound with my tongue; Delilah's ears rotated to hear me, and she picked up a pretty trot. The reins swung loose and long in arcs from her mouth to my hands, and we settled into a practiced rhythm.

Back at the barn, I took my time untacking Delilah. Gently, I unhooked the bridle and lowered the bit from her mouth, replacing the bridle with her purple halter and tying her loosely to the cross-ties before hanging the bridle on a nearby peg. Then I pulled my cross-country saddle from her back, noting the square of sweat left on her where the saddle had been. I took the pad out from underneath the saddle, flipped it sweat side up so it could dry overnight, and hung it on its peg in the tack room.

I led Delilah from the cross-ties to the wash racks and tied her securely before turning on the hose. I sprayed her spindly legs first, then worked the water up across her back. As she got wet, her red coat darkened and shone. I sprayed between her withers, and her muscles shivered in pleasure.

When she was rinsed, I pulled the sweat scraper from my tack bucket and swept the water from her coat, from her neck, down her sides, across her shoulders, down her flanks. There was something supremely satisfying about this activity—all the activities, actually, that went along with taking care of my mare. I didn't even mind cleaning her stall. Keeping her groomed and well fed brought me more pleasure than I ever got from taking care of my own body.

I spread a thick coat of sealant over all four of her hooves. They shone as if polished in the late-afternoon light.

Finally, there was nothing more to do, so I led Delilah to her stall, where a thick flake of hay and some oats awaited her. She pulled eagerly at the lead rope, nickering at her food.

I laughed. "All right, girl, you've earned it." I unfastened her halter and she pushed past me into her stall. I closed its heavy door and latched it securely behind her.

I wasn't alone at the stable, though I would have preferred it that way. Two men were working in the garden, watering and weeding the twin bands of flowers at the stable's entrance.

And Alice was in the office, waiting for me to finish my ride so that she could drive me back to town. I felt a twinge of guilt at how late it was; I knew Alice had a husband and kids waiting for her back home, and I was pretty sure that she would have left by now if she wasn't held up waiting for me.

Cars on the island are a rare commodity, and even though I'd turned sixteen last April, there was no hope of my having my own car anytime soon. There was a long waiting list to bring cars onto the island, and anyone who already had one held on to it fiercely. Around town I walked, or took my family's golf cart through the narrow streets if I was in a real hurry, but the road out to the stable was too far and windy to safely negotiate by golf cart, so I caught a ride with Alice whenever I could, at least three or four times a week.

Before Ronny Died, Alice used to hassle me about taking

so long with Delilah. "Are you still messing with that mare?" she'd call at me across the courtyard. "That horse must be sick of you by now!"

But since Ronny's death, Alice didn't rush me anymore. Even on the days when I came off the trails at twilight, Alice waited patiently in the office, with a light shining like a beacon for me. She never complained about how long I took.

That was no excuse to take advantage of her goodwill, I admonished myself. Alice was not my personal chauffeur. She was a family friend, as close as an aunt, and since my mother had disappeared into the deep cave of her grief, Alice had been the closest person in my life.

I hurried over to the office now. Alice must have seen me through the window because she switched off the light and came out through the door, closing and locking it behind her.

Alice was the kind of lady who made everything look easy. She had to be the same age as my mom—forty-five—because they had graduated from college the same year, but her face was luminous and bright.

Alice wore her light brown hair in a neat bob, the ends turned under, just chin length. Sometimes she pinned one side back with a colorful barrette, but usually her hair fell like wings on the sides of her face, framing it.

Even on the days she was at the stable, Alice did her face. Mascara, lipstick, the works. I harbored a secret suspicion that she ironed her jeans.

Today, her fingernails were painted a pretty pearlescent

pink, and I would have bet twenty bucks that her toenails, hidden in her shiny black stable boots, were painted the same shade.

"Hey, kiddo," she called to me as we both headed to her truck.

I flinched, invisibly I hoped, as I did every time she called me "kiddo," which was what Ronny had always called me. I would have asked Alice not to call me that anymore, but I knew how horrified she would have been to learn that she was echoing my dead brother's nickname for me. All of Alice's actions were governed by her desire to lighten the burden on my heart . . . as if that were possible.

"Hey," I answered, and climbed into the truck.

It was spotless, of course, like Alice herself, and some easy jazz song came on as she turned the key in the ignition.

As we headed down the dusty road, away from the stable and toward Avalon, I could feel Alice's flitting glance landing on my body again and again like a troublesome fly. She'd look at my leg, then back to the road, then at my arm, bare in the pink T-shirt I was wearing, then down at the radio, back to the road, and across to my face.

Her forehead creased with worry, and her lips pursed as if she was deciding whether to speak.

Please don't speak, please don't speak, I silently willed, and I reached out to turn up the volume on the radio.

But Alice beat me to it, and she flicked the radio off.

"Scarlett," she said. "I notice you've been losing weight."

My window was down, blowing the strands of my hair around my face. I pushed them back and tried to flatten them behind my ears, but the wind thwarted my efforts. From her seat, Alice pressed a button, and my window silently slid up. The wind died out at once and the cab was suddenly, unbearably quiet.

I wondered what the most polite way to say "It's none of your business" might be . . . but I found my mouth dry, no words coming.

"It's natural, I'm sure," Alice went on, her words coming faster now, as if the floodgates were open, "when you're going through such grief, to lose your appetite, though for me I guess the opposite is true. Whenever I'm stressed-out or sad, I tend to hit the peanut butter cups pretty hard. So I've hesitated saying anything. But Scarlett, you're starting to look . . . downright scrawny."

I appraised my body the best I could from my position in the truck. "Scrawny" certainly isn't a word I would have chosen, but I couldn't deny that my jeans were much looser on my hips and thighs than they'd been at the beginning of the summer, and my arms, I guess, were skinnier too.

But I wasn't about to admit this to Alice. "I don't know what you're talking about," I said, my voice rougher than I'd intended. "I'm exactly the same as I was six months ago."

I felt the lie in my words, though, and I knew Alice heard it too. Nothing was the same as it had been six months ago. Everything was terribly, permanently different. A whole new version of the future, one that never should have become reality, was playing out now. Ronny should be getting ready to go back to UCLA for the fall. He should be sunburned from all the fishing he'd done with Daddy over the last few months on the island, and he should be contemplating the best way to break up with whichever girl he'd occupied himself with this summer.

Instead, his body was decomposing in a coffin. I wondered grimly if he looked anything like he had when we'd buried him, or if he'd be unrecognizable now. I wondered too if all of him was dead. I wanted to hope that some part of him lived on, but I couldn't feel him out there . . . all I felt was alone.

Thoughts like these came to me often. They were hard to control, and they made me feel sick and breathless, dizzy, like I would pass out. Not much counteracted them, but focusing on the details of living—like how many strokes to brush my hair, how many ounces of water I drank, how many calories I consumed in a day—seemed to take the edge off, at least for a little while.

I considered explaining this to Alice, but I figured it wouldn't really help anything. It would just make her worry more, and maybe even prompt her to share her worries with my parents, who were pretty much incapacitated by their grief over Ronny already. I certainly didn't want to add to their stress with my own problems.

So instead I plastered what I hoped was a sincere-looking smile on my face and turned to Alice.

"You're right, Alice," I began. "I guess I have been losing a little weight. I don't know . . . I guess it's been hard since Ronny died. But I'll pay better attention. I promise. Just . . . don't worry my parents about this, okay? Mom especially . . . she's not doing well."

Alice grimaced, and I knew I'd hit a nerve. My mom was her best friend, after all, and it must be hard for Alice to watch her going through all this. She nodded, tight-lipped. "All right, kiddo," she said. "I won't talk to your mom— yet. But I want to see you filling out those jeans again, you hear?"

I nodded, fighting down the ball of anger in my chest. There was no reason to be mad at Alice; she was just trying to help. But my anger rose anyway, bilious and bitter, and I bit down on my lip again to suppress it.

This is how it was, lately: my emotions were stronger than I was. If I slipped up, even for a moment, they could erupt from me in a spew of ugly words, and if I started to cry and scream, I feared I would never stop.

I pressed the button on my door to lower my window again, and Alice flipped the music back on—then, as if reading my thoughts, she switched the station to something loud and full of bass and turned the volume way up.

We finished the drive to town like that—the cab of the truck full of wind, my hair whipping about my face, blissfully obscuring my view, the screams of the rock music pushing my own thoughts away from my mind.

When we pulled up to my house, Alice turned the volume to low and swiveled in her seat to look me in the eye. "Go on in now, Scarlett, and eat something good—a burger, maybe." Then she smiled, and I saw her eyes were kind. I could see why my mom loved her so much. Alice was a good lady. Still, though, I didn't need a babysitter.

"Sure, Alice, will do," I muttered, and I slammed the door

of the truck a little harder than I needed to after I hopped down. "See you tomorrow?" I asked, sticking my head back through the open window.

"I'll pick you up at ten," Alice said, and she waved at me as she drove away.

Then I was alone, and I sighed with relief. It was hard to be around people. It was like I didn't know what to say anymore, or how to act, to give them what they seemed to want.

I'd always thought I was a pretty good actress; I'd been in Drama Club since freshman year. But this summer, I'd found acting normal to be a challenge that was beyond my skill.

I turned to appraise my house. A 1925 classic Victorian, our large wooden home was all turrets and spindles, wide porches and graceful steps. Three stories tall, the house featured a great room where our visitors could mingle and six guest rooms, each painted a different color, on the first and second floors. The third story was reserved for my family—three bedrooms, one small shared bath with an old claw-foot tub, a small kitchen.

Mom cooked for the guests in the house's main kitchen on the bottom floor. When we had visitors, she prepared amazing quiches and muffins for breakfast, and cheese and cracker plates in the evening, along with complementary wine. When it was just the three of us, we ate cereal in the morning, and I pretty much fended for myself for the rest of the day.

We used to have family dinners most nights, even after Ronny had gone away to college, but since his death his chair at the table seemed even more vacant than it had been when he had been at school; the promise of his return was gone.

Now we ate together on Sunday nights and again on Wednesdays; twice a week was about all we could manage to fake it as a family. I could tell it was as painful for my parents to sit together at the dinner table as it was for me, but we all shared an unspoken understanding that we had to at least try.

Today was a Saturday, so I was free. I knew some of the kids from my class would be meeting down at the mini-golf course in the center of town. I hated mini-golf, but when school started up I'd be seeing a lot of these kids, and though I'd been avoiding them all summer, it would be a lot more uncomfortable avoiding them at close range. It was in my best interest to start trying a little harder to act normal. I wondered if Andy would be there tonight; the idea of seeing him seemed strange, but not in a bad way.

Then, like a vision, I recalled Will Cohen's green eyes, his intense stare, the curl of his dark hair across his forehead. I wondered if he would be hanging out with the crowd at the mini-golf, but the proposition seemed somehow ridiculous.

I looked down at my dusty jeans and dirt-encrusted riding boots. If I was really going to reenter the world of the living, I was going to need a shower.

Steam filled the bathroom as I soaked, shampooed, buffed, and scrubbed. I treated my body as if it were a machine, something that needed regular servicing to keep running. I barely registered the temperature of the water on my skin, only noticed that it was too hot when my thighs turned bright red. I had to focus for a moment before I could decide if I felt pain . . . yes.

I turned up the cold water and watched as the red skin faded to a more normal-looking pink. Then I scrubbed my head, hard, and worked the shampoo into a thick lather before rinsing.

My hair fell like a veil, reaching past my shoulder blades, halfway down my back. I tugged out the tangles in it, trying to remember the last time I'd really brushed it. . . . I must have looked pretty interesting that afternoon on the trail.

As I thought of Will Cohen and the strange encounter we'd shared, a flush of warmth spread across my cheeks. Suddenly I was all too aware of the sensation of the water on my skin, working out the tension in my shoulders, streaming down my back, rivulets caressing the backs of my thighs . . .

My body felt as if it might be waking from a long, deep sleep. On the one hand, this might be a good thing. The numbness I'd strived to maintain throughout the summer couldn't go on forever, after all. On the other hand, the thought of my pain overwhelming me as it had those first few weeks after Ronny's death . . . Perhaps numbness had its advantages.

I didn't want to think about it anymore, not now anyway. So I cranked the water off and clambered out of the bathtub, fighting my way through the plastic shower liner and wrapping myself in a towel.

It was easy to avoid my reflection in the bathroom; the

mirror was steamed up. And as I entered my room at the end of the narrow hallway, passing the closed door to Ronny's room, there was no danger that my full-length mirror would reflect my image; I'd turned it toward the wall.

I don't know why, exactly, but lately the idea of looking in the mirror had seemed repulsive to me. Not that I was repulsive to look at; Andy had never complained, that was for sure, and I knew I'd inherited my mom's easy prettiness, with my straight flaxen hair and light blue eyes. But I didn't want to see myself anymore. I bet the school shrink would have had a field day with that little piece of information.

The jeans I'd worn to the stable today were my smallest pair, a detail I hadn't chosen to share with Alice when she'd started in on how loose they looked. My other three pairs were stuffed in the back of my closet. They all swam on me.

So jeans were out for the night. That left me with the option of shorts, a dress, or a skirt. The evenings were beginning to get cold, so I settled on my favorite skirt, a heavy hemp wrap that skimmed my ankles, and pulled on a blue long-sleeved tee.

I didn't feel like blow-drying my hair, so instead I wove it into a loose braid and fastened it with a thin band of leather. I slipped on my favorite Rainbow sandals and called it an outfit.

My wallet had twenty dollars in fives and ones, tips left in the bedrooms of our B&B by the guests. I earned extra money by helping my mom clean the rooms, so I usually had a small fold of cash to spend around town.

This summer, my take was definitely smaller, due in equal

parts, I thought, to the faltering national economy and my family's private grief. Still, twenty dollars would be more than enough for mini-golf and sodas.

Then I couldn't avoid it any longer. The pull was too great, like a deep treacherous undertow.

I knelt by my bed and reached underneath it, extracting a slender yellow notebook. Before I sat with it by the window, I closed my bedroom door silently.

There was a ritual to maintain. Before I could open the notebook, I had to turn on my overhead light, then turn it off, then turn it on again. It didn't matter if light still streamed through the window; I had to flip the light switch exactly three times.

Then I had to straighten the pillows on my bed. It was an old white iron bed, a double, with a white chenille spread and throw pillows in pastel colors. The yellow pillow had to sit closest to the headboard, then the mint-green one, then the two robin's-egg-blue ones.

After this, I gazed out the window and scanned the back garden. There was Daddy, sitting in his favorite spot near the water feature he'd installed with Ronny two summers ago, just beyond the gazebo. Even from here, I could see the glint of the koi fish as they swam in the miniature pond.

Each time I held the notebook, I would sit in the rocking chair that had been a fixture in my room as long as it had been my room—all my life. It was white too, and it was angled toward the large bay window that spanned one whole wall of my room. I would sit, rock for a bit, and then open the notebook.

But this time, before I opened the notebook, before I even sat in my rocking chair, I heard loud footsteps bounce up the stairs of the front porch. I froze at the sound, as if I'd been caught doing something wrong. Then I waited, perfectly still, for a knock at the front door.

THREE
Andy Bunts

*I*t was a loud, uneven rap. I waited to see if someone else was going to answer it, but silence resonated through the house. A moment passed, and then another knock came, this one beating out a rhythm on the wooden panel of the door.

I cursed quietly and shoved my yellow notebook back under my bed. The door to my parents' room was closed; I pictured my mother in there, as she'd been so often lately, flat on her back on her bed, a pillow covering her face.

I half ran down the steps, wanting to get to the door before whoever it was knocked a third time. Twisting the brass handle and yanking open the door, I caught Andy, knuckles raised, about to rap the door again.

He grinned his friendly lopsided smile that used to thrill me and drawled, "Hey, there, Scarlett."

"Andy." I remembered my manners and twisted my mouth into a fairly good imitation of a smile.

"Hey," he said again, craning his neck past me to look into the house. "Can I come in?"

"Umm . . . sure." I pulled the door open and gestured for Andy to come inside. As he passed me, his arm snaked around my waist and I felt his breath against my ear.

"Mmm," he whispered. "You smell good."

My stomach tightened. "It's the shampoo," I muttered.

"I don't think so," he said, his lips inches from my ear, his breath warm and moist. "I think it's just Scarlett."

I twisted away to close the door, turning my face so that I could arrange my expression. When I spun back around, Andy was sauntering into the main kitchen, pulling open the refrigerator with easy familiarity.

"Always hungry," I chided, following him into the kitchen.

"Gotta bulk up for the season." He grabbed an apple from the crisper and then took a bite, his strong, white teeth cutting into the apple's flesh.

He took a chair from the kitchen table and spun it around, then sat, his arms crossed against the chair's back. His eyes traveled over me, appraising me frankly.

"You look good, Scarlett. Are you feeling . . . better?"

I looked away. "Mmm-hmm," I said. I traced the lines of the tile floor with the toe of my shoe. "It's getting a little easier, I guess."

Andy took another bite. "I'm glad," he said. "We've missed you, Scarlett. I've missed you."

When I looked up, Andy's blue eyes were earnest. I admired his tanned arms, the hair on them as golden as if it had been woven by Rumpelstiltskin. He looked like he'd been lifting weights; his broad shoulders were more muscled, and his neck was maybe a size bigger too. His hair was shorter than it had been the last time I'd seen him, out at the stable . . . it wasn't quite a military cut, but the sides and back were cut close, and a sweep of hair in the front was brushed upward.

My appraisal must have been obvious, because Andy asked, "You like what you see?" in between bites.

"Yes," I answered, feeling bold, and when I met his eyes I was relieved to find that it felt almost normal.

There was that grin again, and this time, when I returned his smile, it felt natural.

"That's my girl," he said, standing, the feet of the chair scraping across the tile floor as he spun it back around and pushed it into place. I noticed he was wearing a button-down shirt with a collar, light blue to go with his eyes, the sleeves rolled up past his elbows. "So what do you say?" he asked. "Come with me to the mini-golf? I know it's your favorite," he teased.

I hesitated. I'd planned on going anyway, but showing up with Andy felt awfully like a date. I knew that was how the other kids would see it, and news travels fast in a school with only two hundred students. By Monday, Andy and I would be practically engaged according to the island rumor mill.

Maybe that wouldn't be such a bad thing. The thought of crossing campus with Andy at my side seemed easier than flying solo. His strong hand at the small of my back, maneuvering me down the hallway, a guaranteed seat at lunch at a table full of athletes and cheerleaders, outgoing people who'd carry the conversation . . .

"Yeah," I said. "Why not?"

Andy smiled again. It seemed so easy for him—smiling, making conversation. Yes, mini-golf would be remarkably more tolerable with Andy close by.

"Just let me tell my mom." I left Andy standing in the kitchen, finishing off his apple. Upstairs, my mother's door was still closed. I hesitated before opening it, listening quietly for any movement. There was nothing.

The door swung open silently, and I found my mother just as I had envisioned her—on her back in the bed, a pillow over her eyes.

For one terrifying moment, I was certain she was dead. But then she breathed, and the pillow shifted, and I let out the breath I'd been holding.

On her bedside table sat the bottle of sleeping pills our family doctor had prescribed. The lid was off.

I pulled the door closed and headed back downstairs, more slowly.

Andy looked at me expectantly. "That was fast."

"Yeah . . . she was sleeping. Let me just leave a note." I took a pad of paper and a pen from the junk drawer and scrawled, *Out with Andy. Home later. Love, S.*

I left it on the counter. I had no idea if my mother would even come downstairs tonight; we didn't have any guests, so there really wouldn't be any reason for her to, but Daddy would probably see the note when he came in from the garden.

• • •

One of the good things about living on an island is that you can walk pretty much anywhere in town. From our B&B, it was a short five blocks to the mini-golf, and as we headed over, Andy took my hand, as if we had tacitly agreed to pick up right where we'd left off last spring.

I knew all the neighbors, of course, and I collected a half-dozen smiles and as many waves from eager-looking islanders who seemed relieved to see me back among the living. Andy returned their greetings, waving broadly, as if he were the grand marshal of the Rose Parade.

The mini-golf was as crowded as it ever got. A mix of tourists with their screaming kids yanking on their arms, begging for quarters for the vending machine, and teenage locals who formed their own little circle a clear step away from the visitors gathered around the ticket booth.

It was understood that tourists go first. Locals held open the doors to restaurants for them, took a step back if a group of them was heading for the ice cream stand, kept the shop lights on as long as they wanted to browse.

The tourists were our livelihood, so I guess it was natural that life on the island kind of revolved around them, but we got pretty tired of it sometimes. It was like we lived in Disneyland; there was very little private space, and almost everything was about making a buck.

Of course we knew the owners of the mini-golf: the Carpenters, a nice older couple who'd never had any kids of their own and seemed to enjoy all of their customers—tourists and locals—equally. That was one of the reasons the island teens liked to hang out here; there were no dirty looks from the proprietors. Most of the island kids were pretty broke, except during high season, when tourist money lined our pockets from summer jobs, so the town's businesses usually viewed us as a burden rather than as genuine paying customers.

To an extent, they were right; after all, our friends were the waiters and waitresses, the tour guides and ice cream scoopers, and we had an unspoken agreement to give each other free sodas and fries, bigger servings of ice cream . . . when the owners weren't looking.

But the Carpenters didn't employ any teenagers. They worked the ticket booth themselves, handing out the putters and brightly colored golf balls. And though Mrs. Carpenter was a kind lady, she kept a shark's eye on the equipment, making sure that no one got a free round unless they scored a hole in one on the eighteenth hole.

"Hey, it's Big Red!" shouted Connell, Andy's closest friend. They played baseball together—Andy was the pitcher and Connell was the catcher. They had a secret language of signs and signals that they employed on the field, and I was pretty sure that they used it off the field too.

I hated that nickname—Big Red. Because my name was Scarlett, Connell seemed to think that any moniker referring to things red was appropriate. Big Red wasn't as bad as some of the names he'd called me over the years; freshman year I'd made the mistake one day of wearing red tights, and he'd called me Fire Crotch for most of the first semester, until I dumped a tray of pasta in his lap one lunch and threatened to smash his face with the tray if he ever called me that again.

The crowd of kids watched me with the full spectrum of expressions on their easily readable faces—surprise, pleasure, concern, pity . . . and, from Kaitlyn Meyers, a mix of resentment and distaste.

I registered their expressions without feeling much about them either way. Kaitlyn and I had been pretty close until Andy and I started dating last year. It was clear from the way she stared at our interlaced fingers, as if she'd like to turn my hand to dust, how she felt about me being here, and with Andy.

Kaitlyn looked great as she always did; her pretty strawberry hair was twisted away from her face into some kind of messy bun at the nape of her neck, and her lip gloss shimmered alluringly on her lips, always slightly parted. She was technically overdressed for the activity, but she pulled it off, anyway; she was wearing kitten-heeled shoes and a fluffy pink ballet-neck sweater with professionally distressed skinny jeans. I got the impression from the way she looked at Andy that she had dressed with him in mind.

Even apart from her shoes, there was something distinctly kittenish about Kaitlyn. The way she smoothed the errant hairs about her temple, the way she tilted her head to an appealingly lilting angle . . . Yes, if Kaitlyn were a pet, she would be a perfect, eternal kitten, playful and soft, full of delightful purrs . . . and unexpectedly sharp claws.

Connell came over to ruffle my hair, and I cringed away from his hand. Andy had me covered, though. He knocked Connell's hand away and said, "Take it easy, man, okay?"

They stared at each other for a beat, and I could practically smell the testosterone boiling. Then Connell's face stretched into a grin and he held his hands palms up, as if surrendering.

"Sure, buddy, sure thing," he said, and ambled over toward the vending machines. There was something about the slope of his shoulders that made me wonder if maybe Connell was getting a little tired of catching for Andy.

He sure had grown over the last few months. He was now taller than Andy, and his face had lost all the soft edges it had had the spring before. His face had kind of a Neanderthal slope to it, though it looked good on him, the wide brow, the shaded eyes, the square jaw. Connell, I mused, was a guy you'd want on your side in a fight.

"I'll get our tickets," Andy said, and he dropped a kiss on my temple before releasing my hand and jogging over to the ticket booth. When I looked up, I counted six pairs of eyes on me, though they all looked away quickly . . . all except Kaitlyn's.

Inwardly, I sighed. It all seemed so silly now, this jockeying for position, these petty jealousies. But I felt angry, too, that familiar burning sensation I'd come to rely on over the last few months. . . . There was no way I would be intimidated by Kaitlyn, not today, not anymore.

I held her gaze and walked toward her. Her eyebrows shot up, revealing her surprise.

"Hey, Kaitlyn," I said smoothly. "What's your problem?"

Her eyes widened, her innocence on display for all the onlookers. "Problem?" she asked. "I don't have a problem. It's great to see you, Scarlett."

She sounded sincere. This confused me. Maybe I was misreading the situation. I adjusted my posture, relaxing my arms and taking a half step back.

"Yeah," I said. "It's been a while."

The others turned away, and Kaitlyn's eyes narrowed. "You and Andy seem pretty friendly," she said.

It was there—the animosity I had suspected, but she had it layered under a saccharine coating.

"Yeah," I answered, keeping the heat of anger inside of me under control. "I guess my absence made his heart grow fonder." I shrugged as if it didn't matter to me either way.

"Hmm," she said. "We'll see, I guess. You're looking . . . skinny."

I couldn't tell for sure if that was meant to be an insult or a compliment, but I decided to take it as the latter.

"Thanks," I said.

Andy returned with our putters and two golf balls. He handed me the red one. His was blue.

"You ready?"

The next hour was a lot less difficult than I thought it might be. Everyone cheered my good shots and consoled me when my putts went wide, in a clear effort to make me feel comfortable. Of course, all the extra attention did the exact opposite, but I knew their hearts were in the right place.

Kaitlyn glued herself to Connell's side, flirting with him outrageously and asking him for tips on how to negotiate the tougher holes. This was completely transparent as Kaitlyn was one of the most dexterous players, but at least it kept her out of my hair for the night.

It felt good to be out, but I couldn't help feeling I was betraying Ronny. I knew he'd want me to be having fun. No one loved a party more than Ronny. He had always made sure that everyone around him was at ease and having a good time.

I gave up keeping score, just concentrating on holding myself together as we negotiated our way around the tight little course. Ahead of us was a family of four—the mom and dad with their two little kids, an older sister and a little brother.

The girl was probably about ten. I could tell that she had a real competitive streak from the way she was vigilant about keeping score. Her baby brother, just four probably, kept messing up her strokes, swinging his putter in wild loops, tumbling on the green, kicking the balls every which way. She tolerated him the best she could, but I could see the strain it was causing her. The parents laughed easily, and took turns trying to distract the little boy.

They looked happy. Normal. As if they had no idea how lucky they all were.

I tore my gaze away from them when the mother caught me staring, and focused on my shot through a haze of tears. Andy must have seen me fighting to maintain my composure, because he leaned in close to me and whispered, "You want to get out of here?"

I nodded, not trusting myself to speak. He took my putter and ball and returned them to the booth. Then he led me by the arm away from the green and called over his shoulder, "Catch you later, guys."

I heard a mix of voices calling out goodbyes, but didn't turn as I raised my hand in a halfhearted wave.

All of a sudden, I didn't have anything else to give. I'd managed to fake it for almost an hour—pretty good for a first attempt. I felt Andy navigating me toward the lights of the boardwalk, though I wasn't really paying attention to where we were headed.

"Hungry?" he asked.

I shook my head.

"Mind if I get something to eat?"

I shook my head again.

Steering me by the small of my back, Andy maneuvered us through the crowded main street toward a little café. I knew it well; my family was friendly with the family that owned it. The Hendersons had five daughters: one off at college, one who'd gotten pregnant during her senior year and still lived at home, now with her baby boy, two who were still in school with me, and one in middle school.

One of the owner's teen daughters, a sophomore named Hailey, was working the hostess stand. There wasn't a line, so after forcing my way through some awkward small talk—*Hey, long time no see, how's it been?*—she seated us at a table in the back corner.

Andy pulled my chair out for me—always the gentleman—before seating himself.

"Can I get you a drink?" Hailey asked, handing us our menus. I put mine down on the table without looking at it.

"I'll have a Coke," Andy said. "Scarlett, what do you want?"

To be at home, tucked into my room for the night, I thought. "Do you have herbal tea?" I asked.

"I think so," Hailey said. "I'll check."

She came back a few minutes later with Andy's icy Coke and a pot of lukewarm water that had a tea bag floating morosely in it.

"You really should eat something, Scarlett," Andy urged. "You look a little . . . I don't know, weak."

Another Henderson girl, Jill, one year above me and Andy in school, came over to take our order.

"Hey, Andy," she said. "Hi, Scarlett."

Andy made small talk, but all I could hear was the drumming of my blood in my ears. I closed my eyes and felt the room spin.

". . . and you'll have . . ."

My eyes opened. Andy and Jill were both staring at me.

"Umm . . . ," I said.

"Bring her a burger too, will you, with fries," Andy ordered.

"Sure." Jill jotted it down on her pad. "Are you okay, Scarlett?"

I nodded carefully, not wanting to move my head too much. I heard her footsteps as she carried our order back to the kitchen.

". . . don't look so hot, Scar."

I forced myself to look at Andy. "I guess I forgot to eat lunch."

Andy shook his head. "Well, no wonder," he said. "I can't go twenty minutes without eating something, or I'm practically crazy with hunger." He went on to break down his diet into minute detail, rattling off fat percentages and calorie counts, grams of protein in his favorite muscle-builder shake, how many ounces of water he drank each day.

I nodded and asked a vague question every minute or two about fat conversion. Andy was thrilled to have an audience, I could tell, and after a while he shifted from diet to nutritional supplements.

"My dad has me taking all these omega-3s," he said. "And I just started popping these acai berry supplements."

I wasn't sure what the right response would be to this, but fortunately Jill arrived with our burgers.

As she set the plate down in front of me, my belly grumbled urgently, and I felt my mouth watering.

Andy was still talking, but it was as if his voice were coming through a tunnel from somewhere very far away. I watched my hands reach out and embrace the burger. The bun was warm, and as I raised it to my lips, droplets of meaty juice rained down on the fries. I closed my eyes as I took a bite.

I chewed, I swallowed, I chewed, I swallowed. My tea went from lukewarm to room temperature as I ate and ate and ate. My burger disappeared and I felt my stomach stretching, distending, and I knew I should stop, but my hands kept bringing salty, oily fries from my plate to my lips until they were all gone. When my plate was empty, I sat for a moment with my eyes closed, remembering the taste of it all.

Across from me, Andy's plate was cleared too, and he was saying something about baseball—his own team or a professional team, I couldn't discern, but I couldn't care less. My mouth felt greasy and my lips tasted like salt.

Jill walked by and I flagged her down. "Can I have a glass of water?"

As I drank the water, I felt my head clearing and my heartbeat returning to a more civilized pace. I wasn't dizzy anymore, and the restaurant seemed somehow brighter, more sharply in focus.

I watched Andy's lips move as he talked, and I forced myself to listen to what he was saying.

"So Jenna dumped Brandon that weekend, and by the next Thursday, Connell and I found her and Kevin making out during their lunch break over at the tourism office. I mean, they were broken up already, so whatever, right? But Brandon didn't seem to feel that way about it. I think he was about ready to pound Kevin when we told him." He slurped the final drops of his Coke from the bottom of his glass.

"Why did you tell him?" I asked.

Andy seemed a little startled by my question. Maybe because he'd gotten used to the conversation being one-sided. "I dunno. I guess we figured he had a right to know."

"What right?" I asked. "I mean, they were broken up, weren't they?"

"Yeah, but still . . ." Andy shrugged. "It seemed the right thing to do."

I doubted that, but I nodded as if I agreed. It seemed to me that Andy and Connell were a bigger set of gossips than two old ladies, and they had wanted to see what would happen if they passed their little gold nugget of information along to a jealous ex-boyfriend.

The lump of meat in my stomach felt as if it was beginning to congeal, and it seemed that I could feel the saturated fat pumping through my veins.

"Are you taking Drama again this year?" Andy asked, probably to change the subject.

I shrugged. "I don't know. I guess." I was signed up for Drama, seventh period, just as I had been the two years before . . . but the thought of getting onstage now made me uncomfortable.

"You should. You're so good in all those little plays. So pretty." And he leaned across the table to brush his hand across my cheek.

"Yeah. Thanks." My eyes flitted over to a small crowd that was waiting over by the hostess stand. "We should go . . . give our table up," I said.

"Sure." Andy pulled his wallet out to pay and I reached into the small pocket on the front of my skirt for my cash. "No, I got it," he said.

"No, you paid for the golf . . . let me at least pay for my food," I argued.

Andy pursed his lips and shook his head. I knew from experience that he wasn't budging on this one.

If there was any question about whether or not this was a date, how this meal was paid for would settle it.

I wasn't sure if the discomfort in my belly was the burger or the pressure from the decision I was about to make. "All right," I said smoothly. "But I'm leaving the tip."

46

I could see from the look on Andy's face that he wasn't quite sure about this turn of events, but he didn't argue.

I didn't know exactly how much the bill was; I left Jill a five-dollar bill. Andy draped his arm across my shoulders and pushed the door open for me.

The air outside was chilly, and the sun had disappeared entirely from the sky while we were eating. Andy's arm felt good, a comfortable weight pressing me firmly to the earth, grounding me.

We walked like that, together, through the town. The water lapped quietly at the shore; the boats in the harbor bobbed gently in their moorings. Above us, a heavy moon sailed across the sky.

My arm hesitated, then wound around Andy's waist. It didn't feel the same as it had before, but it still felt nice.

Andy's face dropped to my hair and he breathed deeply. "Mmm," he said. "I'm glad you came out."

We walked farther and turned up my street. It was empty now, the windows in the front rooms glowing blue from televisions that ensnared the people inside.

Andy walked me to my house, then up the steps of my porch. My father had left the porch light on for me; moths flitted about it in mindless circles.

I knew Andy was going to kiss me now.

I turned and tipped my face up to his. "Thanks for dinner," I said. "And the golfing."

He laughed, low and sweet. "Yeah, you really loved that golf," he said, and then his lips caught mine.

I didn't give him a chance to hesitate; my arms wrapped around his neck and I pulled him roughly against me. I told

47

him with my mouth the things I couldn't bring myself to say—that I was grateful for him, that I was glad he'd showed up at my house, that it was good that he'd waited for me, these long months of summer—that I was back, or trying to be, at least.

He pulled away first and he smiled at me, a wide, boyish grin, as if he'd just won a prize.

"Good night," I said, and I slipped into the house, closing the door softly behind me.

FOUR

Mirror, Mirror

Even though Lily and her family got home three days before school started, I didn't see her until the first day of class. They had all come down with some kind of flu—("Ugh, airports are disgusting" was Lily's explanation of how they got sick)—so even though I wanted nothing more than to spend the last days of summer chilling poolside at Lily's house, I was stuck in my own sad little world.

My mom rarely appeared before eleven a.m. these days, and when she did make it out of her room, I wasn't entirely convinced that she was fully conscious. I know my dad had refilled her prescription for sleeping pills, though his brow was creased with worry when he was talking to the pharmacist on the phone about it. I heard the phrase "developing a dependency," but when he saw me listening, Daddy quickly finished the conversation and hung up.

There were no more guests; I figured my parents must be

dipping pretty heavily into their savings to cover the bills, and I considered trying to find an after-school job to help out. When I mentioned this to my dad, he shook his head firmly.

"Junior year is the most important," he said. "This is the year colleges look at closely. You don't want to be stuck on this island forever, do you?"

Absolutely not. I wanted to go somewhere far, far away for college. This hadn't always been my plan; I had figured I'd follow in Ronny's footsteps and go to UCLA, if I could get in. Maybe we would share an apartment. But with Ronny gone, I found myself yearning for something very different . . . snow, maybe, and big mountains.

So I resigned myself to just doing my best not to spend my parents' money, which was one of the reasons I turned my mom down when she offered to take me to the mainland to do some back-to-school shopping.

The other reason was that I didn't know if I could stand being alone with my mom for a whole day. Our sadness separately was hard enough. . . . Sometimes at night, I heard my mother crying, and I knew that she must have heard my sobs too. Together, our pain threatened to be overwhelming. I think my mom felt the same way. Even around the house we avoided standing too close to each other, and we never touched. Eye contact was minimal. It was as if we each were a highly reactive chemical that, if combined, would explode.

So I spent my last few days of summer much as I'd spent the rest of them—doing chores around the house and hanging out at the stable with Delilah.

Every time she and I rounded a bend on the trails, I found myself expecting to see Will Cohen again. But all I saw was more of the same—dry grass, rolling hills, trees.

I even revisited the trail where I'd met Will. I found the straw cowboy hat that had blown off my head that afternoon; dismounting Delilah, I picked it up from where it lay on the ground, blowing off the dust before putting it on.

But Will did not appear. I began to wonder if he had been a dream, or some sort of hallucination. Except his eyes—the shocking electric green of his eyes, staring at me with such intensity, such bewildered pain . . . I knew I didn't have that good of an imagination.

The day after Labor Day, I awoke to a strange mixture of anticipation and dread. Life seemed to be insisting on moving ahead, with or without Ronny.

Time was a cruel bitch. Either move on with her or get steamrolled; I don't think she cared much either way. My mom seemed to be taking door number two—steamrolled. Myself, I was ambivalent.

Still, I'd get to see Lily today. That was worth getting out of bed for.

There was no competing with Lily's sense of fashion, especially considering that she'd just returned from two and a half months in Italy. So I dressed quickly, pulling on my favorite dress. It was violet, made of soft stretch cotton, with elbow-length sleeves and a pretty lettuce hem. It hung just above the knee. As an afterthought I pulled my jeans on, too. Andy loved to mock my penchant for wearing jeans with dresses. He preferred bare legs, but I felt better in my jeans, less vulnerable.

My standard flip-flops completed the outfit. It occurred to me that I could turn my mirror around to see how I looked, maybe apply a layer of mascara, but my stomach started to feel like I was on a roller coaster, so I just shoved a few dollars into my pocket and yanked a brush through my hair. It was fairly compliant today; I twisted up the front and stabbed it with a couple of bobby pins, then let the rest alone, swinging on my back.

My mom was still in her bedroom—no surprise there—but in the kitchen, my father stood with a cup of coffee, gazing out the window over the sink. When I entered, it took him a moment to focus on me, and then he smiled.

"You look nice," he said. "I like that color with your eyes."

"Thanks, Daddy."

"Do you want me to cook you a couple of eggs?"

I shook my head. "I'll just grab an apple," I said, heading to the refrigerator.

"Just an apple? That's not enough for breakfast . . . especially not on a school day."

"Lily's going to bring some of her mom's famous muffins to school," I lied. "You know, like to celebrate the beginning of the school year?"

He nodded. "That'll be nice." His gaze wandered out the window again. I started to leave, but his voice stopped me. "How are you holding up, honey?"

I rolled the apple I'd taken from one hand to the other, then back again. I didn't turn to look at him. I didn't want to start crying, not now, right before school. "Okay," I said. "I guess."

"All right, baby. We love you. Have fun out there."

I nodded, waiting a minute to see if he was going to say anything else. When he didn't, I left our little kitchen. I couldn't get down the steps and out the door fast enough to suit me. I couldn't think about all that—not now.

"*Ciao, amica mia!*" called the voice I so loved.

I turned to see Lily—at least, it had to be Lily—standing on the sidewalk, clutching a leather satchel.

The outfit she was wearing did not belong in our school. Let me clarify that: the outfit did not belong in our *lives*. Lily was dressed from head to toe in some kind of buttery ivory leather suit. The jacket was nipped in at the waist and seemed to have at least a half-dozen zippers, along with . . . shoulder pads, something I'd seen in old movies from the late 1980s but had never worn in my life. There was a matching skirt, of course, several inches above the knee, and her feet were encased in the hottest leather booties I've ever seen. I didn't think I could have walked the length of a classroom in those shoes, but it appeared that Lily planned to wear them all day.

Her black curls were bouncing saucily about her shoulders, and they seemed to shine even more than usual. Her mouth was painted a daring shade of red, and who knew what kind of eye makeup she'd applied; her eyes were hidden behind sleek gold aviator sunglasses.

I grinned. Only Lily.

She clapped her hands, tucking her satchel under her

arm, and ran toward me. Embracing me quickly, she kissed my right cheek, then my left, then my right, then my left again. I was starting to feel dizzy.

"I missed you too!" I said.

"Oh my god, Scarlett, that's how you say hello in Italy. Can you believe it? I mean, you can totally go up to, like, even the hottest guy and just start kissing him! And he'll kiss you back! I mean, Italy is so civilized! It cuts out all the crap, do you know what I mean, and it just gets right down to the good stuff."

"Umm . . . I'm pretty sure you're only supposed to kiss the people you already know," I said. "I read that you just shake hands there the first time you meet. The kissing isn't supposed to come until later."

Lily shrugged. "Well," she said, "*I* didn't hear any complaints."

She laced her arm through mine and started walking toward Avalon High. "It's beyond beautiful there too, Scarlett. You would have loved it," she moaned. "I've already convinced my parents that they have to send me back when I graduate. This time, *without* parental supervision. And *with* you, of course. You'll go, right?"

"Sure," I said. It was good to know I had plans for after I graduated in a year and nine months . . . even if I didn't know how I was going to navigate successfully through today.

"You look awful, Scarlett," Lily said frankly. "Just skin and bones."

"Easy for you to say," I scoffed. "Not all of us are as . . . blessed as you are." I indicated Lily's generous curves, tucked neatly into the leather packaging of her suit. "You look great, by the way."

"Of course I do. These Italian designers—they really know what they're doing. No more buying American for me, no way, no how. It's European everything from here on in."

"Way to bolster the flagging economy," I said, rolling my eyes. Lily was passionate, but usually only for a few weeks about any one thing before she moved on to the next obsession. I gave this Italian thing until homecoming, tops.

I took a halfhearted bite of my apple. It tasted too soft, mealy. As soon as I spied a trash can, I tossed it in.

The rest of the way to school, Lily filled me in on everything I'd missed in Italy.

According to her, the boys were way cuter than anyone here on the island—"Even Andy, no offense," she said.

None taken.

The food was amazing. And people took hours eating their meals, and dinner didn't even *begin* until after eight o'clock, and the beaches were incredible and—"you'll never guess . . . ," she whispered, conspiratorial now, "I went to this beach, and, like, half of the women weren't wearing their bikini tops . . . and now I don't even *sort of* have a tan line. Look!"

She unzipped her jacket and peeled it apart to reveal her smooth, tan shoulder, unmarred by the customary band of white left by a bikini strap. I had to admit, I was impressed. Public nudity was not something I thought I'd ever be comfortable with. Lately I had a hard enough time being around people even fully clothed.

"Wow" was all I could say.

"I know, huh?"

And then we were on campus. Our school wasn't large. Because our island was so small, kids ages six through eighteen found themselves spending most of their time at the Avalon School.

The kindergarten and elementary kids were in their own section of the campus, the middle schoolers had their own buildings, and then there was what served as the high school—a couple of older Mission-style buildings, a gym that was ours when the littler kids weren't using it, the fields where our teams practiced after school.

I'd bet twenty bucks that no one—teachers included—had ever seen a suit like the one Lily was wearing, but no one seemed surprised to see her dressed in it. If she'd shown up with a live ferret wrapped around her neck, everyone would just think it was the latest in fashion. One good thing about Lily was that I was free to be as invisible as I wanted to be when she was around.

At least, that had been the case last year, Before Ronny Died. Now I noticed that even Lily's amazing leather ensemble wasn't enough to send all the attention her way; I saw a few girls whispering behind their hands to one another while looking me up and down, and more than a couple of teachers gave me sympathetic smiles as they walked by. Mr. Brown, last year's math teacher, even patted me on the shoulder.

My mother's "let the steamroller get you" philosophy was beginning to seem more and more practical, and the first bell hadn't even rung.

"Who is *that?*" Lily murmured. "Scarlett, you've been holding out on me."

Even before I turned to see who she was talking about, I knew Will Cohen was watching me. I looked up, and there he was—tall and angular in jeans and a thin green T-shirt, holding a spiral notebook and a couple of texts, leaning against the wall of the school's main building.

His eyes froze me again, and though Lily was making appreciative sounds next to me, I didn't respond.

His hair was a bit tidier today, though still nothing like Andy's neatly coifed cut. Dark brown waves swept away from his face, and his hair brushed the neckline of his shirt. His jaw looked tense, as if he was holding himself very, very still, and his eyes did not waver from mine. I felt my heart flutter, and for one bitter moment I wished I'd put a bit more effort into getting dressed this morning . . . at least, I could have left the jeans at home.

"He's staring at you," Lily said in amused stage whisper. "Why is that, do you think?"

"We met last week," I murmured. "Out on the trail."

"He rides too?"

"No. He was just . . . standing there."

Will lifted his hand, as if to wave at me.

"Hey there, beautiful." Andy pulled on my hair and peeked his head around my shoulder. I think he must have seen Will looking at me, because when he leaned down to kiss me, his embrace felt . . . territorial. Like a dog marking his property.

I pushed him away and craned my neck around his wide shoulders, but Will was gone.

"Must you do that in public?" I glared at Andy.

"Public, private, anywhere you want me to," he said with a grin. "Hey, there, Lily. Nice threads."

"Thanks," Lily said, but her voice was cool. "Good timing, bozo. You scared away the new kid."

"I don't know what you mean," Andy said.

Sure he didn't. But I didn't feel like a fight. So instead I said, "Hey, save some seats for me and Lily at lunch, okay?" Then I ducked out from under his arm and headed toward my locker with Lily in tow, tottering on her impossible heels.

"Wow!" she said when we were out of earshot from Andy. "The sexual tension is sizzling. Do tell."

Luckily, the first bell rang; Lily would have to wait.

The morning classes were a blur. Lily and I shared European History first thing and French right before lunch, but when she tried to pass me a note in French it was intercepted by Monsieur Antoine. An actual Frenchman, Monsieur Antoine boasted one of those amazing mustaches that practically hypnotized you; it was groomed into two tight points with some sort of wax or pomade, and when he spoke, it jumped up and down like a fish on a hook.

"Mademoiselle Adams," he chastised, taking the note in his manicured hands and tucking it into the pocket of his vest. *"S'il vous plaît, restez après la classe."*

"He wants you to stay after class," I murmured to Lily. Her French was terrible.

"Merde," she grumbled.

So I entered the cafeteria by myself, and I felt my feet

drag as I joined Andy at his table. I tried to keep my eyes from scanning the small gathering of students, but I couldn't help myself. Will Cohen was nowhere to be seen.

Connell was there, though, and he flopped loudly into the seat I was saving for Lily. "Hey there, Red Vine," he said, and plopped down his tray, loaded heavily with pizza. I counted four pieces. He had two cans of soda as well.

"Gotta bulk up," he said, a little defensively. "Where's *your* lunch?"

"I had a big breakfast." There was no way I was eating around all these people.

Andy, seated across from me, looked at me quizzically, but I guess he decided not to push the issue. Instead, he asked Connell, "Hey, what's the 411 on the new guy?"

Connell prided himself on knowing everything about everybody. Once, in eighth grade, Kathy O'Malley had gotten mono from French-kissing her cousin Gabe, who lived over on the mainland. She might have kept the whole thing on the down-low, but somehow Connell found out about it, and the next thing you know, the entire town knew Kathy's secret. She hasn't been on a date since.

"Name's Will Cohen," Connell said, getting right down to business. "He's a Jew."

I felt myself bristling. "Really, Connell? We have to talk about his religion?"

He shrugged, unabashed. "I'm just a conduit for information, Big Red. Information just flows on through me." He turned back to Andy. "He lives over in Two Harbors. His dad is a professor of something or other . . . religious studies, maybe? Anyway, he's some intellectual bigwig from the East Coast, but for some reason he dragged his kid out here right before the beginning of his senior year. His dad is on . . . sabusteron?"

"Sabbatical," I guessed.

"Yeah, that's it." Connell picked up one of his pieces of pizza and took a large bite. A string of cheese swung from his chin as he continued. "Anyway, it's just him and his kid—Will. His wife died a few years ago."

A wave of loaded silence descended over the table. Everyone tried really hard not to look at me.

Finally, Jane Maple, a girl I sort of liked, piped up, "Well, if anyone tried to move me right before senior year, I'd freak the hell out. That's lame."

The consensus at the table was that it was indeed lame, perhaps even bogus, to move someone right before senior year. I guessed it would be even worse to take someone out of a big-city school and bring them to a little tourist trap of an island. But I kept my opinion to myself.

"Anyway, that's all I know about Will Cohen," Connell concluded.

"Well, you left out that he's perfectly *gorgeous*," Lily gushed, making a late entrance and shoving Connell aside to make room for another chair next to me. "And that he seems to have quite the thing for Scarlett."

I felt my face flush red, and I kicked Lily under the table. She laughed. "What?" she asked. "Is it so bad that the cutest guy in school is crushing on you?"

Andy's face was murderous, and Connell looked personally hurt. "You think he's cuter than me?" he asked.

60

"Way," Lily said seriously. She uncapped a bottle of water and took a sip. "He's got that whole ethnic thing going on. You're just an island boy."

The conversation turned to ranking the appeal of the boys clustered at our table, an activity that seemed to thrill the girls and made all the guys squirm in their seats.

"What do *you* think, Scarlett?" asked Kaitlyn. For the first day of school, she'd gone with a "schoolgirl"-inspired outfit: a white button-down topped with a fitted vest, a red plaid skirt, and white knee-highs. *A little too obvious to be ironic*, I thought. "Do you vote Will or Andy?"

"I think I need to go to the bathroom," I answered. "I'll see you all later, okay?"

What I really needed was some air. I pushed my way through the cafeteria doors onto the lawn and took a deep, cleansing breath. Over the last couple of months, I'd spent almost all my time alone or in the company of a rather taciturn mare. The conversation of the last twenty minutes had been so loaded with subtext, so potentially rife with misunderstandings and double entendres, that I felt a little sick. High school seemed to be a world for the healthy, most definitely. It was no place for me, not anymore.

I stood in the sunshine until the curious glances of Mr. Steiner, the vice principal, who was trolling the quad for potential misbehavior, turned more deliberate, and he began walking in my direction. Then I took refuge in the bathroom.

I turned the faucet on cold and splashed my face. It felt shockingly good, a reminder that I was really here. I liked that sensation; it wasn't pleasant, exactly, but it was reassuring, like hunger pains. I am here. I am alive.

After a few moments, I shut off the water and turned around, reaching for a paper towel.

Damn. I'd made a miscalculation. I'd forgotten that the school bathroom featured a full-length mirror along the far wall, and suddenly I was confronted with my reflection.

The girl who stared back at me was thin—*Too thin*, I thought, with the part of my mind that was still able to analyze a situation rationally. Her hair was a pretty color, just as I remembered it, but longer than I'd thought it was. The last time I'd really seen my hair, it just reached the strap of my bra. It was longer than that now, and the ends looked as though they could use a trim.

The face of the mirror-girl was less easy to recognize. The basic features were about as I remembered them: there were still two eyes, a nose, a mouth. But this girl, the one who gazed at me, had eyes laced through with pain. Violet half-moons cradled her eyes; her cheekbones seemed too high, too sharp; her lips pale.

This was not a pretty girl. This was not a happy girl, or a popular girl, or even a fully functional girl. If others saw me that way, it was because their vision was muddled by their memory of the girl I had been. This girl didn't have much going for her. I didn't think I liked this girl—not very much at all.

Calmly, deliberately, I set the edge of my fingernail on the most tender flesh of my arm. Watching the reflection, I drew my nail down and watched with something akin to pleasure as a line appeared on the inside of the mirror-girl's arm, first white, then blush-red. Somewhere, I registered pain.

The mirror-girl smiled.

• • •

When I came out of the bathroom minutes later, I must not have been watching where I was going. I was hurrying because I thought I must be late for my next class, Organic Chemistry.

I didn't see him until too late—by the time I realized we'd collided, our books were intermingled at our feet.

"Sorry, sorry," I said, stooping to collect my stuff. He bent down too, and our foreheads smashed into each other.

This sent me sprawling, and I was glad I'd worn the jeans. I squeezed my eyes closed and rubbed my head, trying to pull myself together.

"What happened to your arm?"

It was Will. I peeled open one eye and looked at him through my fingers. "My arm?"

"It's all scratched." He leaned forward and, without asking permission, grabbed hold of my arm. His grip was uncomfortably tight. One finger of his other hand traced the scratch that extended from the inside of my elbow to my wrist. "What did you do?"

I couldn't speak. His touch was warm and soft, and the line his finger had traced felt lit by fire. I was acutely aware of how close we were; the dark curls of his hair bobbed just above me, and his eyes, looking up to my face from my arm, seared me as surely as a brand.

"I . . ." I felt the beginnings of anger in my chest, and I leaned on it like a crutch. Yanking away from him, I gathered my books and stood. "I don't need to answer to you," I spat. "What are you doing here, anyway, lurking outside of the girls' bathroom? Are you some kind of a perv?"

"I was looking for you," he said.

This made no sense to me. "I have to go to class," I said. "I'm sorry I bumped into you."

Organic Chemistry happened mostly without me, though I was in my seat. My mind was absent—I couldn't stop replaying the scene in the hallway. Why on earth would Will be looking for *me*? And why had he looked so pained when he'd seen my arm? It was just a scratch, after all . . . no big deal.

He had to be some kind of a psycho, I finally determined, as class was coming to a close. And for some reason, he'd set his sights on me. It was a good thing he was a year ahead; at least chances were good we wouldn't have any classes together.

I contented myself with this conclusion for exactly seven minutes, the time I had to gather my books and walk to my last class of the day, Drama. Then I opened the door to the classroom and saw him again, sitting in the seat I'd called my own for the last two years.

My anger boiled again. This was too much. First he'd stalked me on the trail; then he'd practically attacked me in the hallway; now he had infiltrated the only class I truly enjoyed, the one hour of the day I'd been looking forward to.

I stormed across the classroom, crossing in front of Mrs. B's desk, and poked my finger at Will's chest.

"You," I said.

He looked up. "Me," he said. His eyes traveled the length of my forearm, reminding me of earlier, when his finger had traced the same path.

I crossed my arms. The conversations that had been brewing all about me had died out.

"You're in my seat," I said quietly. Tears filled my eyes suddenly.

"I'm sorry." He moved to stand. "I didn't realize."

"No," I said. "Don't. I'm sorry. My name's not on it or anything." I tried my best to smile as I walked to another seat, three rows over and two back. I could almost hear the swivel of heads as everyone watched me negotiate the aisle.

What was wrong with me? Of course he wasn't stalking me; he was just a boy in my Drama class. He hadn't done anything.

My anger was gone, drowned by a sea of sadness, and without a word I stood and left the room, Mrs. B smiling sympathetically after me.

FIVE

The Press of Sand

*A*lice must have seen the answer on my face, because on our drive out to the stable, she didn't ask me how the first day of school had been. Delilah, at least, was a known quantity. She awaited me patiently in her stall, and she nickered same as always when she saw the chunk of carrot I palmed for her.

As she chewed, I rubbed my cheek against her velvety forehead. It had been a couple of days since I'd ridden, so before I tacked her up I loosed her in the arena so she could get out her bucks. She tossed her head in pleasure as she picked up a trot. I chased her with a longe whip, snapping it at her heels.

Her back hoof shot out in a buck, and she broke into a canter. In the sand in the middle of the arena, I swung the long black whip in a series of waves, encouraging her to be wild.

"Come on, girl," I urged. "You can do better than that." Her ears rotated back at the sound of my voice and her run became more muscular and driven. Not far away, one of the gardeners started up a weed whacker. Its sharp growl spooked Delilah and her canter became a gallop. She careened around the arena, faster and faster, leaning slightly inward as she banked the turns.

Her red mane and tail sailed like a wind-fed fire; her hooves flashed and sand flew as they dug into the arena's footing.

"Calm down, girl," I soothed, the whip slack at my side. Her speed was beautiful, but dangerous, too; the last thing I wanted was for her to pull a tendon. "Shhh, shhh," I called. "It's all right, Delilah, easy."

She tossed her head, eyes wild, before her run slowed a half pace, then another, until she'd found a trot and, finally, a walk. I clicked my tongue and dipped my hand into my pocket before holding it out in an invitation. Delilah altered her trajectory and headed toward me in the center of the arena. She dipped her mouth to my hand and took the sugar cube as gently as if it were a communion wafer.

I thumped her neck and clipped the lead rope to her halter. There was another sugar cube in my pocket. I withdrew it and hesitated before placing it on my tongue.

The sweetness burned as the sugar melted. It was grainy, and I held it against the roof of my mouth as it disintegrated. Twenty-five calories. It was nearly four o'clock. This was the first thing I'd eaten today, except for the one bite of mealy apple I'd had before school. So why should I feel shame, as if I'd failed somehow? It was irrational, and yet this felt like the truth to me. In an instant, the sugar's sweetness seemed bitter and I spit into the sand.

Delilah and I rode toward Two Harbors, the only other town on Catalina Island. With just a couple of restaurants, one little store, and one hotel, Two Harbors, on what we locals called the Isthmus, barely counts as a town. More a village, really, only a hundred and fifty or so people live there year-round. Apparently Professor Cohen had chosen the most remote, out-of-the-way spot he could find for himself and his son. I had to admit, I was curious. Who would *want* to live at the Isthmus? *It's bad enough to live in Avalon,* I thought. I remembered what Connell had said about the Cohens moving out from the East Coast, kind of last-minute. I found myself wondering . . . what could have compelled Professor Cohen to drag his kid across the country right before he started his senior year? Maybe Will had been some kind of troublemaker, I mused. Maybe he was part of a big-city gang or something, and his father had decided to get him as far away as possible.

But the flash of Will's intense green eyes came unheeded to my mind. He didn't look like a troublemaker . . . though he did look *troubled,* definitely.

As I came down from the hills to the Isthmus, I surveyed the idyllic scene. Two Harbors got its name from its unique geography; in this spot, the Isthmus's two harbors nipped in tightly like a lady's corseted waist. You could walk from one harbor to the other in under fifteen minutes, a favorite activity of visitors.

The Isthmus attracted a different class of tourists than Avalon did. People who came to this part of the island came for the hiking, the wildlife, the atmosphere—not the shopping or the tourist attractions, like our famous glass-bottom boats.

And the few people who chose to live on this side of the island were different too; they were independent, mostly content to have taken an additional step away from society, and happily navigated their little village by bicycle or foot.

As if on cue, our island's sole school bus pulled into town. My heart leaped as I watched the doors slide open and Will's lanky figure descend the four steps, his backpack thrown over one shoulder. Again, he seemed to me from a distance to be much older than I now knew him to be. It was easier to believe that he was a teacher or a chaperone than a high school kid, even a senior.

He stiffened as he stepped off the bus, and I felt a shock of fear and embarrassment, terrified he'd think I was here to see him, though, of course, he *was* the reason I'd ridden Delilah in this direction today.

But then, without so much as a glance toward me, almost as if he was purposely *not* looking in my direction, Will walked toward the small country store and disappeared inside.

I didn't wait to see him emerge. Turning Delilah sharply, I urged her with my heels back up the trail and disappeared from town.

This was Wednesday. And Wednesday meant a sit-down dinner with Mom and Daddy. I dreaded it the whole way back to the stable, the whole way home with Alice. By the time I got to our house it was after seven, and I allowed my-self to hope that maybe they hadn't waited for me.

But when I climbed the stairs to our little kitchen, of course they were waiting. Daddy sat at the table, working on the newspaper's daily crossword puzzle, and Mom was standing over the stove, stirring something. Her shoulders, even from behind, looked fraught with tension.

"Sorry I'm late," I mumbled, flopping into my chair at the table.

Daddy looked up at me and smiled distractedly. "You have a nice ride?"

I shrugged. "It was okay."

I could smell garlic, and onions, and cooked fish. Salmon, probably. Fish are chock-full of those essential fatty acids. Good for the heart.

Mom carried the pot she'd been stirring to the table and scooped a heavy ladle of rice onto each of our plates. Then came the fish, which she laid across the rice lumps, drizzling the whole mess with some kind of a sauce. My stomach did a slow flip, threatening to revolt.

Daddy set his puzzle aside and smiled at Mom widely. "This looks great. Just great. Doesn't it look great, Scarlett?"

"Mmm-hmm." Great, actually, would have been if the table would have spontaneously combusted.

Mom seemed to try her best to smile back at Daddy. "Do you want something to drink?"

"I'll get the drinks." Daddy practically jumped up. "You did all the slaving over a hot stove; I can get us a few drinks. Scar, you want a glass of milk?"

The idea of pouring a full glass of milk down my throat on top of a meal of overcooked fish and rice sounded absolutely horrifying. "Just water."

"Liv?" He turned to my mom. She looked startled, as if it took her a moment to realize that he was saying her name—Liv, short for Olivia—and not asking her if she intended to continue her existence.

"Just water, John." Her voice was tremulous.

"Three waters it is." He was trying too hard. Sometimes I did that too, at these terrible dinners—sometimes I tried too hard, complimenting the food, telling stories about the barn, asking about business at the B&B—and sometimes I could barely manage to force myself to stay at the table. Either way, it didn't seem to make much difference. The evenings always ended up much the same—the three of us pushed the food around on our plates for ten minutes or so, and then Mom would mumble something about finishing the laundry or paying the bills and she'd wander off to her bedroom while Daddy offered to help with the dishes and I'd refuse, and he'd go out to the porch to finish his crossword and I'd dump the largely uneaten food from the plates into the sink, the disposal masticating it better than we ever could.

When Daddy returned with our waters, we began the charade.

"So, how was the first day of school?" he asked me in a loud, enthusiastic voice.

Mom's eyes, which had been gazing off into middle distance somewhere over my left ear, managed to focus on me.

After a moment she said, "Oh, that's right. You started back up today. How did it go?"

I didn't believe that either of them was really invested in hearing about the mundane details of my high school existence, but it was my turn now, and I wasn't one to miss my cue.

"Fine. Lily showed up in this insane leather outfit. She and I have two classes together, which will be great because she *needs* my help if she thinks she's going to pass French this year, and probably the best part is that I don't have to take PE anymore, now that I'm an upperclassman."

Somewhere in the middle of my monologue, Mom's gaze had shifted again. I turned my head to see what she was looking at; her eyes seemed to be focused on a completely unremarkable section of cabinetry.

"Did you meet the new kid, the Cohen boy?"

Daddy's question snapped my head back around. He seemed nonchalant enough; with more bravado than I could muster, he was scooping a large forkful of the salmon-rice mush and preparing to actually ingest it.

"Uh . . . yeah. Will, I think. He's a senior. We have a class together, actually . . . Drama."

Daddy nodded. "I'm sure you'll help him to feel right at home. Aren't you going to eat your dinner?"

My fork still lay next to my plate of untouched food. I picked it up and tried to separate out a mouthful of plain rice from the fish and the sauce.

"Will's dad called over here while you were out at the stable," Daddy went on, bravely stabbing a large flake of fish.

72

I coughed, shooting out half of the rice grains I had managed to salvage from the fish mess. "What did he want?" I choked out.

"Well, they live way over at the Isthmus, and the Cohen boy doesn't have a car. His father—a professor, isn't that nice—thought that maybe his son might want to rent a room from us here in town every now and again. You know, on nights when he might need to stay late for an activity or a study group or whatnot. That way he won't always have to rush to catch the bus or have his dad pick him up." Daddy coughed. "He made it pretty clear that he didn't want his son to make a regular habit of staying over here. He said something pretty peculiar . . . that Will was *safer* over at the Isthmus, though when I pressed him he didn't seem to want to say any more. I mean, can you imagine? As if Avalon isn't safe enough! I guess when you're coming from a big city like they did, you start to see danger on every corner."

"Where are they from?" Even though I wanted to believe that I didn't care anything about Will or his history, my curiosity compelled me to ask.

"Connecticut. Professor Cohen has tenure at Yale. His wife worked for the university too, before she died."

As soon as death entered the conversation, Daddy's eyes, and mine too, shot across the table at Mom. She had been moving her food around her plate like a child who'd spoiled her appetite with too much candy. At the mention of death her fork stopped moving, just for one long beat, before it continued to stir the food.

After a moment, she cleared her throat and set down

her fork. She blotted her lips with her napkin, though I doubted she'd eaten a bite, and then said, "Well, I am plumb worn-out. I hope you two won't mind if I call it a night and tuck in?"

I looked at the clock over the stove: 7:42.

Without another word, Mom stood up and walked out of the kitchen. She walked slowly, slightly stooped, and if I hadn't known who she was, I might have mistaken her for Miss Agnes, the eighty-two-year-old lady who lived up the street.

When it was just me and Daddy in the kitchen, I moved to clear the plates from the table. His hand reached out to stop me. "You're not finished, are you? You've hardly taken a bite."

"Umm . . . I'm not really in the mood for fish," I said.

"Ah. Well, what sounds good?" he asked. "We can fry you up some eggs."

"No." I sighed and sank back into my chair. "This'll be fine."

It was clear he intended to see me eat the food. Daddy might not have been all that tuned in to my emotional state, but he seemed determined to keep my body functioning on all cylinders, if nothing else.

It wasn't that I didn't like to eat, exactly. It was that I didn't like to *have eaten*. Some might consider this a subtle distinction, but I didn't think so. I had grown to embrace the sensation of emptiness, of being *hollowed out* like a freshly scraped jack-o'-lantern.

I could have pointed to my mother's uneaten food, but I

didn't really want to fight. I just wanted to get to my room. So I chewed, and I swallowed, and I repeated the process until my plate was mostly empty. I tried not to think too much about where the food had gone.

"Okay?" I asked at last.

Daddy nodded. "Okay," he said. "Let me do the dishes tonight. You probably have a bunch of homework to do."

I didn't argue, and I didn't feel the need to remind him that teachers aren't in the habit of assigning much on the first day. I just retreated down the hallway to my bedroom and focused on getting as far away from the rest of the fish as possible.

My yellow notebook called to me, singing its siren song from beneath the bed. The door clicked closed behind me. It was dark in my room, and as I fumbled for the light switch, I was full of unreasonable fear. Something brushed against my cheek like a caress, and I choked back a scream. My fingers found the switch at last and flipped it up; a white moth fluttered in front of my face, then continued its random dance around my room.

My window was open, and the white panels of my curtains reached to me like pale arms on the evening's wind.

I didn't want to, but I had to . . . my fingers switched my room back into darkness for a fraction of a second, and then returned the light.

My bed was next. Even though the pillows were just fine, I crossed the room and straightened them anyway—the fat rectangular yellow pillow, the square mint chenille one, the twin blue cushions.

And then I knelt by the bed and extracted my notebook.

Each page represented a day, and each day I'd recorded exactly what I'd eaten, and when, and with whom. Next to each entry I included a caloric breakdown with a total for the day at the bottom of the page.

The first three days I'd filled in later, after the fact. The very first page was May 11—the day after Ronny had died. It, as well as the two pages that followed, were blank save for the date across the top and a "0" at the bottom.

From there on in, the entries resembled something of a wave pattern. Some days were full; others were less so. Only two other pages besides the first three were entirely empty; the first, a week after Ronny's death, was the day of his funeral. The other was from just a few weeks ago, the day that a package had arrived from Ronny's college roommate, full of his books and some notes his friends had written to us.

One of the notes had been from the girl Ronny had last been seeing, Helena. She had written *Ronny was the smartest, funniest, nicest guy I ever dated. He talked all the time about his family and growing up on Catalina. He especially loved to tell me about his baby sister, who he said was the prettiest girl he knew. I tried not to get jealous. Know that lots of people loved your Ronny, and that he will be deeply, deeply missed.*

I'd taped that note to the inside of the yellow notebook's cover. I knew it by heart, but still I liked to read it.

I turned to a new page and entered the date: September 7. I recorded: *Mealy apple. 1 bite.* An apple is about 110 calories. For one bite, I recorded 5 calories. *One sugar cube:* 25 calories. Then there was dinner. *Rice and fish:*

150 calories for the rice. Salmon is the richest fish; I gave it 300 calories. Then there was the sauce that Mom had poured over it . . . it hadn't tasted buttery, but sort of sweet, like teriyaki. A quick check on my laptop told me that a cup of teriyaki has about 250 calories. She'd poured less than a quarter of a cup on my fish . . . I figured 30 calories. Grand total: 510 calories.

I felt relief course through me. The calorie count was less than I'd thought it would be. Then I felt a flash of panic that perhaps I'd missed something or miscalculated somehow, so I did the math again. But I was right; all I had consumed today was a piece of fish, a scoop of rice, a sugar cube, and one bite of a mealy apple.

Then a flood of emotions hit me, and my notebook slipped to the ground. I collapsed on my bed as heavy sobs rolled through me, burying my face in my pillows to muffle the sound.

What was I doing? Who was I becoming? My body felt weak and tired, my skin felt very, very fragile, my hair felt lank, and my bones ached as they pressed into the firm mattress.

I had to stop this. I needed to stop. Even more, I *wanted* to stop. Maybe this had started off being about Ronny, but I knew that this was not what Ronny would want for me— to whittle myself away like a piece of driftwood until all that was left was too brittle to survive even the slightest fall or jostle.

But even as I thought these thoughts, aware of their truth, I felt compelled to pull myself up to make sure my notebook wasn't bent or twisted on the ground. It lay sprawled like a broken bird on the wooden floor of my bedroom, its cardboard covers wings that would never fly. I picked it up gently and closed it, then slid it back underneath the bed. I was so, so tired. . . .

In my dream, I lay in the sand, the sun warming my face, a slight breeze drifting across my body. My eyes were closed and I felt so relaxed, as if I might never move, as if I was somehow connected to the beach beneath my body.

At first, I didn't realize what was happening when I began to sink. It seemed as if I was just nestling more perfectly into the divot I'd carved into the beach with my body. But gradually, as the taffy-long seconds of my time-distorted dream stretched by, I realized I was sinking.

The sand began to break in little waves over my fingers and toes first, cold and granular, and then my ankles and wrists started to sink, and when I tried to move my arms, lethargically at first, I found that they were stuck, or shackled, weighed down by the increasing pressure of the sand.

Sand is like that. A single grain weighs practically nothing; a handful is a pleasant weight in the palm; but combined, the force of all those little granules is overwhelming, desperately powerful, and inescapably heavy.

My heart began to beat faster; my head thrashed from side to side as I struggled to pull myself out of the mire. The warmth of the sand's top layer was gone now, its cold, heavy weight pressed on my chest like a hand, and I knew in an instant that I would die there, buried in the sand.

Was it relief I felt? I think so. The weight of the sand was making it harder and harder to take a breath, and in a moment, the sand would crest over my nose and mouth, making breathing impossible, anyway. I stopped thrashing and lay perfectly still, considering the press of the sand. It was an embrace—that's what it was, a sweet embrace, an escape, an excuse to stop fighting.

But as grains of sand began to roll across my face, ensnared in my eyelashes, covering my lips, my heart leapt in fear and protest. Adrenaline coursed through my veins, and I felt myself thrashing against the weight of the sand, struggling to free myself, to sit up, to stand.

I'd hesitated too long—the sand was overpowering, its weight too much to fight—but I fought anyway and managed to stretch one hand upward. Still, I couldn't break the surface.

How far had I sunk? I lost all perspective; was I reaching up or down? Where was I? Could I still feel my feet?

My desperation was overwhelming. My lungs burned with my final breath of air, and my fingers stretched hopelessly, searching for something, anything, to grab on to.

And then someone grabbed my hand. The grip of warm, real flesh pulling me to the surface.

Ronny! My heart soared. My brother, my friend. In my dream state, I forgot for half a moment that he was dead . . . that his hand would not be warm and strong anymore.

And then I remembered. This hand could not be my brother's. I felt tears seep from my still-closed eyes, mixing with the sand that shrouded my face.

Andy, then, it must be Andy. I forced my fingers to grasp back, and I felt myself being hauled up, felt the sand releasing me begrudgingly.

Then my arm was free of the sand, and my head emerged next, and my shoulders and my body, and I opened my eyes, blinked away the sand, and smiled up at my savior.

Green eyes looked down at me, full of concern and another emotion I couldn't quite name—bright green eyes, the color of life.

Will.

A curl of his dark hair fell across his beautiful olive-tinted forehead, and his smile blinded me.

In my bedroom, my eyes popped open. The overhead light shone down too brightly, and I shielded my eyes against it. I stumbled to my feet and over to my window, yanking the window down, the panels of my curtains falling still as the wind was blocked.

I was dazed, unstable on my feet. My clock told me it was 2:02 a.m. I shook my head and pushed my hair out of my face. I was still dressed in my jeans from the stable, but I shivered with cold. My dream felt too real—the press of the sand, like the press of death, still lingered on my skin.

It had been Will. Will had rescued me. What should I make of this?

Don't be silly, Scarlett, I admonished myself. *It was just a dream. No one is saving you.*

No one was saving me. The truth of these words resounded in my empty chest, and I forced back the useless sobs that threatened to overtake me. I shook the thought from my head and pulled open the top drawer of my dresser, finding my nightshirt.

I changed quickly and set the alarm for 6:30, just a few hours away, and pulled back the covers of my bed. Then I switched off the light and stumbled into bed, closed my eyes, and slept again, blissfully dreamless this time.

SIX

Coming Undone

*D*ay Two of junior year wasn't all that different from Day One—or from the days that would follow, I guessed. The teachers seemed to be warming up to the idea of homework, and all of my core classes assigned projects that would be due over the next several weeks.

Mr. Blaine, my AP American Literature teacher, dropped well-worn copies of *The Bell Jar* on our desks. "Read the first fifty pages by Monday, people," he told us. "And don't be surprised if there's a quiz."

Most of the other students moaned, but I didn't mind. I was good at this—being a student, answering questions. The right answers came easily to me, and I had always liked the way teachers treated me: with respect and a knowing smile, as if they envisioned big things in my future.

I'd read *The Bell Jar* already, of course—twice, actually. The first time had been during the summer between freshman and sophomore year. At the time, I'd considered Esther to be a big crybaby. I wasn't impressed by her depression. Why bother getting out of your pajamas? Come on. Because there was a whole big, beautiful world out there, and you can't ride a horse in a nightgown, or go snorkeling, or look pretty for the school dance.

The second time I'd read Plath's book had been last spring, shortly after my brother died. This time, Esther's worldview didn't seem so hard to relate to. Death was coming, after all . . . it was just a matter of time before it arrived.

But I hadn't gotten stuck in my bathrobe, at least. I continued going through the motions of life, and I thought that I was doing pretty well, actually, especially compared to Esther.

Mr. Blaine looked at me a bit sheepishly as he set the paperback on my desk. I knew what he was thinking . . . he was wondering how I was going to handle such a downer of a book, considering what had happened to Ronny.

My anger threatened to resurface. If he thought I was so fragile, then why didn't he pick a different book, something more uplifting? And I was tired of the way everyone kept looking at me—like I was going to break, or something, at any moment.

So I gave him a big, broad grin. "One of my favorites," I said, tapping the book.

Mr. Blaine looked relieved. "I figured you'd probably read it already."

"No problem. I'm sure I'll notice new stuff this time through."

"I'm sure you will," he answered, clearly pleased with my attitude.

The rest of the morning passed inconsequentially, save for the uproar caused by Lily's outfit. Today she'd donned a pair of demolished skinny jeans—I think there were probably more holes than fabric—with an off-the-shoulder oversized short-sleeved sweatshirt. It was an eighties style, I gathered, and she did look pretty fabulous . . . but Mr. Steiner said she was breaking about six different dress-code rules and sent her home to change.

When Lily returned at lunchtime, she'd traded the shredded jeans for a skirt that I thought was probably a good three inches shorter than school regulations allowed, but I guess Mr. Steiner decided to let it slide since at least it wasn't held together by safety pins. She had these fabulous sequined high-tops, unlaced, and her tank top was edged with sequins too.

I tried harder today to focus on eating lunch. But the voices all around me, the constant shoving by the boys as they jockeyed for position in the unspoken hierarchy, the raised eyebrows and silent discussions carried on by the girls . . . it was deafening, all of it. I focused on breathing regularly, trying to slow down my heartbeat to something approaching normal.

A tray crashed down on the table at my elbow, and I practically leaped out of my seat.

"Easy, Scarlett." Andy laughed. "You're jumpier than that horse of yours."

I managed to smile. "Hey."

Andy leaned in close and kissed me just beneath my ear. I tried not to count how many eyes were watching us, but I couldn't help wondering if Will had seen.

He was sitting two tables over with a few other people. Today he was wearing a light brown T-shirt with the name of some band I didn't know and low-slung jeans.

I didn't intentionally catalog his outfit, and I didn't really mean to pay such close attention to the way his brown hair fell across his forehead, I didn't want to obsess over whether his eyes would look stormy or clear today . . . but it was like I couldn't help myself. All I wanted to do was stare at him.

Andy must have noticed how often my eyes darted over to Will's table. He frowned.

"Looks like that Cohen kid has made some friends," he observed.

"Some kid," I answered. "He's older than we are."

Andy shrugged. "In years, maybe. But in experience, no way."

This earned a loud laugh from Lily. "Yeah, right, Andy," she said. "You've spent the last sixteen years stuck on this island out in the Pacific, but you've seen more than Will, who was raised in New York."

"Connecticut," I corrected her. Damn. I hadn't meant to say that out loud. One of my worst personality traits was that I couldn't stand to hear incorrect information bandied about. I was, admittedly, a bit of a know-it-all.

Andy raised an eyebrow. "Quite the Cohen experts, aren't you, girls? Well, Lil, for your information, you can learn quite a bit about human nature without ever really going anywhere. This little island is a microcosm. If you pay enough attention, you see things."

"What the hell's a microcosm?"

This from Connell, who was powering through a bag of potato chips in between gulps of soda.

"*Micro*, meaning 'small,' *cosm*, meaning 'world.'" Andy loved to show off his vocabulary. "You know—this island is like a little version of the bigger world. Everything is represented here, in miniature."

Connell nodded. "Got it. Like the tits of most of the girls at this table are a microcosm of the bigger, better tits of the girls on the mainland. Except for yours, Lily. Yours are great."

The girls at the table squealed angrily, some crossing their arms across their chests in embarrassment.

"Take a good look, little man," Lily answered smoothly, thrusting her chest in his direction. "This is as close as you'll ever get."

The table laughed loudly, and Connell blushed red.

Andy wasn't done with his lecture. One of the things I liked best about him was how smart and well-read he was, but one of the things I liked least was how much he enjoyed showing off about it.

"Like I was saying, I'll bet there's nothing Mr. Big City Cohen has seen that I haven't seen represented just as well here on the island, microcosmically."

"You'll bet, will you? How much?" This from Lily, of course.

"Twenty bucks." Andy didn't hesitate.

"Fifty," Lily responded. "And the loser has to do the winner's trig homework for a week."

Andy snorted. "Yeah, like I'd let you anywhere near my homework. I actually want to *pass* trig."

Lily narrowed her dark eyes at him. "Fine," she said. "Loser has to convince his parents to let him throw a killer Halloween party."

"Done," Andy said, sticking out his hand to shake Lily's. "Good thing the loser's parents—the *Adamses*—have such a sweet pad."

This wasn't the first time it had occurred to me that Andy and Lily may have made a better couple than he and I did. They certainly thought alike.

Lily swiveled in her chair and waved at Will. "Hey," she called. "You . . . new kid! Come over here, will you?"

It was clear who Lily was talking to, but Will looked around anyway, before standing and walking toward us. As he came closer, I saw that there were shadows under his eyes, as if he hadn't slept well.

"Yes?" he said when he reached the table. He was there because Lily had called him, but he looked at me as he spoke.

"Umm . . . my friends wanted to ask you something," I mumbled, looking down at the salad I'd bought. It sat mostly untouched on my tray.

"Hey, sit down, will ya?" Andy was smooth now, a host, king of the castle.

Will slid into a chair next to Lily, across from me. Again, his eyes searched my face as if looking for something important, something essential—something I was certain I didn't have.

"Will," Lily said, all business. "We want to hear what it was like growing up in a big city."

"New Haven's not that big," Will said. "It's only about a hundred and twenty thousand people or so."

The rest of us laughed, some with envy. A hundred and twenty thousand people? To us islanders, that sounded enormous.

I considered the anonymity such a populace would provide. Here on Catalina, everyone knew everyone else's business. Secrets were a luxury we just didn't have. But a place like Will's New Haven . . . you could live there all your life and only meet a fraction of the other residents. To me, it sounded blissful.

"Well," Will allowed, "I suppose compared to here, that's a lot of people. What do you want to know?"

Andy leaned back in his chair, confident. "What's the weirdest thing you ever saw?"

Will shrugged. "There was the assistant professor at Yale who tried to hold his office hours in the nude to protest the clothing industry's sweatshops," he offered.

"Mrs. Arugssy," Andy said.

"Who?" Lily asked.

"One of the part-time residents, spends the summers here." He looked over at Connell as if to ask permission. Connell nodded. Andy continued. "She likes to sunbathe naked. Not bad, either, for a woman in her forties with three kids."

"You were spying on her?" I was disgusted.

Andy shook his head. "Hardly. She hired me and Connell the summer before last to paint her house. And she didn't bother covering up while we worked." He and Connell shared a high five.

"I don't think that's in the same class," Lily argued. "Will's story involves someone using his nudity to make an important point about oppressed workers. Mrs. Arugssy is just a MILF who likes to parade around naked in front of horny boys."

"Who you calling a boy?" Connell guffawed.

Will looked puzzled. I filled him in. "Andy has a theory that our island is a microcosm."

"Ah," Will responded.

"Okay," Lily conceded. "I guess your proximity to Mrs. Arugssy makes up for the political intentions of Will's professor example. My turn to ask the questions." She turned to Will. "What about real deviants? You know . . . sickos. Did you ever see anything like that?"

Will seemed to choose his words carefully. "There was Father O'Brian. He taught at the Catholic school just down the road. He was arrested last winter for sexual abuse of some of the boys—his students."

Andy chortled victoriously. "Coach Bradley was diddling those cheerleaders a few years back," he said. "Remember? When we were in, like, the sixth grade? He had to leave the island before the girls' dads pounded him."

Lily shook her head. She was upset—but not by the story Will had shared, I could tell. She was angry that Andy was winning.

What was wrong with these people—with my friends? Didn't they get it? Those boys who were abused by the priest, they weren't pawns in a game. They were real people with real lives that would always be screwed up now, because some prick-head priest thought his desires were more important than their rights. And those cheerleaders—one of them, Amanda, worked at the soft-serve place on Main Street. She was no cheerleader now. Just twenty-three, she was already saddled with two little kids by two different guys, neither of whom was around anymore. Didn't anyone but me think there just might be a connection between what had happened when she was a teenager and the life she had today?

"One more shot," Andy told Lily. "Lunch is almost over."

"Come on," Lily said to Will, her voice pleading. "Didn't you see anything that was really screwed up—like big-time? Anything truly bizarre?"

Will looked at me, his green eyes soft. "There was this one girl," he said, so quietly that everyone leaned in a little to hear him. "She went to my school for a while, before they transferred her somewhere that she could get some help. She used to . . . cut herself. She had little white scars, all over her wrists, all up her arms. Then it got worse, so she didn't wear anything that didn't have long sleeves, and then she took a bunch of pills. After that, she didn't come back to school. This was a few years ago, when I was a freshman. I was just a kid; I didn't know what it meant. I didn't even notice the scars until after she'd been transferred. Then people started talking—people love to gossip," he said meaningfully, "and

I realized what she'd been doing to herself. I didn't know her at all, really. It was a big school. But something like that . . . you remember."

The table was silent for a moment. I felt the weight of Will's gaze on my face, and I wanted to shrug it off, I wanted to disappear—or punch him in the face. I realized my nails were cutting tiny crescents in my palms, and I forced my hands to relax.

Then the bell rang, signaling the end of lunch.

"Shit!" Andy cursed, realizing he'd lost.

Lily held her hand out smugly, palm up. Andy slapped three bills, two twenties and a ten, into it.

"Thanks," she said. "I'll start working on my Halloween costume."

During their exchange, Will stood smoothly from his seat at our table. He seared me with his eyes once more, then turned, and was gone.

"Damn it, damn it, damn it," Andy complained as we left the cafeteria. "I don't know how I'm going to convince my parents to let me throw a rager for Halloween."

"You'll figure something out," I murmured, not really paying attention.

But then Andy turned me down the hallway, pressing me up against a row of freshmen's lockers. He put his well-muscled arms on either side of my head and smiled down at me. "Well," he said, "at least I'll have the hottest date at the party." He kissed me then, and I tasted the onions from the sandwich he'd had at lunch.

Ignoring the threesome of freshman boys who gawked at us, Andy continued. "You know, Scarlett, we've been seeing each other for a while now."

"I guess so," I said, trying not to be obvious about checking the time on my cell phone. I didn't want to be late for Chemistry two days in a row.

"I was wondering," Andy continued, his breath hot against my ear, "when you might want to . . . you know." He ground his hips suggestively into mine, providing the freshman boys plenty to think about that night.

"Can we talk about this later?"

Andy looked at me, eyes hopeful. "Sure, sure, as long as we talk about it." Suddenly, he looked as young and eager as the gawking boys who were waiting uncomfortably for access to their lockers.

"Yeah, we'll talk." I let Andy kiss me again before I ducked away from him, breaking into a sprint toward class.

"Promise?" he called after me.

This time, when I walked into Drama class, I was prepared to see Will. Before I crossed the threshold of the room, my eyes went directly to the seat he'd been in yesterday—*my* seat—and I felt a wave of confusing desperation when I saw that it was empty.

But then I saw him, two rows over, drawing something absently on the cover of his notebook. When I entered the room, he put down his pen and touched his forehead, as if in pain, and his eyes closed. I found my way to my seat and slid into it just as the bell rang. Mrs. B had her back to us and was writing something on the board. I took out my notebook and pencil, preparing to take notes.

Just one look, I promised myself, and slid my glance across to Will.

He wasn't looking at me. His attention was focused on Mrs. B and the board.

My disappointment manifested itself in a sour taste in my mouth. I would be focused too, then. I looked up at Mrs. B and found her watching me.

"Hi, Scarlett," she said warmly. "It's so nice to have you back with us."

My blush was hot on my cheeks. "Sorry I ran out of here yesterday."

"No need to apologize," she said. "We're just glad you're here today."

She started talking about kitchen-sink realism, listing the various elements of the genre on the chalkboard. I fell into a familiar rhythm—taking notes, writing my own questions in the margin of my notebook for later thought and research.

Some kids hate taking notes. Not me. I love it. I get to disappear as the words I hear flow through my body to my fingers where I record them in neat letters on the page.

I have excellent handwriting. Back in elementary school, I won the penmanship award three years running, until the principal decided it was time to give someone else a turn. It soothed me to watch Mrs. B's words transform into rows of writing in my notebook, and my world narrowed and focused as I wrote.

"Okay," Mrs. B said at last, wiping the chalk from her

hands. "Now everybody pair up and take a good look at Arthur Miller's *Death of a Salesman*. I want you to decide—does his play qualify as kitchen-sink realism? Why or why not?"

Ah. Classification and defense. What is something, and why? I was good at this, too, and my classmates knew it. Three people called my name, asking to be my partner.

I looked around, and this time Will was looking at me. He smiled, slow and sweet, and gestured for me to join him. All the kids were moving around the room, breaking into pairs, and as Brandon Becker moved to join Katie Ellis in the back of the room, I slid into his seat next to Will.

"Hey," I said.

"Hey," he replied. "So . . . have you read it?"

"Read what?"

"*Death of a Salesman.*"

"Um . . . yeah. Of course. It was on our summer reading list. Have you?"

He nodded. "I played Biff last year at my old school."

This made me laugh. "You don't look much like a Biff," I told him.

"No," he admitted. "I guess Connell would fit that role better. Or Andy."

I narrowed my eyes at him. "You think so?" I kept my voice casual.

He didn't back down. "Absolutely," he said. "Either of them could play the dumb jock pretty well, I'd imagine."

"Andy isn't dumb," I protested. As for Connell . . . well, I'd pick my battles.

"I didn't say he was dumb . . . just that he could *act* dumb, if it suited him. I'll bet Andy could do just about anything if he thought it was in his best interest."

I wasn't sure what to make of this. It sounded like a veiled insult, but I certainly couldn't prove it. "Let's just get to work."

Will turned to a fresh page in his notebook, divided it down the middle, and labeled the columns "Pros" and "Cons."

"You first," he said.

"Well, I wouldn't really classify *Death of a Salesman* as any kind of realism," I began. "I mean, the play's symbolic meanings form the real depth of the play . . . the expressionistic flashbacks are where most of the substance exists."

"I don't know," Will said thoughtfully. "The reality is that our dreams, our misconceptions, our interpretations of the world around us are every bit as significant as the actual truth. They inform our decisions just as much, don't they?"

Suddenly, I wondered if we were still talking about the play. "They shouldn't," I argued cautiously. "We should make our decisions only on what is *really* real, not on what we *wish* to be real, or what we fantasize about the world."

"So you're saying dreams are meaningless?" As I looked into Will's eyes, I felt the press of the sand from my dream, and I felt again that he was saving me. The classroom, the students, Mrs. B and her blackboard full of terms seemed to melt away.

But then I remembered Ronny in his grave and my yellow notebook waiting for me at home, and I dropped my eyes. "Yes," I whispered. "Dreams are meaningless."

Will's hand reached out and he tipped up my chin. His deep eyes searched my face. "What if you're wrong?" His voice sounded desperate. "What if there is more to reality than you can see, more than you know?"

I was flooded with fear, so I pulled away. "Yeah, and what if the tooth fairy and Santa Claus threw a big party?" My voice was harsh with contempt. "Face it, Will. Loman's fantasies trap him and keep him from dealing with reality. And his wife, Linda? She's just as bad. She coddles her husband and lets him stay stuck in his stupid, vacuous daydreams. They deserve each other."

We stared at each other, and I could tell that Will was as upset as I was, though I wasn't sure why. This was just a stupid class activity, and here we were, all worked up as if any of this even mattered.

Class was nearly over. I would go to the stable, where I'd feel the real, warm, living flesh of Delilah, and I would climb on her wide back, and I would breathe the fresh air and feel the sun on my face.

I started to pack up my stuff, but Will's hand stopped me. "I need you to consider," he said, "that you might not be right about everything."

That did it. Who *was* this guy? He thought he knew me so well—he thought he could see inside me. "I might not be right about everything," I said, "but at least I know when to mind my own damned business."

And then the bell rang, and the class filled with the sounds of the students ending their day, and I turned and left without looking back.

• • •

After that, Will left me alone. In the lunchroom, when he was there, he kept his back to my table, though he appeared at lunch less and less frequently. In Drama class, he paired up often with Katie Ellis, which I tried to convince myself didn't bother me in the least, even when her lilting, flirtatious laugh carried across the classroom toward me.

I buried myself in my schoolwork, going straight up to my room after the stable each afternoon, telling my parents I was too busy to have dinner with them, even on Wednesdays and Sundays. They didn't protest much; I could tell Daddy was getting more and more concerned about Mom, who looked as if she'd aged five years in the last six months.

Daddy decided not to take any more guests until the spring, so our rambling house felt like a ghost town. He spent most of his time out in the garden, tending to the flowers and the fish. Sometimes I wanted to go down and dig in the earth with him, feel the soft ground under my nails, plant something . . . but I just couldn't. My room and the stable felt safe. The rest of the world, even our own back garden, did not.

And though I didn't really want to lose any more weight, three more pounds slipped off of me in as many weeks, and as September ended, I found that I weighed less than I had when I'd started high school, when I'd been several inches shorter.

I was cold a lot now, even though September and October in California often feel like an extended Indian summer, and I took to wearing layers of everything—jeans under skirts, long-sleeved thermals under tees.

And when Andy tried to snake his hand up under my shirt when we were alone together, I pushed him away, not so much because I didn't want his touch, but because I was worried he might be disgusted by the feel of my ribs just beneath my skin, the slight concavity of my stomach, the protrusion of my hip bones jutting against my jeans.

The first Saturday in October, as the leaves were just beginning to change, Andy showed up uninvited on my doorstep after dinnertime. I was annoyed; I had wanted to finish up the final paper on *The Bell Jar*, and I'd planned to start the next trig chapter after that, just to get ahead.

"What are you doing here?" I asked, wrapping my hair in a bun and stabbing it with my pencil as I opened the door for him.

"Nice to see you too," he said, leaning in to kiss me.

"Sorry." I sighed. "That was rude. I was just in the middle of my homework is all."

"Listen, Scar, I know how important homework is. I mean, I get it. I want to go to a good college too. But it's Saturday night! Let's have some fun."

I had three or four good reasons to refuse him, but unfortunately my father overheard. "That's a great idea," he said, overenthusiastic. "Scarlett, you haven't been out of the house in weeks."

"I go to the stable almost every day." It was weak, but it was the best I could do.

"Go on out, be kids, have some fun," Daddy said, and

he dug a twenty out of his wallet and pressed it into my hand. "Go on, I insist."

Andy laughed. "Your dad is cool, Scar," he said, pulling me out of the house before I had a chance to argue.

We found our way down to the beach just as the sun slipped beneath the horizon. The beach was quieter now that summer was over; we wandered over to a small cove and tucked ourselves behind a large rock to get out of the wind.

I knew what Andy wanted. He kissed me and pulled the pencil from my hair. It tumbled down and Andy stroked it gently as he kissed me, his mouth eager but not pushy.

This time, when his hand reached up under the waist of my shirt, I didn't push it away. He paused for a second, as if he couldn't believe his luck, and then his warm fingers splayed against my bare skin. He moaned a little and pulled me even closer, his fingers pressing into my side.

He didn't seem disgusted by the feel of my ribs; in fact, his breathing grew jagged as his fingers wandered tentatively upward, tracing the line of my bra. I considered stopping him then, but I felt strangely numb, as if I were somewhere else, far away. *If my body isn't going to give me any pleasure,* I thought briefly, *why shouldn't Andy enjoy it?*

He managed the hook on the back of my bra, and his fingers caressed the underside of my breast. He moaned again, deeply this time, and pushed me back into the sand.

"Hey, hey, kids, enough of that." Mr. Johnson, out for a walk with his toy poodles. He had three of them—Fancy, Prancer, and Fidget—and they were off their leashes. They growled and yipped when they saw our bodies tangled together in the sand, and Mr. Johnson tried ineffectually to round them up.

Andy groaned in frustration and hauled himself to his feet, turning his back to me and Mr. Johnson while he adjusted his pants. Then he reached down and took my hand to help me up.

Under my shirt, my bra strap swung uncomfortably, but I couldn't think of a way to gracefully reattach it without Mr. Johnson noticing.

"Plenty of time for that when you're older," Mr. Johnson blustered. "You kids head on home, now."

"Yes, sir, Mr. Johnson," Andy answered. "Come on, Scarlett."

We wandered around town a while after that, but clearly all Andy could think about was getting me somewhere alone where he could pick up where he'd left off, so after a while I told him I needed to get home to finish up my paper.

"Okay," he said, "but Scarlett, the night of the Halloween party . . . how about then?"

The numbness I had been feeling at the beach was wearing off, and I felt suddenly panicky and unsure. I nodded anyway, and the smile that lit up Andy's face was almost enough to make me happy too.

That night, though, alone in my room with my yellow notebook, my anxiety grew like a harvest moon, pregnant with anticipation, and I felt my heart fluttering in my chest, and suddenly the hollowness I'd been relying on to keep me calm, to keep me neutral, was no longer enough. It felt that I would burst, so full of every emotion—anger and fear, excitement and anticipation, sorrow and dread.

Will's story returned to me then, the one about the girl with the scars on her arms, and I reached into my little desk for my manicure scissors. Before I could stop myself, I drew its edge, once, across my wrist.

The scissors were sharp, and the cut they made was deeper than I had intended, and blood seeped to the surface. It was a beautiful color, deeply and richly red, and the thought crossed my mind in that moment that I had the perfect name, Scarlett.

And all my worry was gone, and all my fear and excitement and anticipation with it. Even my sorrow and dread receded, and I felt blissfully clear and free, standing there, watching my blood surface.

I took out my yellow notebook and flipped it to a new page. Then I pressed my wrist against the white paper. A thin line of my blood left proof, there, of what I had done.

SEVEN

Fig Leaves

When I woke, the light filtering through my windows was bright and warm. I had a sensation of peace and happiness, as if suddenly everything was going to be okay.

A glance at my alarm clock told me that I had woken up earlier than usual; it was just past six in the morning. I stood and stretched, enjoying the swing of my long hair against my back as I arched.

My wrist, brushing against my side, felt tender. I looked at the mark there; it smiled up at me in a curve of red. It had scabbed over while I'd slept, but it was still pretty fresh. I dressed carefully, pulling my gray thermal gingerly over my arm, then folding up the cuff to keep it from rubbing on my wrist. I put on a second shirt, this one a short-sleeved pink tee with puffed sleeves, and pulled on my jeans and a short, gray fleece bubble skirt.

I braided my hair in a single, long plait, wrapping the end

in a rubber band before flinging it back over my shoulder, out of my way. Pushing my feet into my flip-flops—the air coming through the window portended a warm day—I felt a weirdness in my stomach.

I wondered if I was going to be sick. And then, surprised, I recognized the feeling. It was hunger.

I was hungry. More than hungry, I was ravenous. I made my way out to the kitchen and started rifling through the refrigerator. I found juice and eggs and bacon, and I pulled them eagerly from the shelves.

The smell of the cooking food brought my father out from his bedroom; he looked at me with surprise. "You're up early."

"Mmm-hmm," I answered, focused on turning the bacon quickly, before it burned. In another pan the eggs cooked, and I stirred them often so they wouldn't brown.

Toast popped up from the toaster behind me, and Daddy pulled it out and buttered it.

Soon we were sitting together, a large plate of bacon, eggs, and toast in front of each of us. Steam wafted up from the plates and I closed my eyes as I breathed in the warm buttery smell of it all.

My hand shook a little as I lifted my fork. I looked up quickly to see if Daddy had noticed, but he was busy stirring milk into his coffee.

The first bite of yellow eggs tasted better than anything I could remember, ever. Slightly salty, rich, absolutely nourishing and delicious. Then I bit into the bacon—crisp in one spot, juicy in another. I followed this with a gulp of the cold, sweet juice, and then ate more and more and more.

When I pulled my eyes away from my plate, Daddy was watching me. He smiled. "It's good to see you with an appetite, honey."

I smiled. "Hungry today," I admitted.

"Then eat!" He gestured to my empty glass. "More orange juice?"

I nodded, and he pulled the pitcher from the refrigerator and filled my glass.

He ate too, and after a few minutes I had sated myself enough to talk. "Mom still asleep?"

Daddy's mouth turned down. "Still sleeping. I need to have a little talk with the doctor," he said. "It seems that she's gotten pretty dependent on those sleeping pills he prescribed."

I was going to say something, ask a question, but there was a knock on the door downstairs. I rose to answer it, but Daddy stopped me.

"I'll get it, hon. You just finish your breakfast."

As he left the room and headed downstairs, I scraped the last bits of egg onto my toast. I felt happy and full of energy. It was the best I had felt in a long time, since before . . .

But I wasn't feeling quite well enough to think about that.

I took my dishes to the sink.

"Scar?" Daddy called up to me. "There's someone here to see you. A boy." His voice was quizzical.

I grabbed my book bag and trotted down the stairs. Maybe

it was Jake; he lived just up the street and had trig with me. Last night's homework had been pretty tough . . . maybe he had a question.

But it wasn't Jake. Standing in the doorway, his green eyes flashing angrily, was Will.

I stopped halfway down the stairs. "What are you doing here?"

He smiled at me, but only with his mouth. His eyes were still the same, a dangerous flash of green. His smile, it seemed, was for my dad's benefit. The eyes were for me.

"Can I walk you to school?" he asked.

"You must be Will Cohen," Daddy said. "I talked to your dad a couple of weeks ago."

Will pulled his gaze from my face and forced himself to focus on Daddy. "Yes, sir," he said. "It's nice to meet you, Mr. Wenderoth."

"Just John," Daddy insisted, shaking Will's hand. "We're all pretty casual here on the island."

"John," replied Will. "Well, John, do you mind if I walk your daughter to school this morning?"

"It's fine by me," Daddy said. "So long as Scarlett wants you to."

They both turned to look at me as I stood like a scared rabbit on the stairs. Truthfully, what I wanted was to turn back up the stairs and bolt for my bedroom, but I didn't.

"Sure," I said, trying to make my voice light, friendly. "I'll see you later, Daddy."

"Have a good day, kids," he called after us as we made our way down the porch steps and through the front garden.

I heard the click of the front door closing, and then I was alone with Will.

Suddenly, with something that felt like restrained fury, Will took me by the elbow and led me forcefully out my front gate and down the street, toward the corner.

"We need to talk," he growled through his teeth.

His grasp on my arm was strong, and I felt the heat of his hand through the thin layer of my thermal. Above us, the sun shone brightly. Today would be hot.

I tried to yank my arm away, but Will just tightened his grasp.

"Ow," I said, feeling panicky. "You're hurting me."

Instantly, Will dropped my arm. "I'm sorry," he said.

He stopped and turned to me. His face was anguished, tortured. "What are you doing?" he asked me, running his hands through his hair.

"Me? What am *I* doing? You're the one who showed up at *my* house, totally uninvited. What are *you* doing?" I reached out to push him, but Will's quick eyes found the cut on my wrist and his hand shot out, encircling my arm.

"What's this?" His voice was dangerous.

"It's nothing. A scrape." I pulled my arm back. This time, Will let go, and he watched as I yanked my sleeve down to cover my wrist. I scratched off the scab and I felt my wrist bleeding again, soaking into my cotton shirt.

"How did this happen?" he moaned, and I had the sensation that he was talking about more than just my cut.

"It was an accident." I lied smoothly. "And anyway, what's it to you? It's none of your business."

"That's where you're wrong," Will said. "It's absolutely my business if you get hurt, Scarlett. Even if *you're* the one hurting yourself."

I didn't know what to say, so I spat out another lie—"I don't know what you're talking about. Why would I hurt myself?"

Will ignored my bluster. "I don't know," he said. The anger was gone from his eyes, but he still looked pained, as if it was his fault I was hurt. "But I'm not a kid, not anymore. If you're hurt, even if you're hurting yourself, I won't just stand by and watch."

Then he reached out and brushed my cheek with his hand. I wanted to close my eyes. I wanted to lean into his touch, take the comfort he was offering. But I felt scared and ashamed, so instead I pulled away, wiping the traitor tears angrily from my face.

"Just leave me alone," I said.

"For now," he answered.

I listened to the sound of his footsteps as he headed through town, toward school.

I didn't feel like going to school anymore. Breakfast felt leaden in my stomach now, a heavy ball of food I didn't want to have anything to do with. Who did Will Cohen think he was? What right did he think he had to show up at my house and interrogate me? Had someone put him up to this . . . a teacher, maybe?

Or did he have some kind of hero complex? Maybe he'd heard about Ronny and had decided that he was going to save me or something. Whatever it was, I felt my old bilious friend Anger rising in my chest, forming a crust of bitterness around my heart, protecting me from the other emotions that threatened to flood me—shame, and fear, and inescapable loneliness.

I yanked my cell phone from my bag: 7:32, half an hour still until school started. I punched in Lily's name, hit Send, and waited for her to answer.

"Yo," she said after the second ring.

"Hey."

"Where are you?" she complained. "I went to your house but your dad said *Will Cohen* walked you to school? I don't think Andy's going to like that," she said, singsong and full of laughter.

I loved Lily. "Do you feel like going to school today?" I asked.

"Not really." Always game for anything—that was Lily. She didn't take anything seriously, a quality that sometimes irritated me but right now felt just right.

"I think we're about due for a mental health day," I suggested.

An hour later, when we should have been trapped in European History, Lily and I were instead strolling along the boardwalk, trying to blend in with the tourists. Lily was sipping some chocolatey coffee confection topped with whipped cream, but I'd chosen a mint tea instead. The breakfast that had tasted so good felt like some kind of alien invader. I hoped the tea would settle things down.

Lily was wearing her sunglasses and her eyes darted back

and forth over the crowd as she enjoyed playing secret agent. "We'll have to get off the boardwalk soon," she said to me in a stage whisper, "before we're spotted by the fuzz."

I rolled my eyes at her mock-theatrics, but acknowledged that she was right. Our tiny island was far too intimate to allow us to ditch class so publicly; we'd be ratted out in no time by one of the shopkeepers if we didn't keep a low profile.

"Snitch at eleven o'clock!" Lily hissed, pulling me behind a parked truck and crouching down as Mrs. Antoine, our French teacher's wife, whisked by us on her bicycle.

"That was a close one," I whispered, enjoying the dramatic tension. "Maybe we should go somewhere a little less obvious."

Lily pursed her lips, thinking, still crouched behind the truck. "I know the perfect place."

The thing about an island is that there are lots of beaches. A half mile out of town, there's a piece of shoreline where the tourists gather to snorkel and feed the fish, especially our island's famous orange Garibaldis, who are practically as tame as house cats. Not much farther, if you're willing to climb down a fairly treacherous cliff, there's a little inlet of sand and sun that tourists rarely bother with.

Scrambling down the cliff in my sandals was a challenge, but nothing compared to Lily's descent in her four-inch espadrilles. I suggested she take them off, but she shook her head. "It's good practice," she told me. "If I can make it

109

down this cliff, negotiating the cobblestones in Brazil over winter break should be no problem."

"You're going to Brazil at Christmas?" I felt panicky. Two weeks of vacation without Lily?

"Yeah," she said, hopping down the final couple of feet and landing neatly on the sand. "The twins want to see a river dolphin."

I clambered down after her. "A river dolphin? You have to go all the way to Brazil to see a river dolphin?"

She shrugged. "They've got the biggest kind in Brazil . . . the pink ones."

I shook my head. "Sure," I said. "Why not? Pink river dolphins."

"Wanna come?"

For a moment, I allowed myself to imagine traipsing through Brazil searching for pink river dolphins with Lily, the twins, and their parents. It sounded pretty tempting, and I was sure they'd be happy to have me along to entertain Lily. But missing Christmas . . . I knew it would be torturous to sit in our big, empty shell of a house, knowing that Ronny would not be taking the ferry home for the holidays, but it seemed even more excruciating to imagine my parents with no kids home at all on Christmas Eve.

"Nah," I said. "Not this year."

Lily seemed to understand my thought process. "Maybe next time," she suggested.

The sun was warm on my skin. I lay down on the sand and tried to relax. European History would be over by now; I'd be in trig, a class I shared with Andy. I wondered briefly what he'd make of my absence.

I felt Lily casually plop down next to me on the sand. "Ah," she said. "One more chance to tan before summer's over for good."

Only in places like California can you even pretend that the beginning of October still qualifies as summer. But a tan?

Looking over, I gasped. Last I'd checked, Lily had been wearing red jeggings and a white, belted tunic. "Lily!" I said. "Someone will see you!"

"It'll be their lucky day," she answered, eyes still closed. Aside from her black panties, Lily was completely naked. She hadn't been lying about sunbathing in Italy; except for her rose-colored nipples, her heavy, round breasts were darkened to the same even bronze as her shoulders and stomach. Her belly, even when she lay on the beach, was not totally flat. Instead, like that of the naked beauty in the Art Deco mural on our island's casino-turned-theater, her stomach was gently curved, a little soft, and perfectly lovely.

Her legs, too, were rounded—not fat, but not thin, either. She looked healthy, beautiful, more like a woman than I imagined I ever would. Shading her face with her hand, she peeled open an eye and peered at me.

"Well?" she said. "Are you going to just sit there with your mouth open, or are you going to catch some rays?"

I'd seen Lily naked lots of times before when we got dressed up for parties and dances, when we tried on clothes in shared dressing rooms. But I'd never seen her like this, luxuriating in the feeling of the sun on her skin, fully sensual and completely comfortable. Suddenly, I felt very, very young, and terribly awkward.

"I'm kind of cold," I mumbled.

Lily snorted. "I don't think so," she said, closing her eyes. "But stay dressed, if you want. *I* plan on having a tan for the Halloween party."

I was torn. I wanted to be like Lily, free and cosmopolitan. But I felt frightfully small-town and full of nerves.

The beach was completely deserted. There were a couple of seagulls, but they weren't paying any attention to us. The waves came and went, came and went. The sun felt hot on my head, and I considered how good it would feel on my bare skin. Lily's eyes were closed; she might even have fallen asleep.

"What the hell," I muttered to myself, and reached down to the waist of my shirts, pulling both layers off together. I shoved down my skirt and jeans and kicked them, along with my flip-flops, in a tangled, sandy heap. My hands hesitated a minute before unhooking my bra . . . but I did it, and tossed it on top of the rest of my clothes, then flopped stomach-down into the sand and squeezed my eyes shut.

A breeze passed across my skin. My hair, still braided, fell to one side, and my bare back felt like an offering to the sky.

My muscles were tensed almost to the point of spasm, I realized. So I focused on relaxing—first my toes, then my calves, all the way up my body to my shoulders, my neck, even my face muscles. I relaxed my lips. I relaxed my nose.

As I lay there, warming in the sand, I listened to the drumming of the waves against the shore. The rhythm was soothing, like a heartbeat, reliable and steady. I heard the gulls calling overhead; farther away, above our cove, I heard the occasional rush of an engine as a car sped by.

I felt things too; I felt the crunch of the topmost layer of sand as my body shifted slightly; I felt the cooler, softer sand beneath, molding to my body; I felt the gentle touch of the breeze pushing through my hair, caressing my back, my legs, my feet.

I breathed in the particular salty-wet smell of the seaside and purposely filled my lungs as full as I could, holding my breath for a long moment before releasing it. I felt empty. I felt good.

"Oh, Scarlett," Lily said. Her voice sounded so forlorn, almost horrified. "Why didn't you tell me?"

"Tell you what?" I murmured, on the brink of sleep.

When she didn't answer, I looked up. Lily was sitting, still almost naked, and staring at me. Her eyes were brimming with tears.

"What is it?" I asked, alarmed.

"Scarlett, where have you gone?" she asked, reaching out toward me, her fingers trembling as they ran across my bare shoulder.

Suddenly, I saw myself through her eyes—all angles and elbows, each knob of my backbone pressing against my skin, my ribs threatening to protrude.

It was as if I were suddenly more naked than naked, as if my very flesh had been pulled back to reveal my shame, my hidden horrors, and I reached with shaking hands for my shirt and clutched it to my chest.

It was no use pretending with Lily, not now, when she'd seen me like this.

"I don't know where I've gone," I admitted, my voice as small as a child's. "Far, far away, I think."

This time, when the tears came, I didn't brush them off as I had in front of Will. I let them come, and they coursed silently down my cheeks.

Overhead, a gull shrieked mournfully, circling again and again and again.

"Oh, Scarlett," Lily cried, and she leaned across to me, unabashed in her nudity in a way that seemed so beautiful and yet impossible at the same time. Her warm arms embraced me, her dark curls brushed against my tearstained cheeks, and she rocked me as if I were a baby. "Scarlett, this can't go on. I mean, I noticed you'd lost some weight, but I had no idea it had gone this far. This is, like, nineties heroin-chic, and that really wasn't a good look for *anyone*."

I knew what she was doing—she was trying to make me laugh so I would feel better—but I didn't feel like laughing. I felt like wrapping my arms around my gangly, undernourished nakedness and running and hiding behind a tree.

I pulled away from Lily's hug. "I'm okay," I sniffed. "I'm just not beach-ready right now, I guess, okay?"

I tried to shove my arms into my thermal but the shirt was all tangled and wrapped up in itself, and it was like I was trying to punch through a wall of fabric.

Lily watched me, still gloriously unrobed, her eyes filled with pity. She reached out to try to help me untangle my shirt, but I pushed her hands away and turned my back to her.

"Scarlett, don't be mad," she begged. "I want to help you. . . . I won't tell anyone . . . just let me help!"

But how could I explain that I was angry not at her desire to help me, but rather at the vision she was just then, so completely at ease in her own skin, so beautifully curvy, so obviously in the bloom of life? I felt like a very old lady, withered and preparing to die.

"I'll call you later," I mumbled as I pulled on my jeans and skirt, shoving my bra into my back pocket and stumbling into my flip-flops. "I've got to go home."

I'd tell my dad I was sick. It wasn't a lie; it was all too true.

The rocks shifted beneath my feet as I scrambled back up toward the road. I heard pebbles clattering down the cliff and I struggled to find a toehold. I wasn't going to fall, I would have found my footing after another moment, but suddenly a strong hand reached down and grasped my upper arm, hauling me up to the road.

"I had it," I snapped at the do-gooder, and looked up to glare at him.

After all the times he'd snuck up on me, I shouldn't have been surprised to find Will standing there on the side of the road. He released my arm and took a step back from me, as if it was difficult for him to stand too close.

"You're starting to creep me out," I said. "Find someone else to stalk."

"I wish I could." His mouth twisted in a wry smile. "But it seems that, for the time being, at least, we're stuck with each other."

"Did you follow me here?" I was struck with the image

of myself and Lily, practically naked, on the beach below. "Were you *spying* on me?"

"In a matter of speaking."

The creep didn't even bother *trying* to sound embarrassed!

"Did you see me down there?" I demanded.

His gaze slipped from my face. "I didn't come here to see you naked."

My face blushed hotly. He didn't *come here* to see me naked. That definitely wasn't the same as saying that he *didn't* see me naked.

"I don't think Andy's going to like this very much." I said, throwing Lily's earlier taunt at Will.

His eyes narrowed. "I don't much care what Andy likes," he said, and though his voice stayed calm, his eyes betrayed him. "I don't much care for Andy."

I shook my head. "You have no business coming here, following me like this."

"You don't know what my business is."

"Then tell me," I challenged.

A car sped by, too close, and Will shifted his body so that he was between me and the road. It was just a couple of steps, but it seemed deeply significant.

He seemed to consider my challenge, and then said, "I can't." His voice was tinged with regret. "Just— Scarlett, be careful."

Before I could snap back a poisonous retort, he stepped in and closed the distance between us. The touch of his lips on my temple, just below my hairline, felt so sweet, yet so charged with electric meaning, that without intending to I reached out and took his hand. Our fingers interlaced; his hand was warm, strong, and felt familiar in my grasp, as if we had held hands before, in some distant life.

Then I remembered that I was angry at him, that I had a boyfriend, and I pulled my hand away. He held on more tightly, for such a brief second that I might have imagined it, if not for the regret mirrored in his eyes. But he loosened his grasp and let me go.

EIGHT

Big-Boy Superheroes

That was the last really warm day of the fall. After that, the air had a snap to it, foretelling winter, or at least our California version of it. I wasn't out of place anymore in all my layers. Everyone was more covered up, and I begrudgingly traded in my flip-flops for a pair of Tom's.

Around school, the hot topic of conversation was Andy's impending Halloween rager. It turned out that Andy was in luck; his parents would be off the island on Halloween night, accompanying his little brother to an orchestra performance on the mainland. Andy's brother, Jeffrey, hadn't followed Andy's footsteps onto the field. Instead, he'd picked up the French horn, of all instruments, in the third grade, and now, a freshman in high school, he was reaching the level where other school orchestras routinely invited him to play with them. Apparently, French horn players were a pretty hot commodity.

So Andy was to be left to his own devices Halloween weekend.

"I told them I might have a few friends over to help me pass out candy," he told us at lunch the Wednesday before Halloween.

"That's not too far off," joked Connell, "considering the size of our class."

"Well, the whole class isn't coming." Andy's face looked a little panicky. "I mean, the neighbors are going to notice for sure if sixty-four kids show up."

"Don't forget the seniors," sang Lily, "and a select few sophomores, too." She was practically humming with satisfaction as she watched Andy squirm.

"This is the first time my folks have left me alone for a weekend," Andy protested.

"Don't bet what you can't afford to lose, Mr. Turlington."

Sometimes Lily was a bit much. "I'm sure everyone will keep it pretty quiet." I tried to soothe Andy.

Just then, Mike Ryan, a senior football player who was rumored to have engaged in a threesome with two sophomore girls with low self-esteem, walked by our table and ruffled Andy's hair affectionately. "Rager at Turlington's! I'll bring a keg."

Andy groaned, thumping his head against the table. "I'm dead."

Everyone at the table laughed, and I chimed in too, though my laugh sounded hollow to me. No one else seemed to notice, except maybe Lily, who looked at me curiously from her seat across the table. Without a word, she pushed half of her sandwich across to me.

This is how it had been for the past couple of weeks, since our day at the beach. Lily was keeping her promise—she hadn't told anybody about how I'd looked out there, without my clothes. But she seemed to expect me to do something about it. She still met me outside my house in the mornings, but she was never empty-handed. Some days she gave me a freshly made egg sandwich, wrapped in one of her mom's pretty cloth napkins; other days, it was a muffin. But there was always something, and although she didn't directly talk about it, she didn't leave my side until I'd eaten. She'd make small talk and linger outside the school with me, not exactly watching as I ate, but keeping me company as I downed the food.

And it was working; I felt better, had more energy, didn't find myself dizzy or light-headed nearly as often.

So I accepted the sandwich as she had offered it—silently—and took a bite.

I knew he wouldn't be at his table, since he rarely was anymore, but I couldn't stop my gaze from sliding over to the chair Will sometimes occupied at lunch.

Empty.

I knew where he was. I'd seen him there several times over the last few weeks—in the library, in the chair nearest the window, with a book in his hands. Most days, I stubbornly resisted the urge to watch him read. But occasionally, like today, the pull toward him was too strong, like the tide, and I would make my excuses and find him there.

It seemed that I'd eaten enough of the sandwich to satisfy

Lily. She didn't comment as I wrapped the crusts in a napkin and stood from the table. Andy stood too, and waved at our friends.

I shouldn't have been irritated that he wanted to ditch the cafeteria to come with me; he was my boyfriend, after all. But I didn't want his company. I wanted to be alone.

No—that wasn't true. I didn't want to be alone. I wanted to be with Will.

So, on top of everything else, I was a terrible girlfriend, too. My guilt guided my hand to Andy's, and he squeezed my fingers as they interlaced with his.

Andy seemed to think that what I was looking for was some time alone with him, because he led me back around behind the cafeteria, one of the few truly private places on our small campus.

Of course, the reason it was so private is that this was the nook where the large cafeteria trash cans were kept. Not exactly the most romantic locale on the island, but Andy didn't seem to notice.

Emboldened, Andy ran his hands from my waist down across my hips as we kissed. I concentrated on matching the intensity of his embrace, still feeling badly about wanting to ditch him.

Even as our tongues battled fiercely, I felt my mind wandering elsewhere, wondering what Will might be reading today.

Last Tuesday, he'd been laughing to himself as he thumbed through the collected plays of Oscar Wilde; on Friday, he'd held a heavy text in a language that looked ancient and important. Hebrew, I'd guessed. On that day, he hadn't been laughing. Rather, his brow had been furrowed in deep concentration.

Just before he caught sight of me watching him, he'd raised his hand to massage his temple in a gesture I had come to know intimately. Then his eyes, hawk-like, had raised from the page and found me instantly, half hidden in the stacks.

Had he known I was there all along, or had I made some unconscious noise to alert him to my presence? I didn't think so. It was more like . . . he sensed me there.

I remembered my words to him on the cliff above the beach—"Find someone else to stalk"—and I'd blushed hotly, painfully aware of the situation's role reversal.

I broke away from Andy. It was just too weird to kiss him while I was obsessing over Will, replaying our meetings in my head. Besides, the stench of the decomposing trash wasn't helping matters either.

"I've got to get something from the library," I murmured, trying in vain to disengage his hands from my backside.

"Oh, yeah?" he said into my neck. "Like what? Will Cohen?"

I laughed too loud, almost braying. "What are you talking about?"

Andy pulled away, but just slightly. "I see the way you look at him." He shrugged. "It doesn't matter. I get it—new guy from the big city, a senior, all that. And I've seen the way he looks at you too." Andy clenched his jaw, then smiled, but not nicely. "That seems to have stopped, though, since Connell and I had a little talk with him."

I shoved Andy's chest. "You didn't!"

"Course I did. Can't have the new kid sniffing around my girl."

I was seething now. "*Sniffing around?* What am I, your fire hydrant? Nervous some other dog's going to lift his leg on me?"

Andy grinned. "Something like that," he said, leaning in for another kiss.

I turned my head and his kiss landed in my hair.

"Doesn't matter," he said. "I know you like me the most. And Saturday night, I'll show you how much I like you back."

He rubbed his hips against mine, and I felt his hardness pushing against me.

"Go on to the library, get your book," he said softly, letting me go at last.

I stumbled away from him, straightening my clothes and pushing my hair back from my face. My heart fluttered in my chest like a trapped bird.

Saturday night.

I hadn't given too much thought to my virginity. My parents weren't religious and had never really tried to convince me and Ronny that we should wait until we were married to have sex. I knew from old pictures and the way Daddy sometimes teased Mom that she had lived with someone before they met, an artist type named Kenneth.

But I hadn't thought I'd be one of those girls who did it in high school, either. I had more important things to think about—taking care of Delilah, getting into college.

Now, though, I'd made a promise. The words were out there . . . Saturday night. Three more days.

Even though my parents weren't abstinence advocates, they were fond of "suggesting" that both Ronny and I wait "until you're eighteen and in love," and my father would always tack on, "and it wouldn't hurt you to wait until after college, either." Smugly, I had always thought that there was *no way* I'd be one of those girls who risks everything just because of hormones, because of some silly boy.

Still, I'd be lying if I didn't say I was curious about what it would be like—not just the act of sex, but being on the other side of that line, virginity. Would I feel different? Would I *be* different?

The idea of being different appealed to me a lot lately. I didn't much want to be what I was. . . . How much worse could different be?

He was there. In his chair, at the library. I wandered around in the nonfiction section, flipping through a collection of Sylvia Plath's poetry, and quietly watched him read.

He had beautiful lips. They were full and soft, and he parted them slightly when he relaxed, which he always did when he was reading. And he had excellent posture. Even leaning back in his chair, there was a quality of straightness about the way he sat, as if he was always paying attention, always ready to react, if he needed to.

When he did rise—to fetch another book, to get a drink of water from the fountain—it was graceful, balanced.

I had thought I was subtle in my observation of him, but when Will looked up, his eyes found mine at once.

"Hello, Scarlett," he said. "Would you like to sit down?"

I tried my best to keep from blushing as I walked across the room, Plath's collection tucked under my arm. I lowered myself to perch on the chair across from him.

"Hey," I said softly. His deep, green gaze seemed to be looking for something in my face. I guessed that he didn't find it, because he finally grimaced and looked away, out the window to the gray sky.

"What are you reading?" I asked. I wanted, desperately, for his eyes to turn back to me.

He closed the book in his hands so I could see the title. *Jewish Mysticism*.

"I didn't know our library had anything like that."

"It doesn't. I brought it from home."

Right. Will's father was a professor of religious studies.

"Is it your dad's?"

He nodded. "I've been reading a lot of his books lately."

Then I noticed the name of the author: Rabbi Martin Cohen.

"Wait. Your dad *wrote* it?"

He nodded again.

"And your dad's a rabbi? That's kind of like a priest, isn't it?"

Will chuckled. "Hardly. Rabbis aren't half men like priests; they get married, have families."

"Whoa. *Half men?* That's pretty harsh, isn't it?"

Will shrugged.

I didn't know what to say next. "Well," I started at last, "does he say anything interesting?"

He looked down at the book's cover, as if considering

something. Then he thrust the book at me. "Here," he said. "Take it. See for yourself."

The book was heavy and smelled both dusty and somehow sweet. I breathed in its scent deeply.

"I love the smell of books," I admitted when I saw Will watching me.

He smiled. "I do too," he said. "Nothing better."

It was nice to sit like that, together, in the library. We looked out together at the gray sky.

"It looks like it might rain," he said.

"Maybe this weekend," I hoped aloud, wondering if rain might forestall Andy's plans.

Will's face was quizzical. "Isn't your big party this weekend?"

"Saturday. Are you coming?"

He ignored my question, asking, "Then why would you want it to rain?"

I didn't know how to answer. "I just like the rain," I offered at last, lamely.

Will clearly didn't buy it, but he didn't press me.

"So, are you coming to the party?" I asked again.

Will grinned. "Your boyfriend didn't invite me. Even though he did want to talk with me last week."

I shook my head. "Yeah," I said. "Sorry about that. I'll tell him not to bother you again."

He shrugged. "I can take care of myself, Scarlett."

My eyes glanced at his arms, toned and strong. I didn't doubt that he could take care of himself, whatever the situation.

"So you won't be at the party?" I was embarrassed to hear sadness in my voice.

"Do you want me to come?"

There was no good way to answer this question. "No" would be rude; "yes" would be too dangerous.

I shrugged. "It would be a good chance for you to get to know some girls," I said at last. "I could set you up with Lily."

I was looking at my feet in their green canvas shoes, but I felt the pull of Will's gaze and looked up. Again, his eyes paralyzed me with their fierceness, their undisguised intention.

"I don't want to be set up with Lily," he said.

I looked at him, and he looked at me. I felt myself pulled forward in my seat. Will leaned forward too. It was as if we were two magnets, intractably pulled toward each other—and then I heard the loud clang of the school bell, calling us back to class, back to Earth.

Will stood to leave, and I rose at the same instant. A wave of my hair fell forward and brushed against his arm.

He closed his eyes, just for a second, and he took a breath. "*Almost* nothing better," he said quietly.

I fumbled to my feet, clutching the book he'd given me, abandoning Plath. "Come to the party if you want," I managed to say, and I fled from the library, Will's magnetic pull still calling me.

Saturday afternoon, thunder rumbled the skies. I'd told Andy that maybe he should cancel the party.

"I can't wait to be alone together too," he said, "but if I cancel, Lily will never shut up about it."

When I'd realized that Andy expected me to keep my promise, party or no party, suddenly I decided that the show must go on.

"Yeah," I said. "Everyone would be pretty bummed if you canceled. You probably couldn't even get ahold of everyone this late in the game."

"But we'll kick everyone out by midnight," Andy promised. "Did you tell your parents yet that you're spending the night at Lily's?"

I had, though I wasn't fond of lying to them, no matter how distracted they seemed.

Mom hadn't even heard me, I don't think, and Daddy had just smiled and said, "That'll be fun."

So here I was, sitting at the little desk in my room, smearing my face with green makeup. My hair was pulled up into two tall, tightly wrapped buns, and it was sprayed green. I had found a green Lycra bodysuit in my mom's workout clothes; I slashed it savagely until it was thoroughly shredded, then splashed green glitter paint randomly across it.

I didn't have any good shoes to wear, so Lily lent me her gold sequined high-tops. A pair of googly gold glitter antennas attached to a headband that I'd found in a tourist shop downtown completed my outfit. I was an alien.

It was easier for me to look at myself like this, in costume, face painted. I turned my tall mirror toward the room and appraised myself. It was pretty cool—not half bad for a homemade costume.

I'd gained back a bit of the weight, thanks to Lily's

persistence, but I was definitely still on the thin side. The Lycra was as tight as a second skin, and my small breasts were smashed nearly flat. The green face paint had kind of a sickly glow to it, and I watched my reflection carefully as I smeared black lipstick across my mouth.

I didn't look beautiful. I looked interesting. I'd seen a movie once where the main character, a high school girl, said that Halloween was an excuse for girls to dress up slutty, and in Halloweens past, I guess I'd enjoyed that myself. Last year, Before Ronny Died, I had dressed up as a sexy pig in a pink leotard, pink tights, a curly little tail, and a pink piggy nose. The year before I'd been a fairy: yellow leotard, yellow tights, wings, colorful face paint.

I wasn't sure what had compelled my costume choice this year, but looking into my mirror eyes, shrouded in green, I smiled. The green face, the ridiculous hair, the antennas: it felt honest. I felt fierce and dangerous and ready to dance.

"Are you ready yet?" Lily called to me from the front door.

"Almost! Come on up," I hollered. Then I slipped behind my open door and listened to Lily's footsteps as she came up the stairs and down the hallway.

Definitely heels, I determined. Of course.

Lily and I had decided to surprise each other this year with our costumes. I couldn't wait to see what she'd put together.

The footsteps stopped just outside my door.

"Scar?" she called into my room.

"Arg!" I yelled, leaping out, my hands fierce claws, my gold antennas bouncing ridiculously.

She wasn't scared, but her loud laughter was almost just as good.

There she stood, her fabulous curves showcased in a red Devil costume. The horns perched saucily in her dark curls; she wore long red false eyelashes; her lips were stained bloodred; the cleavage she was showing, I was pretty sure, could have gotten her arrested in several states. And the skirt was so short that bending over probably wasn't an option. Her legs were probably warm enough, though; they were encased in above-the-knee red leather boots balanced on three-inch heels.

I had to remember to close my mouth. "You look amazing," I told her. Suddenly, my green alien garb seemed a little *too* ridiculous.

"I know, right? I got these boots in Italy, of course. *You* look bizarre," she said. "Fabulous costume."

We grinned at each other.

"That's going to be pretty hard to shimmy out of later, if you know what I mean," Lily said, gesturing to my Lycra suit.

"Shhh!" I said, pointing up the hallway. "My parents!"

Lily shrugged. "I'm just saying."

I grabbed Lily's arm and pulled her out of my room. "Come on," I said, "before you say something even more incriminating."

But our escape from the house was not without incident. Just outside the front door, Daddy was sweeping the falling leaves from our porch. He looked up at us and smiled vaguely.

"Hi, girls," he said. "Lily, you look . . . nice. Neat costume, Scar."

"Thanks, Daddy," I said just as Lily answered, "Thanks, John!"

"You girls will be back at Lily's house by midnight, right?"

I opened and closed my mouth like a fish. Lily jumped in. "Sure, John, absolutely, before the carriage turns back into a pumpkin, ha, ha!"

She yanked me down the pathway, more sure on her tall, pointy heels than I was in the high-tops.

"Way to build a cover story," she whispered.

"Sorry, sorry," I said. "I hate lying."

Lily rolled her eyes. "Good thing I'm here."

It wasn't far to Andy's house, but Lily had her parents' golf cart so she wouldn't have to walk home in the middle of the night. We climbed in after Lily adjusted her ridiculously short skirt, and then she pulled away from the curb.

The night was cool, almost cold, and I shivered in my thin Lycra skin. Little kids were just starting to pour out onto the streets. Tiny angels, various superheroes, and at least three SpongeBobs bounced excitedly up and down, showing off their costumes to each other and waving their candy-collecting bags. Their parents clustered steps behind them, sipping something warm from mugs, probably cider.

Several of the houses on our street had hung orange lights from their trees, and a variety of jack-o'-lanterns, some scary, some funny, glowed on the porch steps in various states of decay.

Somebody on the street had lit a fire in their fireplace, and the smell of it was warm and spicy. I wanted suddenly, desperately, to be one of the little angels or superheroes—hell, even a SpongeBob, if it meant I could be a kid again—when all of this was new and exciting, when I could have raced down the street with a passel of friends, screaming "Trick or treat!" at my neighbors' doors, trading my Tootsie Rolls for my brother's tiny boxes of Nerds.

But Lily's golf cart drove me unalterably away from all that, toward Andy's party, where the dark secrets of adulthood waited to reveal themselves to me.

When we pulled up in front of the Turlington home, the party was already under way. Loud music reverberated through the windows, and I peered at the people wandering toward the house. Lily and I squinted in the dusk, trying to make out who was who behind the masks and face paint.

"That must be Connell," Lily said, pointing at a guy dressed as the Hulk.

"Any excuse to take off his shirt, that boy takes it," I agreed.

"He looks pretty good, though," Lily said, admiringly. "Maybe I'll save him a dance."

"*Connell?*" I was incredulous.

"Well, I can't let you have all the fun, can I?"

I shook my head. "I guess not."

"I can't *believe* you're going to be the first of us to lose it."

"Shhh," I commanded. There was no need for the whole *world* to know.

"All right, all right," she said, lowering her voice an octave. "But you have to tell me *everything*. I want details."

I nodded, a little bit miserable.

"Of course, if Will Cohen shows up, I suppose I could save Connell for another time," she mused.

I narrowed my eyes. "No way," I said.

"Off-limits?"

I considered. Who was I to stake a claim on Will? I mean, he wasn't my boyfriend—Andy Turlington was. Still, I wasn't about to loose Lily on him, even if I had suggested at the library that I could fix them up. I remembered the blaze of his eyes and made my decision.

"Off-limits," I said firmly.

Lily shrugged. "A shame, but friends first. If you want to keep him on the back burner, that's cool."

It wasn't that I wanted to keep Will on the back burner, exactly. It was just that I couldn't stand the thought of another girl's hands around his neck, another girl's lips on his.

"Off-limits."

The house was full of our classmates. Most of the girls had hearkened back to the grand Halloween tradition of grossly underdressing for the weather. Thin scraps of fabric clung to their bodies almost as if to spite gravity, and several tottered on high heels, though none as fabulously as Lily.

The boys didn't grow up quite as quickly as girls; several besides Connell were dressed as superheroes, some even as the same superheroes I'd seen earlier in miniature. I counted two Spider-Men and a Superman. No SpongeBobs, though.

Almost everyone was holding a red plastic cup full of social lubricant, and a few of the bravest kids were dancing, even though the evening was young and they couldn't be drunk yet.

"There's my girl!" shouted Andy. Dressed as a pro baseball player, he wore a red-and-white jersey, tight white pants, tall socks, white shoes. He slung his arm over my shoulder and the liquid in his red cup sloshed messily, threatening to splash me.

"Hey, hey," I protested.

"Sorry, baby," he said, taking a step back. "You want a drink?"

Under normal circumstances, I'd say no. I'd always said no before. Alcohol was not my drug of choice. My drug of choice was racing along a wide, empty trail, wind whipping my hair, Delilah's hooves drumming out a rhythm I loved.

But Delilah wasn't here. As I looked up at Andy to see the anticipation burning in his eyes, I thought that maybe I could use a drink.

So I nodded. Andy practically ran to the keg.

The beer tasted bitter, a poor substitute for the Halloween candy of my lost childhood. But I drank it anyway, trying to stop myself from counting up the calories in the cup.

"Can I have another?" I asked, thrusting the cup in Andy's direction.

"Take it easy, Scar." He laughed. "You can't weigh more than a buck ten. You don't want to get wasted, do you?"

I didn't answer. Maybe that was exactly what I wanted.

Andy shrugged and turned to refill my cup. Lily was gone, dancing unabashedly out in the middle of the living room floor, although not entirely to the beat of the song. All the furniture had been pushed up against the walls to clear some space for dancing, but most of the people at the party were pushed up against the walls as well.

I began to feel warmer, looser. I felt my knees beginning to move with the rhythm, my hips swaying. Andy returned and placed my cup back in my hand. It wasn't as heavy this time; some clear liquid filled it only about an eighth of the way up.

I looked at Andy quizzically.

"Vodka," he said.

Did it matter, really, beer or vodka? I didn't know enough about drinking to have an educated answer, so I shrugged and tasted it.

It wasn't bitter like the beer had been, though it burned my throat and sent a wave of fire across my chest, down into my belly.

But the music didn't seem too loud anymore; it seemed just right. In fact, I felt like dancing. I took Andy by the hand and led him out onto the floor. When I turned to face him, he looked a little embarrassed, and I realized that even though we'd been dating—on and off—for most of a year, we'd never really *danced*, except for that awkward rocking of compulsory slow songs at school shindigs.

It occurred to me that I should feel nervous—but I didn't. I felt weightless and sexy, and completely, utterly fabulous.

The song flowed through me like blood, and beat in me like a pulse. I pushed against Andy, smiling, and he smiled too, and thrust his hips in my direction. I threw my head back and laughed out loud.

The room was spinning, or I was spinning, or maybe

everything was spinning. I didn't care. I let Andy pull me close, and we moved together.

His head lowered to my ear and he whispered, "You look sexy as hell, Scarlett. I'd want to do it with you even if you really *were* an alien."

I shivered a little, and took another sip of my drink.

The party was still going strong when Andy pulled me from the makeshift dance floor and nudged me toward the staircase, up toward his room.

"But all the people," I murmured.

"Connell will take care of it," he answered, steadying me on my feet as I stumbled slightly.

His room was decorated with pendants from various baseball teams. Above his bed hung a poster pulled from a *Sports Illustrated* swimsuit edition. It was of a girl, probably no older than I was, standing under a waterfall, pushing her hair back from her face, her mouth open in something simulating pleasure.

Andy guided me to the bed and gently pushed me back onto it. My heart thudded wildly, and as I lay there, the room suddenly seemed to be spinning too fast, out of control, no longer fun.

The weight of Andy on top of me felt too much to bear—as if I was being smothered. His mouth crushed mine, and his hands roamed my body, finding my breasts through the Lycra costume and squeezing them almost painfully.

He thrust against me, and I was afraid suddenly of the rough push of him, and my hands scrambled against his shirtfront.

He must have taken my anxiety for pleasure, he must have thought my fingers were trying to unfasten the buttons of his jersey, because he lifted off of me and pulled off his shirt, tossing it near the closed bedroom door.

"Scarlett," he murmured, "we've waited a long time for this."

"I don't know—" I started to say "I don't know if I really want to do this," but Andy's mouth crashed down on mine again, almost as if he didn't want to give me a chance to stop him. This time, his hands pushed downward, and as one of them snaked between my legs, I clenched my thighs together, suddenly sure that I was in the wrong place, wanting nothing more than to be at home, in my own bed, alone.

Andy's hands were stronger than my thighs, and with something that sounded like a laugh, only angrier, he pried them apart and wedged himself between them.

"This sure is a hell of a costume you chose, Scar," he mumbled as his hands worked to pull the unitard down off my shoulders. He yanked roughly, and I heard the neckline beginning to tear.

"Wait, Andy, I don't think—"

He interrupted me again. "Don't think, Scar, just feel." His words were garbled, tainted by beer and testosterone, and I felt again as I had felt in my dream, impossibly weighed down and lost, my sense of direction distorted, beginning to suffocate, out of breath, out of time.

The door banged open. Suddenly the music from downstairs seemed louder, even more confusing, without the wooden door muffling it.

Andy lifted his head and swore roughly, turning to see

who had entered. Before he had a chance to swivel all the way around, hands yanked him up and threw him from my body.

The room was spinning again, the music was insanely loud, my heartbeat was wild. Then my eyes found Will's, and my face split into a wide smile. Will smiled back before he turned to Andy, who was rushing at him, his face full of fury.

"You're dead, Cohen," he spat, his arm pulled back to punch Will's face. Will ducked neatly to the side. Andy, who hadn't expected to miss, stumbled forward with the weight of his swing, and Will stuck his leg out and tripped him.

Andy got up twice as mad and swung again. Will's face was angry too, but not in the same rage-filled, thwarted way as Andy's. Will's face was in the same moment both furious and calm. His beautiful mouth was set in a line, and his eyes tracked Andy's attack like a predator's. This time, when Andy swung, Will caught his hand and twisted it, hard, to the left. I heard a sickening crunch, and Andy fell to the floor, making a sound like an animal caught in a bear trap.

Still, he stumbled to his feet again, cradling his injured hand and preparing to hit with the other. Will clenched his hand into a fist and, with a jab almost too fast to follow, he knocked Andy hard in the gut.

Andy made a sound like "oof," something I didn't know people did in real life, and this time, he stayed down, his body curved inward like a fetus, and he rocked a little from side to side, groaning.

Will stepped over him and came to me on the bed. He reached his hand down to me. I took it; it was warm.

"Are you all right?"

I nodded, still feeling spinny and sick, and he pulled me gently to my feet. His arm wrapped around my waist to stabilize me, and together we stepped around Andy's writhing body, and we went down the stairs, and the crowd of dancing bodies parted as we passed.

The sky broke open at last, and the rain washed down on us as we went out, together, into the night.

NINE

Will Speaks

Now that the rain had finally come, it seemed torrential. Will threw his jacket across my shoulders and wrapped his arm around my waist, pulling me against his side. I felt the world vibrating and spinning around me and wondered if we were having an earthquake, but it was all inside my own body; I was shivering terribly, and I was drunk.

Clouds blackened out any stars that might have lit the sky, and the moon was a sliver as sharp as a fragment of broken mirror. Will ushered me silently through the streets toward my house.

I wondered at how empty all the streets were; it seemed not so long ago that they'd been cluttered with eager children and watchful parents. Most of the windows of the houses were blackened too.

And then there was my house, porch light still on, and

I whimpered a little. Will's hand clutched my waist more tightly as he guided me up the steps and through the door.

Inside, though, the warm promise of the porch light felt unfulfilled. No one was waiting for me; why should they be? My parents thought I'd be spending the night at Lily's. I'd told them I'd be back home in time for Alice to pick me up on her way to the stable. The great room to the left of the front door, where guests nibbled cheese and crackers during high season, felt as hollow as a cave, and the long staircase toward the second floor and our upstairs quarters yawned at me like a tongue.

Will walked me toward the stairs and guided my hand to the banister. "You'll be okay now," he said, not a question. He looked at me for a long moment before turning to leave.

"Wait!" My free hand reached out to stop him, and my own sudden movement threw me off balance. "Don't go."

Will turned back around. He seemed to be considering his next move very, very carefully. There was something in his expression that unsettled me; he looked too wise, too old by far to be just a year my senior. But then his face softened into a smile, and I let go the breath I hadn't realized I'd been holding.

"I'm not going far," he confessed. "Just to my room at the end of the hall. Your dad checked me in a few hours ago."

Of course. Why else would Will be on this side of the island late at night? I remembered what my father had said about Will maybe using one of our guest rooms now and again.

"I guess it's lucky for me you decided to come to that party, huh?"

Will's face twisted, as if remembering something unpleasant. "Luck had nothing to do with it, Scarlett. Why don't you go upstairs and dry off? I'll still be here in the morning." Then he touched my hand on the banister, gently, almost shyly, before disappearing down the hall.

I wanted to follow him. But a violent wave of sickness washed through me, and I rushed as quickly as I could up the two flights of stairs, stumbling into the bathroom. I managed to close and lock the door before the nausea overtook me, and then I collapsed alongside the toilet, retching as quietly as I could manage.

I threw up twice, and then felt better. Still dizzy, but with that familiar sense of hollowness I'd come to depend on. Weakly, I crossed over to the sink and turned on the water to rinse out my mouth.

My reflection in the medicine cabinet's mirrored door was startling. The rain had washed away streaks of my green face paint, leaving me with a bizarre, marbled appearance. My bobbing antennas were gone, probably abandoned on the floor of Andy's bedroom, and my tall green buns leaned wildly to one side.

I pulled off Will's jacket and saw that the neckline of my green unitard was ripped across my right shoulder, exposing my collarbone. The torn fabric hung down in a limp flap.

I remembered how it had come to be that way, and my knees trembled badly. Carefully, I lowered myself to the edge of the white tub and balanced there, lowering my face into my hands. Thoughts—lots of them—threatened to over-take me, but I determinedly put them away and twisted the knobs of the bath. While the water heated up, I pulled the bands out of my hair and stripped off the gold sneakers, my socks, and the shredded unitard, which I thrust into the trash can. Then I turned the bypass knob so that the water rained down from the showerhead and I climbed gratefully beneath it.

It was too difficult to stand. Still drunk and dizzy, I low-ered myself to sit Indian-style on the floor of the tub and let the water course over me. It swirled down the drain, green-ish at first, as the spray from my hair and face rinsed away, but eventually it was clear.

I sat there numbly, shivering in spite of the water's heat, wondering several times if I was going to puke again. It was a definite possibility, but at last I determined that I was going to keep it together, and I turned the water off and climbed gingerly from the tub.

In my room, the best I could manage before collapsing was to pull back the covers. Then I fell onto my pillow, still naked from the shower, my damp towel dropped on the floor next to me. But sleep would not come; the room spun be-hind my closed eyes, and I felt the heat from my shower seeping out of me. I was cold again, and restless.

I imagined Will downstairs, in a guest room. Was he awake too? If so, was he staring out at the storm, or was he lying in the dark, eyes focused on nothing?

Sleep was not coming anytime soon. Emboldened by my lingering drunkenness, I pulled on my jeans and a sweatshirt and slipped as quietly as I could from my room, trying to tiptoe past my parents' room, though I had to lean heavily on the wall to keep my balance.

Downstairs, I followed a dim glow from underneath the door of the Yellow Room. I swallowed, and smoothed my hair, damp and heavy over my shoulders. I raised my hand to knock, but before I did, Will's voice greeted me— "Come in."

He was sitting in front of the fireplace, and he'd built a fire. Its orange glow cast tricky shadows on the walls. Will sat in one of the two chairs in front of the fireplace, and when I came in, standing awkwardly and fidgeting with my hair in the doorway, Will gestured for me to join him in the other chair.

I tripped over the edge of the rug and stumbled into the chair. Will laughed a little and shook his head. "Still drunk, huh?"

"A little."

We sat in silence before the fire. Will stared into the flames; I stared at him. I had so many questions, but all of them started with the same word—Why?

Why had he come to the party? Why had he come to my house that one morning? Why had he been waiting for me outside the girls' bathroom? And why, why had he come to me that day on the trail?

At last, Will looked away from the fire and met my gaze. We looked at each other for a long moment, and this time I was the one to look away into the fire.

"Scarlett," he said softly, "can you keep a secret?"

Biting my lip, I nodded. Secrets were what I did best.

"Ever since we met, Scarlett—even *before* we met—I've felt this strange pull toward you."

It was ridiculous how happy those words made me feel. I tried to tell myself that I was relieved to know I hadn't been making it all up, turning a string of coincidences into something meaningful, but there was more to it than that. He'd felt a pull toward me.

"Do you know why I'm here, Scarlett, on your island?"

"I know your mom . . . died . . . a few years ago. I figured your move had something to do with that. You know, like your dad wanting a change of scenery or something." I felt shy, suddenly, mentioning his mother—and nervous, too. Talking about his dead mother was just a step away from talking about my dead brother, and I didn't think I could handle that.

"Or something," Will agreed. "I'm sure my dad did think it would be good for both of us to get away. But not just to escape our memories, though I'd bet that figured more strongly into Dad's decision than he'd be willing to admit. My dad's an interesting guy, Scarlett. You'll see for yourself when you meet him."

I flushed with pleasure, hoping my face was hidden by the half-light of the room. He wanted me to meet his father.

"See, Scarlett, things are different for me." Here he paused, pursing his lips as if considering whether he should really continue. I realized my hands were gripping each other tightly, anxious for him to tell me more. I slid my chair closer and curled my legs under me, leaning in toward him. The fire warmed my hair, drying it.

When Will looked at me, his green eyes burned as fiercely

145

as any fire. "I've never told anyone this, Scarlett, except for my dad, and I'm not really sure I should be telling you. But secrets . . . they eat you up, if you hold them too long." His look was almost pleading, as if he was asking for my permission.

I reached across the distance that separated us and rested my hand on his. Even though his hand was warm, I shivered a little when we touched. The sensation that seemed to jolt through me was so powerful that there was no way I could deny it, no way he didn't feel it too.

Will flipped his hand over so that we were palm to palm. As easy as melted butter, our fingers interlaced. He squeezed my hand, and a measure of the torture that had colored his expression seeped away.

"Ah," he said. "That's better."

Our hands connected, and the shock I'd felt upon our first touch surged between us like a current whose circuit had been completed. My drunken dizziness faded to almost nothing and I felt so present, so *alive*, that I could have stayed just like that, fingers entwined with Will's, for the rest of my days.

"I have this . . . thing," he said. His voice was so low, almost a whisper, that I leaned in even closer to hear him. My hair fell like a curtain between us and the fire. We were in a very private little room. Will closed his eyes as if the telling would be easier if he didn't see his audience. His head tipped forward; so did mine, and our foreheads touched. "I don't know why, or how," he confessed. "But I am drawn to . . . I feel the need to . . ."

He couldn't seem to finish a sentence. I squeezed his fingers to give him courage.

"When something bad is going to happen, somewhere, I have this sensation of impending danger. I'm *pulled*, I guess, to locations where something bad—violent—is going to happen."

He fell silent then, but it wasn't a restful silence. I could tell he was waiting for my reaction. Would I pull away? Would I call him a liar?

But I knew, without question, that his words were absolutely true. Will Cohen was not a liar. How did I know this? I couldn't say. But I knew, as sure as my breath, that he spoke the truth.

"It started a few years ago, not long after my mom died," he said with an air of confession. "The first time I didn't have any idea what was happening. I woke up in the middle of the night, just after my thirteenth birthday. It was like there was a hook in my brain"—here he leaned back from me and touched his forehead in the disarmingly beautiful gesture I'd come to know of him—"and it pulled me like a fish on a line through the dark streets of the city."

He sat back in his chair now so he could see me as he talked. I understood; once you start telling your secret, its lock on you loosens and the words come faster, more easily. Our hands, still entwined, rested together on his knee.

"I wandered down streets I didn't know and found myself in an alley, a place I'd never been. I couldn't tell you the route I took. But I kept speeding up until I was running. When I got to that alley, I stopped. The pulling feeling was gone, replaced with this sense of anticipation, but the hook was still there, ready to reel me in if I tried to leave. I waited, knowing for sure that something was about to happen. And I was going to have to stop it."

"Go on."

"I didn't have to wait long. I heard them before I saw them. There was a whimpering sound and a man's deep voice. As they rounded the corner into the alley, I stepped back into a shadow. They knew each other, that was clear, because the girl—she was probably about twenty or so—was begging him by name to stop. It seemed like he was enjoying her cries, like they were actually urging him on. He had a knife to her throat, and he pushed her up against the brick wall and reached under her skirt, pulling off her underwear. Suddenly, all I could see was this pulsing, rage-filled light, and I knew I had to help. There was a bottle on the ground, and I picked it up and smashed it against the wall. I pointed it at the guy and yelled at him to leave her alone."

I remembered the party at Andy's, the way Will had stridden into the room with such intention, such purpose, and I pulled his hand into my lap and squeezed his fingers.

"He must have just been startled to find that he wasn't alone in the alley. I was just a skinny kid—I'd barely bar mitzvahed, even—but he flinched, just long enough for the girl to kick him, hard, in the groin. He dropped his knife, and she and I both ran, fast, leaving him there behind us.

"The girl ran one way, and I ran the other. It was like, as soon as I'd helped her, the hook in my brain disappeared, and I was free to go. I ran home, scared to death that the guy

148

would follow me. He didn't, and somehow I made it home, though I didn't know the way. My dad was still sleeping. In the morning, I tried to convince myself that the whole thing had been a crazy dream. I didn't really believe that, of course, but how else could I explain it?"

It was silent now outside. The rain had stopped. The fire had consumed itself and was just embers.

Will seemed to be waiting for me to say something. I didn't know which question to ask first. Finally I said, "Is it always . . . you know, girls who you have to save?"

He shook his head. "No, but there are more of those than you'd believe. Sometimes it's a fight gone wrong, or a parent beating his kid. Every now and then it's something even stranger—things I wouldn't like to tell you. But it's always a crime, and a violent one. Robberies, accidents, destruction of property . . . those don't speak to me."

"So you were . . . called to me tonight?" My voice was uncertain, shaky. "But I asked for it, Will. I'd told him I would."

Will shook his head, angry. "No one asks for that, Scarlett. No one has the right to . . . I saw, Scarlett. You were trying to push him off."

My eyes burned. "But I'd told him before . . ."

"That doesn't matter. That doesn't count. It was pretty clear what you were telling him then, in the bedroom. And it wasn't yes."

The tears spilled down my cheeks. I hoped Will wouldn't see them, but the sun was beginning to rise and our room glowed faintly in its light.

He reached out, so gently, and wiped away my tears with his thumb. "It's okay," he said, his voice rough. "I was there."

I nodded and took a deep breath. "Thank you," I whispered.

"You're welcome."

The room turned pink in the sunrise, and I felt the press of our time running out. Daddy was an early riser; he'd be up soon.

My question came out in a rush. "But what about the other times? On the trail? Outside the bathroom at school? I wasn't in danger then."

Will shook his head. "I don't know. The first time I came to you, out on the trail, it was the first time since we came to the island that I had that familiar hook-in-the-brain feeling. I found myself pulled to the trail, and then you showed up. There was something different, though. You weren't in any danger, not that I could see. And there was no one else out there; you were all alone. Even if you would have fallen from your horse—"

"I never fall from Delilah."

"Even if you had, I don't feel pulled to accidents. Only violent crimes. So there was no reason that I should have been out there, on the trail."

"But you were."

"And afterward, I was hit with one of my headaches."

"Your headaches?"

Will nodded. "If I don't respond to the fishhook pull, or if I don't try to stop the crime, I get the worst headache you could imagine. Like a migraine, I guess. Blinding pain for days, makes me want to bang my head into a wall."

"That's why you stumbled off like that," I murmured.

"It's different with you, Scarlett. It doesn't matter *where* you are. The pull is never to a place. It's to *you*. It's as if your body is the crime scene."

My stomach lurched. I imagined my yellow notebook, tucked beneath my bed. I thought of the thin scar across my wrist.

Will looked at me as if waiting for me to say something. Finally, I raised my shoulders in an unconvincing shrug and looked away.

I knew we were out of balance now. Will had shared his secret with me, and I hadn't reciprocated. His fingers loosened, and he withdrew his hand.

There was emptiness where there had been warmth. But unlike the raw, cored-out feeling I craved, this emptiness was just . . . empty. Sad.

Will got up and walked over to the window. He pulled open the drapes and stood with his back to me, so I couldn't see his expression when he talked.

"I don't know about you, Scarlett, but I was raised with a certain outlook on life. In my faith, we're taught that all of us are connected. And each of us has a responsibility to the others. Whether we like it or not. The things we do matter . . . sometimes they matter far more than we can know."

I didn't like where this was headed. "If all of us are responsible to everyone, how could any of us ever move?" I argued. "It would be paralyzing! If I walk to the left, I risk causing someone to suffer. If I go right, maybe someone else falls off a cliff."

"You're being ridiculous."

Of course I was, but I didn't like Will telling me so. "So you're telling me you're just thrilled to bits to be saddled with this gift of yours? You *like* having to drop everything and head off like some superhero?"

"I hate it," Will whispered. "Sometimes I try to ignore it, but—I'm too weak."

A flash of insight struck me. "That's why you're on this island," I accused. "You came here to hide from what you can do, is that it?"

Will nodded. "After my mother died and then this . . . thing . . . started with me and it just kept getting stronger, my father couldn't stand the thought of losing me as well. So here we are—insulated by miles of uninterrupted Pacific Ocean from the nearest big city. My father put his whole life on hold to try to keep me safe from myself." He laughed, but not as if he found it funny. "Imagine how upset he was when I came back that day from the trail and he saw me, completely wrecked."

"What do you mean, wrecked?"

Will's smile was tight. "Well, I didn't save you that day, did I? So the headache came."

"Oh, Will, I—"

He shook his head. "It's not your fault," he said. "You couldn't have known. But now you do. Scarlett, every time you hurt yourself it hurts me, too. I don't know how, or why, but there it is. And I'm not the only one you're hurting."

I didn't know what to say. I couldn't name my feeling. Shame seemed the closest fit.

"I wasn't trying to hurt anyone," I offered lamely.

"Scarlett," Will admonished. He crossed away from the window and knelt beside me. I felt tiny, so insignificant curled into a corner of the chair by the deadened fire. "You were trying to hurt *yourself*."

I opened my mouth to speak, to deny, but the words wouldn't come. How could I explain—hurting myself wasn't ever the end, it was always just the means. A method to distance myself from myself.

"I've got to go," I mumbled, untangling my legs and standing. They felt weak beneath me. "My dad will be up soon."

Will stood too, and I wondered if he was going to stop me. But he just nodded. "Try to get some sleep."

Back in my room, I forced myself to breathe regularly. My heart pounded wildly. I sat on the edge of my bed, then stood, paced the room, then sat again. I replayed what Will had told me in my head. Downstairs with Will, everything he said had been so easy to accept, but up here, alone again in my room, my agitation was overwhelming. Could it be? Could Will be blessed—or cursed, perhaps—to anticipate where violent crimes were going to occur?

I recalled his words—"It's as if your body is the crime scene."

My manicure scissors sang to me from the drawer of my desk. My heartbeat was too fast, too erratic, and it seemed that if I was to grasp those tiny silver scissors in my hand, if I was to draw their sharp edge across my wrist, or down the instep of my foot, maybe, then the beat would slow and settle to a more acceptable rhythm.

But I thought of Will, downstairs in the Yellow Room.

Was he lying in the bed, now that I had gone? Was he staring at the ashes of the fire? And my yearning for the scissors slowly seeped away, and I counted my breaths and forced them to slow, and my heartbeat slowed as well, until it was steady and strong. I lowered myself to my bed, imagining Will lying next to me, the length of his body warm and solid against mine, and the beat of my own heart lulled me to sleep at last.

TEN

Under the Elm

I slept like the dead until ten o'clock, when I heard from outside the window the urgent honking of Alice's truck. At first I tried to block out the sound with my pillow, but it just sounded again, louder and longer this time.

Groaning, holding my head in my hands to keep it from splitting apart, I stumbled to the window and yanked it up. I waved weakly down at Alice. "Coming," I called.

The effort of opening the window and calling to her wore me out completely. I collapsed back on the edge of the bed and tried very, very hard to sit perfectly still. The room seemed to slip sideways, and I did the best I could to bring it back to level with my brain. The effort was disconcerting. I figured the world could be slippery, for a while, if it wanted to be.

Looking down, I saw I was still wearing my jeans and sweatshirt. This realization brought with it a jolt of anxiety. Will had been here, in my house, in the Yellow Room.

"It's as if your body is the crime scene."

Was he still here? Finally, I found the motivation to stand on shaky legs and make my way downstairs, shoving my feet into my boots on the way.

Passing through the kitchen, I grabbed my silver water bottle and filled it from the sink. As an afterthought, I grabbed a bagel, too. The plain bread sounded pretty good, as if it might soak up the alcohol that still seemed to be sloshing inside me.

Mercifully, my parents weren't around. I was certain if they saw me like this, they'd know for sure I was hungover. I hadn't looked at myself, but it couldn't be good.

Downstairs, I walked carefully down the hall toward the Yellow Room. The bed was empty, stripped of its linens, which were piled near the bathroom door.

Will was gone. But the stripped bed proved he had been here, that my memories were real. I wanted to sit in the chair by the fire and replay our conversation in my head, but another impatient honk from Alice's truck compelled me out the door.

Alice was sleek and perfect as usual. She wore a button-down cardigan over a neatly pressed blouse, and her jeans looked as if she'd just picked them up from the dry cleaner.

Unlike mine, her boots were laced tight and done up in neat little bows.

She appraised me over the rim of her sunglasses. "You look like hell, Scarlett. Have a big night?"

I groaned and flopped into the passenger seat, pulling the door closed behind me.

• • •

The drive helped; the air blowing through the window began to wake me up, and I fed myself little bits of the bagel, checking carefully between each bite to see if it was going to stay down. By the time we neared the stable, I'd managed to eat half of it and drain my bottle of water. I was feeling better—not good, but better.

Alice did her best to mind her own business, but she wasn't very good at it. She kept giving me sidelong glances and asking leading questions like, "So, did you have fun last night?"

Finally, my exasperation at her hedging reached maximum capacity. "Yes, Alice," I said, answering a question she hadn't exactly asked. "I got drunk. I am hungover."

Alice tried to arrange her mouth into a stern expression, but it looked to me like she was biting back a smile. "Hungover, are you? Hmm . . ."

And then her hand reached out and twisted the volume knob to high, and she stepped on the gas and swerved at the same time, and she sang along with the music loudly, grinning at me.

I was too weak to fight. I leaned my head against the window frame and my hair whipped out the window, tangling in the wind.

When we made it at last to the stable, Alice grabbed my arm to keep me from leaving the cab of the truck.

She killed the engine and turned to me, pulling off her sunglasses. "I hope this isn't going to become a habit."

I shook my head carefully, trying to keep my brain from

rattling against the sides of my head. "No, Alice. I'm not going to become a drunk. I don't plan on drinking again, ever."

"Good girl. Now, if you're up to it, maybe you could work with Traveler this morning. He could use some time under saddle in the arena."

This perked me up a little. Traveler was the colt out of the same mare that had mothered Delilah. He was going to be big; at nearly three years, he was already well muscled. He was red, like Delilah, but with a more orange cast. His eyes, still, were a little wild.

"Yeah," I said. "I'll take him out first."

"Put the stud chain on him," Alice warned. "Don't give him an inch."

One thing that I really liked about Alice was that she got on with her work and stayed pretty much out of my hair. She trusted me with the horses—and her trust was well placed.

I passed Delilah's stall on my way to Traveler's, and she nickered after me.

"Sorry, girl, I'll get you out later," I called. Now that I was up and moving, my headache was receding.

I visited the tack room first and pulled out the lightest-weight saddle. This would be Traveler's first time wearing tack, so I wanted to be sure to make the experience as pleas-ant as possible. I grabbed a thick, soft saddle pad, too, along with the brush bucket, a halter and lead, and, finally, the stud chain.

I hated to use a stud chain. Alice was old-school; she viewed the nasty metal chain as essential to breaking a horse. Maybe it was, but I was against the whole concept of "breaking" anything. I preferred to look at my relationship with a horse as a building of trust, of reciprocal respect. Still, I put the stud chain, slippery as a snake, into the bucket along with the brushes.

I grabbed a couple of sugar cubes and left the equipment at the cross-ties, taking the halter and lead to Traveler's stall at the end of the barn. He was standing with his head out, rocking agitatedly back and forth, rubbing his chest against the rubber edge of the door.

"Hey, big guy," I called. His ears pricked forward and he lifted his chin as if in greeting. I palmed a sugar cube and held it under his nose. He took it gently with his lips. The other cube I popped into my mouth while I slipped the halter over his head, fastening the buckle and clipping on the lead before sliding open the door to his stall.

At the cross-ties, I took my time about grooming him. I showed him the brush and the hoof pick, holding each tool slightly to the side of his head so he could see them clearly. I explained what I was doing, step-by-step.

It didn't matter if he understood my words; he felt the calmness in my tone, and gradually he slowed his heavy pawing on the rubber mats and sighed, leaning into the strokes of my brush. When he was so calm that his lower lip began to dangle a little, I told him, "Now we're going to try something new, okay, big guy?"

Slowly, I stepped around his side and picked up the fuzzy saddle pad. I showed it to him, and he spooked a little, trying to feint to the right, but the ties attached to the halter held him mostly still. I made soothing little noises and rubbed the saddle pad all over his body, starting high up on his neck, then across his shoulders, along the barrel of his chest, across his flanks, down each of his spindly Arab legs. Slowly, he calmed, accepting the touch of the saddle pad on his body.

Then I balanced it on his back, high up between his withers. Back in the tack room, I'd taken the stirrup irons off the saddle; Traveler didn't need anything thumping around on his sides, not this first time. Gently, slowly, I hoisted the saddle up and onto his back, square on top of the saddle pad.

He quivered a bit, but he did not shy. "Brave boy," I soothed. "Such a big, brave guy."

We stood like that for several long moments, Traveler getting used to the weight of the saddle on his back. I steadied it with one hand and stroked his neck with the other, talking softly to him the whole time.

Then, when his lip began to flap in relaxation again, I maneuvered around to his right side and attached the girth. Back around on his left, I grabbed the girth from under his belly and fastened it on its loosest set of holes, just to get him used to the feel of something rubbing against his belly.

It didn't seem to faze him, which was a good sign, but I waited a long moment anyway before tightening it a notch.

Mares are usually more girthy and irritable about the whole process than their male counterparts, and Traveler was taking his first girthing like a man. He barely seemed to notice as I ratcheted the girth another hole tighter, and then one more.

It was tight enough to keep the saddle from slipping while we worked in the arena, though not as tight as I would fasten it if I planned to climb up on his back.

I moved to grab the longe rope and spied the stud chain curled in the bottom of the tack bucket. I hated the thing, truly I did. So I left it there, winding the longe rope instead through the chin ring on the halter, then looping it up behind his ears before clipping it to the ring on his right cheek.

I unhooked him from the cross-ties and led him toward the arena. We had to pass in front of the office, and I wondered guiltily if Alice would see that I'd eschewed the stud chain.

In the arena, I made my way to the center and let Traveler out several lengths, careful to keep the circle tight so that he couldn't get too wild.

Eagerly, he picked up a trot. He was a gorgeous mover. His hooves flew through the sand, his head dropped naturally into a lovely arch. The weight of the saddle didn't seem to bother him any more than a fly would have.

I couldn't help but feel a little smug after fifteen minutes had passed uneventfully. I kept Traveler to a trot, tugging mindfully at the longe rope when he quickened his pace. He seemed eager to listen and obey, his ears rotating as if to show me he was paying attention.

Finally, I slowed him to a walk and shortened the longe rope length by length until he was beside me in the center of the arena. "Good, good," I told him, thumping his neck with my palm.

• • •

With Traveler put away, I turned my attention to Delilah. It may have been my imagination, but she seemed a little huffy today.

"Come on, girl, don't be jealous," I teased her, rubbing her velvet forehead the way I knew she liked.

Delilah could have something of a temper, but she forgave quickly too. By the time we were out on the trail she moved along happily, graceful and beautiful as always.

The trails were damp from last night's rain; I felt the sponginess of the earth with each step she took.

Though the sun was out and the air was dry, it wasn't warm on the trail. The shadows cast by the trees seemed longer than they'd been just a few weeks ago.

If Ronny were alive, he'd be deep into his first quarter at UCLA. He'd be preparing for his first set of midterms. He'd be able to commiserate with me over my first—and last, I hoped—hangover.

And if I told him about what had happened with Andy, he would have taken the next boat over to the island and kicked Andy's ass.

As if feeling my sadness, Delilah took a deep breath and let it out in a sigh. I stroked her mane, and then gave her a squeeze with my legs, urging her to pick up a canter. We loped down the trail, and the cool air laced like fingers through the strands of my hair, and though my sadness weighed heavily in my core, I breathed deeply of the autumn air and felt joy, the joy of being alive.

• • •

By Monday, my hangover had faded to a sheepish memory, but the incident with Andy had not. He had sent me a string of texts the day before, ranging in tone from apologetic to annoyed at my failure to respond. I had deleted them cleanly, one after another.

Lily—as dependable as she was fabulous—met me outside my house at 7:50 sharp. She handed me a croissant from our local bakery and a mocha. There was whipped cream on top, a gorgeous dollop of white confection. I couldn't remember the last time I'd had whipped cream.

Carefully, I drank a sip of the hot, chocolatey drink, the sweet cream cold against my lips. Ahh.

"Details," she demanded.

Lily had texted me too—hers, I'd answered, though hedgingly. *Left party with Will*, I'd written. *More later.*

Now, apparently, was later. Lily did not look as if she was willing to wait any longer for the scoop. But I remembered Will's question—"Can you keep a secret?"—and I knew I'd be giving Lily the abbreviated version.

As we walked, we nibbled our croissants. I opened with, "So Andy got sort of pushy on Saturday."

"Did he hurt you?"

I remembered my torn unitard, now shoved deep into the trash. "No, not really," I said. "But I don't know what would have happened if Will hadn't shown up."

"I heard a rumor that he punched Andy?" Lily's eyes were bright with the drama of it all.

I hesitated, then nodded. "Yeah, he sure did."

"Oh my god. I saw you leaving the party. Will had his arm

around you like some kind of guardian angel. I called your name, but he whisked you out of there before I could get across the dance floor."

"I didn't hear you. I was pretty drunk," I admitted.

Lily shook her head. "You never should have mixed your drinks," she advised sagely. "If you start with beer, you stick with beer. End of story."

"That would be good advice, if I ever planned to drink again," I said. "But I'm pretty sure I'm going to be a tee-totaler from here on in. Alcohol and I are not a pretty picture." I remembered curling over the toilet, and shivered.

"Well," Lily said, taking a long sip from her mocha, "about three minutes after you and Will left, Andy stumbled down the stairs, looking like hell and sort of holding his stomach, and he yelled, 'Party's over!' He and Connell kind of herded everyone outside. And it was pouring! By the time I got to the golf cart, my dress was completely soaked. Andy had better hope that the dry cleaner can get the water stains out of my leather boots, or I am sending him the bill for a new pair. Those boots are, like, my soul in leather."

I admitted that the boots were, indeed, fabulous, but my heart wasn't really into the discussion of rain-damaged leather. We had reached the campus, and I scanned the small cluster of students.

There he was. Standing slightly apart from the others, Will held his books and shifted his weight, as if nervous. Our eyes caught, and he smiled, a sideways half smile. His hand lifted in a wave.

Lily watched as my mouth widened in a grin. I waved

back, maybe a bit too exuberantly. She raised an eyebrow knowingly.

"So," she said. "Anything else you want to tell me?"

Luckily, the warning bell rang.

When I walked into American Lit, Andy was already at his desk—same row as mine, three seats back. He tried to catch my eye, but I refused to meet his glance.

He must have anticipated this, because resting on my desk was a neatly folded square of notebook paper. *Scarlett* was written in Andy's hand across the front.

Using the edge of my notebook, I scooted the note to the edge of my desk. I felt Andy's gaze boring into the back of my neck, but I didn't turn to face him.

Mr. Blaine was doing some song and dance about the contributing factors of the Jazz Age—soaring stock market, advent of new technology, shockingly short hemlines, Prohibition and speakeasies.

I slipped comfortably into note-taking mode. I was pretty sure I knew where this was all headed: *The Great Gatsby* was one of the landmark Jazz Age novels, and we'd just read some Fitzgerald short stories the week before, so I wasn't surprised when Mr. Blaine opened the cabinets at the back of the room and recruited volunteers to hand out copies of the novel.

Once we each had a copy, Mr. Blaine started making a list on the board of key characters and settings. I tuned out here, preferring to encounter the story on my own as I read.

At last I turned my attention to the note. I unfolded it and smoothed it on my desk. I wasn't interested in the words on it, though; I unfocused my eyes so the letters blurred together, and concentrated on tearing the paper neatly into long, thin strips, ten in all, then piling up the strips and tearing them horizontally, again and again, until I had a nice little pile of apology confetti.

When the bell rang, I gathered up my books and swept the confetti pieces into my hand, dropping them into the trash can next to the door. My heart felt free, like a bird that had flown from its cage, and I floated from the room and down the hall.

Will wasn't in the library at lunchtime. For a moment I felt a surge of anxiety—I had been so sure his smile this morning had meant something. I was embarrassed to admit to myself that I had expected him to be waiting for me in what I considered to be our place . . . the library.

I considered going to the cafeteria, but I had brought a lunch from home, and somehow I knew that Will wouldn't be there, anyway. So I closed my eyes and considered where he might be.

I felt a faint breeze coming from the open door at the end of the hallway. I heard birds too, and then, opening my eyes, I saw another note with my name on it, this one resting on the short table next to the chairs where Will and I had sat.

He wrote in cursive. I couldn't think of another boy I knew who actually chose to write in script; they all scrawled awkward block letters, or at best strung together two or three straggly letters at a time.

I liked the way my name looked written by his hand. This note I read, eagerly. It was short: *Outside, under the tree.*

I knew at once where he meant. At the far end of the

field grew a graceful elm, one of the few semiprivate spots on our small campus.

Tucking the note into my pocket, I went outside.

The ground had dried after the big storm, and I found Will reclining on the grass beneath the tree, resting on his elbows, ankles crossed. His eyes were closed, his face turned up toward the sun, inviting its rays.

My feet were quiet in the long grass, and he didn't hear me coming. This gave me time to study his face. He looked beatific.

His dark hair curled in soft rings and waves across his forehead, over his ears. His whole face looked divinely relaxed, and his mouth seemed plump as ripe fruit. I ran my tongue across my own lips. To kiss him . . .

His eyes opened. My gaze felt suddenly paralyzed, and I was certain he had felt me staring at him.

"Umm . . . hi," I mumbled, suddenly finding something very interesting to examine by my feet.

He sat up and held his hand out to me. "You want to sit down?"

My hand slid into his. It was a good thing I sat down, because my knees were shaky.

He leaned back again under the tree. Marbled sunlight filtered through the elm leaves, and his face was bathed in light and shadow. I leaned back next to him, our entwined fingers linking us together.

"You feeling better?" he asked.

"Mmm-hmm." I frowned. "But you were gone when I woke up."

"I wanted to stay. But I wasn't sure if you'd still want me there . . . after everything I told you."

He was actually nervous! About how *I* might react to *him*!

"I would have liked it if you'd been there," I answered quietly. "It's nice to be with you now."

He smiled, and the tension faded from his face. "It's good to hear you say that," he confessed. "I wasn't sure if you'd think I was crazy."

"I think you're *something*," I said, "but not crazy."

He laughed. I flushed with happiness for having made him laugh.

We sat for a while in companionable silence, watching the breeze stir the leaves in the tree. One drifted gently to the ground.

"Got anything good in there?" asked Will, gesturing to my lunch bag. I let go of his hand and peeled open the bag, pulling out a cheese-and-avocado sandwich, a small plastic bag of pretzels, and an apple.

"Are you hungry?" I offered him half of the sandwich.

"Thanks." He sat up and bit into it. I watched him chew and swallow, and then I took a bite of the other half.

I pulled my metal water bottle from my backpack and unscrewed the lid.

When the sandwich was gone, I took a bite of the apple, more to have something to do with my hands than anything else. Will was watching me, so I held the apple out to him.

"Want a bite?"

His smile was slow. "Are you tempting me, woman?"

I blinked. Then I recalled the Garden of Eden, the fruit, Adam and Eve, and I laughed. "Are you tempted?" I asked.

Will nodded, serious suddenly. He leaned across and put his mouth on the apple still in my hand. As he bit into it, a shudder of pleasure coursed through me.

Something shifted between us. It was as if, without speaking any words, we'd come to an agreement. When we heard the bell, Will stood and offered me his hand. I took it, and we walked back across the field, our tree at our backs, together.

My next two classes passed in a haze, Andy's beseeching glance in the hallways easy enough to ignore. Finally, it was time for drama.

Mrs. B was busy filling the board with information about social satires. I noticed there had been a rearrangement of seats in the classroom: flushing happily, I saw that Will had displaced Brandon Becker in the seat next to mine. Brandon didn't seem too affected by the change; he was hamming it up to Katie Ellis, who did seem less than pleased by the re-arrangement.

I grinned at Will, feeling shy. His returning smile was like the sun—wide, bright, beautiful.

"Okay, people, what can you tell me about Oscar Wilde?" Mrs. B asked.

"Wasn't he a fag or something?" called out Connell from the back of the room.

I rolled my eyes. I still had a hard time understanding what Connell was doing in this class; it could only be that Mrs. B had a reputation for being an easy A.

"Or something," answered Mrs. B. "Rein in the homopho-bia a little, will you, Connell? Oscar Wilde was famously homosexual as well as famously creative and clever. This spring, we're going to do one of his productions—*The Importance of Being Earnest*."

A pile of playbooks rested on her desk. "Connell," she ordered, "make yourself useful and hand those around, won't you?"

As Connell grumblingly did her bidding, Mrs. B continued, "Now, this play pokes vicious fun of the social strata and sabotages that existed in Victorian England. There were the haves and the have-nots, and layers of rules—both spoken and unspoken—that dictated how everything was to be done. Not that different from modern-day high school, I'd wager."

Some noises of assent from the class.

"Browse the cast of characters and see if any of them appeal to you. Casting will begin next week."

As Connell slapped a playbook on my desk, he hissed at me, "You'd better talk to 'Andy. He's a wreck." Then he sneered at Will and said "Not cool" before he moved on.

Clearly, the circle of students around my desk heard him, and no one looked confused. I hated being the object of gossip, but even more, I hated the thought of letting these bullies and leeches have the upper hand—so I scooted my desk closer to Will's and said, in my best stage voice, "I hear the relationship between Cecily and Algernon is pretty steamy. Want to read those parts with me?"

"Whatever you say." Will's voice was liquid.

I heard the papery whispering of the gossip vultures kick into high gear. Good.

I'd be like Oscar Wilde. Fabulously myself.

ELEVEN
The House Behind the Hill

By the end of November, Andy seemed to have given up. He'd tried flowers, endless phone calls, even sending various friends to plead his case on his behalf. ("Come on, Red Hot," begged Connell. "What's the Jew got that Andy doesn't have, only better?") The best thing to come of the whole situation was that Andy did end up paying Lily's dry-cleaning bill—most likely as a peace offering to me.

But as the month wore on, his attempts waned slowly, finally ceasing for a good three days before I spied Kaitlyn Meyers perched like a milk-drunk kitten on his lap in the cafeteria.

Andy's eyes followed me as if attempting to gauge how much this turn of events bothered me. The answer was not at all—though I did hope for Kaitlyn's sake that Andy had learned his lesson the night of the Halloween party. I sent her a text that night, fairly certain how it would be received, suggesting that she might want to be careful with Andy.

She texted back almost instantly—*Mind your own business, Scarlett.*

And my business was plenty to keep me busy. Alice, impressed by my work with Traveler, had recruited me to help with his further training, and he and I had progressed to tentative work in the arena under saddle. Tryouts for *The Importance of Being Earnest* had just ended, and I'd been thrilled to see my name next to the part of Cecily Cardew, and Will's just underneath, next to Algernon.

The day the casting list went up, a Wednesday, Will and I disappeared into the library as soon as we'd finished our lunch. Outside, the day was wet and gray, too chilly for lounging under our elm tree. We sat across from each other in our chairs by the window, thumbing through our playbooks and highlighting our lines.

"We've got a lot of scenes together," Will said. "What do you think about a weekend rehearsal?"

I tried to maintain an air of casualness. "That should be okay."

Will set aside his script and leaned across, running his fingers lightly across my knee. Even through the denim of my jeans, I felt the jolt that always accompanied his touch. He looked at me, his thick lashes framing his green eyes, and suggested, "You could come out to my house for an afternoon—are you busy on Saturday?"

Will's house. I grinned. "I'm not busy," I said. "I'd love to."

He smiled back. "You can meet my dad. He's been asking me to bring you by so he can get a good look at you—whatever that means."

A shiver of anticipation went through me. Will wanted me to meet his dad. And his dad wanted to meet me!

"I've never met a rabbi before," I confessed. "Should I wear something special?"

Will laughed out loud.

The librarian gave him a stern look, and Will flashed her his best contrite expression, which seemed to appease her.

"He's not really that kind of a rabbi," Will said, after the librarian had returned to whatever it is school librarians do. "We're not Orthodox, and Dad hasn't led a service in years, since before he began at Yale."

"Oh. Why not?"

Will shrugged. "Maybe you can get him to tell you," he suggested. "He's never been very clear with me on the issue."

"I don't think I'll be asking him any real intrusive questions the very first time we meet," I said. "I'll just stick with 'How are you?'"

Will laughed again, more quietly this time, and removed his hand from my leg. I sighed. Without the slight pressure of his touch, my knee felt as if something was missing, as if I'd been altered, just from the brief stroke of his hand, and my knee would be yearning from this moment forward for the return of his touch.

More and more of me was starting to feel this way—my left hand, which he routinely held as we walked together across campus; my cheek, where his hand had brushed one afternoon under our tree, in a caress so gentle yet so searing that I'd forgotten to breathe.

But no kiss.

I wanted to ask him what the holdup was; it was going on three weeks that we'd been—what were we? A couple? Boyfriend and girlfriend?—and he hadn't so much as tried to kiss me.

Andy had kissed me on our very first date. In fact, the whole date had felt like a lead-up to the moment when he practically lunged at me on the front porch, his mouth eager and pressing, his hands even then inching away from the relative safe zone of my back up toward my bra line.

So what was wrong with Will? Did he have something against kissing? Was it my breath? What was the deal?

But as comfortable as I was around Will, I wasn't about to ask him any of these questions. I resolved to be patient and wait.

Meanwhile, I had a lot to occupy my mind. There was the test on *The Great Gatsby*, the French midterm, miles of trails to explore with Delilah . . . If Will didn't want to kiss me, for whatever reason he might have, I certainly wasn't going to live or die by it.

"So did he kiss you yet?" Lily hissed at me after school, as Will headed for the bus that would take him back across the hill to the Isthmus.

I shook my head miserably. "Nothing," I complained. "Not even a peck." He *had* kissed me once, that day by the beach . . . but that was before our relationship had shifted. And it wasn't the kind of kiss I yearned for.

Lily, always a friend, immersed herself wholeheartedly in the problem. "Maybe it has something to do with his religion," she suggested. "Maybe he's, like, saving kissing for marriage."

I shrugged. "I don't know. But if he doesn't kiss me by Saturday, I'm getting in the driver's seat."

The rest of the week came and went, and though Will leaned in close to murmur "See you tomorrow" before he climbed on the bus after school on Friday, there was no kiss.

I had arranged for Alice to give me a lift over to the Isthmus after the stable on Saturday afternoon, so I packed heavily for the day, knowing I wouldn't make it home before dark. I took a change of clothes for after my work with the horses, my script, some snacks, and my silver water canister.

I was shoving it all into my backpack at the kitchen table when I heard my mother pad into the room behind me.

"Hey, Mom," I said, tugging on the backpack's zipper. "I'm heading out, okay?"

She didn't answer. I blew my hair out of my face and turned to see if she had heard me. She was looking out the kitchen window, over the sink, her glance somewhere very far away. Her light brown hair was lank, unbrushed. She was wearing a white cotton nightgown and these ridiculous fuzzy pink slippers that Ronny had given her a few Christmases ago. They had little bunny faces on the toes.

Her skin was an unearthly pale; it occurred to me that I didn't know how long it had been since the last time she'd stepped outside.

"Mom?" I asked. She blinked.

Abandoning my backpack on the table, I walked across the kitchen toward her. "Are you okay?"

She turned her head toward me and looked in my direction, but I don't know what she saw—if she saw me at all, or if she didn't focus enough to know that I was even in the same room.

Two things happened then: Alice pulled into the driveway, honking her usual double blast to let me know she had arrived, and Daddy thumped up the stairs and into the kitchen.

"Olivia!" he said, his voice full of forced cheer. "You're up!" He walked over to her and pressed his cheek against hers.

I looked away. The moment seemed personal, intimate in a way that made me feel like an intruder.

I grabbed my backpack from the table. "I'll be home late," I called over my shoulder as I headed out. "I'm running lines this afternoon with a friend from Drama."

There was no answer, and as I rounded the corner into the hallway, I couldn't stop myself from looking back at them. My father had his arms wrapped around my mother's waist, though her arms hung at her sides, and they were rocking, slowly, from side to side, as if to a tune only they could hear.

It was a good day with the horses. I ran Delilah hard, the pounding of her hooves on the trail matching my quickened heartbeat. I wasn't one of those super-shy teenagers who didn't know how to talk to adults, so there was no reason meeting Rabbi Cohen should have made me nervous.

But it did.

Alice let me use her office to change my clothes, and she smiled at me when I emerged. I'd changed into my only non-jean pants, a pair of dark green cords, and I wore a soft gray cashmere V-neck over a white tank. I'd thrown in the tank at the last moment, not wanting to expose too much skin in front of a holy man.

"You look awfully nice," Alice said, turning over the engine of her truck.

"Thanks."

"This Cohen boy . . . is he someone special?"

I remembered what Will had confided in me—the strange hooklike pull he felt toward locations where violent crimes were about to be committed, his compulsion to step in and stop them from happening.

"You could say that," I demurred.

"Well, is he special to *you?*"

Alice did her best to sound casual, but she didn't fool me, not for a minute.

"Yes, Alice," I said. "He's special to me. I like him a lot."

She was practically humming now. "Is that why you're wearing lip gloss?"

"Is it too much?" I flipped down the visor and examined my face.

"No, Scarlett, it's nice. Not too much. Relax!"

"It's just that I'm meeting his dad today," I confessed.

Alice whistled. "Meeting the parents."

"Just the dad," I corrected. "Will's mom is . . . she died."

"I see." Alice was quiet for a moment before she continued. "Well, maybe you and Will can help each other with that . . . with your losses. I'll bet he understands how you must be feeling better than almost anyone else."

I nodded, staring out the window. "We haven't talked about it much," I told her. "But I think Will understands my problems."

We pulled into the village and Alice slowed her truck to a crawl. Turning onto one of the few neighborhood streets, we looked together for the right house: 38 Olive Lane.

There it was. Plain brown shingles covered the face of it, and a climbing shrub of some kind laced through the brown picket fence.

When we pulled to a stop in front of the house, the door opened and Will stepped out.

Alice laughed. "That boy's got it bad," she said. "He was waiting for you."

My stomach was doing that thing again. "Thanks for the lift, Alice."

"How are you getting home?" she asked me as I climbed down from the cab.

"Lily's mom is going to be over on this side of the island having dinner with some friends," I said. "She's going to swing by and pick me up around eight."

"Okay. Have fun!" With a wave, Alice stepped on the gas and disappeared up the street.

Will came through the little gate and greeted me on the sidewalk with a smile. "You're here." He took my backpack from my shoulder and slung it over his own. "Come on," he said. "I'll give you the tour."

Inside, their little house reminded me of a storybook cottage. It was kind of a mess, but in a nice way. There were books everywhere—filling bookshelves that lined every wall in the small front room, piled on the coffee table and the end tables, strewn over the brown leather ottoman, even one perched atop a lamp.

This was definitely a man's house. Both the couch and the oversized chair were made of the same leather as the ottoman, and all looked well used. There were candles here and there, but they looked sturdy and practical, not of the scented variety.

Atop the fireplace mantel, more books were piled precariously. There was a framed picture there too, of three people, all with wide smiles. The one in the center was Will, a slightly younger Will. The woman had to be his mother: her eyes were his same shocking shade of green. Her hair fell to her shoulders in dark brown waves, and her wide smile was warm and lovely. The man standing on Will's other side had his arm thrown across Will's shoulder. He was grinning through an impossibly unruly dark brown beard, and all three of them looked incredibly happy.

"That was the day I bar mitzvahed," Will said. "It was a good day."

"How old were you?"

"Almost thirteen," he said.

"You look older." I peered more carefully at the picture.

"People have always thought Will was older than he is," came a man's voice.

Startled, I jumped back from the mantel and turned.

There he was—the man from the picture, only with a gray streak in his beard and slightly heavier.

"You must be Scarlett." He greeted me warmly, walking

into the room and extending his hand to shake mine. "Will has told me so much about you."

"Rabbi Cohen," I said, wondering what Will might have told him. "It's so nice to meet you."

"The pleasure is all on this end, my dear," he said.

His grasp was firm and friendly. "Well, son, she is at least as pretty as you said." He smiled. "And yes, her hair is indeed exactly the color of freshly harvested wheat."

"Yeah, Dad, thanks for that," Will said, blushing.

Rabbi Cohen chuckled. "What are fathers for?" he asked rhetorically. "Scarlett, please call me Martin."

I nodded, trying to contain my pleasure at hearing Will's comments about me through his father's words. Freshly harvested wheat?

Martin was looking at the picture on the mantel. "Meryl was a beautiful woman too," he mused. "This was our last picture together."

We stood quietly looking at the picture, each with our own thoughts. Finally, Martin shook his head, as if to clear a memory. Then, "You kids have fun," he said. "I'll be in the study doing a little light reading if you need me."

It seemed apparent to me, as he made his way to an adjacent room dominated by a large desk, also overflowing with books, that Will's father meant us to know that he would be nearby.

Will seemed to read my thoughts as he led me to the kitchen. "Dad likes to say that it's not that he doesn't trust me, it's just that he remembers being a teenager very, very clearly."

I laughed a little, wondering if Rabbi Cohen would be a little more trusting if he knew what a perfect gentleman Will had been so far—*too* perfect, as far as I was concerned.

The kitchen was painted a warm butterscotch. The shelves were pine, unpainted, and all the cabinet doors had been removed. Books dominated this room too, but they were largely cookbooks, everything from *Eat Right 4 Your Type* to *The Chocolate Lovers' Almanac*.

"Who's the cook?" I asked, amazed by the sheer number of cookbooks.

"We both are. Every other night, we take turns, and I have to admit, we've gotten pretty competitive. You've come on a good night. Dad's trying a new recipe, something Italian." He gestured to the stove top, where a large red enamel pot bubbled over a low flame. "He's baking fresh bread too," Will said. "You're staying for dinner, right?"

"As long as it's before eight," I answered. "That's when my ride gets here."

"Dinner will be served at six-thirty," called Martin from the other room. The man had ears like a bat.

"Come on," Will said, taking my hand. "I'll show you my room."

Back through the front room and down the hall were a series of doors, all open: a bathroom, what must have been Martin's room, and, at the end, Will's room.

It was neater here than in the front of the house. Will had a ton of books too, but all except two were shelved in the heavy mahogany bookshelf that lined the far wall. He had a double bed covered neatly with a gray flannel blanket. The lamp next to his bed was made of green glass that reminded me of the glass fragments I sometimes found washed up on the beach from old bottles. On the nightstand was a slim MacBook and Will's copy of *The Importance of Being Earnest*, dog-eared already, along with another volume entitled *The Essential Kabbalah: The Heart of Jewish Mysticism*.

A large wood-framed window looked out on an untamed square of yard behind the house. Near the window was an upholstered armchair, brown-and-green plaid, with a tall floor lamp beside it. I imagined Will sitting here in the evenings, the lamp glowing softly above him as he turned the pages of a book.

There were no posters anywhere, though three oil paintings hung on the wall near the closet. I stepped closer and examined them, more out of nervousness than anything else.

All three were simple and beautiful, and though I didn't know much about art, it seemed to me that all had been painted by the same hand. The first featured a fish, drawn from above, swimming in a stream or a river. It was very close up, and each scale was clearly articulated. The next was a landscape, a field of grass at sunrise or sunset, the sky painted in hues of purple and pink, the field awash in yellow. I remembered Martin's comment about my hair and smiled.

The third picture was the loveliest, to me. It was of a tree, though it felt somehow like a portrait, as if the tree were more than a tree. A person, perhaps, or maybe even something more.

"Did you paint these?" I asked.

Will cleared his throat. "My mother," he said.

182

I turned to see him. He was gazing at the pictures too, with a faraway look in his eyes. "They were birthday presents," he offered. "The tree was for my bar mitzvah. She died just a few days later."

I stepped closer to him. "How did she die?" My voice was a whisper.

He blinked twice, as if bringing himself back to the present. "There was an accident," he said simply. "In the car. We were together—the three of us. Mom was driving. I was in the backseat. For some reason Mom stepped hard on the gas and pulled into an intersection. The guy in the other car must have been going over sixty when he hit us. We were all hurt, of course, but Mom didn't make it. Massive internal hemorrhaging, the doctors said."

I shuddered. It seemed as if I could almost see them—his mother, knuckles white as she gripped the steering wheel; his father next to her, yelling for her to stop, too late; a younger Will in the backseat, behind his father, his head buried in a book, unaware of what was even happening until it was all over.

"It's a good thing you were sitting behind your dad instead of behind your mom," I murmured.

Will grew stiff next to me. "How could you know that?" he asked.

Confused, I looked up at him. His eyes were intense, his jaw tight. "Didn't you say you were?"

Will shook his head.

"Oh. I don't know, I guess I just figured you'd have to have been—you know, since you were okay."

Slowly, the intensity of Will's gaze faded, and his face

183

seemed to relax by degrees. "That makes sense," he said at last. "Yeah, it was lucky I was behind my dad."

I wanted to offer him something then, a slice of my pain, so that we would be even. "Ronny went really fast," I said. "The doctors said he never felt a thing."

Will's hands came up to my shoulders and he pulled me against his chest. The rough wool of his green sweater rubbed against my cheek. He rested his chin atop my head, and we stood like that for a long time.

Finally, with a sigh, Will pressed his lips into my hair. Then he stepped back a little, and I unwound my arms from his waist. We looked into each other's eyes, and we might have kissed then, but I think neither of us wanted our first kiss to be colored by our grief. So we parted.

This time, the whole front of my body felt that desperate yearning for the press of Will against me—my breasts tingled, and some place deep in my belly turned with a sensation I hadn't felt before, a kind of urgent desire I'd never experienced firsthand. I tucked my loose hair behind my ears to have something to do with my hands, then turned to my backpack to search for my script.

"I like it when you wear your hair like that," Will said. "Loose and untamed."

"Thanks," I managed to say, though I wanted to say much more. I found the book and turned back to Will. "Do you want to run some lines?"

He hesitated, as if he also wanted to say something else, but instead he nodded.

I curled up in the plaid armchair and Will sat across from

me on his bed. He switched on the bedside lamp and re-trieved his script, flipping it open. "Let's start at the first meeting," he suggested, and I was happy to escape into character—flirtatious, bubbly Cecily Cardew, who had never known real grief and never would, who would simply fall in love, over and over again, remaining eternally young, forever innocent, blissfully pure.

By five-thirty, sounds of clanging pots began emanating from the kitchen. By six, the mouthwatering smell of bak-ing bread wafted down the hallway. And even though I had thought nothing could make me ever want to leave Will's small room, by six-thirty, I couldn't wait to dig into what-ever Martin had prepared.

He'd set the table with a faded but clean red tablecloth, white china dishes, and silver shined to a beautiful luster. The red pot from the stove sat in the middle of the table on top of a potholder. Steam rose from it in tempting waves. Martin stood at the counter, slicing his fresh bread.

Next to each plate was a crystal goblet; on the sideboard was an uncorked bottle of red wine.

"Ah, the actors arrive," said Martin, cheery and red-cheeked from the kitchen's heat. "Son, you're going to be hard-pressed to beat this one, I'm warning you now."

He came around the counter, the basket of steaming bread in his hands.

"Will," he said, "pour the wine, will you?"

I tried to keep my mouth from falling open. The rabbi was serving me wine?

Will chuckled quietly as he poured the red wine into the goblet in front of me, stopping when the cup was just a third full.

"Everything in moderation," he and his father chimed, almost in unison.

"More moderation for some than for others," chortled Martin, tipping up the bottom of the wine bottle as Will filled the cup at the head of the table.

I noticed that Will's cup was also less than half full; he sat to my left, between me and his father.

His father said something in Hebrew, before nodding to Will to serve the food.

And then we ate. The pot was full of vegetables and a heady tomato sauce, fragrant and delicious. We filled our plates with the mixture, shaved fresh Parmesan over the top, and then spooned mouthfuls onto bites of the fresh, hot bread.

After every few bites, I raised my glass to my lips for just the smallest sip of wine. An entirely different drinking experience than the night of Andy's party, tonight was about appreciating flavors, not getting drunk. The wine wasn't my favorite taste of the night—the fresh bread was—but as I listened to Martin talk about the art of viticulture, I started tasting the elements he was mentioning—something woody, a touch of blueberry.

The kitchen was warm and cozy. The food was nourishing and delicious. I listened as Will and his father bantered back and forth about the fate of some college football game they'd watched together earlier that day, but rather than listening to the words, I just heard their tones and inflections—they laughed often, sometimes raised their voices almost to a shout when making a point, they waved their hands around wildly, wine sloshing and threatening to splash on the table-cloth.

The room—the whole house—felt beautifully alive.

I imagined how my kitchen at home must look at that same moment. Meticulously clean, without the papers and books and clutter that dominated every surface of the Co-hens' kitchen, but also cold . . . abandoned. If the kitchen was the heart of the family, ours had ceased beating along with Ronny's. I wished that I could bottle some of the joy I felt all around me and take it home with me, where I'd fling it around our house like pixie dust.

The table had grown quiet. I'd been too still, I realized. Now both Will and Martin were looking at me with con-cern, leaning forward a little across the table.

Then Martin asked, "Are you all done with that, Scar-lett?"

I nodded, and he took my plate. "Thank you so much, Martin. It was wonderful."

"You have to come back on one of my nights," Will in-sisted. "Then you'll see and taste something wonderful."

"Did I raise you to be a braggart?" Martin asked.

"Absolutely," Will answered. "Like father, like son."

Before he cleared the rest of the plates, Martin returned to his seat. He closed his eyes briefly, and half spoke, half sang in Hebrew, "*Baruch atah Adonai, Eloheinu Melech Haolam, Hazan et haolam kulo, b'tuvo, b'chein b'chesed uvrachamim.*"

"What does that mean?" I asked, after he'd opened his eyes.

"It's called the *Birkat Hamazon*. It's a giving of thanks—for the food, the land, Jerusalem, and the goodness of God. We're not Orthodox, so around here we do the abbreviated version. Roughly translated, I said, 'Blessed is the Lord our God, King of the universe, who sustains the entire world with goodness, kindness, and mercy.'"

I'd been on this planet for over sixteen years. The only blessing I'd ever heard at my house was "Rub-a-dub-dub, thanks for the grub." But I didn't want Martin to know how godless we were; he might not like me anymore.

Instead I said, "Well, thanks for everything, Martin. It was really, really good."

"As was the company, my dear." Martin bowed to me, then headed back toward his office. "I've got a date with a radio show," he called to us over his shoulder. "And you two have a date with the dishes."

TWELVE
Turning a Page

$\mathcal{A}$nother day had ended, and still Will and I had not kissed. When Lily's mother arrived to pick me up, honking impatiently curbside, I thought that Will might catch my lips with his own before I left.

We had been in his room, gathering up my books, and as he handed me my script, Will's hand brushed a tendril of my hair behind my ear, and he stared at me intently, his green eyes looking deeply into mine.

I felt a shudder of anticipation, and I leaned in toward him, my eyes fluttering shut . . . but then Martin's voice had boomed down the hallway, almost as if he could hear the chemistry between me and Will threatening to boil: "Well, Scarlett, sounds like your ride is here. . . . Such a pleasure to have you come and visit!"

At least he had called to me rather than just coming into Will's room; when we emerged together, Will shouldering my backpack, Martin's eyes were knowing. He shook my hand solemnly and invited me to visit again soon.

I nodded dumbly, but managed to pull it together enough to mumble a cursory "Thank you for having me" before heading out the door.

Will walked me to the car, his hand on the small of my back so much less of him than I wanted to feel. I yearned to turn to him in the yard and throw my arms around his neck, tilting up my head toward his mouth . . . but instead I allowed him to open the passenger door for me and hand me my backpack.

"Thanks for taking her home, Mrs. Adams," he said, a pillar of respectful politeness. "I'll see you on Monday, okay, Scarlett?"

And then the door was closed, and Lily's mom was stepping on the gas, and we were gone, though I still felt tethered to him, our connection winding out between us as the car crested the hill and the lights of Two Harbors disappeared.

At home, I didn't mind that my parents' door was shut, the muffled sounds of some news channel emitting from behind it, or that our kitchen was sterile and dark, blacked out. I'd wandered rather brainlessly into my room and flopped on my bed, dropping my backpack and kicking off my shoes.

In the darkness, I allowed myself the luxury of remembering the feel of Will's hand on my back as he walked with me through his darkened yard. He had barely touched me, really, yet the sensation that had shot through me had been one of remarkable warmth, total connection.

I remembered the curve of his smile as we ran lines in his bedroom. I remembered the angle of his hand as he lifted his cup of wine to his lips. I remembered the thrill I felt at his laugh, his smile, his touch, the sound of him, the smell of him . . . I was a goner. That much was clear. Completely, utterly lost. A time before Will? Somehow, unthinkable. Unimaginable. I had been a different girl, or at least a different version of the girl I was becoming.

Who was this girl who lay on my bed? She felt . . . happy. Whole. Not like the shattered wreck I'd been all summer and most of the fall. Could love alone create this kind of change?

There it was. The word. *Love*. I had barely thought it before I knew it was the truth: I loved him. I loved Will Cohen, the strange, complicated boy who had somehow managed to come to me, to come to my island. I was no longer alone.

But as marvelous and as true as that was, there was something more. I was no longer alone, but also, I was no longer shattered. How had that come to be? A mirror, once broken, cannot be mended. Yet here I was. I was different than I had been, and I would never see the world in the same way I had Before Ronny Died. Then, it was as if nothing bad could touch me. Now, I knew better. Some of life was downright horrible.

But I was *alive*. I could *breathe*. Somehow, I was whole, if different.

I leaned over my bed and fished my hand underneath it. There it was, its metal spiral cold and wound tight, like a serpent: my yellow notebook.

I sat up and flipped on the nightstand light. For a long moment, I stared at the notebook's cover. And then I opened it.

Not because I wanted to see what it contained, and certainly not because I had something more I wanted to add. But because it was true, and it was part of me.

I took my time. I read each page carefully. I saw now what I hadn't seen before—I saw the weakness that had guided me for months, that had allowed me to take myself to pieces, and even more, I saw the almost unforgivable self-indulgence of it all.

Three figs, a slice of dry toast, and one piece of beef jerky? That is nowhere near enough food for a day! That's not something to be proud of, to record and savor. That is sickness.

To take pleasure from my own deprivation . . . to whittle myself away chunk by chunk, to allow my body to become a dried-out husk—this is not what I would want for a friend, for a *dog*, let alone for myself.

This is not what Ronny would have wanted for me. And if my mother were well, if she could see me, *really* see me, then this would not be what she wanted for me either.

I flipped to the last pages I'd written on. I saw the smear of blood I'd left there. It had dried to an ugly shade of brown. What if that blood were inside me still? What if all the effort that I'd put into denying myself, into harming myself, I'd channeled instead into something else, something *better*?

The thought frightened me. Could I have made that choice? Was the life recorded in this notebook a record of choices made? I knew in my heart that it was. And I knew I wanted to—*I needed to*—make a different choice. I just wasn't sure how. But I knew where to begin.

The room where Will had stayed was vacant, like all the guest rooms. Its fireplace yawned at me, an open mouth. I aimed to feed it.

Gently, I peeled loose the letter Helena had sent and set it aside. Then, I tossed my yellow notebook into the fireplace and touched each corner with the flame from a match. I sat cross-legged in front of it and watched it burn.

It didn't catch quickly; two of the corners blackened and smoked, threatening to go out, but I blew on them gently, encouraging the flames to spread.

And then the flames burst to life, and the heat seared my face, and my eyes filled with tears as I watched it burn and burn and burn, my crutch, my favorite friend, my enemy.

In the end, all that was left was the twisted spiral of metal, blackened and ugly on the fireplace grate, surrounded by ashes.

Sunday morning was cold and dry. The sky shone a particularly beautiful shade of blue, untouched by clouds. I felt jittery and nervous, as if I had drunk too much coffee, as if I were a yearling mare.

That's what it was . . . I felt raw, almost newborn. The sky was too big, frightening in its vastness, and the day felt that way too. Too big. Too many possibilities.

I was scared. I wanted to change, but I didn't know how. I didn't just want to deny myself the pleasure of denial, of hurting myself; somehow, this seemed like another layer of the same sickness. I wanted to not *want* to deny myself; I wanted to not *want* to hurt myself. Can you control your wants, your desires, or only your responses to them? I didn't have the answers to these questions. But I thought I might know someone who did.

It was a perfect day for riding. The ground was dry; the breeze was cool. Delilah's nostrils flared as we trotted down the path. She and I seemed to be of one mind; it didn't seem that I turned her in the direction of the Isthmus, but we headed there together, admiring the colorful leaves on the autumnal trees, the cheerful chatter of a jay, the soothing solitude of the trail.

I had been riding for over ten years now, and my body seemed almost designed for the saddle. As I rode, I felt the familiar stretch of the muscles on the insides of my thighs, down the backs of my calves as I pushed my heels down in the stirrup irons. My back felt straight and strong, and I had the strange sensation of seeing myself as another might see me: I was young, and strong, and confident in the saddle.

Delilah, of course, didn't know that Will Cohen lived on Olive Lane, but it seemed that I didn't need to guide her head into the turn. I felt a little silly, riding a horse down a neighborhood street, but I felt too as if it was somehow right to be making this visit in this old-fashioned, deliberate way.

Behind the brown fence, bent over in a patch of dirt,

turning over the earth to prepare a bed for planting, knelt the person I had come to see.

"Rabbi Cohen," I called. My heart raced with nerves.

He looked up from his work, brushing his graying curls from his forehead in a gesture made familiar to me by his son. "Scarlett." He smiled up at me. "A pleasure to see you again."

He rose, slightly awkwardly, as if his knees were giving him pain, and pulled his flowered gardening gloves off before reaching across the fence to stroke Delilah's mane. I dismounted and pulled the reins over her head.

"What a lovely horse," he said. Delilah stood very still while he petted her neck, her ears rotated forward toward him. "I'm afraid Will isn't home, Scarlett. He's gone off on one of his hikes today. I don't expect him back until dinnertime."

"That's okay. Actually, I came to see you." The words came out in a rush, and I felt myself flushing a deep red.

"Ah," he said. "Well, I am home, and about ready for a break from my work. Would you like to come in for a cup of tea? And please, Scarlett, call me Martin."

I let Delilah loose in the Cohens' small backyard; it was well fenced, and, as Martin suggested to me, the grass could use a trim, a job Delilah seemed happy to take on. I pulled off her saddle and bridle and rested them on the back porch, then unlaced my boots and walked stocking-footed into the kitchen.

Martin had boiled a kettle of water and was steeping a pot of tea. He'd set out a little ceramic cow of cream, a pot of sugar, two cups, and a red plate with cookies laid across it in twin rows.

"Thanks for talking with me," I said. "I know I should have called, but . . ." My voice trailed off lamely.

"No, no, I am glad you came. My knees couldn't have taken much more of that. I'll never understand how the Catholics manage all that knee time!" His laughter filled the room and then cut suddenly short. "Oh, dear. You're not Catholic, are you?"

I shook my head. "I'm not really anything," I admitted.

"Nothing could be further from the truth," Martin told me, pouring out two cups of the rich, fragrant tea. "On the contrary, you are a good deal more than you could possibly imagine." He gazed at me in a way that I couldn't decipher.

"That's nice of you to say," I demurred, "but what I meant is my family hasn't ever really belonged to a religion."

"Ah," Martin said. He scooped an enormous spoonful of sugar into his tea, then poured in a satiny stream of cream. "A modern family."

"I guess you could say that."

Martin offered me the cream and sugar. My first impulse was to refuse them . . . but my impulses hadn't done me much good lately, so instead I said "Thank you" and doctored up my tea just as Martin had done.

The cookies were gingersnaps. They were crisp and delicious. My tea was so hot that it burned my mouth slightly when I sipped it. The whole experience felt luxurious, and if I hadn't been wound so tightly, I would probably have enjoyed it.

As it was, I didn't quite know what to do with my hands, whether or not to cross my legs, how to hold my cup of tea. Martin held his in both hands, and I didn't know if this was a Jewish thing or a rabbi thing or a politeness thing, so I did the same, just to be on the safe side.

After he'd finished about half of his tea, Martin pushed his cup slightly away and asked, "So. What can I do for you today, Scarlett?"

"I—I don't know if you can do anything for me, Rabbi— Martin. But you seemed as good a place to start as anywhere else." I worried this might sound disrespectful. "I don't mean that how it sounds, really. I was just hoping to ask you for some advice."

Maybe it was from years of practice, first as a rabbi and then as a college professor, but Martin was either genuinely interested in what I was going to say or he made an excellent show of it. He said nothing, but the warmth in his dark, deep brown, almost black eyes encouraged me. They looked both wise and full of humor. I forced myself to go on. "I've had a hard time, Martin, since my brother died last spring."

"Ah," he said. "Yes. Will told me about your loss. I'm sorry for you and your family."

"Thank you." I willed the tears in my eyes to recede. I didn't want to get all gushy, I just wanted to power through. "I've started some . . . bad habits, I guess. I want to stop them. I'm not sure how."

Martin nodded. He did not ask for details.

I sipped my tea, more because I didn't know what to say than because I was still thirsty. Finally, I continued. "I don't know why," I half whispered, "but my relationship with food has been pretty challenging lately."

Martin smiled. "Food can be complicated," he said. "Ever since Eve and Adam tasted the forbidden fruit, we humans have been challenged to find balance. Food can nurture, but it can also cause pain."

Adam and Eve. Forbidden fruit. We were entering some uncomfortable territory, at least for me. "Do you really believe in all that? All that supernatural God stuff?" I blurted out, immediately horrified with myself. I'd just asked a *rabbi* if he believed in God!

But to my surprise, Martin didn't look perturbed. "A good friend of mine, another rabbi, actually, is fond of saying that to be a Jew, all you have to do is believe in one god . . . or fewer."

I didn't know what to say to this. "I thought religions were all about God," I said at last.

"Religions, perhaps. But Judaism is more than a religion. It's a philosophy, a people, a shared history. In fact, there are branches of Judaism that interpret the idea of God as the manifestation of the best and highest of human potential, others who view the Bible as metaphorical rather than literal, whole groups of Jews that believe that the important facet of a god is not belief but the idea of awe . . . that the imagery of God and the Biblical stories can still inspire those among us who do not believe the stories to be factually true."

This was all news to me. Religion without God? God as a metaphor for the best of human potential? I felt a little uncomfortable. It seemed that Martin was saying something very, very important, but fragile, too.

"I've heard it said, in response to the question, 'Must Jews believe in God?'" Martin continued, "that the answer depends entirely on how you define four words: *must, Jew, believe*, and *God*. Rabbi Kaplan put it quite nicely, I think. Basically, he argued that to believe in God is to believe that it is our nature to rise above our basest compulsions and to eliminate exploitation and violence from all human society."

"So to Rabbi Kaplan, believing in God didn't mean believing in a thing, like, up in the clouds?" I said, wondering if Rabbi Kaplan was someone Martin knew personally.

"Exactly. By his definition, a belief in God is to believe in the best in all of us . . . and, by implication, that this belief *must* be acted upon, must manifest into deeds rather than remain paralyzed in words. Most Jews, regardless about what they think about God, will agree that ours is a tradition of action rather than faith. For Jews, it's never enough to passively 'believe' in anything. For Jews, our *actions* are what define us, rather than our beliefs."

Martin eyed me. "You look uncomfortable, Scarlett."

I shrugged and picked at the cookie on my plate. "I don't know," I started. "I guess I haven't spent too much time thinking about these things. Like I said, we're not a religious family . . . but since Ronny died, I guess I've wondered what that means. Where did he go?"

Unspilled tears burned my eyes.

Martin looked at me with such gentle kindness that I

couldn't hold the tears back. He let me cry, and I sniffled like a child. Then he passed me a napkin and patted my hand.

As I dried my eyes he said, "These are big questions. Too big for easy answers."

"It's pretty straightforward for Christians," I mumbled. "All they've got to do to get into heaven is believe that Jesus is God, right? But we aren't religious, not in any way that counts." I wiped my nose with the napkin and then folded it carefully, setting it near my plate. I wanted to shift the subject away from Ronny, so I asked, "What about Jews? How do they get to heaven?"

Martin shrugged. "Most Jews aren't too concerned with heaven and hell. We believe the purpose of life is to come to know God, as much as it's possible, and this is done through both study and through living a life that makes us more like God—whatever that is."

It seemed heretical to hear someone talking about God like this—redefining him—it?—and suggesting that God might not be something *outside* of us at all! And for all of this to come from someone I'd expected to give me answers.

"To be honest, Scarlett, I struggle with these same questions. Since Meryl's death—and since Will's abilities have manifested—I have been to some dark places. Dark and lonely. I look to my books for comfort."

He seemed to be considering something, and then he pushed away from the table and said, "Wait here, Scarlett." He walked out of the kitchen, toward his study. I heard him rummaging around and after a minute he returned, a book in his hands. "You came to a rabbi for advice. If you'd gone to see a Buddhist, he might have given you a book about the Four Noble Truths to contemplate. If you'd visited a psychiatrist, she might have suggested Freud, though I hear he has fallen out of favor as of late. But you chose a rabbi . . . and this is what I have to offer. Why don't you borrow this?" he suggested. The book was small, bound with a hard blue cover with golden words that read *A Guide to the Sefirot.*

"What's the Sefirot?"

"It's difficult to translate, but one way to interpret it is *emanation*—that which has been sent forth from God."

"Didn't you just say that the idea of God is up to interpretation?"

"You're a quick learner, Scarlett. Perhaps we could think of it as sent from the best possible version of ourselves to our current, flawed incarnations."

I thought about this. "Like time travel?"

Martin laughed. "That's as useful a metaphor as any, I suppose. But the purpose of the Sefirot, the purpose of Kabbalah, is the same as the purpose of life—to ascend. Again, not theory . . . *action.*"

"Kabbalah?"

"Ah, Kabbalah. It is sometimes easier to define something by what it is *not.* Kabbalah is not a book . . . it is not a single answer . . . it is not supposed to be easy." Martin looked down at the book in his hands, and he seemed troubled, as if hesitating to hand it to me. But he placed it in my hands. I felt a whisper of fear deep inside me as I took the small book.

When Martin spoke again, his voice was hushed, reverent. "Kabbalah has been called the heart of Jewish mysticism; it has been called the Way. Literally, it is an action; in Hebrew, *Kabbalah* means 'to receive.' Remember what I said about Judaism being defined by action rather than faith? Kabbalah is a prime example. Men spend their entire adult lives studying the Kabbalah . . . and this study is not without risk. Kabbalah is a mystical practice. It has been veiled in secret for centuries. In fact, many have prohibited the study of the Kabbalah, saying it is too dangerous for anyone but mature, male Jews—over the age of forty—to even attempt."

"Dangerous how?" The book looked innocent enough to me, not like it was about to explode in my hands.

"It can lead to madness."

We were quiet together then, in the kitchen, and the sense of awe, of danger, seemed almost palpable, and suddenly the golden letters of the book's title seemed to glow.

Then Martin cleared his throat, and clattered his teacup against the table, and the world was ordinary again.

"Read the book," Martin encouraged, and he cleared the table, pouring the cooled tea into the sink. "The Sefirot is a good place to start."

"Thank you, Martin." I stood up too, and helped with the last of the dishes. "Thanks for talking with me."

"I hope it won't be the last time," Martin said. "Please, visit again—bring your questions, and we'll talk together about what the answers might be."

He opened the back door, looking out at Delilah grazing in the tall grass.

202

"Animals are lovely, aren't they?" Martin murmured. "Such grace, such peace."

"Sometimes I wouldn't mind being a horse," I admitted. "It would be nice not to have to worry so much."

"Well, that may be true, but think about all the good things your Delilah will never experience, by dint of her equine nature."

I thought of the brush of Will's hand against my cheek as he pushed back my hair, the spread of warmth his touch brought unfailingly, and my cheeks burned red. I hoped Martin wasn't quite as astute as he seemed; I didn't need him intuiting my thoughts about his son.

Martin watched as I tacked up Delilah and opened the side gate of his yard for me. I noticed she'd left a fresh pile of manure in the center of the lawn. For some reason, I found this desperately embarrassing, but Martin brushed it off.

He laughed. "That, too, is part of life."

As I rode down the street, Delilah's hooves clopping pleasantly on the asphalt, Martin's little book tucked inside the pocket of my coat, I filled my lungs with breaths of fresh, cool air. The breeze carried the ocean's briny smell upon it. Living on an island can be isolating and claustrophobic, but it can be deeply intimate, too. An island is small enough to come to know really well.

I had felt like an island myself, in the past. Perhaps, I considered now, turning Delilah up the trail that would lead us back toward the stable, being an island is not an entirely bad thing. To know oneself, intimately and deeply. To unearth one's own potential. The book in my pocket seemed to emanate its own warmth, as if it were a living thing.

In the last twenty-four hours, I had held two books in my hands—my notebook, which contained a history of self-denial and pain, and now *A Guide to the Sefirot*. I was eager to find out what it might mean for me.

Overhead, a pelican traversed the sky. I urged Delilah into a canter, and the road seemed to fold open before us like the petals of a flower, the turning of a page. My heart was full to brimming.

THIRTEEN

Venetian Unicorn

$\mathcal{A}$t school on Monday, I found a note taped to the door of my locker. *Scarlett,* read the front. Again, I was struck by the beauty of Will's script. It was as if he was creating a little piece of art just by writing my name.

Inside, the note read, *Will you do me the honor of being my date Saturday night?*

Saturday night. I looked up from the note to the signs papering the school's hallway advertising the winter formal. Saturday night.

Homecoming had come and gone earlier in the fall, and really I had had no plans to attend any school functions this year. Ronny had been King of the Undersea Ball his senior year; he had been voted Big Man on Campus two years running; he had won MVP for his soccer team every year he'd played.

It wasn't that I had anything against school dances. I'd

always relished the opportunity to get dressed up. Even if the dancing was mostly of the rocking-back-and-forth variety, there was something kind of dorkishly fabulous about wearing a corsage and having my picture taken.

And the winter dance was always held at Avalon's Casino, the beautiful rotunda built just above the shore at the edge of town.

The Undersea Ball theme was a yearly tradition: the murals in the theater of the Casino set the mood and the high school seemed unable to purchase new decorations, so year after year they hauled out the same papier-mâché starfish and seahorses, the same aqua-colored ribbons and lace, and adorned the island's finest building.

Of course I would go to the dance with Will. I would probably go anywhere with him.

Behind me, my classmates shuffled down the hallway, making their way to first period, jostling and pushing and telling off-color jokes.

"Andy asked me to the dance in the most romantic way," trilled Kaitlyn. It seemed that her voice was intentionally loud. "He came to my house last weekend with a bunch of roses and sang me this silly little song on my front porch. Isn't that *adorable?*"

Katie Ellis, whom Kaitlyn was towing along by her arm, murmured something I couldn't make out, but as she sauntered by, Kaitlyn peered at me with mean, narrowed eyes.

I smiled and gave a little wave, which seemed to both baffle and infuriate Kaitlyn. She nearly yanked poor Katie Ellis's arm right out of its socket as she stomped off down the hallway.

And then there he was—Will, leaning appealingly close, his face just inches away, that achingly beautiful curl falling across his forehead.

"Well?" he asked, his voice sounding a strange mixture of amused and nervous.

"I'd love to," I said, smiling.

"That's a relief," Will answered. "I already bought a suit."

Will in a suit. That was definitely a sight worth seeing. "What color is the tie?"

"Umm . . . blue."

I mentally ran through my wardrobe. Did I have anything that would go with blue? Probably not. But I knew the best place on the island to find a dress.

"Of *course* I'll loan you something," Lily said at lunch. "When can you come over?"

I considered my afternoon. The farrier would be shoeing the horses, so there would be no riding, and my homework was all pretty much under control. "Today?"

"Fabulous!" Lily hopped up and down, her dark curls bouncing. "It's been *forever* since you've been over, Scar."

"I know." I paused. "I haven't been exactly the most fun person lately, huh?"

Lily grinned. "You've been an absolute *drag*," she said. "But I love you anyway. And I understand."

Even though I hadn't been to Lily's house since the spring before, her parents greeted me from the kitchen table, where they sat playing a game of cribbage, as if no more than a weekend had passed.

"Scarlett," boomed Jack Adams. "Tell this woman that she's out of her gourd if she thinks she can beat me at a hand of cribbage. It's been nineteen years now that we've been married, and she hasn't done it yet!"

"You're out of your gourd, Laura, if you think you can beat Jack at a hand of cribbage," I parroted obligingly.

Laura smiled up at me a bit absentmindedly over her cards. "Hello, dear. Good to see you. You and I both know that Jack is full of shit."

I turned back to Jack. "She's right, you know. Everyone knows you're full of shit."

Laura laughed loudly, and Jack did too. Laura was built like Lily: fabulous, full breasts, loose curls that she wore longer and lighter than her daughter's, highlighted to a caramel color that must have cost a fortune to keep up.

But they had a fortune. Jack, even on casual days, kept himself impeccably groomed as well. His short brown hair was thinning on top and around the temples, but it was a good look for him. The twins, Jasper and Henry, would probably grow up to look just like their dad. They worshipped him, and sat on either side of him at the table now, working at building some Lego structure right in the middle of their parents' cribbage game. All the extra little wooden cribbage pegs that weren't fastened to the board were strewn among the Lego pieces, and I wondered how any of them kept their games straight.

"Come *on*, Scarlett!" Dragging me by the arm, Lily headed toward the staircase. "See you guys later," she called.

The Adamses' staircase was painted Tiffany blue, and the wide, white-paneled walls of the front room were covered with black-framed family pictures. The whole house was a shrine to family. There was a table in the far corner dedicated solely to puzzle building—a half-finished picture of the Leaning Tower of Pisa was there now—and next to the couch were a few of those luxuriously oversized beanbag chairs that cost several hundred dollars apiece, just ready to be collapsed into during Family Movie Night.

Under the long, white-framed front window were shelves and shelves of games—card games, board games, video games. Their colorful boxes formed an inviting mosaic that wouldn't have been out of place in a Pottery Barn catalog.

Upstairs, to the left, lay the children's wing, and to the right was the master suite. Jasper and Henry preferred to share their space, so Jack and Laura had taken out the wall between their rooms to create one large room where they could construct, paint, color, and explode things to their hearts' content.

Lily's room was at the end of the hallway. She had her very own bathroom—probably, more than anything else about her family's wealth, her bathroom was the thing I was jealous of. So luxurious, to have her own toilet, her own sink, even her own tub!

Her bedroom was a welcome sight. She had an ornate wood-framed double bed that had been her mother's girlhood bed, and the room's short wall had a built-in desk-and-bookshelf unit. It was cluttered in typical Lily fashion, books and papers spilling off its surface. Behind the desk was a large corkboard, and Lily had pinned up magazine pictures of her current actor-crush alongside a birthday card the twins had made for her.

But the most fabulous part of the room, hands down, was Lily's closet. She turned to it now with a grin and flung open the doors. "Okay, Scar," she said. "Let's do some shopping."

Lily's closet was better than any store our little island had to offer, and better than nearly any shop on the mainland too. Her mother only had one daughter, as Lily liked to point out, and Lily had inherited her love of shopping and fine things directly from Laura. At least once a season, Laura and Lily would head to the mainland to do some serious "bolstering of the economy," as Jack liked to call it, and would return several days later laden with bags for the entire Adams family. They would always pick up something for me—nothing too big, so that I wouldn't feel uncomfortable or indebted, but always something beautiful.

When they'd returned from Italy, they had brought me a little violet unicorn made from Venetian blown glass. I'd held it in front of my window and looked at the play of light through its delicate body, wondering at the artist who had created something so fragile. It was too delicate to exist, really; how had it survived the plane trip all the way across the Atlantic, then across our country, then on the helicopter to the island? I was terrified that I would drop it, after it had come so far, that it would shatter into little violet shards all over the wood floor of my bedroom, so I'd laid it back in its velvet-lined box and tucked it in the top drawer of my bureau, pushed all the way to the back.

Lily pulled open her closet doors with a flourish. "Want to see what I'm going to wear?"

"Sure! Who did you decide to go with?"

Lily had had three invitations to the Undersea Ball: Josh Riddell, who had been harboring a not-so-secret crush for years now; Connell, who'd decided to take a swing at it; and Mike Ryan.

"I haven't chosen yet," she said, pushing aside piles of clothes as she searched for the dress.

"Lily! Today is Monday! The dance is in five days!"

She shrugged. "Then I have four to decide."

I shook my head. Lily was one of a kind. And *I* wasn't about to change her. "Let's see the dress," I said.

"Here it is!" Her voice was triumphant, and she pulled a gossamer confection of white gauze and silk from the hidden recesses of the closet. "It's an undersea theme, right, and this dress reminds me of a mermaid. See how it's gathered at the bottom?" She spread out the skirt and I admired the beautiful beading.

"What shoes are you going to wear?"

"Those." Lily gestured to the ugliest pair of black lace-up boots I'd ever seen. I think they had steel toes.

"Are you kidding?"

"I never kid about fashion," Lily said, deathly serious. "Anything pretty would be way too obvious. These boots give the dress a little panache."

"Whatever you say."

"Fashion isn't always about looking pretty, Scarlett." Uh-oh. Her voice was heavy with the time-for-a-fashion-lecture tone.

"Okay, okay," I interrupted, before she could get too deep

into the history of tulle or something. "So help me pick something. But I, for one, want to look pretty."

"Of course you do," Lily answered, tolerant as if she were talking to a child. "There's no *subtlety* to your style, Scarlett. You're so *obvious*."

"Well, I don't want to be *obvious*, but I do want to be pretty. This is my first real date with Will."

"You still haven't kissed."

It wasn't a question. I shook my head.

"So, pretty it is." And Lily got down to work.

Twenty minutes later, Lily's room looked like an organza bomb had gone off in it. I was reminded of a line from *The Great Gatsby*, which we were still reading in class, from the scene where Daisy finally goes over to Gatsby's mansion and he makes an ostentatious display of his wealth, bragging about his "man" who buys clothes for him several times a year, and he spreads his shirts—silk, flannel, linen, in a rainbow of hues—for Daisy to admire. She collapses in tears, crying something like, "They're just so beautiful! It makes me sad, because I've never seen so many beautiful shirts before."

And that's how I felt, looking at the banquet of dresses lying before me. Pink tulle, like a ballerina's tutu, red sequins, fluffy yellow confections of lace and organza . . . If Daisy had seen this spread, she may have had a stroke.

"I think this would be great with your eyes, Scar." Lily was half buried in the closet, and she emerged triumphant, waving a light blue shift as if it were a prize fish and she had just caught it.

It was probably the simplest dress of the bunch; made of watery blue silk, slightly shimmery, it had long, fitted sleeves and was cut rather high, straight across the collarbones. It was long and straight and perfectly elegant.

"This one was a mistake," Lily admitted. "I thought maybe it would fit me if I wore some serious Spanx, but no matter what kind of heavy artillery I strap on, there is no way I can cram these girls into that dress." Lily gestured to her breasts with a sigh.

She thrust the dress in my direction. The silk was cool and slippery in my hands. "Try it on."

I retreated to Lily's bathroom to change. Last year, I would have stripped down to my underwear without a qualm, but since our visit to the beach, I was feeling less comfortable than before.

I pulled off my sweater and T-shirt and pushed down my jeans, but before I slipped into the dress, I figured I might as well pee.

A streak of blood across the toilet paper stunned me.

My period. This should be no big deal . . . I'd had my period for the last three years. But as I sat naked on the toilet, my white panties stretched across my ankles, I strained to remember the last time I'd had to buy tampons. It had been at least several months—since midsummer, the best I could figure—since I'd last had my period.

I flushed the toilet and rummaged through Lily's medicine cabinet, finding her tampons—not my brand, but they would do.

I had read about girls who stopped getting their periods if

their calorie intake was too low. I just hadn't thought I could ever become one of them.

My reflection in Lily's bathroom mirror stared back at me, wide-eyed. I stepped back to get a better look at my body. Beneath the strap of my bra, each of my ribs clearly showed through my skin. My collarbones, too, were evident.

But there was improvement: My belly, as my fingers traced across it, felt, if not round, at least not concave as it had. My thighs, though they still didn't touch at the tops, were curved again, not just femur bones coated with skin and tendon.

My hair, as I ran my hands along the length of it, felt less brittle, and it shone a bit underneath the bright lights of the bathroom. The scar I had created on the inside of my wrist lay like a white bracelet, a reminder of how close I had come to falling—or rather jumping—off the precipice of health.

My period was back. Normally, this would be an irritation before a school dance, something to groan about. But not today. Today, the red blood that flowed from me was proof of life—proof that my body could heal, that it *was* healing, that I had not irreversibly damaged myself.

Lily pounded on the door. "What's taking so long in there?"

So I unhooked my bra, dropping it on the counter before slipping myself into the silky sheath of the blue dress. It had no hooks, straps, buttons, or zippers, but there was a slight stretch to it that enabled me to fit it across my shoulders and hips.

The dress was several shades lighter than my eyes and it fit me beautifully.

I swerved around to see the back; it dipped low, and I lifted up my hair to expose the bare skin of my back.

"Come in," I called to Lily.

She came in and looked at me appraisingly. "Hubba hubba," she said, and smiled. "Will hasn't got a chance."

Downstairs in the kitchen, the cribbage board revealed that Jack's winning streak had gone unbroken. The Lego project was either completed or abandoned, I couldn't tell which. The four of them were working on making a pizza: Jack was rolling out the dough, Laura was slicing veggies, and the boys were fighting over whose turn it was to grate the cheese.

"Hey, girls," Jack greeted us as he stretched the dough, preparing to throw it in the air. "You pick a dress?"

"Mmm-hmm. Lily's closet is getting pretty full, Jack. Pretty soon you're going to have to build a room addition," I said.

"Or have a yard sale," Jack scoffed.

"Don't you dare, Daddy," Lily said sternly. "You know my clothes are my *life*."

"No, Lil," admonished Laura. "Family is your life. Clothes are just decorations." She turned to me. "You staying for dinner, hon?"

I considered it. Their kitchen was so warm, so inviting; it would be nice to sit down at the table and pretend for a little while that I was part of their family.

But I shook my head. "I should get home."

Lily folded the blue dress and tucked it inside a burlap shopping bag her mother kept stashed in the pantry.

"Come on, Scar," she urged. "What'll we talk about if you leave?"

"Maybe your brothers can help you pick a date," I suggested.

"Oh, Lil, honey, you still haven't told those nice boys which of them you'll go with to the dance? Shame on you!" Her mother shook her head, but Jack just laughed.

"That's my girl," he said. "String 'em along, string 'em along."

Laura slapped his arm. "Funny, I don't remember you being such a fan of that technique when you were on the receiving end of it!"

I could have listened to them banter all night, and watched the twins build and destroy things, and rolled my eyes with Lily, but suddenly I wanted to go home.

"I'll see you tomorrow, Lily," I called as I headed toward the door.

"Okay . . . see you," she answered, sneaking a piece of pepperoni from the pile someone had sliced for the pizza.

It was cold outside. Our last day of school before winter break was this Friday; Lily and her family would be leaving for Brazil the day after the dance, Sunday. They would be gone for two weeks, searching for pink river dolphins.

And Will would be leaving too. He'd told me earlier in the week that he and Martin were taking the ferry to the mainland on Monday, then catching a flight from LAX back home to Connecticut for a visit with old friends.

That was how he'd said it. *Back home*. He and his father had only chosen Catalina Island in the first place because of its remoteness, its isolation, the fact that here Will was mostly free from his strange pull toward violent crimes. It made sense that home to him was still on the East Coast.

I took a deep breath of the cold air. Wisps of fog laced the streets, reminding me of the finely stitched gossamer dresses piled up on Lily's bed.

I couldn't make them stay. I couldn't make anyone stay . . . Ronny, Lily, Will, nobody. The thought weighed heavily on me, and I felt blissfully sorry for myself. Then I shook my head to clear it. Right now, the street around me was beautiful in its soft mist. Right now, Lily was safe at home with her family. Right now, Will was on the island. And right now, I intended to cook dinner.

My good intentions wobbled slightly when I peered into our refrigerator. Mom had always done the shopping, but Since Ronny Died, she didn't make it out of the house that often, and Daddy seemed sort of confused about what to buy. He bought things that didn't go together, like cereal and butter but no milk or bread.

Right now our fridge had some pretty sorry-looking carrots and celery, and half of a roasted chicken left over from the other night.

I checked the pantry; we had rice and chicken broth. Chicken soup, then. I could handle that.

I turned on all the lights and adjusted the dial on the little radio Mom kept on the windowsill, finding a classical station that came through pretty well. Pulling out a cutting board, I dissected the chicken carcass the best I could, slicing away the meat and chopping it into little cubes.

Then I realized I should probably start by boiling the rice, so I started a pot for that, and I fished a hair tie out of the back pocket of my jeans so I could wind my hair up and out of the way.

I hummed as I worked, doing my best to chop the carrots and celery into even pieces, and dropping them in the chicken broth that was simmering on the stove. It was clear to me what I was doing; I was trying to re-create the feeling I'd experienced in Lily's kitchen earlier that evening or Will's kitchen a few nights ago. But even with the lights on and the music up, even with the salty smell of the simmering vegetables and broth, there was an element I couldn't replicate, not alone. There was no family.

Where were my parents? My mother, I was fairly sure, must be holed up in her room again. Daddy had taken away her bottle of sedatives about a week ago, and Mom hadn't said anything, but not three days after that a new bottle was in its place. It seemed that her only trips out of the house were to see the doctor or to fill a prescription at the pharmacy.

I peered out the kitchen window into the dusk of the garden. There he was, sitting on the bench near the koi pond, stirring the water with a stick.

With the sun down, the air was cold enough to make me shiver. I wrapped my arms around my waist and trampled across a bed of fallen leaves to sit beside my father.

He looked over at me and smiled. His eyes were red.

"There's my girl," he said, patting my knee. "Have a good day?"

"Mmm-hmm." I wasn't sure what to say, where to put my hands. "How about you, Daddy?" I asked at last.

"Oh, fine, fine." His eyes seemed unfocused as they looked across the darkening yard. "Another day, another dollar. Well, another day, anyway." His laugh sounded forced.

"Why don't you come inside? I'm making some soup."

"Are you? That's nice, Scarlett. Soup sounds good. What kind?"

"Chicken."

"Your mother's favorite," he murmured. Another long moment passed, and then he turned to look at me again, more focused this time, as if he was really seeing me.

"You look better, Scarlett. Stronger."

"Thanks, Daddy. I'm trying."

"Well, that's all we can ask, isn't it? That we try?"

The question seemed rhetorical, but there was an edge to it too, and I had the feeling he was thinking about Mom.

"Come on." I stood up and pulled on his arm. He rose reluctantly and followed me toward the house.

"Chicken soup, eh? Did you put in any noodles?"

"Rice."

"Your mom's favorite. Good girl, Scarlett. Good girl."

Daddy and I ate at the table, and I helped him finish his crossword puzzle from the day before. Then he kissed me on the head and told me again—for the fifth time—how good the soup had been.

That was generous of him. It wasn't great soup, but it

219

wasn't terrible, either. I headed to my room to get ready for the next day, and Daddy ladled up a bowl of soup to take in to Mom.

In my room, I looked at the small stack of books on my desk. There was *Jewish Mysticism,* the book Will had lent me that day in the library; *A Guide to the Sefirot,* the slim golden-lettered volume Martin had given me over the weekend; and my copy of *The Importance of Being Earnest.*

I picked up the play and began flipping through it, reading through the scenes that my character, Cecily Cardew, did not appear in. The whole play was absurd, which was its charm. It was about two handsome young men and two young ladies, all privileged, and the creative web of lies spun by the men in order to have the freedom to carouse away from home.

I came across a line Algernon, Will's character, speaks to his friend Jack in the first act: "Relations are simply a tedious pack of people, who haven't got the remotest idea of how to live, nor the smallest instinct about when to die."

I felt that familiar twinge that went along with considering death, especially in conjunction with relations, but I pushed it aside to focus on the words. How ironic that Will, who seemed to esteem his father so highly, would be speaking this awful line!

Of course, much of the play's appeal lay in its irony. And it turns out that Jack, Algernon's friend, is actually his brother. How wonderful it would be if my own brother were to surprise me right now by knocking on my bedroom door and poking his head in as he always used to do, his gangly frame seeming half a size too large to fit through.

I pushed the book away. Then I reached into the burlap shopping bag and pulled out the long blue dress. I rested my cheek on its cool, smooth fabric before pulling a hanger from the closet and hanging the dress from the frame of my mirror.

It had been a long day and I was tired. But before I went to sleep I wanted to do one more thing. I pulled open the top drawer of my bureau and fished around in the back of it, my fingers closing around a small velvet box.

I opened it, and there it was—the blown-glass unicorn. I set it gently on the window frame, where the light would shine on it in the morning. It wasn't out of harm's way anymore, but stuck in a box, shoved in a drawer, was no life for my unicorn.

FOURTEEN

Wrist Corsage

$\mathcal{S}$ ix o'clock Saturday morning found me climbing into the familiar cab of Alice's truck. I scrambled into my seat, handing Alice a ceramic mug of steaming coffee to hold for me while I arranged the rest of my stuff—my backpack, my sweatshirt, my water bottle, my cream-cheese bagel—at my feet and on my lap. Then I gestured for Alice to return my coffee mug.

"Since when do you drink coffee?" Alice smirked, amused.

"Since I discovered half-and-half," I admitted. "I'm a little bit addicted."

"Umm . . . it may be the caffeine in the coffee that you're addicted to."

I took a hot sip of the coffee and shook my head. "Nope. Definitely the half-and-half."

"Well, whatever it is," Alice said, looking at me admiringly, "it must be good for you. You're looking pretty great, Scarlett."

I smiled. "Tonight's the dance," I admitted, "and Will is my date. That makes me *feel* pretty great."

"Ah," said Alice. Her voice was full of knowledge. "I remember that feeling."

Alice was happily married, but she sounded nostalgic.

"Don't you still feel that way?" I asked. "About Howard?"

Alice smiled. We'd turned off the main road and dust plumed up around us. "I love Howard," she said. "And don't get me wrong, we're great together. Beautiful kids, strong communication, we both love garlic. But there's something about the first date . . . if it's with the right guy, it can be magic."

She was looking at the road, but I had the sense that she was seeing something else entirely.

My work with Traveler was coming along. I hadn't taken him out on the trail; that was a long way off most likely, but in the arena I had him pretty well in hand. He was learning both basic Western and English commands, and based on the way he moved, I thought he might have the makings of an excellent jumper.

His gaits were smooth and rhythmic—for an Arabian. He had the characteristic rabbit-bounce in his trot, but he was turning into a nice little horse. Not so little, really, and as we worked more and more often—three times a week now—he was starting to pack on muscle.

Today I set out some trot poles in the arena, set evenly apart, about every six feet. I couldn't wait to see how he handled them. I hadn't told Alice yet, but I had high hopes that he might be an even better jumper than Delilah. After tacking up Traveler, I led him by hand into the arena to give him a chance to get a good look at the poles before I climbed on.

He entered the arena naturally enough, but when I took him past the red-and-white striped poles, his nostrils flared in alarm and he shifted quickly to the side.

"It's okay," I soothed, keeping him tight on my right side and stroking his neck as I talked. "It's just a few sticks of wood. Nothing to worry about."

Apparently Traveler didn't agree, because the next turn past the poles was no better—his hooves crossed hastily to avoid stepping over the poles, and I could see the whites of his eyes.

It didn't improve. For close to an hour I trudged through the arena's sand, leading the obstinate, scared horse again and again past the striped poles. Most horses get less spooked the more times you expose them to something they find scary, but Traveler seemed to be wired differently; his response got worse and worse, until I was yanking on the bridle with uncharacteristic harshness as he dug his hooves in the sand, rearing up and striking out with his front hooves when I tried to force him over the poles.

I felt my frustration mounting. I was as obstinate as Traveler as I tried to convince him that the poles were not terrible horizontal monsters waiting to terrorize and destroy him. But he wasn't buying it.

Alice, who had been watching us for some time, called from her vantage point on the rail, "Why don't you try again another day?"

I didn't want to try again another day. I wanted the damned horse to walk over the poles! It didn't seem too much to ask, but no matter what I did, no matter how hard I tried, Traveler refused.

Finally, I noticed that his withers were trembling and a fine, white foam had gathered in the corners of his mouth. All the urgency that had been mounting in me seemed to disappear. It hit me—this horse was really, truly scared. He wasn't trying to make my life difficult; he was terrified.

My posture changed; the shoulders I'd been tensely holding relaxed, the grim set of my mouth gentled, and I loosened my grip on the reins. "It's okay," I whispered, turning Traveler's back on the poles and leaning my forehead against his. "We'll get it another time."

The horse seemed to sense that our struggle was over, and he strained forward toward the gate to get out of the arena, away from the terrible poles.

I walked him to the cross-ties and untacked him. I hadn't even climbed on his back, but suddenly I didn't want to—not today. Suddenly, the day that had seemed so full of promise felt like a lie, and though I had been so excited just an hour ago about my date with Will, somehow I felt different about that, too . . . as if some of the luster had rubbed off already, even though the experience lay in front of me, not in my past, and I wondered if this was a taste of how Alice felt all the time, if this was what life was like in the grown-up world, full of disappointment and worn-out experience.

• • •

Lily came to pick me up from the stable at two o'clock. She'd decided it would be fun to get ready for the dance together at her place. She pulled her father's black Range Rover into the lot and swung her legs down from its high driver's seat. She was wearing black leather boots with some of those ridiculous jodhpurs tucked into them—the ones that have the enormous, ballooning hips—and wore an argyle sweater of course.

I laughed out loud when I saw her, and I felt the shadow that had been lingering over my head all morning begin to dissipate.

"Hello, dahling," Lily called to me. "Are you ready to be transformed from that dusty, dirty workaday girl into the belle of the ball?"

"Hi, Lily. Did you put that whole outfit together just to drive out here and get me, or do you actually intend to do some riding?"

"It's just for looks. Everything I do is just for looks. Come on," she said, grabbing my backpack. "Let's go."

Back at Lily's house, I found that she had transformed her room into a salon. She must have seriously raided her mom's beauty supplies; top-of-the-line curlers, brushes, powders, and creams lined the top of her long dresser. Our dresses, white and blue, hung side by side on the front of her closet door; Lily had swung by my place while I'd been at the stable.

"First," Lily commanded, "a bath. You smell like horse. I'll get snacks." She clapped her hands twice, clearly enjoying bossing me around.

I didn't argue. A bath sounded pretty good.

226

Lily had one of those great tubs, oversized, with curved sides and a high back. I sighed as I poured myself into it and got lost among the bubbles.

In my dream, I was back on the beach. Again, the sand was warm beneath my body, the sun warm above my head. And again, the sand shifted, and I began to sink.

This time, though, I wasn't shot through with panic. I knew Will would come for me, would reach down into the sand and grab my hand and pull me to the surface and save me.

So I lay still as the waves of sand broke over my fingers and toes, as the press of it grew heavy against my chest, as my hair tangled and was threaded through with sand.

And he did not come.

And he did not come.

And the granules of sand invaded my ears, and my eyes, and my nose and mouth, and there was no air for me to breathe, nowhere for me to go, nothing for me to do.

I couldn't believe he wasn't coming for me. The sadness of this realization weighed heavier than the sand. It wasn't until the highest points of my face—my nose and chin—were lost beneath the press of the sand that my eyes opened in the bath. Tears streaked down my cheeks and mixed with the lavender-scented bubbles, and as I stood from the bath, my limbs felt heavy and leaden.

Then Lily rapped at the bathroom door, and I shook my head to clear my thoughts.

What was the matter with me? I was at my best friend's killer house, getting ready for my first date with a boy I couldn't stop thinking about, a boy who'd told me that he was *pulled* to my *body*. And I couldn't stop my thoughts from turning to death and decay.

As I sat in front of Lily, watching in the mirror as she braided and twisted my hair, I was blinded by a flash of intuition.

I was afraid. Because I knew that tonight, Will and I would kiss. And even though I was already head over heels for Will, when we kissed it would become a thousand times more real, more intense, and ultimately, more painful when we parted.

For we *would* part; I knew we would. It didn't feel like pessimism that I thought this, or a bad dream. It felt instead like foresight . . . premonition.

And I looked so beautiful, like a framed portrait in the water-blue dress, my blond hair braided and wrapped in a low twist to show the milky, naked plane of my back.

I looked into the eyes reflecting back at me, and I thought, *Those are the eyes of a girl who has seen pain; those are the eyes of a girl who will see much, much more of it.*

And then I blinked, and the portrait was again a mirror, and I was just a girl all dressed up for a school dance.

Our dates arrived to pick us up from Lily's house right on time. After much deliberation, Lily had decided that the honor of being her escort should go to Connell. Why she would choose Connell was beyond me, but when I'd pressed Lily about her choice, she only said that she thought it might be "entertaining" to go with him. Of course, this meant that they would be having dinner with Andy and Kaitlyn. A few days ago, this had been fine with me—I was looking forward to a long, uninterrupted evening alone with Will. But suddenly I found myself wishing that Lily would be having dinner with us, even if that meant being saddled with Connell's obnoxious company.

We heard the doorbell ring from up in Lily's room, and we descended the long staircase together.

There waited our dates; they must have just happened to get to the house at the same time, because there was no way Will and Connell would have planned to arrive together.

Connell looked like a character out of some cheesy show from the 1970s: his wide-collared pink shirt was unbuttoned, his pants looked a size too tight, and his hair was slicked back. He whistled long and low as we came down the stairs.

Lily looked amazing. Her curls were riotous and her dress floated around her, ending just above her knees so the view of her awesome black boots was unobstructed. I had to hand it to her: the boots totally made the outfit.

Her dress was halter-style, tying behind her neck, and the neckline was at least PG. Her parents didn't seem to notice; they stood at the bottom of the staircase smiling widely and snapping pictures.

Will stood in the door, framed by the dying light of day. Then he stepped inside and closed the door.

He wore a full suit—jacket, tie, the works—and the cuffs of his sleeves glittered with gold cufflinks. His tie was just a few shades darker than my dress, and in his hands, he held a small box.

He smiled at me as I came down the stairs. His green eyes were dark tonight, full of an emotion I couldn't name. "You look beautiful, Scarlett," he said, not embarrassed at all to say this in front of Lily's parents.

"Thanks," I said, reaching the bottom of the stairs. He handed me the box. It was light; inside was a white orchid attached to a thin band of freshwater pearls.

"It's a wrist corsage," he told me, "but after the flower dies, you can still keep the bracelet part."

I slipped it on my wrist. The flower's fragrant smell wafted up to my face. I knew that for the rest of my life, every time I smelled an orchid, I would think of this moment.

"Smile, kids," ordered Jack, who was clearly relishing the role of photographer.

Will slipped his arm around my waist, his jacket brushing against the bare skin of my back. We smiled awkwardly while Jack snapped our picture.

"Okay, okay, let the kids get out of here, they don't want to spend their whole night hanging out with us." Laura sounded like she might start crying. These things always made her so emotional. But as we turned to leave, I noticed her grab Jack's sleeve and whisper something to him.

"Just a minute, boys, before you go . . . ," he said.

Lily rolled her eyes. "Scarlett and I will wait on the porch, okay, Daddy, while you give them your little talk?"

On the porch, Lily asked me if her lipstick was on straight.

"You look great," I assured her.

"I can't *believe* I have to sit through a whole dinner with Kaitlyn Meyers," she groaned. "What will we possibly have to say to one another?"

"I'm sure you'll think of something," I answered. "Hey, what's your dad saying to them in there?"

"Just the usual. You know. Keep your hands where they can be seen at all times, no heavy petting, yada yada."

My eyes widened. "You're kidding."

Lily shook her head, her dark curls bouncing prettily around her face. I had the feeling she knew exactly how charming that gesture looked. "Nope. Daddy'll put the fear of God in them, all right."

The door opened and Will and Connell joined us on the porch, Will looking amused, Connell swallowing nervously.

"Ready to go?" Lily reached out to take Connell's hand, but he got suddenly busy looking for something in his pocket.

Will took my hand easily, and I waved goodbye to Lily as we headed in opposite directions with our dates. She and Connell were headed downtown to the island's fanciest restaurant, a seafood place on the water.

I didn't know where Will and I were going.

"So, where exactly are we headed?" I asked.

Will smiled. "You'll see."

"How about a clue? Just a little one?"

"You're awfully impatient," Will said.

"Yeah, well, I'm not really a big fan of surprises."

"You'll like this one."

He led me down several blocks, and it seemed to me that I'd willingly go wherever he led, as long as he continued to hold my hand and rub his thumb back and forth across the palm of my hand.

How was it that such a tiny movement—the brush of his thumb, featherlight, against the center of my palm—could

231

ignite such a blazing fire of indescribable yearning in the pit of my stomach?

There was my house, up the street on the left. Probably we were just taking the long way into town, to avoid walking with Lily and Connell.

But then we reached my front gate and Will stopped.

"Here we are," he said.

I blinked. "Are you kidding?"

He grinned. "Come on," he said. "I promise you'll love it."

At least he didn't lead me up the steps to my front porch. Instead, he led me down the path that twisted around the house, to the back garden. There was our white gazebo, threaded thick with white lights, a table for two set in the middle of it. Soft music filled the garden, and little twinkly candles floating on the koi pond made the whole scene magical.

I turned and gazed at Will. His green eyes were shining in the moonlight, in the candlelight. "You're right," I said. "I do love it."

"Wait till you taste dinner." He led me up the gazebo's steps and pulled back a chair for me. Then he sat across from me. He hesitated for a moment, then said, "Don't be mad."

"Why would I possibly be mad?"

And then my dad came out the back door, a white apron tied around his waist, carrying the tray we used for serving cheese and crackers to our guests.

"My dad is the waiter." It wasn't a question.

"Are you mad?"

I shook my head.

"Good. He volunteered. He thought it might be fun."

That cleared up one thing that had been bothering me—why my father had been okay with me getting ready for the dance at Lily's house.

"Hi, Daddy," I said as he climbed the steps to the gazebo.

"Good evening, miss," he answered, doing a pretty good job of keeping a straight face. "Would you care for a sparkling water?"

"Sure."

He placed a tall goblet in front of each of us. "Dinner will be served shortly."

He turned to go, but before he made it down the stairs, he turned back to me. "You look great, Scar," he said.

"Thanks, Daddy." I turned to Will. "I hope my dad didn't cook dinner. He burns everything."

"Nope. He's just serving. I cooked."

The image of Will working in our kitchen came to me like a flash—bubbling pots, sizzling pans, fresh produce piled in the sink.

"Have you been here all day?"

"Since ten this morning."

"You got ready here and everything?"

"Your dad put me in the Yellow Room again."

So he was staying the night.

"I think he puts me in the Yellow Room because it's the farthest from the stairs up to yours," he confided.

"That didn't stop us last time," I reminded him.

"Well," he said, "I get the feeling he may be up listening for us tonight." And he leaned across the table and into me, his lips soft and warm on my neck, just below my ear. I shivered at his touch.

My dad banged the back door open loudly, and Will sat back, smiling crookedly.

Dinner was delicious. There was salad with a dressing Will had made himself; thin-sliced fillets of steak drizzled with some kind of marinade; fresh, steamed vegetables from Martin's garden; and a basket full of steaming heart-shaped rolls.

"Did you make these?" I asked, holding up one of the rolls.

Will nodded, sheepish. "I know they're corny," he said, "but I couldn't help myself."

Dad disappeared after he'd served the food, letting us know that he'd be upstairs for the rest of the night. I was glad my bedroom, not his, overlooked the garden.

When we'd finished eating, Will stood and reached out his hand to me. I dabbed my mouth with a napkin and joined him. We walked down to the pond and watched the flickering candles floating on the water. Will's hand was on the small of my back where the dress dipped to its lowest point. His touch was warm and exquisitely gentle.

Then a new song started to play, something achingly beautiful and slow. Will grasped my hand with his and turned me toward him, and we began to dance—not well, but together, and the warm length of his body pressed against me in my thin water-dress, and I felt the scratchy fabric of his coat sleeve against my back, and the hot exhalation of his breath against my ear.

I closed my eyes and still saw the fire of the floating candles behind them, and when the song ended and Will stopped moving, his green eyes gazed down into mine. He cupped my cheek in his hand so gently, as if I were sacred. He leaned in closer, and I was sure he was going to kiss me.

But just before his lips brushed against mine, Will must have sensed me stiffening in his arms, because he stopped, his mouth just inches from mine, and asked, "Do you want me to kiss you, Scarlett?"

I did. I wanted his kiss so desperately. But I said, "If you kiss me, Will, then everything will change. And if you leave me, then it might hurt too much to bear."

"Oh, Scarlett," Will said, his voice husky with emotion, "I'm not the leaving kind. I'm the hero type, remember?"

And so I tilted my face up toward his, and when his lips touched mine, the current that coursed through my body shifted me inexorably, and I felt like someone who had only half seen the world and awakens one day to find that it is much more beautiful, more rich and deeply articulated than she could have ever dreamed. But as the kiss deepened and Will crushed me against his body, I knew too that this kiss sealed me to Will in a way that would make it infinitely more painful when he left.

I tangled my hands in his beautiful curls, and I shut my eyes, and I gave myself over to the kiss, to Will, to the night.

When we finally arrived at the dance, we found that the party was well under way. A disco ball hung in the center of the Casino's ballroom, flashing dazzling points of light across the dancers.

Lily was dominating the dance floor, spinning herself in wild circles around a completely embarrassed Connell. He didn't seem to know what to do with his feet or where to put his hands, though I'd bet that the latter problem had more to do with Jack's "little talk" than a lack of imagination on Connell's part.

Lily's body looked like a smorgasbord of places for a teen-age boy to put his hands, actually. Her dancing had loosened the bow of her dress and its neckline had gained at least a couple of inches since I'd last seen her, definitely ratcheting up her earlier PG rating to a solid PG-13, and some of her moves put her dangerously close to an R. Her wild curls flew as she tossed her head and laughed, and she was doing this thing with her hips that even seemed to be distracting the male teachers who were chaperoning the dance.

"Hey, Scar's here!" Lily called out when she caught sight of me, and she waved me over. I pretended she was just waving to say hi rather than indicating that I should join her, and I pulled Will toward the punch bowl, hoping Lily would lose focus and forget I was there.

No such luck. Lily sashayed through the crowd and leaned in to kiss my cheeks in her favorite Italian gesture. "What took you so long?" she asked, teasingly.

"Hi, Lily. Having fun?"

"Always," she answered. "Come on, dance with us."

"I don't think so," I started to say, but to my amazement, Will said, "Okay. Come on, Scarlett."

"You want to dance out there?" I said, indicating the mad crush of overdressed revelers.

"Why not?" Will had to raise his voice to be heard over the din. "You only live once, right?"

So onto the dance floor we went.

Will wasn't a terribly good dancer. Neither was I. But Lily was good enough for all of us, and after the first thirty seconds or so, I gave up on feeling awkward and embarrassed and decided to just have a good time.

It's amazing how much the way you approach a situation impacts how the situation develops. Deciding to have fun did not magically make me a better dancer, but it did make me care a lot less what everyone around me might be thinking. I even tried Lily's patented hip move, and noticed that Will's eyes tracked me carefully. He didn't seem to mind that I wasn't exactly a rock star out there; I could tell from his eyes that he liked the way I moved.

I felt beautiful under Will's gaze, I felt brave and strong and sexy in Lily's water-blue dress, and I felt my smile bright on my face. I felt *happy*, and alive.

It was after midnight when Will and I walked home through the sleepy village of Avalon. His jacket was thrown across my shoulders. The petals of my orchid were beginning to wilt, though the flower's fragrance was just as heady.

We were quiet together, which felt nice after the thrumming music of the dance, and Will's hand held mine again, his thumb doing its distracting thing against my palm.

We got to my house and I turned the key in its lock. Then we were inside, together, and the house was quiet. Daddy had left a light on upstairs, and at the end of the hall I could see a light glowing in the Yellow Room, but here in the foyer it was all shadowy and private.

I turned to Will and wrapped my arms around his neck, his jacket falling to the floor behind me. His fingers were strong and warm on my back, and the hunger of his kiss matched mine.

I kissed him again and again, pressing my body against him, stepping so close that our legs tangled together and I lost my balance, Will's arms all that kept me upright.

"Scarlett," he murmured into my neck as he kissed a path along my throat, and one of his hands found the pins in my hair and pulled them free, and my hair fell loose around us.

I was dizzy with the heat of his kiss, the feel of his hands on my hair, on my back, on the silk-smooth fabric of my dress. I wanted to feel more of him. I wanted him to feel more of me.

It was Will who ended our kiss, pulling away just a fraction of an inch and breathing raggedly. "You should go upstairs," he told me, his voice rough, but he dipped his mouth back to my throat and kissed me again, then again.

"Why?" I half moaned in response.

This time he stepped back a little farther, brushing his hair away from his face and trying to control his breathing. "Because your father is trusting me in his house," he said at last. "I don't need a speech like the one Jack gave tonight to know what's right."

"But I thought you felt . . . pulled to my body," I replied, only half joking, closing the distance between us and tipping back my head for another kiss.

Will obliged, tracing his tongue along my bottom lip and

tightening his grip at my waist, bunching the fabric of my dress in his hands as if he were going to rip it free of my body. And I knew he could if he chose to, that the thin fabric would shred in his hands, and I stood perfectly still, hoping that he would do it.

But Will managed to even his breaths, and slowly, gently, he released the handfuls of silk and stepped away. "Good night, Scarlett," he said, stooping to pick up his jacket from where it had fallen. "Thank you for being my date."

He kissed me once more, lightly, and his hand touched the wave of my hair, following its length down to my waist. He sighed then, and said again "Good night" before walking down the hallway, toward the light in the Yellow Room.

My heart felt so fragile, as if it might collapse into a million pieces, and though I tried to convince myself that he wasn't going anywhere, just to the end of the hallway, it seemed instead like he was going somewhere far, far away, where I could not reach him.

Alone now, in the shadows of midnight, I brought my wrist to my face and breathed deeply of the orchid's sweet scent, and I wondered what would become of me now.

FIFTEEN
Tree of Life

All too soon, Will was gone from the island. Only temporarily, I tried to tell myself, but it really did feel like he would never return. I had the orchid from my corsage by which to measure time; I placed it in a little pink vase on my bureau and watched each day as its waxy white petals softened and lost their luster.

Lily was gone too, a separation that ordinarily would have been difficult but was made easier to bear by its comparison to the heavier loss of Will. As I had predicted, his kiss had sealed me to him in some way that I didn't fully understand. It felt, with him away from the island, that some vital part of me was gone too, and as I went about my business—working at the stable, rehearsing my lines for the play, trying my best to keep house—I did so at a deficit. I felt delicate, like the Venetian unicorn in my window I'd come to love, shot through with such beauty given to me by Will's kiss, but also hovering on the precipice of shattering into uncountable fragments.

My role of Cecily Cardew seemed deliciously inconsequential. Like a Persian cat, bred to look good but never expected to really *do* anything, Cecily is a lovely, clever girl who enjoys the idea of love and doesn't take anything too seriously.

I said her lines down by the pond where Will and I had kissed, and I imagined him across from me, wittily snapping back Algernon's responses.

There's a scene at the beginning of the play's second act, before Algernon comes to the country manor, and Cecily and her governess, Miss Prism, are speaking about writing. Cecily tells Miss Prism, "I keep a diary in order to enter the wonderful secrets of my life. If I didn't write them down, I should probably forget all about them."

I thought about my own secret diary, reduced to ashes in the fireplace of the Yellow Room, and I felt a desire to record some new secrets of my own. Unlike Cecily's, my secrets had not been wonderful, but I had loved them all the same, and missed them achingly.

How could that be? Why would I miss the pain and denial I had inflicted on myself? Alone, and bored, and anxious about our first Christmas without Ronny, I found it difficult to keep from returning to my old habits. I forced myself to eat but took little pleasure from it.

I wondered, as I had the day I drank tea with Martin, if it was possible to make yourself stop wanting something. You can deny yourself what is bad for you, sure, just as I had become an expert at denying myself what was good . . . but I had still not found a way to shift my mind away from the desire to do myself harm. Was this new way of being just a permutation of my old habits?

What was more, did it matter?

I remembered something Ronny had said to me when I was little, just seven or so. He'd gone to a sleepover with some of his soccer buddies, and they'd watched a series of horror movies. When he came home, he bragged to me about having seen them, of course, and I told my parents that I wanted to see them too.

But Ronny was adamant that I shouldn't. "Don't do it, Scar," he said to me. "Once those pictures are in your head, you can't ever take them out again."

Was my struggle with food, with denial and pain, much the same? I never had watched the horror movies Ronny had warned me against, yet I'd still managed to fill my head with ugliness.

I guess that's what innocence lost is.

There were good things, though, also crowding my brain: the feel of Will's thumb brushing my palm, back and forth; the touch of his lips to mine; the particular sensation of his hair in my hands as we kissed and kissed and kissed. . . .

Still, as the first week of winter break ended, and I watched my orchid fading, it felt that those images were losing the battle against my darker inclinations.

To compound my sulky mood, Delilah threw a shoe and couldn't be ridden until the farrier could make it out to the island, which he wouldn't be able to do until after the New Year.

Delilah seemed as irritated by this turn of events as I was, and she picked up the bad habit of rocking back and forth against the door of her stall, bowing out the door with her weight.

So I continued to work with Traveler, though I decided to wait a while before bringing out the trot poles again. By Christmas Eve day, Traveler seemed secure enough under the saddle to venture out a bit on the trail—not far, I promised Alice, and I'd keep him to a walk, *and* I'd be sure to run him hard in the arena before we left to get all his jiggies out.

It was a cold day. I had a thermal on underneath my sweater and a down vest over that. I wore my jeans and zipped my leather chaps over them to cut the wind. I chased Traveler in the arena, stiff in all my layers, until he'd gotten all his bucks out, and then I tacked him up.

"Wear a helmet," Alice called as I prepared to mount.

Groan. I hated wearing a helmet. Usually Alice let me slide, but I could see her point. It was Traveler's first time on the trail and all. So I strapped the hateful black helmet to my head, smashing my ponytail to the nape of my neck.

"Okay, boy," I said, patting his fire-red mane. "Let's do this thing."

Traveler moved to walk toward the arena out of habit, but I turned his head the other way, toward the trailhead. His ears perked up, and I felt his steps grow springier, as if he sensed adventure ahead.

"Don't get too excited," I told him. "Just a little nature stroll."

I kept him on a short rein. He was a good horse, but there was no sense in taking any chances. His nostrils flared at all the new smells, and once he spooked a little when a bird flew unexpectedly out of a bush in front of us, but he calmed down quickly.

We were only on the trail for about twenty minutes, and when we turned back into the open area in front of the barn, I saw Alice peering anxiously out the window, looking for us. She ducked her head back after she saw me, as if she didn't want me to know she'd been watching.

But I didn't mind; it felt nice to know that someone was keeping an eye on me, that someone would miss me if I didn't come home.

Back on our street, I looked at the Christmas lights strung up and down our block. Our house was the only one without lights, and as evening rolled around, ours would look like a tooth knocked out of an otherwise smiling mouth.

Mom hadn't wanted to celebrate Christmas at all this year, but after a hushed argument I heard through their bedroom door—shut almost all the time—Dad emerged and suggested that we keep our celebration simple. No tree or stockings, just a nice meal and a few gifts.

I could see that he felt terrible about this, but it had sounded fine with me, at the time. What did I need, anyway? Nothing that comes in boxes.

But now Christmas Eve was here, and suddenly it wasn't okay not to have all the traditions. Yes, Ronny was dead. That wasn't changing, whether or not we had a tree.

We were an artificial-tree family. Most of the families

on the island were, for obvious reasons. So our tree, already woven with tiny white lights, was just a matter of a trip down to the basement.

Dad was at the store, getting food for tomorrow's dinner, and Mom was in her room—of course. I found the box under a layer of dust and managed to haul it up the stairs by myself, though I did bang my shin pretty hard against the water heater.

I had never put the tree together. That was always Ronny's job. But how hard could it be? I fitted the three pieces together and managed to stand the whole contraption in the base, then bent layer after layer of fake plastic pine branches into place before plugging it in.

It was a little crooked, so I pulled and tugged until it seemed straight. Then I returned to the basement and found the ornament boxes. They were dusty too; I burst into a sneezing fit as I made three trips up the stairs to the great room, where the tree waited for me.

Inside one of the boxes, I found the Christmas CD that we had listened to every year for as long as I could remember. I slid it into the CD player and pressed Play. "Blue Christmas" filled the room, Elvis Presley's voice mournful.

Appropriate, I thought, almost laughing. And I dug into the boxes.

When my dad stumbled in an hour later, his arms loaded with groceries, he found me sitting in front of the decorated tree staring up at the twinkling lights, listening to the last song on the CD—"I'll Be Home for Christmas."

He dropped the bags at his feet and blinked, staring at

the tree. And then the last strains of the song played, so poignant: "I'll be home for Christmas . . . if only in my dreams."

He sat down next to me on the floor. The CD spun for a moment, then stopped. The room was heavy with silence.

I saw my father's shoulders shaking as he cried, watching the ornaments illuminated and shaded as the lights blinked, on, off, on, off.

The tree read like a story of my childhood: old, half-crumbled flour-and-water ornaments Ronny and I had made in preschool, yearly ornaments sent by our grandparents in Northern California, each adorned with our name and the year. There was an ornament that a family who had stayed with us two summers ago had sent to us: it was a group of four Christmas geese, each with a differently colored scarf, and our names—John, Olivia, Ronny, and Scarlett—written in script beneath them.

No one had sent us ornaments this year.

Poor Daddy.

I hesitated a moment, then rested my head on his shoulder. Daddy put his arm across my back and rested his chin on the top of my head.

The room softened into night, and the tree was lovely.

I spent the evening alone in my room. I heard a TV show reverberating through the wall that separated my bedroom from my parents'.

On the little table next to my bed rested the two books I had been meaning to open for weeks now, but for some reason had resisted exploring: *Jewish Mysticism* and *A Guide to the Sefirot*.

The first title seemed too expansive to start with, so I slid the second book from the stack and sat curled with it on my bed.

Inside, I found a strange sort of diagram that looked like a spiderweb with a tail hanging down from the bottom, or a tree with a very short trunk. There were ten circles connected by lines, and in each of the circles was a strange word, none of which meant anything to me: *Malchut, Yesod, Hod, Netzach, Gevurah, Chesed, Tiferet, Binah, Chochmah,* and *Keter.*

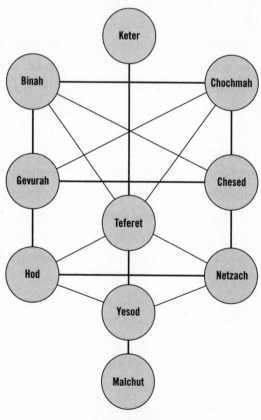

Tree of Life

Beneath the diagram were the words "Tree of Life."

The next page described the diagram of the Sefirot, of the Tree of Life, as the ten emanations of God's "qualities" here on Earth. It went on to say that the Kabbalist—anyone who studies the Kabbalah—would exert himself to perfect, or embody, each quality on the tree. He could even go so far as to think of the tree as his own body, and at the same time, as a kind of a blueprint of the energy makeup of the entire universe.

In the first pages of the book, I was reacquainted with Martin's statement that perhaps God is the best within all of us, as the writer explained that the essence of each of us and that all of Creation is one and the same . . . and this means that the Tree of Life is within each of us, just waiting to be tapped into. When a person does this, he taps into the nature of God.

I didn't fully understand what I was reading, or why Martin might have wanted me to read it. But I pushed on, repurposing my excellent note-taking skills to try to untangle the complicated rhetoric that was so foreign to me.

I made a list of the ten emanations of God, and next to each I wrote a modern, English translation as I found them in the book:

Malchut: Kingdom
Yesod: Foundation
Hod: Awe
Netzach: Victory
Gevurah: Judgment

Chesed: Lovingkindness
Tiferet: Balance
Binah: Knowledge
Chochmah: Wisdom
Keter: Crown

I stared at the list, rendered in my neat handwriting. I knew what each of these English words meant . . . at least, I *thought* I did. But placed in a list like this, these words seemed to be more meaningful together than any one of them would be on its own.

I felt a tingle in my spine, a strange sensation like the one I sometimes got just before a moment of déjà vu. Curious, I turned to the next page of the book.

In the morning, I woke, groggy, to the smell of a turkey in the oven. I took a deep breath . . . Christmas.

I found Daddy at work in the kitchen, chopping up potatoes and dropping them into a pot of water on the stove.

"You must have gotten up early to get the turkey started," I said.

"Crack of dawn," he answered with a smile, but something about it didn't seem sincere.

"Daddy? What's the matter?" I felt wary, almost scared.

He looked at first as if he was going to deny that anything was wrong, but then his face fell and he sighed. "You're going to find out; I might as well tell you. Your mother went downstairs last night, after you'd gone to bed. . . . She saw the tree, Scarlett."

"So? It wasn't supposed to be a secret." I felt a hard knot forming in my stomach.

"You didn't do anything wrong," Daddy said.

"What are you talking about?" I felt tears springing to my eyes and I fought back a panicky sensation.

He shook his head, miserable, and I saw his eyes dart to the window over the kitchen sink. I pushed past him and peered out down onto the yard.

There was our Christmas tree, still decorated, pine branches akimbo, thrust up against the trash cans.

It was one of the saddest things I'd ever seen. Hot tears streaked down my cheeks and I felt the knot in my belly spread to a tightness in my chest.

"She had no right," I seethed, teeth clenched. "She's not the only person who matters in this family."

"Your mom is in a lot of pain right now, Scarlett." Daddy's voice was strained and nervous-sounding, like he was trying really hard to keep things together.

"I'm sick of Mom's pain," I said. "I'm sick to death of all of our pain."

I stormed out of the kitchen and down the hall to my mother's room. I hated her closed door; I hated the dark shadow of sadness that seeped out from under it. I thought maybe I hated my mother, too.

I saw my hand on the doorknob; I saw the doorknob turning; behind me, I felt my father's panic rising to a palpable level, his desire to keep the peace at all costs suddenly costing much too much.

My hand dropped to my side. I trudged down the stairs

and retrieved the ornament box from the front hallway before going outdoors to the tree.

One by one, as if picking fruit, I plucked the ornaments from the plastic branches, wrapping each one in paper and then placing them gently in the plastic bin.

That was Christmas. None of us mentioned presents, and when Daddy presented the turkey dinner at two that afternoon, I wasn't home to eat it. I wandered down to the seashore, watching the gentle drift of the waves against the sand, and I counted, over and over again, the days until Will would come home to me.

At last, New Year's Day came and went, and then school resumed. Will had sent me a text from the road, telling me that he wouldn't make it to school because of the ferry schedule but he would be back on the island in time for rehearsal after school.

He had never sent me a text before. I tried not to let it bother me that he was sending one now instead of calling, but then I decided that if it bothered me so much, I should just call him. So I did—but he didn't answer.

Mrs. B had scheduled rehearsals for three afternoons a week over on the Casino's stage. Our high school plays were kind of a big thing for island locals; even people who didn't have kids at the high school turned out to watch us perform.

Brandon Becker and Katie Ellis had been cast in the other leading roles, along with Will and me. Brandon was playing Jack Worthing, and Katie was his fiancée, Gwendolen Fairfax.

Mrs. B had posted a list of which scenes we'd be practicing on which days; today we'd be rehearsing scenes from the second act, so the four of us—Will, Brandon, Katie, and me—all had to be there, as well as Amanda, who played my governess, Miss Prism, and Connell, who'd been cast as John's manservant, Merriman. Mr. Steiner, the vice principal, was playing the Reverend. Mr. Steiner had earned a Drama minor back in the mid-eighties, and he loved to get involved with the school plays whenever he could swing it.

Will rushed into the theater just as Mrs. B was staging the first scene between me and Katie. My heart leaped to my throat when I saw him shutting the doors against the windstorm outside and slipping into a seat in the second row, his script in hand.

My hand shot up in a wave, and I heard Connell snickering offstage. He murmured, "Big Red's got the hots for the Jew, all right."

His comment barely registered with me; what I was focused on was Will's awkward half wave in return, the way his gaze glanced off of me and settled somewhere on stage left.

Nausea churned through my stomach. Something was wrong.

I spoke all my clever lines with Miss Prism, but I was distracted, and Mrs. B kept stopping the scene to tell me that I was rushing. Finally, after what felt like hours, she dismissed Amanda from the stage.

"All right, Will," she called out. "You're up. Let's start with the engagement scene, shall we? Get that out of the way. Places!" She clapped her hands sharply, obviously relishing her role as director.

I sat demurely in the garden chair and Will stood over me. This was the scene where we were to pronounce our love. I tried to catch Will's gaze, to smile at him, but he wouldn't meet my glance. He ran his eyes across his lines, though if I'd had to guess, I'd have said that he wasn't seeing the words.

His brow was furrowed, and his dark lashes hid his eyes from me.

"Whenever you're ready," Mrs. B called out, motioning with her hands for us to get going.

I knew for a fact that Will had all his lines memorized. Still, he didn't lift his eyes from the script as he spoke his first line: "I hope, Cecily, I shall not offend you if I state quite frankly and openly that you seem to me to be in every way the visible personification of absolute perfection."

And though his words were, most certainly, the words every girl longs to hear from the boy she loves, his tone was flat and distant, tinged with despair.

The scene went on like that until Will knelt at my feet to declare, "What a perfect angel you are, Cecily."

I was to reply "You dear, romantic boy," and then we were to kiss, and I was supposed to run my fingers through his hair.

He said his line, and I said mine, full of fear, and then our mouths came together in a kiss.

But it wasn't a kiss. Our lips touched, my hand found its place in his hair, but that was all. The electric spark I had come to associate with Will's touch was all but extinguished, and the press of his lips felt mechanical against mine.

My eyes swelled with tears, but when we pulled apart I managed to murmur, right on cue, "I hope your hair curls naturally, does it?"

"Cut there," called Mrs. B, dissatisfied, from her seat in the audience.

"The Jew's not much of a kisser," I heard Connell mutter to Brandon offstage. Next to me, it seemed that Will stiffened, but he didn't turn.

"I don't know, I'm not really buying the connection," Mrs. B said. "No romantic energy. Let's try it again, just the last part, with the kiss."

She ran us through the scene four times. Each time, the kiss felt more plastic, more distant, until at last, during the fourth run-through, I clutched Will's hair desperately in my hands and forced my mouth hard against his, pressing my body into his cold embrace. And then, as if against his will, his hands slid around my waist and his mouth grew soft and warm. I clung to him as long as I could, as if by prolonging this moment, I could force away his coldness to me.

But at last Will pulled away, his green eyes troubled.

My line came out breathy, all in a rush—"I hope your hair curls naturally, does it?"

"Yes, darling, with a little help from others," murmured Will, and he untangled himself from my arms, taking a deliberate step away from me.

"That's the way," applauded Mrs. B. "All right, people, we'll call it a day. On Wednesday, get ready to run lines from act three."

The others gathered up their scripts, books, and jackets, and filed out of the theater, chatting happily.

Mrs. B followed them, and called out over her shoulder at us, "Be sure to pull the door tight when you leave." Then she was gone, and we were alone.

I turned to Will. He seemed guarded, as if determined to keep his distance from me. *Probably in case I decide to attack him again,* I thought bitterly.

"What happened?" I asked.

He shrugged. "You didn't do anything wrong, Scarlett."

His words echoed my father's from Christmas morning. I felt a flush of anger rising in my stomach.

"I know that," I said. "What's wrong with *you?*"

He seemed to choose his words carefully. "It's nothing you can change," he began at last. "It's just . . . we're a bad idea, Scarlett, you and me. I'm not good for you."

"But you said . . . you promised you wouldn't leave me." I hated the way I sounded. Whiny, grasping, like one of those girls I couldn't stand.

He shook his head. "It's nothing you can change," he repeated.

"You lied," I seethed, and I stumbled offstage, blinded by my tears. I yanked my jacket off the chair and fumbled for my bag.

As I slammed through the doors, out into the windy evening, I heard his voice saying something, but I couldn't hear his words over the sound of my sobs. The wind wailed too, and it pushed at my back, driving me away, along the edge of the sea, away from Will.

SIXTEEN

The Muddy Path

The time after the New Year is a paradox. It's supposed to be all about a fresh start—eager resolution-makers counting calories conscientiously and eating leafy greens and trying to quit bad habits—but at the same time people are trying to start something, it's the dead of winter.

This would be a pretty good reason to live in Australia; there, at least, New Year's happens during summer. But on my island, New Year's and January are cold and lonely times. Right after my scene with Will in the theater, this seemed fine by me.

Since the day on the stage, I had avoided Will as much as I could. Lily had returned to her former habit of appearing at my house before school with some sort of pastry or breakfast sandwich. I could tell she was worried that I was going to backslide and start shedding the pounds I'd put on over the last couple of months.

Truth was, I'd considered it. I remembered what Will had said: "It's as if your body is the crime scene."

Since I'd burned my yellow notebook, Will had gradually looked less and less pained . . . as if a burden had been lifted from him. I remembered what he'd revealed to me the night of the Halloween party, about the fishhook in his brain pulling him to the scenes of crimes. And I knew that if I was to refuse the breakfast sandwich that Lily offered me, or go even further—break my mirror and run a shard of its glass down my thigh or across my stomach—that Will would sense that decision, and he would come to me.

My body could be a crime scene again, anytime I chose to make it so. I could hurt myself. I could hurt Will if I wanted to.

But I didn't want to.

I wanted to protect him from pain, even though he had hurt me terribly. And I didn't want to hurt myself, either. I was sick of pain. So I chewed the egg and bread; I stayed at arm's length from my mirror and blinked at my forlorn reflection.

I kept reading Martin's book. Some of it I understood; much of it I didn't, though as I read the words I felt pulled into their world of mystery, even if their meaning eluded me.

I came across a passage that discussed the purpose of practicing Kabbalah—"*The dedicated Kabbalist can come to see the face of God*"—but what I read next caused my breath to catch in my throat. "*The result of his practice can transform the Kabbalist; in a moment of divine contemplation, the Kabbalist can be shaken by an ecstatic flash of light, an experience that illuminates the body, bathing it in light, in lightning and thunder."*

Here, I stopped reading. I remembered the force of Will's touch on my hand, the press of his mouth. It was as if these words were written to describe the experience I'd had with Will—the electric charge, the shocking pleasure of his touch.

But remembering his kiss was painful. I got lost in the memory, and when I shook my head to return to my lonely room, the absence of him was too sharply focused, knifelike.

January wore on—a cold, wet, foggy month. Lily invited me to spend the weekend at her house, but she didn't seem surprised when I turned her down. I didn't want to be social; I wanted to be alone, all alone.

"That history paper is due," I offered lamely for an excuse.

"Yeah, and next week it'll be the science test, and I'll bet after that you'll have to memorize some poem for English."

"Sorry if my homework is inconvenient for you, Lil," I said. I heard the brittle undertone in my own voice.

"It's not that I don't get it, Scar," said Lily, and I felt a coldness in my chest. I knew that she was about to say things that I didn't want to hear. "I know how hard it's been for you—Ronny dying. I can't imagine what you're going through, blah, blah, blah, and then Will dumping you obviously really blows too. But Scar—I miss my friend."

Of course her "blah, blah, blah" was totally unnecessary, but I got the basic gist of her complaint. I had become a lousy friend. I tuned out when she started to analyze the various possible implications of Josh Riddell's gestures and comments (she'd started seeing him right after winter break), and clearly, I took more than I gave.

"Lil," I said. "I know I suck right now. I'm sorry. I really am. I want to be better. But this is all I have." I held out my empty hands, palms up.

She looked at them, then up at my face. "There's nothing there, Scarlett."

I shrugged.

She looked miserable. "I'll just ask Kaitlyn, I guess."

I groaned. "You wouldn't."

A smile. "Okay, maybe not Kaitlyn, but someone else. I'd rather have you."

"I'm working on it, Lily. Really, I am."

So that became my resolution: work on it. Only I wasn't sure what "it" was, exactly. It occurred to me as I sat early one morning in the gazebo in our garden, wrapped in a blanket over my fleece pants and sweatshirt, that Martin's book could help me.

Malchut: The Kingdom of this world. The book said something I'd heard many times before: The greatest tree is contained within the tiniest seed, its potential latent until it germinates. What lay inside of me—what desires, what hopes, what possibilities?

What did I want? The answer seemed painfully obvious: I wanted Ronny to be alive and I wanted Will to want me in return.

I felt pitiful. What had happened to all the things I'd wanted *Before* Ronny Died and *before* Will had come to the island?

It was difficult to remember, as if I were looking through a thick, soupy fog.

I wanted to go to college. I wanted to travel the world. I wanted to breed Delilah and raise her foal.

And there was more: I wanted to go to France to meet the far-off second cousins I had heard about from my grandparents but had never met. I wanted to write a book one day, about something.

I wanted a career—maybe in medicine, maybe as a literature professor. I wanted to make my family proud.

How could it be that these desires had faded away? Was I really one of those mewling girls now, whose sun rises and sets on some boy?

Not that Will was just *some boy*, I admitted to myself begrudgingly. Even aside from his impossible ability to sense the future, he was absolutely amazing. He was unlike anyone else I knew . . . it was as if he'd somehow passed over the whole teenage thing, as if he transcended it.

Still, though, he wasn't my universe.

I wandered back into the house. After the cold fogginess of the garden, our kitchen felt warm and almost tropical. I fished a new notebook out of the desk in the corner and flipped it open to the first page.

Its blankness was scary. The white lined paper seemed to issue a silent challenge. I pulled back a seat from the table and sat down.

What I Want, I wrote neatly, deliberately, across the top.
Ronny, my heart cried. *Will*.

I ignored it. Instead, I watched my hand write steadily:

> *Meaning*
> *Happiness*
> *To not be in pain*
> *Family*

Here my hand grew less steady. Family. Could we still be one? My mother was completely checked out. My father's everything seemed tied up in my mother. And me? I didn't know anymore. No longer a sister, not quite a daughter . . . where did that leave me?

I sighed and closed the notebook. It all seemed far, far too complicated, way out of my reach.

Malchut. The Kingdom of this world. It was so much to grasp, the whole world. But if we are all God, and all of everything can be contained in the smallest seed, then it seemed to follow that my body must be full of unseen potential too. I had tried starving it; I had tried hurting it. These things had not brought me joy. I might as well try something else, something different.

If my mother was unable to mother me, and my father too distracted to take care of me, then I would become my own family. I would care for my body as if it was a sacred object—as if it was the whole of everything, as if I really believed it carried God within it.

And so I began new rituals, purposely this time. I set my

alarm clock an hour earlier than I needed, to five-thirty. When I woke, I wrapped myself in warm clothes and slipped from the house, winding my way down to the beach where I would sit, cocooned in a blanket, and watch the sun rise. Then I would stretch, bending myself in half and letting my hair split and fall over my shoulders to pool at my feet in the sand as I pressed my face into my knees. I practiced sitting very still and breathing slowly, in and out.

At home, I took long, hot showers, and I used the pricey shampoos and soaps I used to save for special occasions, and I tipped my face into the steamy water and concentrated on feeling each drop of water as it hit my skin. I took my time shaving my legs. I loofahed my elbows and heels. When I dried off, I paid attention to the nubby fabric of the towel, and I filled my lungs with the hot, moist air that stirred around me. I massaged fragrant oils and lotions into my skin, caressing myself gently.

In the kitchen, I ate simply, but well. Eggs, fresh bread, fruit.

I focused intently, deliberately, on doing things mindfully. When I girthed Traveler at the barn, I watched my fingers tighten the straps and work the metal hooks through the punched holes in the leather straps. When I pulled down the stirrup irons, I felt peculiarly satisfied when the metal reached the end of the leather.

When I braided my hair at night, I watched my fingers twisting the blond strands in the mirror, and I allowed myself to think the things we are told are vain—My *hair is so beautiful. I have pretty hands*.

And I kept reading. On the second of February, a Friday night, I was curled up in bed, the bedside table lamp glowing in the evening's dimness. On page 142, I read: *"The Kabbalah tells us that there are people who walk among us, people with gifts the rest of us can only imagine. These people—Tzaddikim—are sages who have extraordinary levels of perception, some even able to see into the future or the past. Among these Tzaddikim, a very few have achieved Ruach HaKodesh—the 'spirit of holiness,' which is a state of the soul that makes prophecy possible. However, since the age of classical prophecy has passed, no one has achieved Ruach HaKodesh."*

I blinked. The words seemed to move on the page in front of me. I read them again. *Tzaddikim. Ruach HaKodesh.* These didn't even look like real words; they seemed to me as if from some made-up language.

But the meaning behind them felt eerily significant: There are people, though rare, who can see the future.

It was Will the book was describing. I knew so instantly. The book I held in my hands was speaking about the boy I loved—for I loved him still, even if he wanted nothing to do with me.

Early the next morning, I drove with Alice to the stable.

Delilah was still out of commission; the farrier had caught the flu and hadn't made it out to the island yet. So it was Traveler I pulled from the barn; it was Traveler I saddled and bridled and rode out of the yard at a fast trot toward Two Harbors.

Behind me, I head Alice call, "You forgot your helmet!"

But I pretended not to hear her as I pressed Traveler forward with my heels, and I rounded the bend up the winding path, and I felt strong, and brave, and determined to find answers.

Thirty-eight Olive Lane was just as charming as I remembered. The winding plant in the picket fence had filled in even more since I'd last visited the house, the front porch looked neatly swept, and the house was quiet.

It could be that nobody was home. I didn't know where Will was, or what his plans for the weekend might be. We barely spoke these days, other than at rehearsal, when we carried out the charade of being in love.

Truthfully, it was no charade for me, but saying my flirtatious, lilting lines into Will's wary countenance took all my acting ability. What I really wanted to do was shake him, and wail my hurt and disappointment into his face, or press myself against him and *make* him want me again.

The plain little brown shingled house didn't seem concerned with my angst. Its wide windows stared back at me, unblinking; its door did not open to tell me any secrets.

Traveler's nostrils flared as he took in this new environment, and he did kind of a half hop in place that revealed his nerves.

I slid down from his back and pulled the reins over his head. Patting his neck, I told him what a good boy he was, and gradually he quieted.

I didn't know what I had expected. Since discovering the term—*Tzaddikim*—the night before, I had felt such urgency to go to Will's house. I wanted to share with him what I had found.

But now it seemed foolish. What had I thought—that I'd stumbled upon some piece of information, some clue, that Will and Martin hadn't already discovered?

Who was I—just some girl who'd spent a few hours reading one book about the Kabbalah! What could I possibly know that they hadn't already considered from every angle?

But if it was true—if Will's abilities to sense impending crimes really came as a result of being one of these *Tzaddikim*—why hadn't he told me this?

It seemed that the house would not be yielding any answers today. I stood, leaning on the front gate, gazing intently at the little yard, but the door did not open, and neither Martin nor Will emerged.

I felt Traveler's warm breath on my back. As I turned to stroke his muzzle, a car pulled up to the curb in front of Will's house.

It was an old forest-green Jeep—and behind the wheel sat Martin. I felt the warmth of hope course through me, and my hand shot up in a wave. But though he raised his hand in return before he shut off the engine, his mouth did not turn up in a smile.

Martin climbed out of the Jeep and pulled a couple of grocery bags out of the backseat before heading across the sidewalk toward me.

"Scarlett," he said. "How have you been?"

I considered how to answer Martin's question.

"Not great, but I've found out that I'm stronger than I thought I was." It seemed we were equally surprised by my answer. It was true—I wasn't broken.

Martin's face softened. "I'm glad to hear that, Scarlett." He hesitated before asking, "Would you like to come inside?"

"I can't. Traveler wouldn't be comfortable alone."

"Yes . . . this is a different horse." Martin lowered his grocery bags across the picket fence into his yard and stroked Traveler's velvety nose.

"Is Will here?"

Martin's hand stopped midstroke, just for a moment, before he answered. "He is," he said cautiously. "But he's resting. He has a headache today."

I had to fight back the urge to push past Martin and barge into the house. In my mind's eye an image flashed—clear as a photograph—of Will in his room, lying on his bed, eyes closed.

"Is something wrong?" I asked. "Somewhere on the island . . . is something going to happen?"

Martin's eyes were troubled. "It would be better, Scarlett, if Will hadn't told you these things. It's too much for you to have to process, along with all your own troubles."

"I think I can handle it, Martin." My voice sounded steely. "I want to help him."

Martin laughed, but there was no humor in it. "Yes," he said. "I know how you feel. I'd like to help him too. But I seem cursed to watch as those I love suffer. I don't wish to share that burden with you, Scarlett."

I brushed away his concern. "Why is Will just lying there?" I asked. "Why doesn't he do something?"

Martin seemed torn between answering me and dodging my question. He looked in my face for a long moment, and he must have seen something there, for finally he answered, "It's different this time. He doesn't know where to go. It's just the headache . . . no pulling feeling."

"Did any other *Tzaddikim* report the same kind of experiences—being pulled to certain places, feeling compelled to help?" Probably I mispronounced the strange word, but I didn't care.

Martin raised his eyebrows speculatively. "You have been doing your homework," he murmured. "No, I've come across no record of anything quite like what Will experiences, though of course I've been researching for years now."

He didn't deny what I had suspected—that the Kabbalah had a name for people like Will.

"Martin," I said. My voice was strong and steady. "I love your son. It doesn't matter how he feels about me. I want to help him."

Martin's smile was sad. "I can see that, Scarlett. But you can't help Will. All you can do is to take care of yourself, and do your best to leave him alone. Will doesn't need your help."

I felt embarrassed, chastened as though I was a little girl caught doing something naughty.

"Go home, Scarlett," Martin said, and though his face was gentle and his tone was kind, his words stung me like a whip.

I couldn't see clearly as I pulled myself onto Traveler and turned him up the road, but I called to Martin as I urged Traveler forward, "Tell Will I came." And there was power behind my words—they were not a plea, but rather a command.

I knew as I rode away that Martin watched me, and I held my back straight, my head high. I saw again in my mind Will on his bed, and he sat up, and his green eyes opened and stared into mine.

The wind stirred the leaves on the trail as I rode toward the stable. Dark clouds blowing in from the sea cut the sunlight into shadow. I smelled a storm coming; the air felt electric. Traveler felt it too. His ears flicked back and forth and his step was light and high.

On an island, weather can change very quickly. It had been cold this morning, and overcast, but now it was clear that a storm was imminent.

I didn't want to run Traveler on the trail, but I did want to make it back to the stable before the storm, so I cued him to pick up his pace. I resolved to keep it to a slow lope, reminding him with the reins to keep it mellow.

The storm clouds were faster than we were. With a warning clap of thunder, the sky opened and rain poured down.

I had to hand it to Traveler; though he quickened his gait when we began to be pelted by rain, he didn't bolt. I felt his muscles tighten beneath me, and I worked at keeping my seat steady, my hands supportive and controlling, so that he wouldn't spook and take his canter into a gallop.

I felt proud of my work with Traveler. He was young and pretty green, but I had him well in hand during what might have been dangerous trail conditions. I felt keyed up too, and in spite of my interaction with Martin, in spite of the knowledge that Will did not want me—that he might never want me in the way that I wanted him—I felt *good*. A wide, foolish grin split my face. The air smelled earthy and wet, so *alive*, and Traveler's hooves splashed through the mud and puddles that were forming on the trail.

Perhaps it is impossible to feel anything but free on a running horse. Perhaps I really *was* stronger than I thought I could be. But I knew, in the moment before the accident, that life was beautiful in spite of the pain that is its constant, sometimes hidden, shadow. I knew all the pieces existed within me. I might still be fractured, but the pieces were knitting back together, and I would be stronger in the places where I had broken and healed. How I knew this, why I felt this so surely, I don't know. But my own, beating heart—my own, heady gulps of air—this was life, and I was glad for it.

And then Traveler spied a downed branch on the trail.

It must have recalled for him the trot poles that had terrified him back at the stable. Had we been walking, or even trotting, I would have had time to steady my seat. And if the trail had been dry, I could have predicted better what would happen when he saw the branch, when he grunted with fear, when he dodged fast to the left to avoid it, then swerved right to keep from colliding with a tree.

But there were too many factors, too fast, and nothing I did could right the situation. The slime of the mud beneath his iron shoes threw Traveler off balance, and he stumbled to his knees, and I felt myself unseated in that queer, slow-motion kind of way, and as my body flew from the saddle, I almost had time to tuck my head to my chest, I almost had time to cover my bare head with my arms, and then I hit the muddy trail, and my head struck a rock with painful force, and then my world closed around me.

SEVENTEEN

In the Gloaming

I woke, shivering, to rain. I lay on the trail, next to the rock that had knocked me out. Sitting up too fast, my first thought was Traveler—where was he? I swung my head around to find him, but the movement struck me down again. Too much pain. I retched in the mud, rain plastering my hair to my head, and when I touched my brow to push my hair out of my face, my hand came away red with blood.

The horse was gone. Lightning split the sky. I was alone.

I wanted to cry; little sniveling sounds came out of me but there were no tears, though my face was wet with rain. I sat, sprawled in the mud like a broken doll. My heart pounded furiously in my chest; I felt terribly afraid.

Looking around, I tried to situate myself. Time had passed since I'd been thrown; the sun, shrouded by the rainclouds, was lower in the sky. It was late afternoon.

I felt confused, as if my thoughts were swimming through

dark, murky water. Which way was home? I remembered again the horse. Where was Delilah?

No—Traveler. I'd ridden Traveler. But why, and where? It was difficult for me to link any facts together to form a chain of thought. Too much effort was required; after a moment I gave up and closed my eyes.

I was shivering, and my teeth clanked against each other. I knew these things meant that I was cold, but it was as if I was observing myself from very far away. It felt better to have my eyes closed. The weight of my body seemed too much to bear, so I let myself slip back down to the muddy path and I curled myself into a ball. The rain seemed to slacken before redoubling.

I did not sleep, but I was not quite awake. I was still.

Inside my head, or outside of my body, it was impossible to tell which, the world swirled like water down a drain. Images streaked by me and I tried to grasp them—Delilah, trotting gracefully in the arena; Ronny as a young boy, muddy and grinning widely after a soccer game; Lily tossing her curls in that particular way. And Will—Will, eyes serious and eager, slipping the orchid corsage onto my wrist. Will, across from me in the Yellow Room, entrusting his secret to me. Will, next to the pond, his arm at my waist, asking, "Do you want me to kiss you, Scarlett?" And Will, his mouth slanted across mine, the feel of him against my body. And as I lay in the rain, it seemed as if I were in his arms again, as if I were whirling in circles in a dance rather than dizzy and bleeding on the muddy earth, and I said his name—whether aloud or not, I did not know—*Will, Will, Will*.

• • •

A loud rumbling sound brought me awake again, and I opened my eyes into the bright, staring headlights of a truck. Except for the lights of the truck, the sky was darkening on the precipice of night. I was blinded by the headlights, my headache redoubled by their glare, and I brought my arm across my face.

The rain pounded down, and I heard someone running toward me through the mud.

"Scarlett," he called, aghast, and I forced my eyes to open. It was Will. Behind him, his father's green Jeep still ran, its engine grumbling like some monster, its headlights frightening in the rain. The driver's-side door was open. Irrationally, I found myself worrying that the upholstery would be ruined by the rain.

Will dropped to his knees beside me. His hand, fire-hot, touched my cheek. "Scarlett, look at me," he begged.

Even though I wanted to, I found it nearly impossible to focus on his penetrating gaze. My eyes kept slipping to the side, like marbles on a slanted floor. But I breathed in the smell of him in the rain—warm, like he'd been sitting next to the fireplace in his front room. Somehow spicy. My eyes closed and I pictured myself in his arms, and I felt myself slipping away again into unconsciousness.

I felt my body shifting, and I knew that Will had me in his arms, and that now I would be safe.

"You came," I murmured into his shirtfront.

And before I passed out again, I heard him reply, "You called me."

• • •

When I woke again, it was no longer raining. That was my first thought, before I opened my eyes. And then I heard a sound, a steady ping, ping, ping. It sounded medical.

My eyelids felt as if tiny weights were attached to the lashes, making opening them a struggle, so I left my eyes closed. I knew I was in a hospital bed. My head ached, though it was more of a dull throb now than the gripping pain I'd felt on the trail. Working my way mentally down my body, I felt tenderness in my left shoulder, and both elbows stung as if coated with antiseptic. My left hip felt deeply bruised, achy all the way through, but the rest of me seemed all right.

There was someone next to me. I heard quiet sobbing. It was a woman.

I had heard this woman cry before. I had heard her muffled cries through my bedroom wall; I had heard her keening sobs at her son's funeral. I had heard her silent, pervasive sadness that was even worse to me than the sounds of her despair.

I opened my eyes. There she was, in a chair pulled next to my bed. Her head was in her hands, her hair wild and lank about her shoulders. My mother.

Opening my mouth to speak, I found it dry and bitter. How long had I been here, in this bed? How long had my mother been crying over my body?

My eyes scanned the room. Bouquets of flowers covered every surface; three large, brightly colored balloon arrangements shifted in the air, their ribbons leashing them to chairs.

Mom's overnight bag squatted in the corner. It was open, a sweater spilling out of it.

A window. Outside, the sky was dark. Was this the night of the same day or was it another?

I shifted in the bed. Mom's eyes, red-rimmed and puffy, shot up and found me awake. Her mouth opened into a little O; had this been any other situation, I might have laughed at her expression.

Instead, I felt tears filling my eyes. "Hi, Mom," I tried to say, but my voice didn't work quite right, and it ended up sounding like a cough or a quack.

"Scarlett," she said, and she leaned across my chest, dropping her head onto me. "Thank God."

Her words made me remember Martin's book. *God . . . if God is all of us, everywhere, all the time*, I wondered, *then was my mother thanking herself? Thanking me?*

I brought a shaking hand up to my mother's head and rested it on her hair. I had comforted my father in front of our Christmas tree while he cried for Ronny; now I felt my mother's sobs on my chest as I ran my fingers through her hair.

Who was the child? Who was the parent?

I didn't know the answers. Maybe after a family has suffered a loss such as ours, everything needs to be renegotiated.

"I thought I'd lost you, too," Mom murmured into the sheets before drawing a long, quivering breath and sitting up. She smiled into my eyes, and then it was her hand smoothing my hair from my temple, carefully avoiding the left side of my hairline.

I raised my hand and felt my head gingerly, remembering

the blood in the rain. There was a gauze bandage taped to my forehead.

"Scarlett," my mother said. "I'm so, so sorry."

I didn't need to ask what she was sorry about. How many months had it been now that she'd been lost in her own grief, lost in the bottles of pills she lined up on her bedside table?

How many meals had she missed, how many of my silent cries had she ignored? Did she even know that I had stopped seeing Andy? Was she aware that I'd been cast in a lead for the spring play?

Did she have any idea that I was in love—unrequited or not—with Will Cohen, and did she know that his eyes were the color of life?

Did she know anything about me anymore, anything at all?

And I knew I had a choice. I could be angry. I could refuse my mother what she needed, as she had refused me.

Or I could forgive her. The choice was mine. I felt a great sensation of peace. To know that I had power—real power—and that I could decide how I wanted to feel, how I wanted to react, brought me a palpable wave of peace. I could be angry. I could blame my mother for my choices, my silent suffering over these many months.

I remembered Martin's book on the Sefirot, and the Sefirah of *Yesod*, particularly. The book said that if the Sefirot is a map of the human body as well as the soul, and even of God, *Yesod* finds its parallel in the male reproductive organ—the penis. This had made me laugh when I'd read it, but as I read on, I came to understand the metaphor. The penis is a bridge that can transmit genetic material from one person to another. Likewise, *Yesod* can be seen as a bridge—one that connects our inner world and outer reality.

And though it seemed ridiculous that I was thinking these thoughts while my tearful mother sat beside me in a hospital room, so ridiculous that I wondered what kind of damage I might have done to myself when I fell, it also felt very real, and undeniably right. I had power. I could be a bridge if I chose to, and I could close the gap that loomed between my mother and myself.

I brought my hand up from the blanket and found my mother's, and my grip was strong as I squeezed her hand. "I know, Mom," I said, and this time when my voice cracked, it wasn't because my throat was dry, but because it was thick with emotion. "But you're here now."

"I am," she cried. "And I'm not going anywhere."

Though it was dark outside, just a sliver of the moon cutting through the velvet of night, there was light in my room. I was tired, so tired, but I knew that when I woke again, my mother would be at my side.

And she was. I awoke to sunlight pouring through the narrow hospital window and both of my parents talking quietly over cups of coffee.

My mother had brushed her hair back into a neat ponytail—a little higher on her head than she usually positioned it. It looked hopeful this way, and pretty. Her hair, though darker than mine, was thick and straight, and she wore it longer than any of the other moms. Her skin was pale, and there were dark circles under her eyes, but she was smiling.

My dad looked absolutely radiant. He leaned in toward my mom and kept finding excuses to touch her—straightening the collar of her sweater, brushing a wisp of hair from her face, smoothing the line of her pants.

"That coffee smells great," I said, and both of them swiveled around to smile at me. "Can I have a cup?"

"You're too young to drink coffee," Mom said at once.

"I've been drinking it every morning for months now."

She looked over to my dad, who verified my statement with a shrug of his shoulders. For a second, she looked embarrassed, as if she should have known this about me. And then she seemed as if she might want to argue about all the reasons I shouldn't have caffeine. But instead she said, "I'll find you some. How do you like it?"

"Cream and sugar," I said. "Same as you."

"Well, that's something, anyway," she mumbled. "Back in a sec."

"Good to see you awake, Scar," said my dad. "You gave us a scare, all right."

"Yeah. Sorry about that, Daddy."

He nodded, sipped his coffee. "It's a good thing that Will found you when he did," he said. "You'd already lost a lot of blood."

I pushed the little button on my bed, which brought me slowly up to a sitting position. "Tell me everything," I said. "But I should probably go pee first."

He shook his head. "You've got a catheter for that."

"No way." I dug through the blankets and sheets to verify his statement. Yep. Disgusting.

"That's what happens when you ride without a helmet," he said. "We're all lucky it wasn't worse."

"Okay, Daddy, let's let the injury speak for itself, all right? No lecture."

I could tell he wanted to say more on the matter, but I cut him off. "I'll never go on the trail again without a helmet, okay?"

This seemed to satisfy him. "Okay," he said. "No lecture then."

I settled in to listen to the story of my rescue. "So tell me everything," I said.

"Well, you can imagine how upset Alice was when that horse you had ridden came galloping into the stable yard with no Scarlett," my dad began.

"He found his way back? What a good boy." I was relieved to hear that Traveler had made it safely home.

"Good boy, my foot. That horse almost got you killed."

"No, it was my own fault. I never should have taken Traveler out. It was too soon . . . and he was too spooked still. But I needed . . ."

I had needed to see Will—that was what I was going to say.

"Well, the horse is fine, though he wouldn't have been if *you* hadn't been all right." His face took on a funny cast, as if he were thinking thoughts he shouldn't be thinking.

"Moving on. . . ." I motioned with my hands for him to keep going.

Mom came back into the room and handed me a cup

of coffee. "The doctor will be in soon to check on you," she said. She tried to sit back in her seat, but Daddy pulled her into his lap. She laughed a little, and didn't pull away, but her exuberance didn't match my dad's. She looked like someone who was convalescing from a long illness. I had the strange sensation of seeing myself in her . . . the weakened, brittle self I had been not so very long ago.

"Daddy was just telling me about what happened after I fell," I said.

Mom picked up the story. "Well, Alice was a wreck. That horse you were on came tearing into the stable, and you weren't on him, and Alice didn't know what to do. She called the sheriff to go out and look for you, but they had no idea which trail you'd been on, so they didn't know where to start. If it weren't for that Cohen boy—"

"Will." His name tasted like candy in my mouth.

"If it weren't for Will," she continued, "I don't know when we would have found you."

"He told the sheriff that he just had a bad feeling," Daddy said. "You'd been at his house, I guess?"

I nodded. I didn't want to tell them about my conversation with Martin; they didn't need to know *everything*.

"So he took his dad's Jeep and followed the trail he figured you'd take back toward the barn. He found you there, and you were disoriented and bleeding, of course. He hesitated to move you because he wasn't sure if you'd hurt your spine, but you were bleeding so much. . . ." Daddy shook his head. He cleared his throat before continuing. "Anyway, he loaded you into the back of the Jeep and drove you to Two

Harbors. The hospital airlifted you out of there, in a storm and everything, and here you are, two days later." He smiled at me. "It's good to have you back, Scar."

Two days had passed. It didn't seem like it.

"Was I unconscious the whole time?"

"You were in and out. You talked some, but it wasn't coherent—mostly about trees. And a couple of times you seemed scared, something about quicksand, it sounded like. Nightmares."

How strange that I had said things that I had no memory of.

"Will was here yesterday. He took the morning ferry over to see you."

I smiled into my coffee. Will had come. He had come for me on the trail. He had come to see me at the hospital.

"Alice was here too, of course. She feels just terrible. And Lily hasn't stopped calling since she heard. I'd imagine you'll have a lot of visitors when you get home," Daddy said.

"They won't need to visit me, I'll see them at school," I said.

Mom shook her head. "Not this week, at least. Doctor's orders. You need to take it easy. You suffered quite a concussion."

I raised my hand gingerly to my head. Despite the caffeine in the coffee I'd drunk, I felt woozy, a little tired. My eyes closed heavily.

Mom took the cup from my hand. "Just rest," she soothed. "We'll talk more later."

• • •

When the hospital finally released me, it was late afternoon. Lily's parents had offered up their helicopter service to fly us back to the island. My parents had to help me into the helicopter; my legs were shaky and weak, like a newborn foal's.

As the helicopter's blades rotated through the sky, spinning faster and faster until their whirring blur lifted us into the sky and out across the water, I watched the sun, giant and fiery and orange, dipping into the ocean. It seemed as if it would steam and extinguish in the horizon.

We had read the lyrics to a song last spring in English class, right after Ronny had died. The song struck me deeply. I had memorized it, and though I hadn't thought of the song for months, as we crossed the ocean back toward our little island, the sky shifting from day to night, it came to me all at once:

> In the gloaming, oh my darling
> When the lights are soft and low
> And the quiet shadows, falling
> Softly come and softly go
> When the trees are sobbing faintly
> With a gentle unknown woe
> Will you think of me, and love me
> As you did once, long ago?

The gloaming, that peculiar time just after the sun has set, before it is yet dark—neither day nor night, life nor death, waking nor sleeping.

Will had come to me in the gloaming. If there were faeries, this is when they would appear. If there was magic in the world, this is when it would happen.

"You came," I had said to him.

"You called me," he had answered.

I struggled to remember, to cast my line back into the storm.

Yes—I had called to him—*Will, Will, Will,* my need for him as steady as my heartbeat. But he could not possibly have heard me all the way from his house, even if I'd shouted his name—and I felt fairly certain that I hadn't even spoken his name aloud, though my heart had pounded it fiercely.

And I remembered what he had told me—he was pulled, always, toward the scenes of violent crimes that have yet to be committed. No crime had occurred on the trail; Traveler was no criminal. It had been an accident—foolishness on my part, but an accident all the same.

Even more, he hadn't gotten there in time to prevent my falling. He had arrived much later, after I'd lain for some time in the mud and the rain.

But I had called for him . . . and he had answered.

I sat huddled against the window of the helicopter. My father sat in front, next to the pilot. My mother, next to me, saw me shiver. "Are you cold, Scarlett?" Her face was creased with worry. "Maybe you should have stayed at the hospital one more day. The nurses were concerned about you getting sick, after spending all that time in the rain."

"No, it's not that," I murmured. "I'm not sick. Tired, I guess." I gave her a half smile.

She pulled her scarf off of her neck and wrapped it around mine. "Just for good measure," she said.

The island grew larger and larger as we approached it. Will was down there, somewhere, on that little speck of green and brown. I felt him out there, and I knew without a doubt that he was thinking my name.

My arms longed to twine around his neck; my mouth yearned to tip up for his kiss.

Will, I thought, *I'm coming.*

EIGHTEEN

The Arrival of Will

My mother seemed determined to make up for lost time now that I was home. She wouldn't let me get out of bed the first couple of days—"Doctor's orders," she said—but she had Dad move the TV and DVD player to my room from hers and kept me supplied with a stack of brainless comedies.

I guess she and Dad didn't need the TV to keep them busy at night anymore; I heard them talking softly in the evenings, and I heard them crying together, but I also heard their laughter, and once a passion-filled moan that totally embarrassed me. I rushed to turn up the volume on the TV.

It wasn't like everything was magically better thanks to my accident. Twice, when Mom set my tray on my lap at mealtime, I noticed her hands shaking badly—withdrawal from all the pills she'd been downing, I guessed. And though her face looked more animated and present, sometimes her gaze would drift out the window or toward the wall as she sat with me in my bedroom, and I knew where her thoughts had gone.

Not everything was great about having Mom back on task either. She told all my friends that they couldn't visit until Friday, and though I heard Lily arguing her case loudly over the phone, Mom wasn't budging.

But on my second day home, three full days before Mom would officially lift the prohibition on visitors, I heard the doorbell ring downstairs. It was Will—I was certain of it.

I strained my ears to hear what my mother was saying, and after a while, I heard the door swing shut and footsteps climbing the stairs.

Two sets of steps—Mom said outside my door, "Just let me see if she's awake before you go in."

And Will—"Sure, Mrs. Wenderoth. Thanks."

He was here! I straightened myself on the bed, pushing a pillow behind my back and trying to arrange my hair. Mom slipped into my room and smiled when she saw the state I was in.

"I guess you're up," she said. "There's someone here who wants to see you. Refusing to let him in proved more difficult than putting off Lily."

"Let him in!" I said in my best stage whisper. Then, "Wait! Can you get my brush for me first?"

Mom found my hairbrush on my bureau and sat beside me on the bed. She ran the bristles down the length of my hair, smoothing it with her hands as she went.

"You seem excited," she said.

I rolled my eyes. "That's an understatement."

She finished brushing my hair and scooted around so she could see my face. Her fingers tucked my hair behind my ears. "He seems like a nice boy?" Her voice was searching, full of unasked questions.

I could tell she was being careful with me. She didn't know how much to press me, how much it was fair to expect me to reveal. Before Ronny Died, I had told my mother everything—or nearly everything, anyway.

But I could tell from the cautious look in her eyes that she saw the changes in me. Could she see the dark places I had gone? Could she see that I was back now, but changed, forever changed?

She could. She had gone places too, alone in her room, places I couldn't know. No man is an island, that's the expression, but it's not entirely true. Each of us *is* an island, though we can build bridges between us, if we want, if we know how.

"We'd better not keep the young man waiting," she said at last, though it seemed that there were other things she would have liked to have said. And she stood, the place where she had sat on my bed indented from the weight of her.

She opened the bedroom door, and there was Will. I smiled at him, grinning stupidly, so overwhelmingly glad to see him there, in my bedroom.

"I'll just be in the kitchen if you need me," Mom said, and though she pulled the door behind her, she didn't close it entirely.

"Scarlett," said Will, and I saw now that he'd been holding himself together for my mother's benefit. He strode across my room in three steps and fell to his knees at the side of my bed. "Oh, Scarlett," he said, and his fingers wound through mine, and his lips were hot against the backs of my hands, and then he was on the bed with me, pulling me against his chest.

His green eyes gazed into my face, looking at the white bandage at my temple. His face was haggard: bruiselike crescents darkened his face under his eyes, and his hair, always untidy, looked positively disheveled.

I traced the line of his jaw with my hand, and I couldn't stop my fingers from brushing against the softness of his lips. My own lips parted, and my need for his touch was too great to disguise; he could read it in my eyes, on my face, and I saw it mirrored back at me in his expression.

His first kiss was so gentle, as if he was afraid I might break in his arms. His lips and breath, warm and feather-soft, were so tender that tears welled in my eyes. His hands, cupping my face, just barely touched my skin as his mouth reverently explored mine.

I wanted him to never stop kissing me. I wanted to taste more of him, feel more of him. The room spun around me, but it was his touch that was disorienting me, not my concussion. I clung to him, the soft curls at the nape of his neck brushing against my wrists, and my hands wanted only to grab him more tightly, my kiss wanted only to open to him more fully.

I heard my mother clanging pots in the kitchen, but as if from a great distance. Out in the yard, my father was running the lawnmower, but its growl seemed muted as well.

The sound of our breaths tangled together filled my head; the taste of his kiss intoxicated me.

But too soon Will shifted his weight away from me, and he unwound my arms from his neck, though he held my hands in his lap.

"Scarlett," he said. Nothing more—just that, my name.

I hadn't had nearly enough of him. My quickened pulse emboldened me, and I leaned across to kiss him again, not gently as he had kissed me, but full of my desire for him, and as he kissed me back, he abandoned his sense of propriety—at last. The weight of him pressed me down against my mattress, and my chest flattened underneath him, and I groaned as he kissed me again, this time with the intensity I yearned for so badly.

I was dressed for my bed rest in a tank top and yoga pants, and as I felt the press of Will atop me, the thin fabric of my clothes and his jeans and sweater still seemed a frustrating barrier between us.

One of Will's hands found its way into the hair at the back of my neck and his other wandered down my bare arm, resting on my hip, squeezing me roughly before his thumb found the exposed half-inch gap of bare skin between the bottom of my tank and the top of my pants and traced a line there, brand-hot and not nearly enough.

He made a sound then too, a rough groan into my mouth as his kiss deepened. On fire now, I pulled at his sweater and found the broad, warm plane of his back. I pressed him even harder against me, wanting every inch of our bodies to touch.

"Your parents," he murmured.

As if on cue, my mother loudly dropped a pan and called, "Oops!"

I couldn't bring myself to care. I had Will again in my arms, and as far as I was concerned, my parents, my teachers, the entire junior class could line up to watch us kiss. I didn't think I'd even notice.

But when my mother called from just down the hall, "You kids need anything? It's awfully quiet in there," Will pulled away.

Mom picked a fine time to rejoin the living, I thought as I struggled to sit back up. "We're fine, Mom," I called, though my voice betrayed me.

Will had shifted from the bed to the rocking chair, though at least he'd scooted it close to me. I could still reach him, and our hands interlaced.

It took us a minute to calm our breathing and rearrange our faces into something resembling normalcy, but when my mother popped her head through the doorway minutes later, we looked tame enough—though I could tell from the glint in Will's eyes that he was still as inflamed by our kisses as I was.

"You kids want a soda?"

"No thanks," I said at the same moment that Will answered, "Yes, please." We laughed awkwardly while my mom's gaze traveled from Will to me and back again.

"Okay, I'll bring you something." She chose Will's response, probably because it would give her another opportunity to check in on us. This time, when she went to the kitchen, she left the door open behind her.

"I think your mother suspects something," Will said, full of mischief. "She doesn't seem as trusting as your father."

"Yeah, Mom remembers being a teenage girl, I guess. She must know what I'm thinking."

"And what exactly *are* you thinking, Scarlett?"

I was thinking so many things—mostly about kissing Will again—but I knew my mother would return in moments, so I picked a safer topic of discussion. "I'm thinking how glad I am that you're here," I confessed.

Will's face grew serious. "Me too," he said.

"But why *are* you here?" I blurted out. "I mean, didn't you break up with me?"

Will opened his mouth to respond, his face full of emotion, but then my mother came back in with a tray of sodas and chips.

"Here we go," she sang, and she angled the tray conveniently between us.

"Thanks, Mrs. Wenderoth."

I had to hand it to him—Will's manners were impeccable.

And then we were alone again. Ignoring the snacks, Will turned to my question. "I didn't want to break up with you, Scarlett. I just didn't want to end up hurting you."

The idiocy of this concept caused me to bark a harsh laugh. "So you hurt me to avoid hurting me?"

"Something like that. Let me explain. Scarlett, my trip back east over winter break . . . I learned some things."

A shiver passed through me, like a cold draft. My eyes darted over to the window, but it was closed; the curtain panels hung still on either side of it.

"Tell me," I said.

"On the flight back east, I was telling my father about us . . . about how I feel about you."

He didn't seem embarrassed that he'd confided in his father, though it did make me feel a little strange to imagine Will and Martin talking about me.

Will continued, "Scarlett, my dad knows lots of things. Things I'm still learning. And there are things from my past that he's kept from me. He didn't think it would do me any good to know them until I told him about the connection I feel when I'm with you, like electricity—"

"You feel it too?" I interrupted.

He nodded. "It's as strong as the fishhook feeling, only in a good way. A way that distracts me from everything else. Since coming to the island, Scarlett, I've felt pulled closer and closer to you . . . like you're the earth, and I'm the moon caught in your orbit. I can't pull away. I don't *want* to pull away."

"Then why did you break it off with me that day in the theater?" Even remembering the event caused tears to spill from my eyes.

Will wiped them from my cheeks. "I got scared, Scarlett," he confessed. "Maybe you should be scared too."

"What are you talking about?" I *did* feel scared—scared that he would leave me again. But I also knew that I had pulled myself together in the wake of his departure, and if it were to happen a second time, I would not die. I would not break.

"My dad told me about my mother's death."

The room seemed to grow fractionally more still. I waited as Will gathered his thoughts. He cracked open a soda and handed it to me, then opened another and took a long drink.

"Remember how I told you I'm pulled to certain situations?"

I nodded.

"Well, I always thought that there was something wrong with *me*—in the way I was wired. It didn't start until after my mother's death . . . did I tell you that?"

"Yeah, just after you turned thirteen." Every word of the conversation we'd shared in the Yellow Room was imprinted in my mind.

"And I told you how she died?"

"In a car crash. You and your dad were with her."

Will nodded, his face twisted in a way I couldn't translate. "There was more to the story, it turns out. If I had known sooner . . . but my father just told me the rest of it, over winter break. Listen, Scarlett, we didn't just happen to be in the wrong place at the wrong time. My mom put the car exactly where she intended it to be."

I was confused. "She *wanted* to be in an accident?"

"She wanted to stop a crime." Will was quiet, letting his words sink in. Then he continued. "After the accident, when we were all at the hospital, a police officer who was interviewing my dad was trying to comfort him. He told my dad that even though Mom's death was a terrible tragedy, she probably saved the life of a pregnant lady who was walking up the street." Will's eyes were looking into middle distance, as if he was remembering the scene. "The driver who hit our car—the driver whose car Mom blocked with ours—was an angry ex-boyfriend, and he'd threatened the woman twice before. Of course they couldn't know for sure, but it looked awfully suspicious that his car was barreling at sixty miles an hour down a residential street just where his ex-girlfriend happened to be walking."

I didn't know what to say. "But that means—"

"That my mom knew what she was doing. Do you see, Scarlett? My mom, she had it too. She must have. The pull . . . I'm not the only one to feel it."

"What else did your father tell you?"

"That night with the car wasn't the first time," he said. "It had been going on for years, ever since her pregnancy with me. It started off slowly, just with people right around her, in our neighborhood. Domestic violence, mostly. Dad thought there was something wrong with her, some un-diagnosed mental illness. What kind of a pregnant woman gets herself in the middle of a knife fight?" Will's laugh was brusque, humorless.

"He thought it got better after I was born, but later he figured out that she'd just been ignoring the pull. I was a baby—she didn't want to be a hero. She just wanted to be a mom. But the headaches must have been just terrible, Scarlett." He looked at me, his eyes pleading—for what? "I didn't understand any of that," he confessed. "I thought she was lazy. Selfish. She spent so many hours in her room. . . ."

The image of my mother's closed door flashed in my mind. "But you didn't know," I said, trying to comfort him.

Will shrugged. "I was a pretty normal kid, I guess, until

after Mom died. I didn't spend too much time trying to see things from my parents' perspective. I was all wrapped up in my own problems." He laughed again, more gently this time. "Like I had any idea what problems were. Grades, friends, girls . . ." He shook his head. "After Mom died, then I knew about problems. The fishhook worked its way into my brain not long after the accident. Or the not-accident, I guess."

My head was spinning. So Will's mother had experienced the same drive to protect the innocent that compelled Will. I could understand why he was upset to learn this, but what did it have to do with me?

Will seemed to guess my question. "Dad told me all this over winter break," he said. "He wanted me to understand how it could be dangerous for you to be close to me."

"What do you mean?"

"Well, my mom wasn't alone in that car when she crashed. Dad and I were there too."

"I still don't get it," I said.

"Don't you see? My mom was willing to risk her own family to stop that guy from running over that lady—a total stranger! What if I was to do something like that to *you*?"

His face looked tortured, as if he were envisioning me, broken and dead, his fault somehow. "I couldn't bear it, Scarlett, if anything I did hurt you."

"That's ridiculous," I said. "You'd never—"

He cut me off. "I might. Look at who my mother saved—an unborn baby, a mother. She did the right thing. I'm glad she did it. I may not have been old, but I'd already lived thirteen years. If I died, at least I'd have had something. That baby never would have even seen the light of day."

"I'm sure your mother must have known that you'd be okay," I argued. "After all, you said you were sitting behind the passenger seat, right? So your mother must have known that she'd take the brunt of the accident."

Will shrugged. "Maybe. But it was a gamble. I don't want to ever gamble with you."

I felt anger rising in my cheeks. "That's awfully chivalrous of you, Will," I said, "but I'm no princess in an ivory tower, you know. I get to make my own decisions. And I don't want to be protected from you. I want to be *with* you."

Will smiled, and he curled a strand of my hair around his hand. "I want to be with you too," he admitted. "Obviously. I'm here, aren't I? I shouldn't be. But Scarlett, the connection I feel to you . . ."

"You came to me on the trail," I whispered.

His brow furrowed. "That's something I don't understand," he said. "And my father doesn't either. There's no reason I should have known that you were out there in the storm, that you were hurt." He looked at me, his green eyes piercing. "But I did. I was lying there in my bed, and clear as anything I heard you calling my name."

I remembered something. "Your dad said you had a headache that day."

Will nodded. "I didn't know why, at the time. Now, I think maybe I was supposed to go out on the trail and stop the accident. I know it's different than anything I've experienced before—it was an *accident* with the horse, not

296

a crime—but it's the best explanation I can think of." He shrugged.

"Maybe your head hurt because you should have come to me before that," I suggested. "Maybe your heart was trying to tell you to do this." And I leaned across the space that divided us and pressed my lips against his.

"Maybe," he said, his voice husky, when we broke apart at last.

"Your head doesn't hurt now, does it?" I teased, kissing him again.

He shook his head. "Nope. Feels pretty good, actually."

We kissed some more, but my mother must have thought that we'd grown too quiet, because she began whistling in the kitchen and banging the dishes as she unloaded them from the dishwasher.

Will laughed quietly. "Your mother's not big on subtlety, is she?"

"Not one of her stronger traits," I agreed.

"There's something about you, Scarlett," Will murmured, leaning his face into my hair. "Something wonderful."

I rested my face on his shoulder. "You too," I said. I could have said more—so much more—but I didn't want to talk. I just wanted to be there, with Will, and breathe in the scent of him, and be warmed by the press of him against me.

Of course, our silence brought Mom back around again. "Knock, knock," she said before she pushed open the door the rest of the way.

Will and I straightened and separated. The places where my body had been touching his felt the loss of him.

"Well, Will, I think it's best if we let Scarlett get some

297

rest," my mom said. I would have argued, but the set of her mouth convinced me that she wasn't budging.

"Okay, Mrs. Wenderoth." Will seemed to agree that I looked tired. "I'll call you later, okay?" He stood and leaned over to me, placing a kiss on my forehead even though my mother was right there, watching. "Thanks for letting me in to see her, Mrs. Wenderoth."

After he had gone, my mother looked at me appraisingly. "I missed quite a bit, I can see now," she murmured. Then she pulled my blankets up around me. "Get some rest," she said. "We'll have dinner soon."

This time, in my dream, the sand rose more quickly around me. I felt the tiny grains caught in my eyelashes, seeping into my nose, mouth, and eyes. My hand struggled for the surface, finding no purchase in the sand.

At last, something gripped my hand. It felt like a stick or a branch, but with strong fingers that grasped my wrist.

I held on and felt myself emerging from the sand. I gasped for air and wiped sand from my eyes, spat it out of my mouth. Finally, I looked up—and bit back a scream as I stared into the face that peered down at me.

It had the hair of a woman, long and brown, loose curls, and the eyes—green eyes, beautiful and bright—but aside from those two features, the face was just bone, a sun-bleached skull.

With the grace of a dancer, the skeleton woman knelt beside me, her flowered dress pooling at her bone feet. She reached out as if to touch my face, but I recoiled, reanimated by my fear.

The skeleton woman tilted her head as if she was asking me a question. She sat very still, her arm outstretched, her long bone fingers extended toward me.

This was all wrong. The skeleton woman had pulled me from a sandy grave, as if she was the living and I the dried-up, husked-out remains of a finished life. Perfectly still, the skeleton woman waited. By measures, I controlled my breathing, harnessed in my fear. Her wide, unblinking green eyes watched me.

At last I extended my hand and brushed the tips of her bony fingers. They were neither warm nor cold. Somehow my touch was too much, even though I had gripped her hand as she pulled me from the sand; it was as if my touch released her, and I watched in shock as her bones disintegrated right before my eyes. For a moment her form was held together by memory, I guess, of what it had once been—and then a breeze, just the slightest breeze, ruffled her dress, and her body, now no more than sand, rained down on the beach. The breeze became wind, and her dress lifted off into the sky like a kite.

And then I was awake, but I didn't open my eyes. I knew who the skeleton woman was, and I wanted to hold on to my vision a little longer.

Mom made steak for dinner, with her signature mashed potatoes. It was nice to sit at the table with my parents; I listened to them making plans for the spring season. Mom wanted to get new quilts for three of the guest rooms, and Dad made noises about buying a few new koi for the pond.

When we were finished, Dad insisted on doing the dishes.

Mom looked at me with a strange expression—bashful, almost. "We never did open our Christmas presents," she said.

"We can always save them for next year," I answered.

She laughed. "No, no. Come on downstairs. I want to show you something."

I was a little wobbly on my feet as I made my way down the stairs. I grasped the handrail and descended like an old lady, one step with one foot, then bringing my other foot to the same step before taking another.

Mom led me down the porch steps and around the side of the house to the back garden. I saw some sparkling lights, but it took me a moment to figure out what she had done.

There was a little tree just next to the gazebo; Mom had wound lights around the trunk, and then threaded them through the foliage. And she'd hung our Christmas ornaments—all of them—on long ribbons so they dangled at different lengths from the tree's branches.

Our little pile of gifts rested at the base of the tree, and Mom had spread a quilt just near them for us to sit on.

The twinkling lights shone too brightly when seen through my tears. "It's beautiful, Mom," I managed to say. "Thank you."

And as we sat together to open our presents, two months late but still in time, I noticed a new ornament, dangling somewhat lower than the others. It was a family of reindeer—three of them—labeled *John*, *Olivia*, and *Scarlett*. And in the sky above them flew a white bird, with *Ronny* written across his wings.

NINETEEN
Two Roses for Scarlett

One thing I'd learned from Ronny's death was that life moves on regardless. So although I had been absent from school for a whole week, and returned the following Monday feeling that I had been gone a whole lot longer, I wasn't surprised that the high school machine had trudged on just the same without me.

Banners and flyers decorated the hallways and the cafeteria; Valentine's Day was almost upon us, and with it the requisite flower and candy deliveries sponsored by the sports teams. For two dollars you could have a single rose sent to your crush during fourth period; for fifty cents, the girls' basketball team would deliver a box of those disgusting, chalky heart candies to your boyfriend during homeroom.

The hallways were stuffy and hot as the school's antiquated heating system worked overtime in what was shaping up to be one of the coldest winters in our island's history.

The Young Republicans of America club members were giddy over this "proof" that global warming was just a big myth. On the morning of my return, when I walked through the hallway with Lily, the crush of the students threatened to overpower me completely. It seemed I had more friends than I'd been aware of; everyone wanted to hug me and hear firsthand how I'd been knocked silly on the trail, how Will had found me and rescued me in the storm.

"That's so romantic!" gushed Katie Ellis, and she eyed Brandon as if wishing *she* could suffer some mishap so that he would have a chance to save her from it.

I found the whole thing embarrassing. I mean, needing to be rescued means that you've screwed up pretty bad; I'd miscalculated Traveler and had eschewed a helmet, so it felt like I'd gotten what I deserved. But when I tried to explain this, no one seemed to want to hear it. They just wanted to know if Will had given me mouth-to-mouth.

"Just make up something juicy," Lily encouraged. She didn't know that I wouldn't have to fabricate anything; Will's visit to my house had been sexy enough to satisfy any of our classmates.

I hadn't shared with Lily the details of Will's visit earlier that week. Usually, Lily and I told each other everything. But when she asked about Will, all I said was "We're back together." And though she'd screwed up her mouth kind of funny, she didn't press me for details.

I was glad; it seemed that my time with Will was too precious to risk tarnishing by speaking of it with Lily, or anyone else. My mom had tried to get me to talk about Will too, but all I said to her was "He and I get each other, Mom." I could tell she wasn't satisfied, but I guess the set of my chin was stubborn enough that she knew that was all she was going to get.

Even Andy approached me. He came up to me at the end of lunch when Will and I were walking back in together after eating under our tree. It was cold out there, but it was worth the privacy.

When Andy came up to me, I felt Will's fingers tighten their grip on my hand. I squeezed his fingers in return, letting him know that I was okay, that he should calm down.

"Hey, Scarlett," Andy said, completely ignoring Will.

I raised an eyebrow.

He continued, "Umm . . . I just wanted to say, Scar, I'm glad you're okay. I heard about your accident. I would have been pretty bummed if you'd have been hurt real bad."

"Thanks, Andy," I said, my voice even. "You know, Will found me out there."

Andy's eyes shifted over to Will, then down to our interlaced fingers. "Yeah," he said. "I heard." He cleared his throat. "Anyway, I'm glad you're okay." He seemed to grow bolder. "And, you know, if you ever want to . . . hang out or anything, you have my number." He grinned at me, and I felt his eyes take their time roaming across my body before he turned away. "See you later, Scarlett," he called over his shoulder.

I could feel Will bristling beside me. "Lot of nerve," he murmured through clenched teeth.

I laughed a little. "Will Cohen," I teased, "are you jealous?"

"Not really jealous so much as enraged. What gives that creep the idea that he can talk to you?"

The ferocity of his response surprised me. "Will," I said, "it's okay. He only wanted to say hi."

"The only thing that guy should be saying to you is 'I'm sorry,'" Will seethed. "Short of that, he should keep his distance."

I looked more closely at Will. The tendons on his neck were standing out, and his whole body seemed to be leaning forward, as if he were pushed from behind by a gale I could not feel.

I turned to him and pressed my forehead against his chest. "Calm down, Will," I whispered. "It's okay."

By degrees, Will relaxed his body. It seemed purposeful, as if it took great effort, but slowly he reined in the anger, the aggression that looked as if it might overtake him.

The late bell rang, startling us. "We'd better go," I murmured, and Will nodded.

Thursday was Valentine's Day. Right after lunch I had Chemistry. The boys' soccer team pushed and shoved their way into the classroom five minutes after the bell, each holding one or two roses to distribute.

Mr. Graham rolled his eyes and pulled off his glasses, pinching his nose between his fingers as he gave up on maintaining control over the class. "Okay, guys," he said. "Just try to make it quick."

They spread around the classroom, reading the names on the little tags affixed to each flower. Brandon Becker, who was on the soccer team, laid two roses across my desk. "Pretty popular, Scarlett," he teased.

Each rose was long-stemmed, with red petals still wrapped in tight buds. Affixed to each stem was a tag. On the front of each tag was my name written in two different scripts, each of which I knew very well.

The first was from Will. I smiled and smelled the rose before reading the note on the back of its tag—*Be mine*, it read simply. I already was.

The next gave me pause. It was addressed in Andy's hand. After a moment, I flipped its tag over and read what it said—*I'm no quitter*.

I knew what his words meant, even before I registered the reddened, teary eyes of Kaitlyn Meyers across the room, whose desk was bare. But I wasn't about to let Andy's ridiculous competitive machismo spoil my thrill over Will's rose.

I knew I wasn't a prize to be won. Andy could suffer under his own ridiculous delusions if he wanted to.

Will was waiting for me outside of Drama class. I walked right up to him, roses in my hand, and wound my arms around his neck. "Thanks for the rose," I said. "I'd love to be your Valentine."

Our lips touched in the lightest of kisses, but still I was shocked by the force of my body's response to him.

"Who's the other flower from?" Will asked as we walked into the classroom.

Before I could answer—before I had time to dissect why, exactly, Will's question made me nervous—Connell called out from his seat at the back of the class, "Hey, Big Red, I guess the bigger rose is from Andy, right? The Jew gave you the cheap one?" followed by his trademark guffaw.

The muscles of Will's jaw tightened, though the rest of him stayed unreadable. With the politest "May I?" he withdrew the rose with Andy's tag on it from my hand, then weaved his way through the rows of desks to Connell's seat.

Connell was a big guy, bigger than Will, but for some reason he still looked nervous as Will approached. Will didn't stop until he was right up in Connell's face; then, he held the rose over Connell's desk and slowly, deliberately, peeled the red petals, one by one, from the stem, until all that was left was the naked, sad heart of the flower surrounded by the short spiky green leaves that encircled it. Each petal he dropped onto Connell's desk.

The rest of the class watched silently. Even Mrs. B was watching, the stack of papers that she'd been looking through forgotten.

When the last petal had drifted down to the desk, Will said, "Tell Andy that next time I won't stop with just the flower."

He didn't wait for a response, and he didn't look at my face as he made his way past me, out the door, and down the hallway.

I was stunned.

Around me, the students began to talk in whispers, and I could tell from Connell's stormy expression that this wasn't over, not as far as he was concerned. Connell was like a bulldog—a big, gaping mouth that looked like a smile, but when he got his teeth into something, he wouldn't let it go, shaking it until it was limp in his jaw.

"All right, everyone, show's over," Mrs. B called, clapping her hands.

I fell into my seat, eyes focused on Mrs. B but oblivious to whatever she was saying. All I could picture was Will, his jaw tight, as he peeled petal after petal from the rose.

When Will called me that afternoon, I didn't answer the phone. He didn't leave a message, and he didn't call again. I could feel him out there, the pull of him from the other side of the island. I knew he was miserable. But what he'd done wasn't okay. As the evening wore on and my initial shock began to fade, I found myself growing angrier and angrier.

That had been *my* rose, regardless of who had given it to me, regardless of how irritating Will might find it that Andy had sent it to me. Will had no right to take it from me and destroy it.

"I think it's positively romantic," Lily gushed the next morning while we walked to school. "I mean, it proves he's willing to stand up for you, right?"

"Standing up for me is fine," I argued, "but I didn't *need* any standing up for. I mean, it wasn't like the rose was about to bite my hand or anything."

"The rose was a *symbol*, Scarlett," Lily said, as if I were an idiot.

"I get it," I said. "But the rose was *mine*."

Lily seemed to think that this was a technicality. After all, Will's note had read *Be Mine* . . . so I was Will's, right? In a way, she argued, the rose was actually his too.

This didn't sit right with me. Not by a long shot. "'Be Mine' doesn't mean 'Be my property,' Lil," I argued. "It means 'Be my Valentine.' Those are very different things." I could understand Will losing his temper with Connell. After all, Connell had consistently been a dick to him since the beginning of the year. But destroying my rose? It felt to me that Will had crossed a line.

Lily shrugged. "All I know is, if a guy did that for me, I'd be all over him."

For Lily, things were pretty straightforward. Any attention equaled good attention.

"If I were you—" She stopped abruptly. There was Will, leaning against the school's main building as he had been the first day of school, still smolderingly handsome. Today he was wearing his jeans and a thin V-neck sweater to keep away the chill; that day in September he'd worn a T-shirt.

I remembered what he'd been wearing on the first day of school. How lame was that?

"There he is," Lily hissed at me, as if I didn't see him. "What are you going to say?"

"Nothing," I answered. "He owes me an apology."

"For defending your honor?" Lily sounded horrified.

"My honor wasn't threatened, Lily . . . not this time, anyway."

Lily looked prepared to argue her case further, but Will pushed off from the wall and crossed the courtyard with the smooth, easy grace that made my stomach leap in spite of my anger.

"Hi, Scarlett. Hey, Lily." There were dark smudges under his eyes, as if he hadn't slept. "Do you mind if I talk to Scarlett privately, Lil? That is, if that's okay with you, Scarlett?"

I shrugged as if I didn't care, but of course I did.

"I'll see you later, Scar," Lily said, and as she walked away she gestured furiously behind Will's back, kissing the back of her hand to show me that I needed to forgive him.

"She's still back there, isn't she?" Will asked. I could tell Lily's antics amused him, in spite of everything else.

"Yep."

"Listen, Scarlett, about yesterday . . ." Will's eyes were pleading. "I don't know what came over me. I was totally out of line."

"Completely."

"I was a jerk. I'm so sorry."

"You should be," I said, but I was softening.

"I am." He stepped closer, putting his hands on my arms.

In spite of my lingering anger, I warmed to his touch. I sighed. "You know, Will, I thought you were better than that."

"I am! I mean, I thought I was too. I don't know, Scarlett. I just . . . reacted." He looked disturbed, as if his own actions confused him.

"Okay, Will," I said. "I forgive you. Just don't make a habit of it, all right?"

His smile was reward enough. "Absolutely. Of course not. I swear."

He took another step closer and we kissed. From her vantage point on the stairs, Lily clapped and hooted at us.

"Oh, Lily," Will murmured, stepping back from me.

"You should be thanking her," I told him. "She argued eloquently for you."

"In that case . . ." As we walked up the steps toward class, Will smiled at Lily. "Thanks, Lil," he said, dropping his arm across my shoulders.

"Any time," she said.

I had a surprise for Will that Sunday. I had him borrow his dad's Jeep and meet me at the stable. The day was beautiful—bright blue sky, crisp air. When Will pulled into the yard, I had two horses saddled and ready to go.

Delilah was wearing my usual English saddle, and I'd tacked up Bojangles in the heavy Western saddle that sat, dusty and largely unused, in the back of the tack room. Riding Bojangles was kind of like riding a couch, so I figured Will would be fine on him.

As Will crossed the yard toward where I waited with the horses at the cross-ties, I could see that he was nervous.

"Umm . . . we going somewhere, Scarlett?"

"Yep," I said, grinning. "Let's find you a helmet that fits."

As I tried various helmets on his head, Will said, "You know, Scarlett, I've never ridden a horse before."

It was sweet to see him so nervous. I tried to make him feel better; I said, "I'm really the one who should be nervous. After all, I haven't been on a horse since I was thrown."

"*Are* you nervous?"

"Nope." The fourth helmet was a good fit. I snapped the strap under Will's chin. "Ready to ride," I told him.

True to my promise to my dad, I pulled on my own helmet before leading Bojangles to the mounting block. "Just climb up those steps," I directed, leading Bojangles in front of them.

Will looked about to protest, but instead he climbed the steps.

"Slide your right leg across the saddle, and hold on to the reins," I said. "After his first few bucks, he'll calm right down."

The look on Will's face made me burst into laughter. "I'm kidding," I reassured him. "I'm pretty sure Bojangles hasn't bucked in the last decade or so."

This seemed to reassure Will some, because he did as I'd directed and slid atop Bojangles, gripping the saddle horn in one hand and his reins in the other.

I adjusted his stirrups, then led him into the arena. "So, Bojangles 'neck reins,'" I told him. "To go left, just press the rein against the right side of his neck; to go right, press the rein against the left side of his neck. And to stop, pull back and say 'Whoa.'"

"People actually say 'whoa'? I thought that was just something they said in the movies."

"Don't be a smart-ass. Just try it. And squeeze him with your heels to get him to walk forward."

Will did as I ordered, nudging Bojangles forward, then turning right, then left, then calling out a mighty "whoa" and pulling Bojangles to a stop.

"See?" I said. "You're a natural. Just walk around some more while I get Delilah."

Will looked pretty pleased with himself, maneuvering the horse around the arena, but after I'd mounted Delilah and we'd headed out on the trail, he looked a little less certain.

"You sure this horse won't bolt?"

"Nah, you're pretty safe with Bojangles," I assured him.

We rode in silence for a while, Bojangles following amiably behind Delilah. It was nice, combining two of my favorite things—riding and being with Will. I was content to keep Delilah to a walk today; despite my bravado with Will, I was a little nervous about being on a horse again, even my mare.

After we'd been riding for about twenty minutes, Will said, "You know, my mom would have really liked this."

My dream came back to me—the skeleton woman pulling me from the sand, then turning to dust in front of my eyes.

"Tell me about her."

"Well, she was funny," Will began. "Really funny. She was always coming up with these ridiculous puns, and she loved to play practical jokes. There was this one time when I was just a baby—my dad told me about it—when he came home from work and she was holding me in her arms, rocking me, you know, all wrapped up in a baby blanket, and then she asked my dad to hold me . . . only it wasn't *me* in the blanket, it was a chicken—plucked and headless, ready for the oven—and when Dad peeled back the blanket and said, 'Where's the baby?', she freaked out and ran for the oven, like she'd mixed us up, you know? Of course I was sleeping in my crib the whole time. Dad didn't know whether to laugh or have my mom committed."

I laughed, and Will laughed too, but I could tell he was thinking about something. After a few more minutes, he continued. "Actually, Dad told me that having her committed was always sort of on his mind. He wasn't sure why she had these compulsions to go to all these dangerous places, interfere where she didn't belong in other people's problems. And, of course, she wasn't *always* like that. It wasn't until she got pregnant with me that it started for her."

Though he rode right next to me, he was far away, lost in his thought.

"It's strange how the pulling didn't start for me until after Mom died," he said at last. "Almost as if her abilities passed to me, like an inheritance."

"Maybe . . . ," I said. "But I think it's really strange how she didn't feel pulled to crimes *until* she got pregnant with you."

Will nodded. "Yeah. Maybe I gave her a virus when she got pregnant . . . like I was an infection."

I shook my head. "You're not an infection, Will. But it is like the two of you shared something important, something special."

We rode a while longer, and then Will asked, "What about Ronny? Do you think your brother would have liked me?"

I laughed. "Probably not, if he knew how I feel about you. Ronny wasn't a big fan of me being with boys."

"How *do* you feel about me, Scarlett?" He grinned at me.

"I'm crazy about you," I admitted. "You drive me crazy."

Will whistled, long and low. "Then I'm a lucky guy," he said.

I felt myself blushing. To change the subject, I said, "Other than how I feel about you, Ronny would have liked you a lot. He was pretty easygoing. He liked to hang out with his friends, and he loved to play soccer, but he was a reader like you. I'll bet you two would have found a lot to talk about."

"It would have been nice to know him."

The sky was bright above our heads. It felt good to talk to someone about Ronny. This was the first time I'd really managed to have a conversation of any substantial length about him since he'd died. I could tell Will felt the same way about his mom; after a few minutes he said, "You know, my mom was always trying to get me and Dad out of the house more, out into nature. I've spent more time hiking in the last six months than in my whole life back east. She'd be happy seeing me here, riding with you."

I remembered the skeleton woman from my dream; again I felt the touch of her bone hand. I thought too of Ronny. It seemed as though he was close, yet drifting softly away . . . and maybe this was okay. Maybe I could let him go. Maybe I could let him turn to dust. The wide world around me—the trail, the trees, the grass, the open sky—seemed to shimmer a little, or shift, and I felt my heart softening, relaxing, letting go. Next to me, Will seemed to feel it too, and when he looked across at me, his smile was so dear, so open and pure, that I could almost hear its song.

We reached the top of a hill and stopped the horses,

looking out onto the open ocean together. Each wave crested, beautiful in its moment, brilliant in its singularity, before it broke, rejoining the ocean, becoming part of the whole again. The waves weren't lost . . . they were still there. We just couldn't see them anymore.

TWENTY

Break a Leg

The night before the play, Will invited me over for dinner. He drove the Jeep to collect me from my side of the island, and then took me back to his home.

Martin was there. When he heard us getting out of the Jeep, he came outside to greet us. "Ah, Scarlett returns," he said, and he embraced me. He seemed genuinely glad to see me, but I was still kind of nervous. The last time I'd seen him, he hadn't seemed to think too much of my relationship with his son.

He must have read the apprehension on my face, because he said, "I'm truly glad you're here, Scarlett. Not only because you are special to my son, but also because I like having you around." And then he patted my shoulder, as if everything that had passed between us before was completely dissolved now, and he disappeared back into his study.

Quietly, I wondered what had brought about his change

of heart. My accident, perhaps? Or the undeniable fact that Will looked so happy and well? I got the feeling that Martin wanted more than anything to keep his son healthy, and after that, happy. If it seemed to him that I was a detriment to those goals, then it was better if I was not around. If, on the other hand, I helped Will to be healthy and happy, then I was welcome.

This seemed a pretty cynical way to view Martin, that he was interested in me only as a means to his ends, but it struck me as true. Here was a man who had abandoned his home and career, moving his son across the country to an island where he thought he could be kept safe. How upset Martin must have been when it had all seemed useless, when even on this island Will had been pursued by his headaches and his compulsions.

I followed Will into the kitchen, which was busy with the sights and smells of his cooking. He had roasted meat for tacos, and he sat me down in front of a pile of tomatoes and onions to chop up for salsa.

Quoting from our play, he said, full of bluster, "You can't possibly ask me to go without having some dinner. It's absurd. I never go without my dinner. No one ever does, except vegetarians and people like that." With a flourish and a bow, he handed me a chopping knife.

"Eloquently said."

"Thank you." He pulled up a stool across from me and set to work dismantling avocados: cutting them open, splitting them in two, discarding the pit, and spooning out the soft green flesh.

"You have the hands of a surgeon," I said.

"I've thought about a career in medicine," Will said. "But I'm also interested in this other major—Peace Studies."

A silence fell across us, not an entirely comfortable one. Will was a year ahead of me in school—a senior. He'd be leaving in the fall for college. It seemed absurd to talk about this, as our relationship was still so fresh, but somehow it seemed that we'd known each other for a very long time . . . or so deeply that our hearts spoke the same language.

I knew he'd applied to universities all over the country. There was time, still, before he'd hear back from them. I didn't intend to think too hard about what the future would bring.

We lost ourselves in preparing the salsa and the guacamole. Will had bragged that his tacos were absolutely amazing. I figured they'd better be, what with all the chopping it took to prepare them.

Not that I really minded. I was happy to be there, in the Cohens' little cottage.

"Are you nervous about tomorrow night?" Will asked.

"Sort of," I admitted. "I've never done a kissing scene in front of an audience before."

Will lay down his knife and came around to my side of the table. "Maybe we should practice some more."

But just as his lips were about to connect with mine, we heard Martin whistling as he crossed the front room on his way into the kitchen.

Will murmured something that sounded like a curse, sinking back onto his stool and picking up his knife again just before Martin entered the kitchen.

I wasn't as smooth as Will; I couldn't hide the flush on my cheeks as I bent over the tomatoes, chopping furiously. I felt Martin looking at me, but he said nothing as he poured himself a glass of iced tea from the pitcher in the refrigerator. He took a long sip, then asked, "So, son, what time is dinner?"

"Just gotta fry up the tortillas," Will said, standing up and stretching as if he'd been in his seat the whole time. I didn't think Martin was fooled, though.

Will retrieved the cooking oil from a cabinet near the stove and poured a long stream of it into a frying pan. A stack of white corn tortillas rested on a plate nearby.

Martin wandered back toward his study. I had finished chopping everything Will had set in front of me, and I combined it all in a large bowl and mixed it together. Then I settled in to watch Will fry the tortillas.

He had a system. After tying on an apron, he got his fingers wet in the sink, then flicked drops of water into the oil to see if it was hot enough. When it sizzled and popped, he lowered the first tortilla into it with prongs. After a few seconds, he flipped the tortilla over and folded it in half all in one motion, then flipped it again before transferring it to a paper towel–lined plate and sprinkling it with sea salt.

"Are you good at everything?" I asked.

He grinned. "Not everything," he admitted. "I've been known to put pleasure ahead of responsibility—that's what my dad says, anyway."

"That seems hard to believe," I said. "You seem pretty responsible to me."

He flipped the last of the tortillas onto the paper towels. "I guess I am more so now than when I was a kid. But when

I wasn't quite thirteen, I threw a fit to have my bar mitzvah scheduled a couple of weeks early so I could still make the big Boy Scouts campout that conflicted with it."

I must have looked confused, because Will continued, "You're not supposed to have a bar mitzvah until you're thirteen. But the weekend of my thirteenth birthday was the campout, so I petitioned my rabbi to let me do my ceremony early. You know, so I wouldn't miss the trip."

"That sounds like a pretty good quality, the ability to argue your case," I said.

He shrugged and placed the tortillas on the table. "Depends on how you look at it, I guess. My rabbi was pretty cool about it . . . we aren't Orthodox or anything . . . but my dad was annoyed. He's never been a real big fan of rule-breaking."

"Well, if it was okay with the rabbi . . ."

"Anyway, it really doesn't matter when the ceremony is. A boy isn't considered a bar mitzvah—a full man, a member of the Jewish community—until he actually turns thirteen. The ceremony is just a rite of passage."

"So you got to do the ceremony and go on the campout," I said. "Sounds like a pretty good solution to me. The best of both worlds."

Will shook his head. "No, I didn't go on the campout. Just before I was supposed to leave—the day before my birthday, actually—we got in the car crash. I spent my thirteenth birthday mourning my mother."

It felt to me like all the air had been sucked out of the room. There was a thought coming to me, but just barely; if

I sat very still, I had the feeling that I would come up with something.

"Scarlett?" Will asked.

I held up my hand to quiet him and closed my eyes. "Will," I said, slowly, after a moment. "Tell me more about bar mitzvah."

"What do you want to know?" He poured chips from a bag into a bowl, then sat down across from me and dug one into the guacamole.

"How does it work, exactly? Becoming a man?"

"Pretty straightforward, I guess. When a boy is thirteen years old, he's a man. Bam. End of story. And as a man, he has rights—he gets to be involved in decisions at temple, he can marry"—Will wagged his eyebrows at me—"but he's got responsibilities, too."

"Like what?"

"Well, when he's just a kid—a boy—it's his parents' responsibility to make sure that the kid follows Jewish law. It's kind of like his parents are holding his jacket for him. When he turns thirteen, his parents help him into his jacket, and he'll wear it for the rest of his life. He bears his own responsibility as part of the community, and he must uphold Jewish law, traditions, and ethics."

"So until thirteen, the parents sort of safeguard the boy's role? And then it's all on him?"

"Uh-huh."

He kept eating chips, as if nothing had changed. Was it possible that he really didn't see what I saw?

"Will," I said. "I don't think you infected your mother.

I don't even think you shared something with her. I think she held your abilities for you, like a jacket, until you were old enough to take them on for yourself. Until you turned thirteen."

Will stopped chewing. He held a chip with a bite taken out of it, and after a moment he lowered it to the tablecloth.

"I was thinking about it backwards," he murmured, but he wasn't talking to me. He was talking to himself. "I thought that she handed me her abilities after she died, but I had it all wrong." He was silent, staring off into space, but then his gaze snapped back to me. It was fevered, intense. It scared me. "But you must be right. They would have transferred to me, if she would have lived, when I turned thirteen. Maybe she would have been okay, free—if only she had lived one more day."

I swallowed hard; this wasn't where I had intended this talk to go.

"It's not your fault she died, Will," I whispered.

"Of course it is." His voice was harsh. "You must be right. She was holding my curse, bearing its weight until I was old enough to take it from her. But it was too much. It crushed her."

I wanted to say something to comfort him, but I had no words.

When Martin entered the kitchen, it was clear that he'd heard everything we'd said. He walked over and placed his hand on Will's shoulder, but Will shrugged it off and stood. The feet of his chair screeched as they slid across the floor.

"I'm not so hungry," he murmured.

He untied his apron and dropped it on a chair, then fled

the room as if pursued—which, perhaps, he was—by memories, by theories that I had foisted upon him.

"Martin, I'm so sorry," I said. Martin sighed heavily, dropping into the chair where Will had sat.

"It's not your fault, Scarlett. He would have found out eventually."

"So . . . you knew? But why didn't you tell him yourself?"

Martin looked at me pointedly. "Did you see how he took it?"

"Okay. But the truth's got to be better than a lie, hasn't it?"

"Not always, Scarlett."

There was a feast in front of us—salsa, guacamole, beans, fried tortillas, meat—but neither of us reached for any of it.

"What does it mean, Martin?"

"I'm still trying to learn," he confessed. "But I'll tell you what I know. And Will should hear, also. The time for keeping secrets has ended."

He left the kitchen. I imagined Will in his bedroom, and his father entering; I wondered what words they would say. Would Will feel the need to apologize, as if he was to blame for his mother's death? Would Martin be able to convince him that he wasn't culpable, that none of this was Will's fault?

They were gone for a long time, and when they came back, Will's eyes were red and Martin's arm was draped across his shoulders. Will smiled at me, a tired smile, and then he sat at the table. This time, he chose a seat next to me, and he held my hand, squeezed it.

"No reason for this good food to go to waste," Martin

said, and he passed around the tortillas, helped himself to the meat, and encouraged us to do the same.

"No prayer?" Will asked when Martin ripped into his taco.

"Not tonight," Martin answered. "I tire of ritual."

So we ate, and it was as if we had tacitly agreed to finish our meal before we talked. Martin ate leisurely, as if to forestall discussion, but at last he had to push away his plate.

"Well done, son," he said. "What was that spice you added to the meat?"

"Cumin," said Will.

"Ah, cumin," mused Martin.

He was quiet for a moment, contemplating the fine attributes of cumin, I guess, and then at last he said, "Son, when a man and a woman decide to have a child, they accept responsibility for whatever may happen as a result of that choice. If the child is born with a disability, or if the child is sickly, or becomes injured in some way, the parents accept responsibility for that with open and happy hearts."

"So whatever is wrong with me is a sickness, is that what you're saying?"

Martin held up his hand. "Let me finish."

Will looked as though he was going to say something else, to argue, but under the table I rested my hand on his knee.

Martin continued. "And the parents, too, they accept whatever gifts the child might bring to the family. If he is a gifted musician, the parents must foster that gift. If he has a deep interest in the sea, the parents must try to take him to the sea. Of course, the parents are proud of their child, whatever his weaknesses, whatever his gifts. But I think your mother, Will, was especially proud of you. She knew that you were different . . . special. And it was her honor to hold your talents for you until you came of age."

"How do you know? Did she tell you that?"

"Not exactly. She never spoke of it to me. She did her best to hide what troubled her, so as not to worry me. That was one of your mother's few flaws . . . her irrational desire to spare me from anything she thought might hurt me." He regarded Will shrewdly. "I guess she and I share that weakness," he admitted. "Years ago, I should have told you what Scarlett just discovered. I didn't know it myself, until after your mother died and I discovered a journal she had kept. She wrote about you, Will, about how she had felt when pregnant with you . . . *As if I am carrying something great and precious*, she wrote. I'll give you the journal. It should be yours."

"I'd like that." Will's eyes were on the table, his voice barely more than a whisper.

And then Martin continued. "After your mother died, it was just days until you had your first episode. I didn't put the pieces together until much later, when you finally confided to me what was happening to you, and even then I was too consumed with my grief to think rationally. I didn't put it together—your mother's death, your turning thirteen, your seemingly inherited need to go to these dangerous places, do these impossible things. And I watched it grow in you, Will, as you got older. I could tell the radius of your sensitivity was growing. It got to be that a week wouldn't pass without you appearing for breakfast or showing up late in the evening with that look in your eyes—either the pain of a headache that mirrored the headaches your mother used to get, or the half-wild look of someone who's done something far too risky. I didn't know which look to dread more. All I knew was that I had to get you out of there. So here we are, on an island. And you still manage to find trouble."

He smiled at me to soften the impact of his words, but still they stung. He thought I was trouble.

"But what does any of this have to do with the bar mitzvah?" I asked. "And why Will?"

"I've spent many hours wondering these things," Martin admitted. "Do you know, Scarlett, what a mitzvah is?"

I shook my head.

"A good deed, basically," said Will.

"That definition will do, for our purposes," said Martin. "You see, Scarlett, once a boy has become a man, in the Jewish culture he becomes responsible for performing mitzvahs—good deeds—both within the community and in the greater world. Will's particular gift—"

"Or curse," Will interrupted.

Martin shrugged. "Semantics. Either way, gift or curse, Will's abilities enable him to perform mitzvahs above and beyond the range of a normal person. And at thirteen, since he *can* perform these mitzvahs, it becomes his duty to do so."

"But you moved him out here, to the middle of nowhere," I argued. "Isn't that preventing him from doing his duty, as you called it?"

Martin smiled slyly. "Perhaps I've found a loophole."

"But why Will?"

"That's a question we all ask about our lots in life, isn't it, Scarlett? 'Why me?' is a question each of us raises to the sky many times in our lives. Certainly, I've been guilty of asking it myself."

"So you don't know?"

Martin shrugged. "I don't know for sure. I have my theories, of course. I have long thought, as you discovered in your own reading, that Will is one of the *Tzaddikim* and that he possesses *Ruach HaKodesh*, that state of the soul that allows him to see, or feel, some aspects of what is yet to come. Understanding the implications of this, and trying to discover ways to keep him safe, has been my work while we're here in self-imposed exile on this island of yours. I'm attempting to understand why Will has the gift—or curse—that is uniquely his."

"And?" My one-word question sounded rude, but I wanted Martin to show all his cards. I had the feeling he still knew more than he was telling us.

Martin looked distinctly annoyed. I pressed on anyway. "I mean, is it a genetic abnormality? Like being born left-handed?"

"Hardly," Martin scoffed. He looked at us appraisingly before continuing. "There are some among us," he said at last, "who believe that we do not come to this earth just once, but many times, until we have manifested six hundred and thirteen mitzvahs. I theorize that Will has been here before. His is an old soul; I think he can see the future because as he's visited and revisited this place, his soul has grown richer and more closely attuned to *Ein Sof*—the Infinite."

I looked at Will. His expression was difficult to decipher. But I knew how I felt: dubious. "Wait a minute," I said. "*Ein Sof* . . . is that another name for God?"

"It is."

Finally, Will spoke. "I've been here before?"

Martin looked worried. "It's just a theory, son."

But then Will grinned. "Does that mean that I'm older than you? I guess that's the end of my curfew, then, huh?"

Martin's face relaxed into a smile, and his rich laughter filled the kitchen. "Like I said, just a theory. Too soon to go making any major changes."

But Will's countenance had shifted. His face seemed brighter, more hopeful.

Martin looked at the clock. It was after nine o'clock. "It's late," he said, "and tomorrow is your big night. Will, why don't you leave the dishes to me? Drive Scarlett home so she doesn't look too tired onstage."

"Let me get my coat," Will said, and he headed back toward his bedroom.

"Martin," I said. "There's something else I've been meaning to ask you. You're a rabbi. . . ."

"Not so much these days," he qualified.

"Okay," I continued, "but I read something in one of the books I've been studying about nightmares, and rabbis . . ."

"The *Hatavat Halom?*" he asked. "The rite to transform disturbing dreams into something pleasant?"

"How did you know?"

He smiled. "You're not the first to want me to fix a bad dream," he said. "It was a request I got more than once when I led a congregation."

"So it works?" I felt hopeful. "Because I keep having this dream, only it changes, and it's always really disturbing."

"I don't know if it works," Martin admitted. "I don't know what I believe anymore. But this is what I suggest—and it's connected to the idea of *Hatavat Halom*—the next time you have the nightmare, try not to be afraid. Let your subconscious tell you what it wants you to know. You have the power, Scarlett, all on your own, to make your dream a good one."

Opening night was a madhouse. Lily came backstage with me to help me with my costume and hair. I got to wear this fantastic gown made of pink lace with a pinched waist and a fabulous bustle. Lily and I curled and piled my hair on top of my head, using about three hundred pins to hold it in place. Then Lily turned my back to the mirror and took it upon herself to do my makeup. Jane Maple was the official makeup artist for the show, but Lily gave her one of her patented Lily looks and Jane left us to our own devices.

Across from me, Will was buttoning his coat. He looked absolutely gorgeous: gray wool trousers, an evening jacket with tails, a silver silk cravat. Shiny black wingtips and his hair arranged into artful, deliberate curls completed his nineteenth-century look.

He caught me looking at him and dropped me a wink. Had I actually been a socialite named Cecily Cardew, I absolutely would have fallen for him. After all, here I was in the twenty-first century, and I was gone, gone, gone on Will Cohen.

The footlights were blinding at the beginning of the

second act, when I appeared onstage for the first time. I blinked against them, trying to forget that practically the entire town, including all my friends and my parents, was out there on the other side of those lights . . . and then I spoke my first line in my best British accent—"But I don't like German. It isn't at all a becoming language. I know perfectly well that I look quite plain after my German lesson."

And then my jitters left me, and I became Cecily, and I flirted shamelessly with Will—Algernon—and I lost myself in his words, his embrace, his kiss.

"I hope, Cecily, I shall not offend you if I state quite frankly and openly that you seem to me to be in every way the visible personification of absolute perfection."

I was not offended in the slightest.

"Cecily, ever since I first looked upon your wonderful and incomparable beauty, I have dared to love you wildly, passionately, devotedly, hopelessly."

This was fine with me.

And when he took me into his arms, slanting his mouth across mine, it was as if we were all alone far, far from the stage, and the hoots and hollers from the audience might as well have come from owls and jackals. I threw my arms around his neck and kissed him deeply, and I never wanted to stop.

The audience gave us a standing ovation, and Will and I got to step forward from the line of actors and take a special bow. After the curtain dropped for the final time, Mrs. B was beside herself with pleasure.

"Absolutely, without a doubt, the finest production our

school has put on," she gushed. "Will, where were you last year when we were doing *My Fair Lady*? All right, everyone, go get out of costumes. Cast party at the Hendersons' café in half an hour. Chop, chop, everyone! Well done!"

Before I changed, I slipped outside to say hi to my parents. They were waiting for me with a bouquet. I noticed they were holding hands.

"Oh, Scarlett, that was just so much fun to watch." My mom hugged me and kissed my cheek. "And honey, you look just beautiful in that dress, but don't you think you could pull it up a little in the front?" She pinched the bodice of my dress and attempted to hike it up.

"Too late for that, Mom," I said, swatting her hand away. "Play's over."

My dad looked a little bashful, seeing me all made-up and fancy, I guess, and he said, as he had on the night of the winter dance, "You look great, Scar."

"Thanks, Daddy."

I explained to them about the cast party and promised to be home before midnight. They didn't seem too worried about curfew; as they walked away, hand in hand, it occurred to me that they might be pleased to have the house to themselves. They took my flowers with them to put into water for me back home.

I grabbed the handle of the stage door and tried to pull it open so I could go inside and change, but it was locked.

"Damn," I murmured, and then I slammed my palm against it a few times, yelling, "Hello? Anybody there? I'm locked out. . . ."

"Need some help, Scarlett?"

331

I turned around slowly, arranging the features of my face in practiced casualness. "Hey, Andy," I said. "No, I'm okay. I just need to go around to the main entrance. I got locked out."

He stepped in closer to me. I smelled beer on his breath as he dipped his face down close to mine, snaking his arms around my waist. "I don't think you need to go anywhere just yet," he said.

I shoved against his chest, hard. "Step off, Andy." My voice was strong. "I'm not interested."

He looked offended, but he took a half step back. "Tell me, Scar, what does Will have that I haven't got?"

I had a list of attributes I could have rattled off—sincerity, patience, thoughtfulness, gentleness—but before I could say a word, the stage door slammed open and Will appeared, still dressed in his suit, almost too beautiful to look at, his face contorted in anger.

He didn't stop to listen to reason—"I've got it under control, Will, it's okay"—but slammed into Andy's chest full force, knocking him to the asphalt and pounding him again and again.

Andy tried to punch back at first, but Will's anger fueled his strength, and finally Andy gave up trying to fight, curling into a ball and covering his face with his hands.

"Will, stop it, stop it!" I screamed, but he was deaf to my cries. At last, three more guys from the play, including Mr. Steiner, who'd played the Reverend, spilled out of the theater. It took all three of them to peel Will off of Andy, and even with his arms pulled behind his back, he continued to try to throw punches.

Will's suit was rumpled and dirty, spattered with blood, and the skin on the knuckles of his right hand was busted open. His face was contorted with anger, with pain, as Mr. Steiner and the boys hauled him away, back into the theater.

A few girls who had followed the guys out of the theater fell into a semicircle around Andy, helping him to sit up, to stand.

He touched the back of his hand to his lip and looked at the blood. "Hell of a guy you've got there, Scarlett," he said. Then he limped away, shrugging off any help from the girls. Finally, I stood there alone, too shocked to move, shivering in my thin costume.

All the elegance, all the refinement and beauty in the world . . . was it nothing more than a mask, a fragile overlay that hid our true nature?

TWENTY-ONE

Field Trip

I found my way back through the theater and into the changing room. It was abandoned now; costumes lay across the backs of chairs, open cases of makeup and hair supplies cluttered the countertops.

I managed to unfasten the buttons down the back of my dress and I let it fall to the floor. I found my sweatshirt, jeans, and tennis shoes. Pulling on my sweatshirt, I dislodged several hairpins. I sat in one of the makeup stations and pulled out the rest of the pins. It took forever; every time I thought I'd removed the last one, I found another. When they were finally all out, I pulled a makeup wipe out of a little plastic case on the counter. I rubbed it across my mouth, a streak of red lipstick smearing my cheek, reminding me of Andy's face.

Finally I was myself again: hair pulled back into a low, messy bun; face bare. I blinked at my reflection. *It wasn't long ago*, I thought, *that I couldn't stand to look at myself in the mirror.*

I hung my dress on the rack, then gathered up the other costumes and hung them up as well. Then there was nothing else for me to do, so I switched off the light and left the theater.

I didn't want to go to the café for the postperformance celebration, so I headed home instead. As I turned onto my street, though, I remembered the look on my parents' faces; I didn't much feel like walking in on their private party.

I felt paralyzed, standing on the corner of my block. It was full night. The moon was above me. There was nowhere for me to go.

Party or home. Neither appealed to me. Then I saw him, sitting on the steps of my porch, his head in his hands. He looked up at me before he could have heard my steps.

Still dressed in his costume, Will looked just right sitting in front of my Victorian house. Instead of him being the anachronism, it was as if I had somehow stepped through a portal back in time. In my sneakers and jeans, I seemed like a visitor to some far away, simpler time. In this version of reality, Will was my suitor, and I was his intended, and our life unfolded quite simply and beautifully—a wedding, a child, a country estate, and a flat in the city. He would read his paper in front of the fire, and I would work on a pile of darning from a basket at my side.

But then I blinked, and the misty version of some other reality dissipated, and I was just standing on my street again, and Will was a boy in a bloodstained costume.

He held his hands out to me, palms up, supplicating. I walked to him and stood before him on the footpath that led up to our house. He leaned his forehead against my stomach. My hands reached out to touch him—then hesitated, floating just above his head—before they rested on his hair, and Will leaned his weight more fully against me, and he sighed.

After time had passed like that, I slipped into the house and pulled some blankets from the Yellow Room. Will and I circled the house and spread a blanket on the floor of the gazebo, then lay on it together and pulled the thicker quilt across us.

We didn't talk for a long time, or kiss; we just lay there, my head on his chest, his hand pulling my hair loose from its bun and tracing the length of it from nape to hip.

Finally, Will whispered into my hair, "I'm so sorry, Scarlett. I don't know what happened. It's like—I lose myself, for a minute, and all I see is my anger."

"Have you always been like this?" I found that I was scared to hear his answer.

"No. I've never started a fight in my life. I've been in lots of them . . . you know, when I have to . . . but I've never wanted to fight. Until now."

I thought about his words. He'd never wanted to fight before, but now he did.

"Maybe I'm no good for you." I didn't want to say the words, but they seemed so true to me.

"That's absurd."

"No—listen. First I give you these insane headaches, and

then I point out things about your mom that you probably never needed to know, and then I bring out the worst in you. I mean, what's changed? Nothing except for the fact that I'm your girlfriend."

In spite of the depressing nature of my words, I felt Will smiling. "You're my girlfriend, are you?"

I was glad the night hid my blush. "Or whatever," I mumbled.

Will sat up and pulled me up, as well. He tilted up my chin so that I looked into his green, green eyes. "No 'whatever,'" he said. "Scarlett, *will* you be my girlfriend?"

Considering all we'd shared, all the different ways Will had saved me, it seemed ridiculous that he would even ask. But I realized, before I answered, that though he had been saving me from the first moment we met on the trail, I hadn't yet had the chance to save him back.

"Yes," I murmured, and we kissed in the moonlight.

We settled back in the blankets, comfortable in a different way, and after a time I broached the subject of Will's anger again.

"If you're so sure that I'm good for you," I said, "then you need to let me help you. Like you've helped me."

"I've never been adverse to help."

"So tell me, then . . . what is it that happens, right before you get so mad?"

Will shifted, as if even thinking about his anger made him uncomfortable. "It's a lot like the pull I feel to step into violent crimes," he said at last. "Only instead of being pulled to help someone, it's as if I'm being pulled to attack—to smite someone, or something. And I don't feel better until I do."

I found his choice of words interesting. Pulled to smite someone . . . I'd never heard anyone actually use the word *smite* in conversation. It seemed a word from antiquity.

"Do you get the same headache if you refuse the pull?"

Will shook his head. "No, it's not as bad as that. It's more just . . . something I really want to do, and when it hits me, it's like I don't think in words anymore. Just colors. And I mainly see red." He paused, then said a bit begrudgingly, "And, as you've probably noticed, it always has something to do with you. So far, anyway."

Of course, I didn't like this very much. But I tried to keep my tone light and said, "Yeah, I've had that effect on lots of guys."

"I'm sure that's true," Will answered, "but it's certainly not your fault. It's mine, for allowing myself to be led by my emotions."

We thought about this for a while, each of us on our own private island, so close together, though, that it seemed if I tried a little harder, I could extend a bridge of light between us and we could combine our thoughts.

"Maybe," I said at last, "next time you start thinking in colors, you could focus really hard on choosing a different color."

"I could pick blue," he said, scooting down a little so we were face to face, our noses practically touching, "and I could focus on your eyes." So tenderly, he kissed me twice, once upon each of my eyelids.

"Or I could pick gold," he continued, his hands tangling in my hair, "and concentrate on your hair."

Another moment passed, as Will's hands caressed my hair. Then, "I could choose pink," he said, "and meditate on your lips." Our kiss was sweet, and soft, and so warm in the cold night.

As if from a great distance, I heard the back door open. "Scarlett?"

It was my mother.

"Damn," I cursed, then pulled myself away from Will's embrace. "Yeah, Mom," I answered.

"Scarlett Wenderoth, what on earth are you doing out there?"

It was like pulling teeth after that to get my parents to agree to let me go on the trip to the mainland the next month with the school. They both felt *very* strongly that things between me and Will were moving too fast.

"Come on, Mom," I argued. "It's just a day trip. And we'll be with the class the whole time."

Because it was a trip to see a special collection at the museum that would be dismantling in the spring, all upperclassmen were going instead of just the senior class. There was no way I was going to be only upperclassman left at school.

"You could just stay home and help your mother refresh the rooms," Daddy suggested. "Our first guests of the season will be arriving in another week."

But the withering glance I shot him put an end to that discussion.

Finally, they agreed that I could go, but made me promise that I'd stay with a group. I could see how hard it was for them to let me go, both away from the island and further and further away from my childhood.

The morning of the trip was beautiful. It was mid-March, and I could taste spring in the air. As the unwieldy ferry pulled out to sea, our island seeming to shrink behind us, Will and I stood at the very front of the boat. His father had urged him not to go, also—but not for the same reasons as my parents. Long Beach was a big city, known in part for its gang violence. I knew, as we took the ferry to the mainland, that Will was taking a chance by leaving the island. Still, I couldn't help but feel hopeful as we plowed through the sea. Will stood behind me, his arms wrapped around my waist, and though I'd pulled my hair into two French braids to keep it manageable in the wind, still strands of it were blown in my face in the salty air.

I filled my lungs with the sea air. I had never been one of those people who get seasick. It was a good thing, being a lifelong islander as I was; anytime we wanted to travel any substantial distance, crossing the water was a necessity.

I loved it out there—watching the dolphins chasing the ferry, feeling the spray of salt water that shot up from the bow of the boat. As a kid, "ship captain" had made my list of possible professions. And days like this one made me toy with the idea once again.

"I think I could travel the world like this," I said.

"Tucked in my arms?" asked Will.

"That too. But I meant by boat."

"Sailboat or yacht?"

I considered. "Well, a yacht would be luxurious, but maybe it would feel too much like traveling in my living room. I'd choose sailboat."

"Mm. Do you know how to sail?"

"Not really. But I'm a quick study."

Will laughed, the deep, rich laugh I so loved. "I'll sail the world with you," he said. "I'll be your first mate."

"You're gonna mate, Big Red?" For such a big guy, Connell was remarkably adept at a stealth attack. Before I even knew Will and I weren't alone, he had sidled up right next to us.

"Hi, Connell. Bye, Connell," I said. I felt Will's arms tighten around my waist. I ran my fingers down his arm with the lightest of touches, trying to remind him without speaking to think of a different color.

Connell stayed next to us, his fists tight as if he was hoping Will would give him a chance to even the score. I knew how the dynamic worked: Connell was catcher to Andy's pitches. He had Andy's back.

But good to his word, Will wasn't biting. After a moment, he even managed to loosen his grip on my waist. His face was turned in to my hair, and I felt his hot breath as he exhaled.

Connell tried again to bait him. "You know, you only took Andy down because you caught him off guard. Pretty sneaky, but not much of a surprise, considering your background."

Will answered, but without turning his face away from

my hair. "Connell, are you insinuating that because I am Jewish, I am a sneaky, immoral fighter?"

I wasn't sure Connell knew what *insinuating* meant, but he got the general idea. "You said it, *Cohen,* not me." He managed to make Will's last name sound like a dirty word.

"Do your research, White Bread. You ever hear of *Krav Maga?*"

Connell looked confused. He was about to spit out a response, but Mr. Steiner, chaperone for the day, joined our little party.

"Everything okay here?"

"Right as rain, sir," answered Will.

Connell slunk off, his hands shoved deep in his pockets.

"Just watch it, Cohen," warned Mr. Steiner.

When we were alone again, I said, "That was pretty good, Will. I'm proud of you."

He kissed me just beneath my ear. "It wasn't so hard," he admitted. "Once I made up my mind to control myself, it got a lot easier."

"So it wasn't meditating on my lips that did it for you?" I teased.

"Well, that certainly helped too."

I turned to kiss him but, true to his word, Mr. Steiner had his eye on us.

The museum was a large, brown shingled building perched on a cliff on the edge of the ocean. We had to take a bus from the port, and by the time we finally arrived, half of the kids were grouching about being hungry for lunch.

Mr. Steiner caved and let us take our lunches, which we'd each brought from home, across Ocean Boulevard to a park for a quick picnic.

The grass was damp, so the students spread out across the park to claim the various cement tables. At the far end of the grassy area was a skate park, and a bunch of the guys, and some of the girls, migrated over there to watch the local talent.

Mr. Steiner followed them to keep a watchful eye. He didn't seem keen on any interaction between us islanders and the big, bad Long Beach locals.

Will and I sat near the edge of the park where we could glimpse the ocean. Even if we did live on a small scrap of land surrounded by water, I never could tire of the sea. Will didn't say anything, but his body was stiff next to mine. He seemed on edge, keyed up. And then I heard the siren.

At the sound of the siren, my spine stiffened. After its first mad scream, the siren seemed to fade away, and I let myself pretend that I had imagined it. Then it came back stronger than before. There was a neighborhood nearby, populated with small cottages mixed together with apartment buildings, and from up the street, a small flood of people headed toward the park.

I smelled something in the air—acrid and smoky.

Will stood from his perch at the picnic table and walked away as if hypnotized, his eyes unwavering in their gaze as he made his way toward the street.

"Will?" I said, but it was as if he didn't hear me. I stood

and followed him. He crossed Cherry Avenue, not even looking to see if any cars were coming in his direction. A man pulled up short, leaning on his horn. Will didn't turn his head. I waited for the car to pass, then trotted to catch up with Will.

Just ahead of me, he started to jog and then flat-out run, his hands cutting through the air.

"Will!" I called, desperately anxious and scared.

He didn't turn.

I felt the heat before I saw the fire. It was on the corner— a tall, thin wooden house, with two unit letters on its side— A on the downstairs unit, B on the upstairs apartment.

The flames licked the structure, spilling out the upstairs windows and consuming the plank siding. Lengths of the building's gray paint curled back like birthday ribbon.

Behind us, the whine of the fire engine crested, intolerably piercing, before cutting short suddenly midwail. Firefighters shoved past us, rolling out their long, heavy hose.

"Back off!" they yelled at us, shoving us roughly into the street, away from the building. And then they turned on the hose and a fierce spray of water shot into the flames.

I put my hand on Will's arm. "See, Will?" I said. My voice sounded frantic. "It's okay. They have it under control."

Will didn't answer. Not once had his focus veered from the building—from one of the windows, specifically. He stood stock-still, as if paralyzed. Then, as if he'd come to a decision, he turned to me. "Stay here," he implored.

And then he was gone, running around the corner toward the back of the building.

Too stunned to move at first, I looked at the spot where Will had been standing just a moment before. Now he was gone.

That was how it was. . . . One minute, someone can be standing right next to you. The next, they can be gone. Irreversibly. Intractably. Forever.

This last thought—*forever*—seemed to propel me into action. I followed the path Will had taken, making my way around the rear of the building. Will was nowhere to be seen. He had disappeared, and three firefighters had barreled around to the back entrance.

I tried to push past them, but of course they stopped me. "There's somebody in there!" I screamed.

"Back away, miss," one of them ordered, his voice stern. They looked like three fierce aliens in their helmets and heavy fire gear, and their faces were serious and absolutely immovable.

"You've got to get him out!" I was crazy with fear. Black smoke poured from the window that had so hypnotized Will. I beat my fists against the firefighter's chest, sobbing, and coughing from the smoke.

"Calm down!" The firefighter grabbed my hands and forced them to my sides. "Everyone is out. We asked the residents."

But his logic did not assuage my fear. Will was in there—I knew it—and when the window exploded, shooting glass shards down upon us like spiked confetti, and the firefighter tucked me against him, turning his back on the flames to protect me, my howl was wild and piercing and my heart felt like it would explode too.

And then the door behind us flew open, and there he was—Will, clutching a baby close to his chest. His clothes were blackened, the curls around his face singed.

The baby shrieked loudly, his fat little arms flailing. At first I thought the baby's skin was darkened from soot. Then I realized I was seeing his burns. Wordlessly, Will handed the baby to the firefighter who had sheltered me from the falling glass.

Our classmates, chaperoned by Mr. Steiner, returned to the island on the ferry. But Will and I were shepherded into an ambulance to be examined at the hospital. The emergency-room doctor was puzzled; somehow, Will had made it through the fire unscathed. The baby was burned but would survive . . . thanks to Will. When the doors to the emergency room opened again to admit a motorcyclist who had crashed, the doctor had to cut his examination short. As he turned away from Will, he said, still puzzled, "Well, you're a very lucky young man."

The baby had been forgotten by his babysitter, who watched three small children every weekday in her one-bedroom apartment. She had been drinking—"Not a lot, I swear!"—and had left her cigarette burning on the arm of her couch when she went to answer a telephone call in the kitchen. She'd fled the building with two of the three children. Whether she'd actually forgotten that there was a third child in the apartment or whether she'd chosen not to mention him because of fear or stupidity, no one knew.

Will pulled his sweater back on—it reeked of smoke—and

stood up from the examining table. Our parents would be coming to collect us; we were to wait at the hospital for them.

We found seats in the crowded waiting room. A television mounted high in a corner played the canned laughter of a sitcom, but neither Will nor I heard the dialogue.

I wanted to ask Will about what had happened back at the fire. What he had done went against everything he had told me about his abilities . . . there had been no violent crime, for one, and for another, nothing he had told me had hinted that there was any reason he should have been able to walk unharmed through a burning building.

But I felt shy somehow, and I waited for Will to share with me whatever he could, so I pretended to watch the show.

At last, Will spoke. "It was different this time," he said. His voice was hushed, and his eyes were wild as he remembered the fire. "I knew there was a problem, but it wasn't like I had to go. It was different. I had a choice. I *wanted* to go. I could have walked away. But I didn't. And inside, in the building, I heard him, Scarlett. I heard him calling to me."

"You mean you heard the baby crying?"

He shook his head emphatically. "No. I heard his *voice*. I don't really know how to describe it. It was as if some part of him was calling out to some part of me, guiding me. And there he was, sitting in a playpen tucked in a corner of the bedroom, by the closet. Under the window that I'd seen from outside. And when I came in, he reached his arms up to me. He knew I had come for him."

I didn't know what to say. I took Will's hand and caressed his palm with my thumb.

"It felt good, Scarlett. It felt wonderful. Not just to save him . . . I've saved people before. But to *choose* to do it."

"You could have been killed," I murmured.

Will shrugged. "But I wasn't," he said. "It's different, Scarlett. Things are changing for me. Since Dad told us his theory about me—his idea that maybe I've been here before—I've been thinking a lot about what happens to me. And I've started to see things differently. Do you know how I talked about responsibility being like a jacket?"

I nodded.

"It's like this. This curse—this gift—was always mine. I guess I've accepted it, and by owning it, by not fighting it anymore but recognizing that it's part of me, it's part of who I am, I've changed it. I can feel things, things I wasn't aware of before."

"You can feel *more* than before? Are you in pain, then, all the time?"

Will shook his head earnestly. "No," he said. "It's weird. I still feel pulled, but it's not painful anymore. And it's coming from all different directions. Over the last few weeks, it's been like nothing I've ever experienced. Sometimes I hear voices speaking in my head, calling for my help, but I don't know where to turn to help them. Some of them seem to be coming from really far away, way farther than anything I've experienced before. But the urgency, Scarlett, the headaches, the pain . . . it's all gone now. In its place, there's this . . . I don't quite know how to put it . . . there's this *knowledge* that there is suffering out there, all around me . . . and that I can end it, or help to end it, if I can learn how."

I didn't know what to say. "How are you going to learn how to save the world, Will? You can't stop *everyone's* suffering, you know."

He shrugged. "I don't know. I don't know everything, not by a long shot. But, Scarlett—it's okay. It's okay that I don't have all the answers. I'm going to find them."

He looked so sure—so strong, so absolutely certain that the answers were out there for him. Perhaps they were.

"The thing is, I didn't choose this—this calling, this curse, whatever it is. But that doesn't mean that I don't have a choice. I *do*—I can choose to embrace it. It can be a burden, or it can be a blessing. *I* get to decide."

I opened my mouth to speak, but I didn't know what I would say. Will's eyes were shining with the truth of his words, the hope he seemed to feel. And then the doors to the emergency room slid open. In came our parents—my mom and dad, with Martin right behind them—and for a moment Will and I were just kids again, safe in the warm embrace of family.

TWENTY-TWO

A Way

By the time our parents had filled out the requisite paperwork and ushered us out of the hospital, the last ferry of the day had left for the island.

The five of us—an awkward party—made our way downtown to dinner. The evening air was moist but not as cold as it had been on the island. I wondered if this was because we were on the mainland or because spring was upon us.

The restaurant our parents chose was loud and crowded. There was a half-hour wait before we'd get a table, but after conferring briefly, our parents decided that every restaurant would have the same crowd this time of night.

So we waited; knee to knee, we were packed like sardines on the wooden bench at the front of the restaurant. Will and I were flanked by Martin and my mom and dad, and they attempted small talk across us.

My parents asked Martin how he liked island life—very

much, thank you—and what kind of research he'd been in-volved with back at Yale—Kabbalah studies, he answered, and though I knew for a fact my parents had no idea what that meant, they did not ask for details.

At last the waitress led us to our table—a booth. Once more we slid into position, re-creating the seating arrange-ment we'd formed on the bench.

I ordered pea soup and a salad. Will had the same. The food took forever to arrive, and when it finally came, it wasn't very good. Still, we managed to work our way through the meal.

Finally, the check arrived and Martin reached into his jacket pocket to retrieve his wallet. "Ah," he said. "I almost forgot. This came for you today."

He extracted a thick envelope and laid it on the table in front of Will.

Mr. Will Cohen, read the envelope. *38 Olive Lane.*

The return address was Yale's.

I watched Will open the letter, and though the restaurant was still crowded and loud, I could clearly hear the sound of the envelope tearing.

Dear Mr. Cohen, read the letter. *We are pleased to inform you . . .*

That was enough. I knew what the rest would say. The words blurred and I tried to disguise my reaction with a chirpy tone that sounded transparent to my ears. "That's great, Will!"

Will looked at me. My parents echoed my congratula-tions, sounding more sincere than I had been able to. Mar-tin thumped his son on the back.

From the restaurant, it was a short walk to the hotel where we'd be staying the night.

My parents checked the three of us into one room with two queen-sized beds. Martin and Will were on the first floor, several floors below us. I took the bag my mom had packed for me into the bathroom and showered, washing the smell of smoke out of my hair, forcing myself to concentrate on my hands massaging my neck, the warm rain of water on my skin. I refused to think about anything else—the fire, Will's letter. After I dried off, I searched through the bag Mom had packed. There were yoga pants and a tank for sleeping in, and a fresh pair of jeans and a thermal for the next day. I didn't hesitate to pull on the jeans and thermal.

When I emerged from the bathroom, I found my parents tucked into bed together watching television. They raised their eyebrows at my clothes, but neither really looked surprised.

"Going somewhere?" my dad asked.

"I won't be long," I said, but I wasn't asking for permission.

"Take a key," my mother called after me.

The elevator descended smoothly. I found Will and Martin's room—137—and rapped sharply at the door.

Will answered. He'd changed his clothes too, and his hair was wet from the shower. He smiled and called back into the room, "I'll be back, Dad."

We took the elevator to the top of the hotel. On its roof was a Japanese garden, probably the inspiration for the hotel's name—Bonsai—and the plants and grass were woven through with pebbled paths and curved benches. The paths were lit with softly glowing lanterns that swung just a bit in the night air.

We settled on a bench that gave us a view of the lights below. So much life down in the city—so many stories, so many possibilities. You could get lost down there. You could lose someone.

"Scarlett," Will began, "about Yale—"

I shook my head. "Let's not talk about it," I said. "Not right now."

"Scarlett, I—"

Will might have said anything next. Maybe he would have said that he *had* to go to Yale—such an opportunity! Or maybe he had been about to say that he'd stay with me on the island, if I wanted him to, if I asked him to. That being together was more important than anything else.

But I stopped him again. "Look at all the lights," I said. They twinkled below us in a mosaic of oranges and yellows and whites. "One thing I'm coming to learn," I said, "is that it's better to be happy than not."

"You're just learning that?"

"Maybe I'm not explaining myself clearly," I said. "What I mean is, here we are." I gestured at the garden, at the lights, at the star-bright sky. "We might as well enjoy it. After all, who knows where we'll be tomorrow, or what we'll be doing. We have this, right now. And it's beautiful."

Will understood what I was saying. I could extract a promise from him, if I wanted to. He would most likely offer one to me willingly. But I didn't want a promise. I didn't want assurances. I wanted this moment. It was all any of us could hope for.

We kissed then, the electric current of our connection looping through us, weaving us together. I closed my eyes and disappeared into the kiss, and I thought, *We have six months. Or six weeks. Or six minutes. We have this moment.*

That night, I had the dream again. Once more, I lay on the warm sand, and the crust of it split, and I sank down into it—my legs, my hips, my stomach, arms, and head—but I did not struggle. I didn't fight. Instead, as I sank deeper and deeper through the sand, I focused all my energy on lifting just one hand—slowly, by inches, through the pressing weight atop me.

And when the warm, strong fingers found my hand, I wrapped my fingers around them in turn, and I surfaced, slowly, gradually, without thrashing or panicking. My eyes were closed to keep out the sand, but when I broke through to the surface at last, when I brushed the sand from my eyes and looked up to smile at my savior, I knew exactly who I would see.

There she was—tall, strong, her long hair loose behind her. Her smile was wide and healthy. Her eyes were blue and clear. She was beautiful.

She was me.

ACKNOWLEDGMENTS

Many wonderful women helped make *Sacred* a reality, and I want to thank them all. First, my sisters—Mischa Kuczynski Erickson, who helped me brainstorm the initial outline poolside with pretzels and cheese sauce, and Sasha Kuczynski, my tireless first editor, who was there when I wrote the last words. Paige Davis Arrington, thank you for helping me learn how to finish a project and how to feel like a writer. Laura Jane, thank you for watching the kiddos while I wrote. Amy Antoine, you gave me the idea in the first place. Thank you.

Rubin Pfeffer, who pulled my manuscript out of the slush pile and wrote to me the very next day—not to mention came up with the title—you are the agent of my dreams. Deborah Warren, how lucky am I that you and Rubin are a package deal? Thank you for your support and enthusiasm. And deep gratitude to the people at Delacorte Press who had a hand in bringing *Sacred* to fruition—first of all my editor, Françoise Bui. Thank you for loving my story, and for your eagle-eyed line edits. Thanks too to Kenny Holcomb, who designed *Sacred*'s beautiful cover. I love it so much. And I'm grateful to Jody Revenson, copy editor, who taught me what "roller-coastering" is and why not to do it.

I am thankful as well to my family of origin, who supported my dual fascinations with horses and books. See, it paid off after all!

And inexpressible thanks and love to my husband, Keith, who loves me, and my children, Max and Davis, who gave me a reason to prove it can be done.

ABOUT THE AUTHOR

ELANA K. ARNOLD thinks everyone has a story to tell. It took her a long time to find hers. She grew up in Southern California, where she was lucky enough to have her own horse, a gorgeous mare named Rainbow, and a family who let her read as many books as she wanted. She lives in Long Beach, California, with her husband, two kids, and a menagerie of pets, including her chicken, Ruby. *Sacred* is her debut novel. Visit Elana at elanakarnold.com.

Splendor

THE SEQUEL TO *Sacred*

COMING FALL 2013!

• • •

AND READ ON FOR A PEEK
AT ELANA K. ARNOLD'S NEXT NOVEL,

BURNING,

AVAILABLE JUNE 2013!

BURNING

Small-town boy. Gypsy girl. Desert summer.

Ben: Having just graduated from high school, Ben is set to leave Gypsum, Nevada. It's good timing, since the gypsum mine that is the lifeblood of the area is closing, shutting the whole town down with it. Ben is lucky; he's headed to San Diego, where he's got a track scholarship at the University of California. His best friends, Pete and Hog Boy, aren't as fortunate; they don't have college to look forward to. So to make his friends happy during their last days in town, Ben goes with them to check out the hot chick parked on the side of Highway 447.

Lala: She and her Gypsy family make money the way her people have been earning it for centuries—by telling fortunes. Some customers choose Tarot cards; others have their palms read. The thousands of people attending the nearby Burning Man festival spend lots of cash—especially as Lala gives uncanny readings. But lately Lala's been questioning whether there might be more to life than her upcoming arranged marriage. And the day she reads Ben's cards is the day everything changes for her . . . and for him.

Told from alternating points of view, *Burning* brims with the passion of two young people, both at crossroads in their lives, and both forever altered by a moment in time.